# ARCH-ENEMIES

# ARCH-
# ENEMIES

## MARISSA MEYER

FEIWEL AND FRIENDS
NEW YORK

A FEIWEL AND FRIENDS BOOK

An imprint of Macmillan Publishing Group, LLC

175 Fifth Avenue, New York, NY 10010

ARCHENEMIES. Text copyright © 2018 by Rampion Books. All rights reserved.

Printed in the United States of America.

Our books may be purchased in bulk for promotional, educational, or business use.
Please contact your local bookseller or the Macmillan Corporate and Premium Sales Department at
(800) 221-7945 ext. 5442 or by email at MacmillanSpecialMarkets@macmillan.com.

Library of Congress Cataloging-in-Publication Data is available.

ISBN 978-1-250-07830-8 (hardcover) / ISBN 978-1-250-31144-3 (ebook)

ISBN 978-1-250-31742-1 (international)

Book design by Patrick Collins

Feiwel and Friends logo designed by Filomena Tuosto

First edition, 2018

1  3  5  7  9  10  8  6  4  2

*For Garrett and Gabriel, future superheroes*

# CAST OF CHARACTERS

## THE RENEGADES: SKETCH'S TEAM

SKETCH — Adrian Everhart
*Can bring his drawings and artwork to life*

MONARCH — Danna Bell
*Transforms into a swarm of monarch butterflies*

RED ASSASSIN — Ruby Tucker
*When wounded, her blood crystallizes into weaponry; signature weapon is a grappling hook formed from a bloodstone*

SMOKESCREEN — Oscar Silva
*Summons smoke and vapor at will*

## THE RENEGADES: FROSTBITE'S TEAM

FROSTBITE — Genissa Clark
*Creates weapons of ice from water molecules in the air*

AFTERSHOCK — Mack Baxter
> *Causes the ground to move with earthquake-like force*

GARGOYLE — Trevor Dunn
> *Mutates all or parts of his body into solid stone*

STINGRAY — Raymond Stern
> *Delivers venom via a barbed tail*

## THE ANARCHISTS

NIGHTMARE — Nova Artino
> *Never sleeps, and can put others to sleep with her touch*

THE DETONATOR — Ingrid Thompson
> *Creates explosives from the air that can be detonated at will*

PHOBIA — True Name Unknown
> *Transforms his body and scythe into the embodiment of various fears*

THE PUPPETEER — Winston Pratt
> *Turns people into mindless puppets who do his bidding*

QUEEN BEE — Honey Harper
> *Exerts control over all bees, hornets, and wasps*

CYANIDE — Leroy Flinn
> *Generates acidic poisons through his skin*

HAWTHORN — Name unknown
> *Wields deadly thorn-covered tentacles*

# THE RENEGADE COUNCIL

**CAPTAIN CHROMIUM** — Hugh Everhart

*Has superstrength and is nearly invincible to physical attacks; can generate chromium weaponry*

**THE DREAD WARDEN** — Simon Westwood

*Can turn invisible*

**TSUNAMI** — Kasumi Hasegawa

*Generates and manipulates water*

**THUNDERBIRD** — Tamaya Rae

*Generates thunder and lightning; can fly*

**BLACKLIGHT** — Evander Wade

*Creates and manipulates light and darkness*

# ARCH-ENEMIES

# CHAPTER ONE

ADRIAN CROUCHED ON THE ROOFTOP, peering at the delivery entrance behind Gatlon City Hospital. It was early morning—the sun hadn't risen yet, though hints of light were turning the sky from charcoal gray to pale violet. The dimness made it difficult to see anything ten stories below, beyond a couple of vans and a supply truck.

"I have eyes on the getaway vehicle," said Nova, who was watching the quiet streets through a pair of binoculars.

"Where?" he asked, leaning toward her. "How can you tell?"

"That van on the corner." She swiveled her view from the vehicle to the hospital door and back. "Nondescript, blacked-out windows, engine still running even though it's been parked since we got here."

Adrian sought out the van. Steam was rising from its exhaust pipe in great white clouds. "Is there anyone inside?"

"One, in the driver's seat. Could be more, but I can't see into the back."

Adrian lifted his wrist toward his mouth, speaking into his communication band. "Sketch to Smokescreen and Red Assassin.

Suspected getaway vehicle is parked at Seventy-Ninth and Fletcher Way. Set your stations to the south and east escape routes. Still waiting on internal recon from Monarch."

"Roger that," Oscar's voice crackled back at him. "We're on the move."

Adrian tapped his fingers against the rooftop ledge, wishing the back entrance to the hospital had better lighting. There were six street lamps, but three of them were burned out. Shouldn't someone have taken care of those?

"Can I see?" he asked.

Nova held the binoculars out of his reach. "Get your own pair."

Though he wanted to be irritated with the response, he couldn't help a twitch of a smile. It was fair enough, he supposed, as Nova had spent twenty minutes that morning explaining to Oscar all of the modifications she'd made to this particular pair of generic binoculars. They now sported autofocus and stabilization functionality, motion targeting, night vision, a video recorder, and computerized lenses that could display GPS coordinates and weather forecasts. And because that evidently wasn't impressive enough, she'd also added software that combined targeted facial recognition with the Renegades' prodigy database.

Evidently, she'd been working on them for months.

"Fine, I will get my own," he said, pulling his fine-tip marker from the sleeve of his Renegade uniform. He started to sketch a pair of binoculars onto the side of a metal utility box. "Maybe I'll give mine X-ray vision."

Nova's jaw tensed. "Were you always such a one-upper?"

He beamed. "I'm only kidding. I would need at least some basic knowledge of how X-ray vision works. But I'm definitely giving them that motion-targeting feature you talked about. And ergonomic handholds. And maybe a flashlight . . ." He finished his sketch and capped his marker. Pressing his fingers against the metal surface, he pulled the drawing from the utility box, transforming it into a functional, three-dimensional reality.

Kneeling beside Nova again, he adjusted the width of his new binoculars and peered toward the street. The van hadn't moved.

"There's Danna," said Nova.

Adrian swiveled his view toward the delivery bay, but the doors were still closed. "Where—"

"Third story."

He readjusted and saw the swarm of Monarch butterflies pouring out of an open window. In the darkness, they looked more like a colony of bats silhouetted against the building. The butterflies converged over the hospital's parking garage and morphed into the figure of Danna.

The communication band buzzed. "They're heading out now," came Danna's voice. "Six altogether."

"Seven with the driver," Nova corrected, as the van pulled forward. It turned the corner and came to a stop in front of the delivery doors. Seconds later, those doors were thrown open and six figures came pouring out of the hospital, loaded down with enormous black bags.

"Citizen status?" asked Adrian.

"All clear," replied Danna.

"Roger. Okay, team, we are cleared to engage. Danna, stay on—"

"Sketch!" said Nova, startling him. "There's a prodigy."

He blinked over at her. "What?"

"That woman—the one with the nose ring. She's showing up on the database. Alias . . . Hawthorn?"

He racked his brain, but the name wasn't familiar. "Never heard of her." Adrian watched through his binoculars again as the figures threw their haul into the van. The woman with the nose ring was the last to climb in. "What's her power?"

"Evidently she has . . . thorn-covered extremities?" Nova shot him a baffled look.

Shrugging, Adrian spoke into his wristband again. "High alert, team. The targets have a prodigy with them. Stay with your assignments, but proceed with caution. Insomnia and I will——" A bang startled Adrian and he turned to see that Nova was already gone. He lurched to his feet and peered over the side of the building. The sound had been Nova landing on the first level of the apartment's fire escape. ". . . take the north post," he muttered.

Tires squealed. The van lurched away from the hospital. Adrian raised his wrist, adrenaline coursing through his body as he waited to see which direction . . .

The van took the first left.

"Smokescreen, you're up!" he yelled.

Tossing aside the binoculars, Adrian raced after Nova. Overhead, Danna swarmed again and chased after the van.

Nova was halfway down the street by the time Adrian dropped down from the fire escape, his boots pounding on the pavement. He raced after her, his long legs giving him some advantage, though he was still trailing behind when Nova jutted her finger to the right. "You head that way!" she yelled, taking off in the opposite direction.

A block away, he heard the screech of tires again, this time accompanied by the slamming of brakes. A cloud of thick white fog could be seen rising over the roof of an office building.

Oscar's voice came through the wristband. "They're reversing—heading north on Bridgewater."

Adrian turned the corner and saw red taillights blazing toward him. He reached for a piece of white chalk in his sleeve, pocketed beside the marker. Crouching down, he drew a hasty nail strip on the asphalt. He finished the illustration as the smell of burning rubber invaded his nostrils. If the driver could see him in the rear-view mirror, he showed no sign of slowing down.

Adrian tugged on the drawing. The four-inch spikes emerged from the ground, and he lunged out of the way seconds before the van blurred past him.

The tires blew with a series of deafening pops. From behind the blackened windows, Adrian could hear the occupants of the van cursing and arguing with one another as the deflated wheels dragged to a stop.

The cloud of butterflies swirled overhead and Danna dropped down onto the roof of the van. "Quick thinking, Sketch."

Adrian stood, still gripping the chalk. His other hand reached for the Renegade-issued handcuffs clipped to his belt. "You are under arrest," he called. "Come out slowly with your hands up."

The door clunked open, parting just wide enough for a hand to emerge, fingers spread in supplication.

"Slowly," Adrian repeated.

There was a hesitation, and then the door was thrown open the rest of the way. Adrian spotted the barrel of a gun moments before a volley of bullets started to pepper the building behind him. He yelped and dived behind a bus stop, throwing his arms over his head. Glass shattered and bullets pinged against stone.

Someone shouted. The gunfire stopped.

The rest of the van doors were flung open in unison—driver, passenger, and the two at the back.

All seven criminals emerged, scattering in different directions.

The driver bolted for a side street, but Danna was on him instantly: a cyclone of golden wings one minute, and the next, a zealous superhero, clamping one arm around the man's throat and throwing him to the ground.

A woman from the passenger seat sprinted south on Bridgewater and vaulted over the strip of nails, but she hadn't gone half a block before she was struck in the face by an arrow of black smoke. She dropped to her knees, choking. Still struggling to breathe, she offered little resistance as Oscar emerged from behind a parked car and clamped cuffs around her wrists.

Three more thieves rushed through the van's back doors, each weighed down with their bulging plastic bags. None of them saw the thin wire strung across the length of the road. Their ankles caught, one after the other, sending them crashing into a heap on the asphalt. One bag flopped open, spilling dozens of small white pill bottles into the gutter. Skipping out from behind a mailbox, Ruby made quick work of binding the three, then went to retrieve the red hook at the end of her wire.

The last two criminals emerged from the side door. The woman with the nose ring—Hawthorn, according to Nova's binoculars— was gripping the automatic rifle in one hand and a black garbage bag in the other. She was followed by a man with two more bags flung over his shoulder.

Adrian was still crouched behind the bus stop when the two shot past him into a narrow alley. He sprang to his feet but hadn't gone two steps before something whistled past him and he saw a glint of red from the corner of his eye.

Ruby's spiked bloodstone sliced through the bag over the woman's shoulder, cutting a narrow slit into its side. But her wire was too short. The woman was just out of reach. The gem rebounded, clattering to the concrete. A single plastic bottle tumbled from the tear in the bag.

Growling, Ruby reeled the wire back in and began to swing it overhead like a lasso as she charged forward, preparing for another throw.

The woman stopped suddenly and turned to face them, aiming the gun. She released another round of bullets. Adrian threw himself at Ruby. She cried out in pain as they both tumbled behind a dumpster.

The gunfire stopped as soon as they were under cover. The criminals' footsteps clomped away from them.

"Are you all right?" said Adrian, though the answer was obvious. Ruby's face was contorted, both hands gripping her thigh.

"Fine," she said through gritted teeth. "Stop them!"

Something crashed down the alley—the ear-splitting noise of breaking glass and crunching metal. Adrian poked his head around the dumpster to see a destroyed air-conditioning unit on the pavement. He scanned the roof of the surrounding apartments just as a second unit was hurled down at the thieves. It smashed onto the ground steps in front of the woman, who let out a strangled cry and opened fire again.

Nova ducked back. The bullets burst across the top of the building, marring it with a series of tiny craters.

Adrian didn't stop to think as he stepped out from behind the dumpster, out from Ruby's view, and raised his arm. Even beneath the dark gray sleeve of his uniform, he could see his skin start to glow as the narrow cylinder he'd once tattooed onto his flesh sprouted along the length of his forearm.

He fired.

The concussion beam struck Hawthorn between her shoulder

blades, launching her over one of the smashed air-conditioning units. The rifle clattered against the nearest wall.

Adrian studied the roof line, heart pounding. "Insomnia?" he yelled, hoping his panic didn't show in his voice. "Are you—"

Hawthorn let out a guttural scream and pushed herself up onto all fours. Her accomplice stumbled a few steps away, still gripping his two bags of stolen hospital drugs. He shook his head. "Rein it in, Hawthorn," he said. "Let's just get out of here."

Ignoring him, the woman turned toward Adrian and snarled.

As he watched, a series of limbs sprouted upward from her back, not far from where his beam had struck her. Six appendages, each one a dozen feet long and scattered with sharp barbs. They reminded Adrian of octopus legs, if octopus legs had been covered in vicious-looking thorns.

Adrian took a step back. When Nova had mentioned thorn-covered extremities, he'd pictured unusually sharp fingernails. Whoever put the database together really needed to work on being more specific.

Hawthorn's accomplice cursed. "I'm out of here!" he yelled, and took off running again.

Ignoring him, Hawthorn reached her tentacles toward the nearest fire escape and hauled her body upward, as quick and graceful as a spider. When she was still a platform down from the top, she reached one tentacle up and over the side.

Nova cried out. Adrian's lungs expelled a horrified breath as he watched the woman haul Nova off the roof. She held her aloft for a second, then threw Nova down.

On instinct, Adrian launched himself upward. He didn't think about using the springs on his feet—the others weren't supposed to know about his tattoos—but there was no time to question it. He intercepted Nova's body before she struck the building on the other side of the alley, and they both crashed down on top of the dumpster.

Panting, Adrian pulled back to inspect Nova, still in his arms. There was something warm and sticky on her back, and his hand was red when he pulled it away.

"I'm fine," Nova grunted, and she looked more angry than hurt. "Just scratched up by those thorns. I hope they aren't poisonous." She sat up and spoke into her communicator band, informing the rest of the team what they were up against.

Adrian scanned the building, afraid that another attack was imminent, but Hawthorn wasn't coming after them. As he stared, she used her tentacles to swing from the fire escape to a drain pipe, then slid back down to the alley. Two of her tentacles stretched out, snatching up the dropped bag and the single pill bottle that had fallen from it, before chasing after her accomplice.

"I'm going after her," said Nova. She slipped over the side of the dumpster, her boots thudding on the ground.

"You're hurt!" said Adrian, landing beside her.

Ruby stumbled out from the shadows. She was limping, but where there had been blood before, now a series of jagged red crystals had burst like stalagmites across her open wound. "I'm going after her too," she said, snarling.

Nova spun away from them both, but Adrian grabbed her arm and held her back.

"Sketch! Let me go!"

"Two seconds!" he yelled back, pulling out his marker. He used it to draw a quick cut into the blood-soaked fabric of her uniform, revealing the wound on her lower back, not far from her spine. More a puncture than a scratch.

"Adrian! They're getting away!"

Ignoring her, he drew a series of crisscrossing bandages over the wound. "There," he said, capping the marker as the bandages knitted together over her flesh. "Now at least you won't bleed to death."

She grumbled something, exasperated.

They took off running together, though it soon became clear that Ruby wasn't going to be able to keep up. While Nova sprinted forward, Adrian grabbed Ruby's shoulder, stopping her. "We'll handle the prodigy. You head back, make sure the others are secured."

Ruby was about to argue when Danna's voice crackled over their communicator bands. "I have eyes on Hawthorn and the male suspect. They're doubling back toward the hospital, heading east on Eighty-Second. Probably going for the river."

Ruby fixed a stern look on Adrian. "Don't let them get away."

He didn't bother to respond. Turning, he sprinted down a narrow side street. Maybe he could cut them off. Had Nova gone back to the main road, or would she make her way to a rooftop and track them from above?

When he was sure Ruby was out of sight, he used the tattooed springs on the soles of his feet to launch himself forward, covering the distance ten times as fast as he could by running. Reaching the end of the alley, he spotted both criminals as they barreled around the next corner.

He ran after them and turned the corner at the same time Nova did, coming from the other direction. She stumbled in surprise when she saw him. "That was fast," she panted.

They kept pace with each other, sprinting side by side. The criminals were a block ahead. Every once in a while Adrian spotted another pill bottle from the slit in Hawthorn's bag, rolling off toward a gutter. It made an easy path to follow.

Ahead, the road ended in a T, and Adrian saw the two criminals start to split up. They intended to separate—and to drive Adrian and Nova apart.

"I'll take Hawthorn," said Adrian.

"No," said Nova, pulling a wide-barreled gun from her tool belt. Without slowing, she aimed and fired. The bolt of energy struck the man just as he was heading for the next street. It sent him flying through the window of a small café. Shards of glass rained around him as he tumbled over a table and disappeared from view. One of the garbage bags caught on the broken window, sending a flood of plastic bottles across the sidewalk.

"You get him," said Nova. "*I'll* take Hawthorn."

Adrian huffed. "Now who's a one-upper?"

Though Hawthorn hesitated when her cohort was blown through the window, she didn't stop. If anything, she ran faster, using both her legs and the six tentacles to skitter down the street.

Adrian hadn't fully made up his mind whether to apprehend the man or stay with Nova when a scream brought them both skidding to a stop.

Adrian's attention swiveled toward the shattered window of the café. It wasn't the window, though, but the front door that burst open, crashing so hard against the side of the building that the CLOSED sign fell to the sidewalk.

The man emerged. He had abandoned the garbage bags and instead had one arm wrapped around the throat of a teenage girl wearing a checkered apron. His other hand was pressing a gun to the side of her head.

# CHAPTER TWO

T HE AIR LEFT ADRIAN as he stared at the gun and the girl's petrified face. A collage of small cuts shredded her right arm. She
must have been standing by the window when the man had
fallen through.

"Listen close!" the man yelled. Though his outward appearance
was tough, with a tattoo snaking from his jaw down into the collar
of his shirt, and arms that had clearly seen plenty of barbells—there
was undeniable fear behind his eyes. "You're going to let me go.
You're not going to follow either of us. You're not going to attack.
You follow those *real* simple instructions, and I'll release this girl
as soon as we're free and clear. But I get one hint of being chased,
and she's dead." He shoved the barrel of the gun against the back of
the hostage's head, forcing her neck forward. His hand was shaking
as he began to sidestep along the building's wall, keeping the girl
between himself and the Renegades. "We have an understanding?"

The hostage started to cry.

Adrian's heart drummed. The code revolved through his
thoughts.

*Civilian safety first. Always.*

But every second they stood there, capitulating to this criminal's demands, Hawthorn was getting farther and farther away.

Beside him, Nova deftly wrapped a hand around the small gun tucked into the back of her utility belt.

"Don't," he murmured.

Nova paused.

The man continued to slink down the street, dragging the hostage with him. Twenty more steps and they'd be around the corner.

If Adrian and Nova did nothing, if they let him go, would he really release the hostage?

The code said to take the chance. Don't give him cause to attack. Placate and negotiate. Don't engage when civilian lives are at stake.

Fifteen steps.

"I can hit him," Nova said under her breath.

The girl watched them both, more horrified with each passing second. Her body was acting as a shield, but there was enough of the man's head showing that Adrian believed Nova. He had seen her shoot plenty of times. He didn't doubt that she *could* hit him.

But still, the code . . .

Ten steps.

"Too risky," he said. "Don't engage."

Nova made a disgusted sound in her throat, but her hand lifted an inch away from the gun.

The hostage was sobbing now. The criminal was practically carrying her as he backed away.

There was a chance he would kill her as soon as he was out of range. Adrian knew it. They *all* knew it.

Or he might hold on to her until he reached . . . wherever it was they were heading to.

Two criminals would still be on the street, including a dangerous prodigy, while pounds of stolen medications that were desperately needed at the hospital entered the city's drug trade.

Five steps.

Nova looked at Adrian, and he could feel the frustration rolling off her in waves. "Seriously?" she hissed.

He tightened his fists.

The criminal reached the corner and smirked at Adrian. "You best stay put, now," he said. "Like I said, I'll let her go when I'm free and clear, but if I get one hint that you Renegades are after us, I'll—"

A stick appeared from behind the corner and struck the side of the man's head. He cried out and started to turn, as another blow snapped his head back. His grip loosened on the hostage. With a wail, she wrenched herself free of his grip.

Ruby dropped down from a door canopy, releasing a banshee scream as she pounced on the man's back and knocked him to the ground. Oscar appeared, gripping his cane like a club. He stood over Ruby and the criminal, prepared to strike a third time, but Ruby had already secured a pair of handcuffs over the man's wrists.

"And that's what we in the biz call teamwork," said Oscar, holding a hand toward Ruby. She locked forearms and let him help her to her feet.

Dazed, the hostage collapsed against the building wall and slid down to the sidewalk.

"Sweet rot," Nova murmured, echoing Adrian's thoughts exactly. Ruby's wounds had continued to bleed, and her uniform was encrusted in sharp red crystal formations sprouting from the bullet wound on her thigh and encompassing her leg down to her knee and up over her hip.

Adrian shook off his surprise. "Where's Danna?"

"Tracking the prodigy," said Ruby. "If she hasn't caught up to her already."

"I'm going after them," said Nova. She shot a sour look at Adrian. "If that's in line with the *code*."

He returned the glare, but without much force behind it. "Be safe. We'll meet back at the hospital."

Nova took off in the direction the prodigy had gone. Adrian watched her go with a twist of uneasiness in his gut. They still didn't know much about Hawthorn or what she was capable of.

But Danna would be there. And Nova knew what she was doing.

He forced himself to turn away. "The others?"

"All secured," said Ruby. "And I've already called for convict removal and a cleanup crew."

Oscar stepped toward the hostage. She was gaping at the three Renegades, trembling.

"You're safe now," said Oscar, using his cane for support as he crouched in front of her. "A medic will be here soon to tend to your injuries, and there are counselors on staff if you need someone to talk to. In the meantime, is there someone you'd like us to call?"

Her shaking body stilled as she met his gaze. Her eyes widened—not with fear this time, but rather a delirious sort of awe. She opened her mouth, though it took her a few tries before words started to form. "I've been dreaming of this my whole life," she whispered. "To be rescued by a *real Renegade*." She simpered, regarding Oscar as if he were the eighth wonder of the modern world. "Thank you . . . thank you so much for saving my life."

His cheeks reddened. "Uh . . . yeah. You're welcome." Oscar glanced at Ruby, uncertain, but when he stood up, his chest was puffed out more than it had been before. "All in a day's work."

Ruby snickered.

The wail of a siren echoed through the streets. The ambulance and Renegade squad cars would be arriving soon. Adrian glanced in the direction that Nova had gone, his anxiety returning in force.

How far had the prodigy gotten? Where was she headed? Had Danna caught up to her yet? Had Nova?

Did they need help?

"Hey, guys?" he started, feeling the pulse of adrenaline all over again.

"You're going after her," said Ruby. "Yeah, we know."

"Better be fast about it," said Oscar. "You know Nova's not going to save any of the glory for you."

Adrian's lips flickered in a grateful smile, and he ran.

THE SUN HAD risen over the buildings now, throwing long shadows across the streets. The city was coming to life. More cars on the roads. Pedestrians casting curious, even excited looks at Nova as she sprinted past in her oh-so-recognizable Renegade uniform. She ignored them all, dodging around the shop owners who were rolling garbage bins toward the street. Vaulting over sandwich boards that advertised seasonal sales and grand openings. Weaving around bicycles and taxis, street lamps and rusted mailboxes.

Their job was difficult during the daytime. Things were easier when there were no civilians around, as the hostage situation outside the café proved. That's when the infamous Gatlon code authority came into play. The whole protect-and-defend-at-all-costs thing. It's not that Nova disagreed with the intention—of course they should be working to protect innocent bystanders. But sometimes you had to take risks. Sometimes you had to make sacrifices.

For a greater good.

Ace never would have spared one life when doing so could have put dozens, even hundreds, more at risk.

But that was the code the Renegades lived by, and now a prodigy with thorn-covered extremities was on the loose, and who knew when she would strike again?

If Nova didn't stop her first.

Given that she was a superhero and all.

She smiled wryly at the thought. Oh, if Ingrid could see her now. How mortified she would be to see Nova, her Anarchist cohort, working with the Renegades—siding with them over another rebellious prodigy, even. Ingrid would have encouraged Nova to let Hawthorn go, maybe even to try to turn her into an ally. But Ingrid was shortsighted. She couldn't fathom the importance of Nova earning the Renegades' trust.

Ace understood. He had always understood.

Earn their trust. Learn their weaknesses.

Then, destroy them.

Hawthorn was headed for the river, just as Nova would have done to cover her tracks if she'd been fleeing from the Renegades—which was, admittedly, a scenario Nova had spent plenty of time preparing for over the years. Three blocks from where she'd left Adrian and the others, she spotted a white pill bottle in a gutter. Hawthorn had changed directions, and two blocks later Nova saw another bottle caught in a storm drain.

She spied a dark, fluctuating cloud over a community garden and it took her a moment to recognize Danna's swarm. The butterflies drifted back and forth, fluttering over a side street, then up and over the roofs of a narrow strip of boarded-up shops.

Nova had the distinct impression that they were searching for something.

She hopped over the fence and jogged through the muddy

garden. When she reached the street on the other side, the butter-flies had begun to alight on the power lines and gutters. Thousands of them, wings twitching as they searched and waited.

Nova's palm thumped against her handgun, but she changed her mind and grabbed the shock-wave gun instead. The alley was almost empty but for half a dozen metal trash cans and piles of heaped-up garbage bags overflowing against each wall. The smell was putrid—rotting food and dead fish. Nova kept her breaths shallow, fighting the urge to gag as she ducked through a throng of houseflies.

A noise made Nova jump and she spun around, shock-wave gun leveled at one of the trash bags. A scrawny cat yowled and darted through a broken window.

Nova exhaled.

A battle cry rang out, echoing through the alley. The lid of a trash can blew upward as Hawthorn launched herself out. A thorny limb snatched the gun from Nova's hand, leaving a burning welt on her palm.

Hissing, Nova reached for her handgun as Hawthorn took the shock-wave gun into her hand.

Nova drew her gun, but Hawthorn fired first.

Nova was thrown back into a pile of garbage bags, her body vibrating with the concussive blow.

Hawthorn ran the other way. Danna formed in the woman's path, her body poised for a fight. Hawthorn aimed for her, too, but Danna dispersed into butterflies before the crackling energy could hit her.

The insects cycloned. A heartbeat later, Danna dropped out of the sky onto Hawthorn's back.

Three of Hawthorn's six limbs wrapped around Danna's body, slicing across her back. Danna screamed as the thorns dug long gashes into her skin. Hawthorn hurled her at the wall and Danna crumpled to the ground.

Struggling to her feet, Nova grabbed the nearest trash can and threw it as hard as she could.

Hawthorn cocked her head and whipped out one of the tentacles, easily batting away the garbage can. Another limb reached into a nearby pile of trash bags and pulled one off the top—Nova recognized the slit in its side. Hawthorn began her spidery climb up the wall, her extra limbs reaching for the bars on windows and bracketed lights. She reached the roof and disappeared.

Nova raced down the alley. Hawthorn's goal became clear the moment she burst onto the street and saw the short bridge spanning Snakeweed River. Hawthorn was already at the bridge's railing. She shot one hateful glower at Nova, then hurled herself from the bridge.

Though Nova's legs were burning and her lungs felt ready to collapse, she pumped her arms faster, urging her body forward. She only had to see where Hawthorn surfaced and she would be in pursuit again.

But when she reached the bridge, her heart sank.

Hawthorn hadn't fallen into the river.

She'd landed on a barge.

It was plowing steadily through the waves, putting more distance between Nova and the criminal with every heartbeat.

Surrounded by shipping containers, Hawthorn waved tauntingly back.

Nova curled her fists around the rail of the bridge, envisioning the river's path. There were four more bridges before it emptied into the bay. Hawthorn could depart at any one of them, but there was no way for Nova to catch up and find out which one.

Nova cursed. Her knuckles whitened as she squeezed her hands into fists.

There had to be another way to follow. There had to be another way to stop the prodigy. There had to be—

Pounding footsteps caught her attention.

Nova spun around. Her pulse skipped as she saw the man in a shiny armored suit charging straight for her.

The Sentinel.

Skin prickling, she reached for her gun, preparing for a fight.

But the Sentinel ran past her and launched himself into the air with the force of a jet engine.

Nova's jaw fell as she followed his trajectory. His body arched up and out over the river and for a moment he seemed to be flying.

Then he descended, graceful and sure, his body braced for impact.

He smashed down onto the deck of the barge, inches from its ledge.

The Sentinel stood, briefly striking a pose straight out of a comic book.

Nova couldn't refrain from rolling her eyes. "Yeah, yeah, show-off."

If Hawthorn was shocked, she didn't show it. With a shout, she sent all six brambled limbs driving toward the vigilante.

Nova sort of hoped she was about to witness the Sentinel being impaled, but then he extended his left arm. A bonfire exploded from his palm, engulfing the tentacles. Even from so far away, Nova could hear the woman's screams as she reeled her limbs back.

Extinguishing the flames around his hand, the Sentinel tackled Hawthorn with such force that both of them rolled behind the stack of shipping containers.

Nova pressed her body against the rail, squinting into the morning light. For a long time, she could see nothing, as the barge clipped through the water.

Before it reached the next river bend, though, Nova spotted movement on its deck.

She grabbed the binoculars from the back of her belt and found the barge. The lenses' programming zoomed in on the deck.

Nova's eyes narrowed.

Hawthorn's clothes were singed from the Sentinel's flames. Blood splattered her bare arms. The left side of her face was swelling around a cut on her lip.

But she was still standing. The Sentinel, on the other hand, was sprawled at her feet, his body wrapped from shoulders to ankles in the barbed limbs.

As Nova watched, Hawthorn dragged the Sentinel's body to the back of the barge and dumped him over the edge.

The heavy armor sank immediately into the murky water.

Nova drew back. It happened so fast, she was almost disappointed by how anticlimactic it was. She was no great fan of the Sentinel, and yet, there had been a small part of her that had hoped he would at least catch the thief, as he'd caught any number of criminals over the past few weeks.

Hawthorn glanced up once more in Nova's direction, her smirk caught dead center in the binoculars' view.

Then the barge rounded a bend in the river and she was gone.

Sighing, Nova lowered the binoculars.

"Well," she muttered, "at least I won't have to worry about him anymore."

# CHAPTER THREE

A DRIAN SURFACED BENEATH Halfpenny Bridge. He struggled to the shore and collapsed, startling a hermit crab who darted beneath a lichen-covered rock.

He attempted a deep breath of blissful air, but it caught in his throat and led to a bout of coughing. His lungs were burning from holding his breath for so long, he was light-headed, and every muscle ached. Grit and sand clung to his drenched uniform.

But he was alive, and for the moment, that was enough to bring a grateful laugh mingling with the erratic coughs.

It seemed that every time he transformed into the Sentinel, he learned something new about himself and his abilities.

Or, lack of abilities.

Today he had learned that the Sentinel's armor was not watertight. And also, that it sank like a rock.

His memories of the flight were already starting to blur. One moment he'd been on the barge, preparing a ball of fire around his gauntlet, sure that he would soon have Hawthorn begging for mercy. Those brambles of hers *looked* flammable, anyway. But the next thing he knew, he was entangled in her tentacles, which turned out to be as strong as iron. One of the thorns had punctured the plate of armor on his back, though it luckily hadn't made it through to his skin.

Then he was sinking. Surrounded by blackness. His ears clogging with the pressure, and water leaking in through the joints in his suit. He'd been halfway to the bottom of the river when he retracted the suit into the tattooed pocket on his chest and started kicking toward the shore.

The coughing fit finally stopped and Adrian rolled onto his back, gazing up at the bottom of the bridge. He heard a heavy vehicle crossing overhead. The steel structure trembled from its weight.

The world had just fallen quiet again when he heard a chime on his communicator band. He grimaced.

For the first time, he began to think that his decision to transform into the Sentinel might not have been the best idea. If he'd caught Hawthorn and retrieved the stolen medication, he'd probably feel differently, but as it was, he had nothing to show for his risk.

His team would be wondering where he was. He would have to explain why he was soaking wet.

Sitting up, he reached for the pocket sewn into the lining of his Renegade uniform, but there was nothing inside.

No marker. No chalk.

Adrian cursed. They must have fallen out in the water.

So much for drawing himself some dry clothing.

The wristband pinged again. He rubbed the water droplets off the screen with his damp sleeve, then pulled up the messages. There were seven of them. Three from Ruby, one from Oscar, one from Danna, two from his dads.

*Great.* They'd gotten the Council involved.

No sooner had he thought it than he heard a roar of water. His eyes widened and Adrian scrambled to his feet—too late. A wall of foaming river water crashed down, drenching him all over again. He barely maintained his balance as the surging wave rolled back out into the riverbed. Spluttering and pulling scraps of snakeweed from his uniform, he watched as a second wall of water built up on the other side of the river, rising impossibly up over the far shore. A wave, thirty feet tall, with all the scattered boats perched deftly on its crest. The floor of the river could be seen, all slimy plant life and built-up trash. The wave hung, motionless for a moment, before sinking back down and surging toward the bay.

Tsunami, Adrian guessed, or one of the other water elementals on the force, combing the bottom of the river.

Searching for *him,* he realized.

Nova must have seen the Sentinel being dropped into the water, and now they were searching for the body.

Turning, he stumbled for the small cliffside. He grasped at weeds and rocks and exposed tree roots as he scrambled up the bank. By the time he reached the top, he was not only soaking wet but muddy too.

There were signs of recent life in the shelter of the bridge—a tarp, a couple of blankets, an abandoned shopping cart—but no one was there now to witness Adrian as he dashed around the abutment and up to street level. Below him, the river roared again as another unnatural wave began to rise up from the depths.

He was preparing to climb over the guardrail when he heard a familiar, booming voice coming from the bridge.

Heart leaping, Adrian ducked down.

"—keep looking," said the Dread Warden, one of Adrian's dads and a member of the Renegade Council. "Magpie will be here soon.

She might be able to detect the suit, even if it's buried beneath the silt."

Adrian exhaled. He hadn't been noticed.

"I'll see if I can find anything from the next bridge too," said Tsunami. "It seems unlikely he would have gone much farther than this, but it won't hurt to look."

Adrian lifted his head and peered over the guardrail. He could see Tsunami and his dad standing on the deck of Halfpenny Bridge, the wind fluttering through Tsunami's royal blue skirt and snapping at the Dread Warden's black cape. They were both watching the river.

Tsunami flicked a finger, and he heard the crash of water below.

They started to make their way in his direction. Crouching, Adrian scurried back beneath the bridge.

"Sketch?"

Gasping, he spun around. Nova stood on the other side of the street, peering at him like he was an unknown amphibious species she was preparing to dissect.

"Nova," he stammered, hurrying back up the hill and stepping over the guardrail. "Er—Insomnia. Hi."

Her frown deepened. She had changed out of her uniform into drawstring pants and a healer-issued tank top. Adrian could see the edges of bandages wrapping around her right shoulder.

"Where have you been? Ruby's worried sick," she said, strolling across the street. Her eyes scoured his uniform. "Why are you all wet?"

"Adrian?"

He cringed and faced the two Council members as they reached the end of the bridge. They appeared as surprised to see him as Nova had, though more curious than suspicious.

So far.

"Hey, everyone," he said. He forced a smile, but then wiped it away, urging himself to stop aiming for nonchalant. Nothing about this was nonchalant. He licked his lips, which still tasted like sludgy river water, and gestured toward the bridge. "Find anything?"

"Great skies, Adrian," said the Dread Warden. "Oscar alerted us about your disappearance more than half an hour ago. One minute you're telling your team that you're going after a prodigy criminal, and then—nothing! We didn't know if Hawthorn had attacked you, or . . . or . . ." He paused, his expression wavering between worried and angry. "What were you doing all this time? Why aren't you responding to your messages?"

"Um. I was"—Adrian glanced at the river, sunlight glinting off its surface—"searching for the Sentinel." He ran a hand over his hair. "I was on one of the side streets when I saw Hawthorn throw him in the water. So I went down to the shore and have been waiting to see if he would surface." He didn't have to fake his chagrin. "I wasn't expecting you to start combing the water so soon, hence . . ." He gestured at his uniform, which was still clinging uncomfortable and cold to his skin. "And, uh . . . messages?" He tapped at his wristband. "Oh, wow, seven missed messages? That's weird. I didn't hear them come through. But you know, my band has been acting up lately. I'll have to get the folks in tech to check into that." He dared to peek at Nova. Her eyes were still narrowed in suspicion.

"Yeah," she said slowly. "You should look into that." Her expression cleared as she turned to the Council members. "The cleanup crew is here, along with Magpie." Her tone carried a definite sourness when she mentioned Maggie's alias. Though Adrian had a lot of sympathy for the kid, he knew Nova had never quite forgiven her for trying to steal her bracelet. He glanced at her wrist, searching for the clasp he'd once redrawn on her skin, but it was hidden beneath the sleeve of her uniform. "She wasn't sure where you wanted her to get started."

"I'll talk to her," said Tsunami. "Should I have Smokescreen brief the cleanup crew, or"—she inspected Adrian—"is the team leader prepared to do that?"

Grateful for the opportunity to move on from this conversation, Adrian was about to say that he would love nothing more than to point out all the locations in this neighborhood where windows had been broken, walls had been destroyed, and bullets had been fired, but the Dread Warden responded first. "Have them talk to Smokescreen. Adrian needs to head to the medical tent and be checked for injuries."

"And let the others know you're okay," said Nova, "before Ruby assembles her own search party."

They followed Nova into a connecting side street, and Adrian spotted two ambulances emblazoned with the Renegade R and a handful of transport vehicles. The media was arriving, too, but they were being held back behind a banner of yellow security tape.

Down the street, he saw the cleanup crew awaiting instructions. Adrian was glad to see Magpie among the crew. It would be good for her to apply her powers to something more productive than pickpocketing. The kid had potential, he knew, even if her personality was as prickly as Hawthorn's extra limbs.

As if she could hear his thoughts, Magpie spotted Adrian across the street and her bored expression turned sour. He waved jovially and she turned his back on him.

A white tent had been erected in front of a small electronics repair store. Oscar, Ruby, and Danna were each on a stretcher, being attended by the healers who had arrived on the scene. One of the healers was pulling encrusted jewels from Ruby's thigh with a pair of heavy-duty pliers. Ruby flinched each time a new one was pulled, the wound immediately covered with thick gauze to stanch the bleeding and keep new bloodstones from sprouting.

Danna was lying flat on her stomach. The back of her uniform, from her neck to her hips, had been cut open, allowing a healer to access the wounds crisscrossing her flesh. Her back looked like it had been mauled by grizzly bear. Adrian suspected that Hawthorn's barbs were to blame. At least the healer working on her appeared to be practiced in flesh wounds, and even from a distance Adrian could see the cuts slowly knitting together in the top layers of her skin.

"Adrian!" Ruby shouted, startling the healer who was trying to extract the final bloodstone from her leg. Ruby yelped in pain as the gem dislodged. She scowled at the healer, who scowled back. Ruby grabbed a roll of bandaging and began wrapping the wound herself. "What happened?" she asked, returning her attention to Adrian and Nova. "Where were you?"

Adrian opened his mouth, prepared to give his explanation again and hoping it would become more believable with repetition, when the healer held up his hand, still gripping the pliers. "There will be time for reunions later. We need to get all of you back to headquarters for follow-up treatment."

"Has Smokescreen been cleared?" asked Tsunami. "We'd like him to debrief the cleanup crew."

The healer nodded. "Yes, fine. His injuries were negligible."

"Negligible?" said Oscar, holding up his forearm, which was wrapped in white bandages. "Their getaway driver scratched me when I was getting out the handcuffs. What if the guy had rabies or something? This could be a mortal wound here."

The healer eyed him warily. "You can't get rabies from finger-nail scratches."

Oscar huffed. "I said, *or something.*"

"Have you checked him for an overinflated ego yet?" teased Ruby. "I'd hate for him to float away on us."

Oscar cut a glare toward her. "You're just jealous."

"Yes, I *am* jealous!" said Ruby. "I helped rescue that girl, too, but she didn't even notice me. She was just all—*Oh, Smokescreen! I've been dreaming of your smoldering smokiness all my life!*"

Adrian's cheek twitched. Ruby's impersonation wasn't exactly how he remembered the barista from the café, but close enough.

Oscar nodded. "I've found that my smoldering smokiness does have that effect on people."

Ruby snorted, and Adrian sensed that she was trying to annoy Oscar and was frustrated that it didn't seem to be working.

"What girl?" said Nova. "The hostage?"

"Yep," said Oscar, idly swinging his cane. "She's pretty much in love with me."

"Who isn't, right?" said Danna, flashing a cheeky grin.

"Exactly. Thank you, Danna."

She gave him a thumbs-up from the table.

"Oscar is always telling us that these uniforms are a love beacon," said Adrian. "I'm surprised it doesn't happen more often. Although . . . no girl has ever swooned over me like that. And now I'm jealous too. Thanks, Ruby."

"It's not just the uniform," said Oscar. "I mean, I did save her life."

"*We* saved her—" Ruby started, but it fizzled into an angry growl.

"Maybe I should have asked for her number," Oscar mused.

Ruby gaped at him, cheeks flushing, and Adrian felt a little bad for her. But then, she had been the one to try to tease Oscar in the first place, so maybe she deserved it.

Slamming her mouth shut, Ruby turned her head away. "Maybe you should have. I'm sure she would love to date a *real Renegade*."

"Who said anything about dating?" said Oscar. "I just thought she might want to be the president of my fan club. Good help is hard to find."

Ruby guffawed, but as she looked back at Oscar, her expression softened with suspicion. "Are you saying you *wouldn't* go on a date with her?"

"I hadn't thought of it." A short silence hung between them, and there was a hint of uncertainty as Oscar ventured, "Do you really think I should have asked?"

Ruby gaped at him again, speechless, trapped by her own taunting. After a long silence, she cleared her throat and shrugged. "You can do whatever you want."

Adrian bit his tongue, trying to hide his smile at the nonanswer.

Ruby turned her focus back to her wounds, studying them with renewed interest as her cheeks turned scarlet.

Oscar, though, was still watching her, flummoxed, and maybe a little hopeful. "Well . . . maybe I will ask a girl on a date," he said. "Someday."

"Maybe you should," said Ruby, without looking up.

"Maybe I will."

"You already said that."

"Right. Well." Oscar climbed down from the table, and Adrian could see that Ruby was no longer the only one blushing. "If you'll excuse me, I have important debriefing responsibility things to take care of. So I'll, uh . . . see you guys back at headquarters. Good job today, team."

Straightening his uniform, he headed toward the cleanup crew. Tsunami followed, with an almost-unnoticeable sigh.

Danna whistled under her breath. "You two are impossible," she muttered. "In fact, all four of you are driving me nuts."

# CHAPTER FOUR

T HE DREAD WARDEN SIGHED, making Adrian jump. He'd forgotten his dad was there. "I don't miss this age," he said, and one
of the healers gave him a knowing look. "Dr. Grant, could you
also examine Sketch when you have a minute?"

"I'm fine," Adrian said. "Don't waste your time on me. Focus on
Ruby and Danna."

"Adrian—" the Dread Warden started.

"Honestly, Pops, I just got splashed with some river water. It's
not like I almost drowned or anything. Don't worry about it." He
added a grin for effect. He'd gotten lucky lately, not having experienced any dire wounds since he'd started giving himself the tattoos
that imbued him with the Sentinel's powers. The last thing he
wanted was for a healer to notice the curious designs inked into his
skin and start to make inquiries, especially to his dads.

"Fine," said the Dread Warden. "Let's get everyone back to
headquarters, and"—he turned toward the gathered journalists and
their flashing cameras—"start figuring out what to tell *them*."

"Wait, wait, wait!" yelled Danna as two assistants wheeled her gurney toward one of the ambulances. She propped herself up on her elbows. "I'm not going anywhere until someone tells us what happened. Adrian disappears and no one can get ahold of him, the Sentinel shows up, Hawthorn gets away, and now they're saying the Sentinel might be *dead*? And what is this about Adrian getting splashed with river water?" She spread her fingers toward Adrian, like she would grab him and shake him if he were within reach. "What were you doing?"

"I was chasing the Sentinel, and after Hawthorn threw him in the water, I was waiting to see if he would surface." He shrugged, relieved that, in fact, it *did* sound more believable this time.

"You'll all be filled in after the healers have released you from the med wing," said the Dread Warden. He snapped his fingers and Danna and Ruby were loaded up into the ambulance, grumbling to themselves.

"Nova?" said the Dread Warden. "I'd like to have a private word with Adrian. You're welcome to assist Oscar and Tsunami with the briefing."

Nova glanced at the group and noticed Magpie among them. Her own lips wrinkled in distaste. "Actually, I think I'd better head home before the news stories get too convoluted. I like to give my uncle the story from my point of view before he hears it all third-hand." Her gaze swooped over Adrian's wet clothes one more time and he found himself standing straighter. "I'm . . . glad you're okay," she said, sounding almost uncomfortable to be admitting it. "You did scare us for a minute."

"We're superheroes," he said. "We wouldn't be doing our job if we didn't scare people from time to time."

Nova didn't respond, but her expression softened before she turned away and started heading back toward the river. It was a long walk to her home, Adrian knew, and he was about to call after her and suggest she wait. Maybe they could take one of the transport vans together. But the words didn't come and he knew that the invitation would be declined.

Most of his invitations were declined where Nova was concerned. So what was the point?

His shoulders sank, ever so slightly.

"About that," said his dad.

Adrian turned to him. The Dread Warden peeled the black domino mask from his face and it was as if his dad had transformed. It wasn't just the costume. The shift was in the relaxing of his posture. The ironic tilt of his mouth. Where the Dread Warden, famous superhero and founding member of the Renegades had stood, now it was just Simon Westwood, concerned parent.

"About what?" said Adrian.

"It is not our job, as superheroes, to *scare* people from time to time."

Adrian chuckled. "It may not be written into our job description, but come on. What we do is dangerous."

Simon's tone hardened. "You're right. And because it is so dangerous, it is of utmost importance that our behavior never veers into *recklessness*."

"Reckless?"

"Yes, reckless. You can't just leave your team behind like that, Adrian. Why do you think we organize recruits into teams in the first place? It's your responsibility to look after one another, and your teammates can't do that if they have no idea where you are."

"We were all following the same objective." Adrian gestured in the direction Nova had gone. "Nova ran off after Hawthorn too."

"Yes, Nova McLain's penchant for making rash decisions has

been well documented, and to be perfectly honest, I hoped that spending time with you and your team would help her grow out of it." Simon pushed his cape back from his shoulders. "Besides, in this particular case, it's not a fair comparison. Nova still had Danna to watch her back. Whereas no one had any idea where you'd gone off to. It's not like you, Adrian, and it's got to stop."

"I was trying to catch up to Nova and Hawthorn. I wasn't sure what direction they'd gone, so it took me a while to find them, and then there was the whole Sentinel thing that threw a wrench in my plans, but . . ." He rubbed the back of his head. "It's not like I ran off to Casino Jack for an afternoon without telling anyone. I was doing my job!"

"I'm not trying to start a fight about this," said Simon. "You're a great team leader, and we're really proud of you. I just want to remind you that there are no lone wolves in the Renegades. There is no *I* in *hero*."

Adrian rocked back on his heels. "You've been holding on to that one for a while, haven't you?"

"*So* long!" said Simon, a smile brightening his face. "Actually, I'm pretty sure it was one of those sayings your mom used to say."

Adrian chuckled. "She did like her two-cent parables."

Though Adrian's mother, the brave and wondrous Lady Indomitable, had been killed when he was a kid, her cheesy sayings still came back to him sometimes. Unbidden, but when he needed to hear them most.

*Superheroes are only as good as their conviction.*

*Sometimes, a smile is the most powerful weapon we have.*

*When in doubt . . . fly.*

Easy for her to say, of course, given that she could actually fly.

Adrian turned toward the cleanup crew. There were a dozen or so Renegades gathered around Oscar as he gave an animated reen-actment of the fight with Hawthorn and the rest of the criminals. He was currently using his cane to swipe at an invisible enemy, which Adrian thought might have been his explanation of how he'd knocked out the guy who had taken the café server hostage.

They had worked as a team then, hadn't they? And they had successfully rescued the girl.

He appreciated his team. Respected them. Even loved them.

But he wasn't convinced that a superhero didn't sometimes have to go off on their own. Maybe there weren't any lone wolves in the Renegades, but . . . the Sentinel wasn't a Renegade, was he?

"So," said Adrian, turning back to Simon, "if you and Tsunami were looking for the Sentinel, who went after Hawthorn?"

"Hugh and Tamaya," said Simon.

Hugh Everhart—Adrian's other dad, the invincible Captain Chromium. And Tamaya Rae, Thunderbird. The only founding member other than Adrian's mom who had the power of flight.

"Have we heard anything?" he said.

Simon checked his wristband and shook his head. "I'm worried the trail had gone cold by the time we got here. But her accomplices are in custody and we'll begin interrogations immediately. One of them will talk."

"What do you think they wanted all that medication for?"

Simon heaved a sigh. "The drugs they took are used to develop a powerful opioid. It's a pretty lucrative business for those who are willing to produce and deal it. And of course, for every street dealer doling out these drugs, there are plenty of sick patients at the hospitals not receiving the help they need. The bag Hawthorn had was mostly painkillers, and it's going to be difficult for the pharmaceutical industry to replenish the supply on short notice. It's been hard enough to bring back legitimate drug production as it is." He pinched the bridge of his nose. "Luckily, your team managed to keep a lot of those drugs off the street. It could have been much worse."

Adrian wanted to accept the compliment, but he couldn't help but focus on their failure more than their successes. They should have been able to stop Hawthorn. "Will you let me know once they have Hawthorn's location? If you're going to send a team after her, I'd like to—"

"No," said Simon. "If Hugh and Tamaya don't bring her in today, we'll be assigning another unit to the case. Your team has sustained too many injuries. You're taking a few days off."

"But—"

"Don't." Simon held up a hand. "This is non-negotiable."

"Are you saying that as my dad, or my boss?"

"Both, and also as someone who cares for Ruby and Danna. They need time to recover, Adrian."

"Fine, then let me, Nova, and Oscar be a part of it."

Simon scratched the dark whiskers on his chin. "Is this going to be Nightmare all over again?"

"We found Nightmare, didn't we?"

"You almost got killed."

"Yeah. I'm a superhero, Pops. How many times have *you* almost gotten killed? And you don't hear me complaining about it."

Simon groaned good-naturedly. "What now? Why do you care about Hawthorn? It was just another mission, Adrian. You guys stopped six of the seven perpetrators. We got back *most* of the medicine they took. You did well."

"I like to finish what I start."

"Is that all?"

Adrian drew back. "What do you mean?"

"I just wonder if maybe you're trying a bit too hard to prove yourself these days, after what happened at the carnival."

Adrian scowled. He hated being reminded of how he had failed at the carnival. True, he had found the Anarchist known as Nightmare, but he had also allowed the Detonator to play him like a pixilated character in an old video game. He had replayed those moments with the Detonator a thousand times in his mind, trying to figure out what he could have done differently to stop her. His hesitation had allowed the Detonator to set off two bombs, resulting in dozens of innocent people being hurt, and Adrian couldn't help feeling responsible for each and every one of them.

It was Nova who had shot and killed the Detonator, putting an end to her terrorism. If Nova hadn't been there, Adrian didn't know what might have happened. He should have done more to stop her. He should have figured out sooner that killing the villain would deactivate the explosives.

Maybe it was because he had the Gatlon code authority echoing in his thoughts. *Killing an adversary should always come as a last resort.*

Nova had recognized that they were at the last resort. She did what needed to be done.

Why hadn't he?

"I'm sorry," said Simon, squeezing Adrian's shoulder. "That was thoughtless of me. You and Nova both handled yourselves well, given the circumstances. I'm sorry you couldn't save Nightmare, but no one regrets that we no longer have to worry about the Detonator."

"*Save* Nightmare?"

Simon lifted an eyebrow. "Isn't that what you wanted?"

Adrian's shoulder jerked and Simon dropped his hand. "I wanted information on my mother and her murder. I thought Nightmare might have that information. It had nothing to do with *saving* her. So she's dead—it's not exactly a tragedy."

"Right. That's what I meant. And I know . . . regardless of who she was and the things she'd done, her death was a disappointment to you. To all of us, if she truly did have information that would have solved Georgia's murder."

*Disappointment* didn't begin to describe how Adrian felt at losing that tenuous connection to his mother's killer. He knew Nightmare wasn't the murderer—she was far too young for that—but he was convinced that she had known who it was. Even now, months after he had fought Nightmare on the rooftop overlooking the parade, her words often echoed through his head.

*One cannot be brave who has no fear.*

The same words that had been found on a small white card on his mother's body, after she fell seven stories to her death.

"Yeah, well, I'm not giving up on finding my mother's killer. Nightmare was an Anarchist. If she knew something, then maybe another Anarchist will, too, or another villain who was around at the same time."

"Someone like Hawthorn?"

Adrian didn't try to disguise his bemused grin. "Was she around back then? I haven't had time to confirm that yet."

Simon lifted a finger, nearly jutting it against Adrian's nose. "I'm only going to say this once, Adrian. Do not try to go after Hawthorn by yourself. Or any of the Anarchists, for that matter. You understand? It's dangerous."

Adrian pushed up his glasses and opened his mouth to speak.

"And don't try to tell me that *dangerous* is how superheroes are supposed to operate."

Adrian snapped his mouth shut.

"We have methods in place for a reason," Simon continued. "To help mitigate threats and damage. If you hear something about Hawthorn or any other villain, you call it in and wait for instructions. I want to find out who killed your mother as much as you do, but I'm not about to lose you in the process."

Adrian forced himself to nod. "I know, Pops. I'll try to be less . . . *reckless*."

"Thank you."

Adrian pressed his lips into a thin smile, biting back the words he really wanted to say. The suspicions that had been filling his head for weeks.

Despite the bomb that had supposedly killed her, despite the amount of destruction that had been wreaked at the carnival fun house that day, despite the fact that Adrian himself had witnessed the fight between Nightmare and the Detonator . . . despite everything, he had doubts.

His dads would call it denial. His team would call it his typical, uncanny optimism.

But Adrian couldn't help it.

The truth was, he did not believe that Nightmare was dead.

# CHAPTER FIVE

ADRIAN AND THE TEAM had been left off the patrol schedule for the rest of the week, owing for time to "recover from injuries and trauma," so there was no reason to head into Renegade Headquarters in full gear today. Normally he wouldn't have had to come in to headquarters at all, except that morning the Council had sent out a global communication to all Renegades in the Gatlon City division, requesting their presence at a mandatory meeting.

It was a mysterious message. Adrian couldn't recall there ever being a meeting for the entire organization. Sometimes they implemented new rules in the code and summoned the patrol units to discuss them, or had department meetings with the administration, or the research and development teams, and so on—but *everyone*?

Unfortunately, his dads had already gone when he woke up, so there was no hope of needling information out of them.

Adrian turned a corner, walking beneath a strip of construction scaffolding as he approached the north side of headquarters. It was an overcast morning and the top of the building was lost in clouds, making the skyscraper appear endless.

His attention caught on a vehicle parked at one of the side entrances. It was an armored van, its back doors heavily fortified, and its sides lined with short, tinted windows. The side of the van read CRAGMOOR PENITENTIARY: PRISONER TRANSPORT.

Adrian slowed to a stop. Cragmoor was a prison located off the coast of Gatlon City that had been built to hold prodigy criminals, as most civilian prisons weren't sufficiently equipped to handle a wide array of extraordinary abilities.

Maybe they were picking up a prisoner from one of the temporary holding cells inside headquarters. Although transfers like that were generally made at night, when the streets were empty of curious onlookers.

He continued walking, gazing into the windows of the van as he passed. He couldn't see into the back at all, and the driver's and front passenger's seats were empty.

Shrugging to himself, Adrian made his way to the front of the building, where tourists were gathered around the main entrance, snapping photos of everything from the revolving glass doors to the nearby street sign and the place where the building disappeared into thick cloud cover high above. Adrian wove his way through the crowd, ignoring a couple of gasps and one low muttering, *Was that Adrian Everhart?* The fame wasn't really his, anyway. People didn't care so much about Adrian Everhart as they did about the son of Lady Indomitable, or the adopted son of Captain Chromium and the Dread Warden.

Which was fine. He was used to the attention, just like he was used to acknowledging that he'd done little to earn it.

He shoved through the revolving doors, smiling at the fellow Renegades he passed and jovial Sampson Cartwright at the information desk. He surveyed the lobby for any sign of Oscar or Nova, but when he didn't see them, he headed up the curved flight of stairs to the sky bridge that connected to Max's quarantine.

Max was almost always inside the glass gallery during the day, working on the extensive glass model of Gatlon City he'd been constructing for years, or watching the TV screens that dotted the lobby's many pillars, but today Max was nowhere in sight. He must have been back in the private quarters tucked behind the enclosed rotunda.

Raising his hand, Adrian thumped hard on the wall. "Hey, Bandit, it's me. Are you—"

Max appeared all at once, standing mere inches in front of Adrian on the other side of the glass.

Adrian yelped and stumbled backward, colliding with the sky bridge's handrail. "Great skies, Max, don't *do* that!"

Max started to laugh. "Your face!"

Glowering, Adrian pushed himself off the rail. "Very clever. I'm sure you're the first prodigy with invisibility to *ever* do that to someone."

"Originality is overrated," said Max, pressing down his sandy-blond hair, though it puffed right back up again. His goofy grin didn't fade. "That was so worth it."

As his heart rate returned to normal, Adrian found himself starting to smile, even as he shook his head. Max was only ten years old, but he could be uncannily serious for his age. It was refreshing to see him pulling a childish prank and getting such an enormous kick out of it.

"I'm glad to see you've been practicing," said Adrian.

"I'm getting really good at the invisibility thing. And also, I was able to fuse a penny to a nickel, which is cool because it's harder with two different metals. Your power, though?" Max made a sour face. "I drew a worm yesterday and all it did was wriggle around for, like, five seconds, then died. I mean, come on. A two-year-old could draw a *worm*."

"You didn't get that much of my power," said Adrian. "Maybe you'll never be able to get your drawings to do much."

Max grumbled something that Adrian couldn't make out.

Max had been born with the rare gift of power absorption, meaning he stole the powers from any prodigy he came in close proximity to, hence why Adrian had long ago dubbed him "the Bandit." Most of his abilities had been taken when he was just a baby: metal manipulation and matter fusing from his birth parents, who had been part of a villain gang; invisibility from the Dread Warden; and even telekinesis taken from Ace Anarchy himself during the Battle for Gatlon. Max had been too young to remember any of that, though. More recently, he got a touch of Adrian's ability when Adrian had pulled Nova out of the quarantine that kept Max separate from the rest of the Renegades. Max said that he was sleeping less lately, which probably meant he'd gotten a bit of Nova's power, too, though he had no interest in staying awake twenty-four hours a day, even if he could. He got bored enough as it was in his solitude.

For years, Max would experiment with his abilities only in secret, keeping the extent of them private, even from Adrian. He had been surprised to learn that the kid was actually a lot more talented than anyone had guessed, largely thanks to his own self-training. Adrian knew Max felt guilty for having a lot of the powers he had—like he didn't have a right to any of them. But lately he seemed more eager to practice, and even to show off a little bit. Adrian was happy to see it. Max was the closest thing to a little brother he'd ever known, and he hated to think that Max might feel guilty for something he couldn't control. No prodigy should be made to feel guilty for what they could do.

"Where's Turbo?" Adrian said, scanning the city at Max's feet.

"In the top of Merchant Tower." Max gestured to one of the taller glass skyscrapers. "I made him a little bed in there and now he sleeps, like, all the time. I think you might have made him part sloth."

Weeks ago, Adrian had drawn a tiny dinosaur, a velociraptor, to prove to Nova that Max hadn't taken his powers from him. The creature had disappeared for a while, then one day showed up unexpectedly inside the pastries case of the small espresso stand in the lobby. There had been a great commotion over it and a lot of screaming, and someone from the janitorial crew ended up chasing the creature around with a broom for almost twenty minutes before Adrian heard about it and claimed the dinosaur as one of his creations. Max had asked if he could keep it, and just like that, he inherited a thumb-size pet.

"Eat, sleep, hunt," said Adrian. "That pretty much covers all the dinosaur instincts I know of, so I doubt he'll ever do much more than that."

"If by hunting, you mean gnawing on the leftover meat from my dinners. By the way . . ." Max gestured to something over Adrian's shoulder. "Did you know you're dead?"

Adrian turned to see one of the screens playing a video of the Sentinel being thrown off the barge and disappearing beneath the water. It had been recorded from Nova's fancy binoculars and was the clearest footage that anyone had managed to catch of the Sentinel so far.

"Were you worried?" said Adrian.

"No."

"What? Not at all?"

Max started to respond and Adrian knew it would be to deny it again, but he hesitated and admitted, "Maybe for about five seconds or so, but I knew you'd be fine."

"Thanks for the vote of confidence." Adrian glanced around and, though the sky bridge was empty, lowered his voice. "Of course, we really shouldn't talk about this here."

"Yeah, yeah," said Max, unconcerned. He was the only one who had figured out Adrian's identity, a conclusion he reached after watching Adrian leap more than halfway across the quarantine in an effort to save Nova. It really was a shame that he was stuck in here all the time, because the kid would have been a great investigator. "Do you ever think about telling them?"

Adrian gulped. He tried to meet Max's eyes, but Max was still watching the news footage.

"Every single time I see them," he admitted. "But every time I see them, it gets a little bit harder."

Adrian had never intended to keep this secret for so long. In the beginning, he'd been excited to tell his dads about his tattoos and how he could use them to give himself new powers. But since then, things had gotten out of control. As the Sentinel, he'd broken a lot of rules. He'd endangered civilian lives. He'd damaged public buildings and infrastructure. He'd searched private property without the "evidence" of wrongdoing that the Renegades would have required. He'd used violent force to apprehend criminals when maybe— *maybe*—he could have found a way to stop them without causing harm. The list went on.

But he couldn't bring himself to regret any of it. Breaking those rules had allowed him to do a lot of good. In the past month alone he'd single-handedly captured seventeen criminals, including two prodigies. He'd stopped car thieves, house burglars, drug dealers, and more. Yes, he'd gone against the code at times, but he was still a superhero.

Somehow, though, he didn't think his dads would see it that way. What would they do if they found out his secret identity? If they showed him leniency, when anyone else would be arrested, it would be a blatant disregard for the Council's laws. *Their* laws.

And Adrian didn't want to put them in that position. He didn't want to make them have to choose between him and the Renegades.

To be honest, he also wasn't sure he wanted to know what their choice would be.

"Maybe . . . ," Max started, though his voice was quiet. "Maybe you won't have to tell them." He gestured up at the television. "Given that the Sentinel is dead."

Adrian blinked. It hadn't occurred to him that *this* could be the end of his alter ego, but . . . Max was right. This would be an easy way out. If he never transformed again, everyone would assume that the Sentinel had drowned. No one would have to know.

But the thought of never becoming the Sentinel again made his stomach lurch.

The Renegades weren't enough. Gatlon City needed him.

"Do you think that would be best?" he asked.

"It would be easiest," Max said. "Also . . . highly disappointing."

The corner of Adrian's mouth twitched. "That would be the worst thing of all."

Max sighed. "No Sentinel, no patrol . . . you're going to be so bored."

Adrian cast him a weak smile. "That's not entirely true. I have . . . some idea of how to fill my time." At Max's curious expression, he leaned closer to the glass. "There are still three Anarchists out there, right? Queen Bee, Cyanide, and Phobia. I may not be on the official investigation team, but with all this free time, I figured maybe I could do a bit of side research."

"Have the patrols found anything since they abandoned the subway tunnels?"

He shook his head. "No. But they're out there somewhere."

And with the Nightmare investigation gone cold—what with her probable death and all—he needed a new direction if he was ever going to find his mother's killer. The Anarchists were his best hope for bringing the murderer to justice.

Adrian's wristband chimed with an incoming message. He tapped the screen and Oscar's text started to scrawl around his arm.

> Ruby just got released from med-wing. Heading to
> meeting room. Any word from Nova?

"I have to get going," said Adrian. "The Council called everyone in for a big meeting this morning. You don't happen to know what it's about, do you?"

Max's expression turned strangely vacant. "I might," he said.

"Oh?"

Max shook his head. "I might be wrong. I don't know. Come tell me when it's over, okay?"

"Can do." Adrian pulled a new marker from his back pocket—a replacement for the one that had fallen into the river—and sketched an earthworm onto the glass wall. He pushed it through, sending the wriggling creature into Max's open palm. "A snack for Turbo when he wakes up."

◇◇◆◇◇

HE FOUND OSCAR, Ruby, and Danna in the hall outside the grand meeting room. "You're free," he said, beaming.

"I know!" said Ruby, throwing her arms gleefully into the air. "I should have gone home yesterday, but there's that antiquated twenty-four-hour waiting period. I don't understand why the healers think they know how our powers work better than we do. My grandma was worried sick."

"Well, you look good," said Adrian, inspecting the place where Ruby's leg had been covered in bloodstones last time he'd seen her. Though she was wearing denim shorts, there was no longer any sign of her wounds. Not even bandages, for that matter. "Being covered in vicious rock formations is cool and all, but I prefer you without."

"Aw, you're making me blush," said Ruby, though one look at her freckled cheeks proved that he definitely wasn't.

Danna, on the other hand, kept flinching when she moved, and he could detect a white bandage peeking out of her sleeve.

"I don't want your pity," said Danna before Adrian could say anything. "I'm actually becoming fond of the covered-in-bandages look. It's like a fashion statement."

"Is the statement that you're a total badass?" asked Oscar.

"Do you even have to ask?" she said, grinning at him. "Anyway, the cuts were deep and not all of them were clean, but another couple of days and I'll be fine. Besides, those injuries were nothing compared with the burns from the Sentinel."

Adrian winced and immediately hoped that no one had noticed.

It occurred to him that the strangest thing about seeing his teammates right then wasn't the fact that their severe wounds were nearly gone—the Renegades kept the best prodigy healers in the world on staff—but that they were all wearing civilian clothing. Even Oscar was in a vest and dress shirt, his sleeves cuffed at his forearms.

Together they seemed almost . . . normal. It was actually kind of nice, for a change.

"Oh! Before I forget . . ." Ruby pulled a handful of cards from a pocket. "You're all invited."

Adrian took the card from her and flipped it over. It was an announcement for the annual Sidekick Olympics happening that weekend at City Park.

"Sidekick Olympics, awesome," said Oscar. "I've been thinking the superhero gig has gotten to be too much pressure. A sidekick role sounds much more laid-back."

"Too bad it's a non-prodigy competition," said Ruby. "My brothers are competing in it. They've always been a little jealous that I'm this totally cool and semi-famous superhero and every-thing. I mean, proud, but still jealous."

"Hold on. You're a superhero?" said Oscar, feigning shock. Then he leaned against her shoulder, batting his eyelashes. "Did you know, I've always wanted to be rescued by a superhero?"

Ruby laughed and shoved him away, even as her cheeks red-dened. "You make a terrible damsel, Oscar."

Danna rolled her eyes at them.

"Anyway, I'd get major big-sister points if you guys came," Ruby finished. "And before you ask, yes, Oscar, there will be food trucks."

Oscar made an approving okay with his fingers.

Adrian scanned the invitation. He'd never been to the Sidekick Olympics before—a series of lighthearted competitions for non-prodigy kids. It wasn't exactly how he'd planned to spend his Saturday afternoon, but it could be fun.

"I have an invitation for Nova too," said Ruby. "Has anyone seen her today?"

"Not yet." Adrian checked the time on his wristband. There were still ten minutes before the meeting was supposed to begin.

He glanced through the open doors, where he could see hundreds of Renegades milling about as they waited. "Maybe she went in already?"

"We checked," said Danna. "No sign of her. But we should go sit down before it gets too crowded."

"We'll save her a seat," said Ruby. "Does anyone know what they called us in for?"

"Do you think it could have to do with yesterday?" said Oscar.

"You mean about the Sentinel being dead?" Adrian asked.

Oscar cast him a strange look as they started heading toward the doors. "No. I mean about Hawthorn getting away with all those drugs."

"Oh, right," said Adrian, feeling sheepish for jumping to the Sentinel thing. "They would have started questioning her accomplices already. Maybe they learned something."

"Guys!"

A spark flickered inside Adrian's chest. Nova was jogging toward them, her cheeks flushed.

"Oh, good," she said, slightly out of breath. "I only saw the message an hour ago. I had to run all the way from Wallow—uh—past Wallowridge. I thought for sure I'd be late." She drew up short as Ruby thrust the invitation beneath her nose. "What's this?"

"My brothers are competing in the Sidekick Olympics."

Nova made a face—instinctive, Adrian knew. But before she could say anything, Oscar piped up, "Don't fret. We've been guaranteed food trucks."

Her aversion was immediately replaced with an amused smile. "Well, in *that* case . . ."

She met Adrian's gaze, and for the briefest of moments all he could think about was how her blue eyes were brighter than usual, from the morning air or the exercise or maybe there was just really good lighting on this floor, and . . .

He really needed to stop thinking about it.

Gripping the card, Nova peered into the meeting room. "Do we know what's going on?"

"No idea," said Danna, waving her arm. "But we'd better get in there before all the good seats are taken."

# CHAPTER SIX

NOVA HAD NEVER been inside the main conference room at Renegade Headquarters. According to the others, it wasn't used much. Oscar had once mentioned an annual meeting in which the Council liked to bore everyone to tears with statistics on their successes over the past twelve months, and lengthy discussions of their priorities for the future. When he told her this, Nova attempted to act sympathetic—how awful, how boring, how can anyone stand it? When in truth, she would have loved nothing more than to sit in on some of the Council's upcoming plans for Gatlon City.

Danna led the way into the room, which consisted of a platform at the front facing hundreds of plastic chairs set into rows. The seats were filling up fast as Renegades poured in. Nova tried to eavesdrop on their huddled conversations, but it seemed the rest of the organization was as baffled as to the purpose of this meeting as her team was.

Though she'd been a Renegade for months now, Nova still found herself growing anxious when she was surrounded by so many superheroes at once. She calmed herself with practice observations—counting exits, determining what objects in the room would make decent weapons, estimating potential threats, and developing a mental escape route should anything happen.

Nothing ever happened, though. She was beginning to feel like all her preparation was unwarranted—the Renegades were as clueless to her true motives as they had been the day she entered the trials. But she couldn't make herself relax. Any small slipup could reveal her identity. Any little clue could end this charade. An attack could come the moment she let down her guard.

It was exhausting to maintain her vigilance while still acting as though she belonged there, but she was getting used to being on edge. She couldn't imagine being any other way, at least not inside headquarters.

"There are five seats together," said Danna, pointing toward a row not far from the front. She moved to stake their claim.

"Nova McLain?"

Nova spun around. Evander Wade, one of the five Council members who was more generally known by his alias, Blacklight, sauntered through the crowd. "Do you have a second?"

"Um." Nova glanced at Adrian, then at the platform at the front of the room. A microphone and a stool were waiting for a presenter, but the stage was empty. "I guess so."

"I'll save you a seat," said Adrian, with the faintest, almost unnoticeable brush of fingers against her elbow, before he followed the rest of the group.

*Almost* unnoticeable.

Nova and her traitorous nerves, of course, noticed it keenly.

"I wanted to discuss the request you submitted a couple weeks ago," said Evander, folding his arms over his chest. The stance was not so much defensive as it was a display of innate power. Nova had seen Evander Wade standing like this a number of times—feet planted into the floor, chest ever-so-slightly lifted. Unlike the rest of the Council, who could at least feign normalcy on occasion, Evander never seemed to be able to turn off his "superhero" self. The fact that he was currently dressed in his iconic uniform made the effect even more pronounced: all black Lycra formed to each muscle, white boots, white gloves, and a glow-in-the-dark emblem on his chest.

To Nova, it made him seem pompous and a little ridiculous, but the crowds of giggling girls who always followed after him at public events must have felt otherwise.

"My . . . request?" she said.

"About doing some part-time work in the artifacts department."

"Oh! That. Right. Is it . . . still under consideration?"

"Well, I'm sorry it's taken us this long to get back to you." Evander tilted his head toward her as if they were in a conspiratorial conversation. "Been busy around here, you know?"

"Of course."

"But . . . well, when can you start?"

Nova's heart expanded. "Really? Uh—now! Or, whenever. As soon as you'd like me to."

"Excellent." Evander flashed a smile, his white teeth visible beneath a curled red mustache. "I've already talked to Snapshot about it. She heads up the department, and she's excited to have you onboard. I think you two will get along well."

*Snapshot.* Nova knew that alias. Simon Westwood, the Dread Warden himself, had mentioned the name to her when he'd told her that Ace's helmet was not strictly available for public viewing, *but . . . "Maybe if you made a really great bribe to the people in weapons and artifacts. I hear Snapshot is a sucker for sour gummies."*

Nova wasn't sure if he'd been making a joke or not. What she did know was that Ace Anarchy's helmet was somewhere in that department. Most of the world believed that Captain Chromium had destroyed it, a lie perpetuated by the Council themselves. They even kept a damaged replica in a display case outside their offices. But the real helmet was actually somewhere in this building and, presumably, this Snapshot knew how to access it.

"Now, that does leave one conundrum," said Evander.

"It does?"

"Honestly, it's part of the reason we've hesitated for so long. There are some people"—he faked a cough and spluttered, "Tamaya," then another cough—"who worry we're putting too much on your plate." He gestured toward the front of the room, where the other four Council members were chatting together beside the platform. It was startling to see them *all* dressed in their traditional super-hero garb, down to the capes and the masks, which made Nova even more curious to know what this meeting was about. "You may not know that Tamaya's been pushing us to start drafting labor laws for the city for . . . I don't know, six years now? It's not exactly a top priority with everything else, but we all have our passion projects. Anyway, we're aware that you're currently on a patrol unit and we want you to stay on patrols. Plus, you've been called on to do investigative work and data entry for incoming acquisitions, and that's asking a lot of you. So you need to let us know if it starts to feel like too much. You want to take some time off, set some limits on your work hours, that sort of thing, you come talk to me . . . or go to Snapshot and she and I can discuss it. Just, please"—he lowered his voice—"for all the skies, don't complain to Tamaya without talking to me first, because she is an adamant abuser of the phrase 'told you so,' and no one needs that, you know what I mean?"

Nova stared at him. "You really don't have to worry about that.

I'm so excited for this opportunity. Believe me, I want to be involved in . . . well, as much as you guys need me for. And I have so much free time on my hands, it feels good to be using it for something productive." She grinned brightly, and it was made easier by the fact that she hadn't had to tell a single lie. Given that she never slept, she *did* have a lot of free time on her hands, and having access to the artifacts department would be very productive indeed.

"Great to hear," said Evander, slapping her on the back, hard enough to make her stumble in surprise. "Adrian really knew what he was doing when he picked you out at the trials. That boy has great intuition." Stepping back, he pointed his fingers at her, like shooting pretend pistols. "You can report to artifacts tomorrow morning. I'll let Snapshot know you're coming."

She turned away, newly energized.

All of Nova's previous attempts to learn more had been met with dead ends and unknowns, to the point where it made her want to attack something with a crowbar. She was supposed to be a spy. She was supposed to be the Anarchists' secret weapon. Now, she could get close to Ace's helmet and start making a plan for how she was going to get it back.

Most of the crowd had found seats by the time Nova made her way toward her team.

"What did Blacklight want?" Adrian whispered as she sat down between him and Danna.

"He wanted to know if I'm still interested in doing extra work in the artifacts department," she said. "I start tomorrow."

Adrian looked surprised and, she thought, a little disheartened. "Artifacts? But . . . what about . . ."

"I'll still be doing patrols. Remember, I have a lot more hours in my day than you guys have."

Adrian nodded, but she could still see a shadow of concern behind his glasses. She knew exactly what he was thinking. Just because she never *slept* didn't mean she shouldn't occasionally *rest*. It was an argument she heard a lot. But people who needed sleep and rest couldn't possibly understand how lack of action only made her irritable. She needed movement, work, momentum. She needed to keep busy during those long hours when the rest of the world was sleeping in order to drive away the anxieties that were always encroaching on her. The constant worry that she wasn't doing enough.

"It's fine," she said. "I want to do this." Remembering the faint way Adrian had touched her elbow, Nova braced herself and went to place a hand on his knee. But in the space between her brain telling her it was a good idea, and her hand actually making the move, it turned into an uncomfortable balling of her fist that knocked clumsily against the side of Adrian's thigh, before immediately withdrawing into her own lap.

Adrian stared down at his leg, brow furrowed.

Nova cleared her throat and wished that she'd been gifted with the power to stop blushing at will, rather than eternal sleeplessness.

A hand thumped against a microphone, reverberating through the speakers. The five Council members had taken the stage: Evander Wade, Kasumi Hasegawa, Tamaya Rae, Simon Westwood, and Hugh Everhart.

Hugh stood at the microphone. Though the Council pretended they didn't have a hierarchy among themselves, most people felt that Hugh Everhart—the invincible Captain Chromium—was the figurehead of the organization. He was the one who had defeated Ace Anarchy. He was the one who had rallied countless prodigies to their side and fought against the villain gangs who had taken control of the city.

He was also, of the entire Council, the one who Nova felt deserved her wrath the most. If anyone should have rescued her family when they were killed more than a decade ago, it should have been Captain Chromium.

But he hadn't stopped the murders from happening. He hadn't been there when she needed him most.

Nova would never forgive him for that. She would never forgive any of them.

"Thank you all for coming today on such short notice," said Hugh. His Captain Chromium uniform was comprised of skintight fabric that made it seem like even his neck muscles had been lifting weights. The classic costumes were generally reserved for special occasions—big celebrations or big announcements. It suggested that today, the Council were not only the leaders of this organization. They were the superheroes who protected the world.

And, in doing so, controlled the world.

"We hadn't intended to conduct this meeting for another couple of weeks," Hugh continued, "but due to recent events, the Council has agreed that immediate action must be taken. As I'm sure you're aware, the Renegade organization has come under recent scrutiny, beginning most notably with the Puppeteer's attack on our parade, and more recently, the Detonator's bombing of Cosmopolis Park."

Nova traded a glance with Adrian, but as soon as their eyes connected they both shifted away.

"Add to this the rising crime rates and the growing black-market trade for weaponry and drugs, and we understand why the public has been demanding a response from us. They want to know how we plan to protect and defend our citizens in the face of so many threats. The Council is doing everything we can to ensure the people that their safety is our utmost priority, and that we require their continued support and cooperation in order to serve them. On that note, I must remind you all that it is of utmost importance that all prodigies who carry the Renegade banner uphold the Gatlon code authority, both on and off duty. The pursuit of justice is integral to our reputation, but the safety of civilians must always be our top priority. On that note, I want to briefly address the rise we've been seeing in vigilantism."

Adrian started to cough sporadically. He ducked his head, burying his mouth in his elbow.

Nova pat his back and he winced. "I'm okay," he muttered. "Just . . . inhaled wrong."

"We want to see justice served," Hugh continued, "but it is a thin line we walk between justice and revenge. The code is in place so that we can always know what side of the divide we must adhere to. It's selfish to risk the lives of innocent people in order to serve our own agendas. It's thoughtless to put civilians at risk so we might achieve glory. That might be the course of villains of the past, or vigilantes like the one who recently called himself the Sentinel. But that is not who *we* are."

Adrian sank lower into his seat. Nova remembered him once talking about the code, and how the rules set forth by the Council could be hypocritical when, during the Age of Anarchy, they themselves had had no problem endangering innocent lives, so long as they caught their enemies in the end. Back then, the Renegades were notorious for causing catastrophic destruction or engaging in fights that led to plenty of innocent onlookers being wounded, but it hadn't seemed to bother them at the time. They would have done anything to ensure their side was victorious.

Sometimes Nova felt like the Renegades of the past had more in common with the Anarchists than anyone dared to admit.

"But of course," said Hugh, "there are times when a peaceful solution cannot be reached. There are times when a criminal must be stopped, as quickly and effectively as possible, to prevent them from causing even more devastation. And so long as stopping that criminal does not interfere with the safety of our citizens, then Renegades who embrace their duty must be celebrated and praised." He took in a deep breath, and the furrow that had appeared between his eyebrows relaxed. "Which is why, today, we would like to take a moment to honor one of our own." His eyes scanned the crowd. "Would Nova McLain, alias Insomnia, please stand?"

# CHAPTER SEVEN

**N**OVA JOLTED IN HER SEAT, not sure she'd heard correctly.

Danna swatted her on the back, nearly pushing her out of the chair. The crowd was already applauding as Nova stood uncertainly in their midst. Even the Council was clapping. Captain Chromium was beaming at her with . . . *pride?*

Nova felt like she'd just stumbled into one of those bizarre anxiety dreams she'd heard people talk about. The ones where you were put on display in front of your worst enemies, only to discover you'd forgotten to put on pants that morning.

But she wasn't asleep. This wasn't a dream.

She blinked at Adrian, whose dark expression from before had disappeared. He was grinning—that open, heart-stopping smile that she absolutely loathed.

Oscar let out a whoop of pride, while Ruby wiggled both hands in the air.

Once the applause had settled, Hugh continued, "I am sure most of you have heard how Nova McLain subdued Ingrid Thompson, an Anarchist more commonly known as the Detonator, with a single, merciful shot to her head, during the altercation at Cosmopolis Park. Had she hesitated, or failed to strike her target, many more bombs would have exploded inside the carnival that day, and we estimate that hundreds of people would have been injured or killed. It is because of McLain's bravery and quick thinking that this catastrophe wasn't far worse. Insomnia, we are proud to have you as a Renegade."

Nova tried to look pleased while cheers started up around her again, but she thought it might have come off as more of a grimace. The look Hugh Everhart was giving her, she couldn't help but notice, seemed borderline . . . fatherly.

He had no right to be proud of Nova or any of her accomplishments, when it was because of him that she didn't have her own father to look at her that way.

*We are proud to have you as a Renegade.*

Her skin prickled.

She knew she should feel elated—she had earned the trust and respect of her enemies, just like she'd wanted to. Like Ace wanted her to. But in this case, their admiration wasn't due to her cunning and duplicity. It was actually warranted. She *had* been a Renegade that day, hadn't she?

The Detonator was an Anarchist. They had been on the same side. For a long time, Nova even would have called her a friend.

But in that moment, Nova had sided with the Renegades.

She hadn't just betrayed Ingrid. She had *killed* her. She could call it self-defense, but there had been more than self-preservation in her mind when she'd pulled the trigger. She'd been afraid for the children and families at the carnival. She'd been furious with Ingrid for tricking her, again.

She'd been worried for Adrian.

Nova knew that sometimes sacrifices had to be made to force society down a different path. She knew thousands of people had died when Ace started his revolution. But Ingrid's casualties wouldn't have been sacrifices. Those would have been murders.

Nova couldn't have stood by and done nothing.

In the weeks since, Nova had retraced her steps from that day a thousand times in her mind, trying to determine if there was something she could have done differently.

Except . . . she didn't regret killing Ingrid.

She wasn't proud of it. Her stomach curdled each time she recalled the squeeze of the trigger and how, for the first time in her life, she hadn't hesitated. The words had been in her head, as they had been since she was a child, staring at the unconscious body of her family's murderer.

*Pull the trigger, Nova.*

The next thing she knew, Ingrid's head had snapped back and she was dead.

The most surprising thing was how easy it was. If that made her a Renegade, fine.

Because she believed it made her an Anarchist too.

The applause died down and Nova collapsed into her seat. Her cheeks were hot. Two aisles ahead, she caught sight of Genissa Clark and her minions: Mack Baxter, Raymond Stern, and Trevor Dunn. Or, as the world knew them, Frostbite, Aftershock, Stingray, and Gargoyle, whom Nova had had the great pleasure of defeating during the Renegade trials. All four of them were sneering at Nova, and Genissa didn't hide her disgusted eye roll as she turned to face the front.

Danna must have seen it, too, because she made a face at Genissa's back. "Jealous," she whispered.

Nova smiled faintly in response. Genissa's team was one of the

Renegades' most well-known patrol units and also the squad that Nova despised the most. Not only because they were cruel and arrogant, but also because they exemplified the corruption that came with handing a bunch of superheroes too much unrestrained power. So Genissa's hostility hardly fazed Nova. If anything, she would have been more concerned if Frostbite actually *liked* her.

Oscar reached around Adrian and knocked his knuckle into Nova's chin. "I remember when she was just a fledgling Renegade wannabe, getting challenged at the trials. And look at her now."

Nova pulled away, but she couldn't quite get her scowl right.

Onstage, Hugh Everhart cleared his throat. "One more order of business before we get to the reason why we requested you here today. As you know, there was a recent theft at Gatlon City Hospital, in which life-saving and expensive medications were taken. We're doing everything we can to find the perpetrator and retrieve the stolen drugs, but in the meantime"—he gestured at Blacklight—"Evander has had the brilliant idea of including a fund-raiser portion to our annual gala next month, where we will be raising both money and awareness for the growing need for medications, especially as our pharmaceutical industry continues to flounder without proper funding. I know there's a . . . a preconception among our civilians that prodigy healers will be enough to aid them should they require medical treatment, but . . . well, there simply aren't enough of them to go around, and their abilities can be limited. We need to put more focus on our medical field. As such, we'll be asking for memorabilia donations for a live auction in the coming weeks. Please mark your calendars if you haven't already, as I hope to see strong support from our entire community."

Nova frowned. If prodigy healers weren't enough to cure the sick and injured patients at the hospital, why didn't they just *say* that? Why didn't they encourage more civilians to study medicine?

Why were the Renegades so determined to act as if they really could save everyone, when they knew perfectly well they couldn't?

"And now," said the Captain, "it's time to discuss the main reason we called this meeting today." He gestured toward the Council. "Kasumi?"

Kasumi Hasegawa, or Tsunami, stepped onto the stage and took the microphone while Hugh disappeared through a nearby door.

Pulling a handful of index cards from the sleeve of her uniform, Kasumi said, "To expand on Captain Chromium's introduction, the Detonator's attack was a reminder that we cannot allow villains like Ingrid Thompson to remain in full possession of their abilities, without any regulation or preventative measures being taken to ensure these sorts of attacks don't continue to happen. When prodigies abuse their powers, it is our duty to address the threat they pose— to innocent people, to us, and to themselves. As the Captain said, our citizens are demanding a response to such threats, and today, we will demonstrate for you precisely what that response is going to be. Please note, what we are revealing here today is confidential and to be kept exclusively among Renegades personnel until further notice."

Nova perked up with interest. She had been following the media's recent coverage and growing disillusionment with interest. For a decade, people had believed that superheroes would always come to the rescue when needed. Though Nova had long known this to be false, Ingrid's stunt seemed to have opened other people's eyes too. The Renegades wouldn't always be there.

It was time that society realized they'd given all the power to the Renegades and were receiving only empty promises in return.

"We are assembling a press release that will make this information available to the media as soon as we feel it is safe to do so." Tsunami turned over a card. Her cheeks had become flushed and it occurred to Nova that Kasumi Hasegawa wasn't comfortable talking in front of large crowds.

How ironic. A superhero, an original Renegade, who must have faced off against guns and bombs and any number of criminals, to be afraid of something as mundane as public speaking.

"For years now," Kasumi continued, "our talented team of lab researchers have been working on some exciting developments that will serve to assist us in our responsibility of keeping our city safe from prodigies who refuse to follow the code authority. We have developed a tool that is harmless to our non-prodigy population, and therefore puts no civilians at risk, while offering a safe and efficient way for us to neutralize prodigies who refuse to abide by our laws. We intend for this tool to become our most practical means of dealing with prodigy noncompliance. We call it . . . *Agent N.*"

Nova's breathing quickened. She recalled Blacklight's words at Cosmopolis Park, after the threat of Ingrid's explosives had been subdued. *"This is proof that not every prodigy deserves their powers. It's because of villains like her that we need Agent N."*

This was it. Whatever Agent N was, they were revealing it here, now. Her heart thumped so hard against the inside of her rib cage it felt like it was trying to escape.

It wasn't just a hypothetical, an experiment constrained to their laboratories. It was real. Their so-called *antidote*. The weapon that Blacklight said would make the world a safer place.

But safer for who?

"To tell you more and to give a demonstration of this tool," said Kasumi, gesturing to the side of the stage, "I invite Dr. Joanna Hogan to the stage."

Obviously relieved that her part was over, Kasumi returned to her seat.

Dr. Joanna Hogan was older than anyone on the Council—

somewhere in her fifties, Nova guessed—though she had a youthful prance to her step as she made her way to the microphone. Her lab coat, stark white and neatly pressed, was contrasted by a pixie haircut dyed bubble-gum pink.

"Good evening," she said, "and thank you for that introduction, Tsunami. I am Dr. Joanna Hogan and I have been one of the leading researchers here at HQ since its inception. It is my pleasure to tell you about this new advancement, and I'm grateful for everything the Council has done to encourage our work." She paused to take in a long breath. "Today, I will be telling you more about the product called Agent N and giving a demonstration of its abilities, so that you can see and understand its effectiveness firsthand. I know that some people will want to label Agent N as a weapon, but it is important to keep in mind that this is, at its core, a *nonviolent* solution to a problem that has been plaguing us for more than thirty years." She opened her arms wide to indicate such an expanse of time, and a few people in the audience chuckled in uncertain agreement. "In addition to being nonviolent, Agent N is portable and its effects are almost instantaneous. It is completely safe to be used around non-prodigy civilians. I really think you're all going to appreciate its real-world applications."

Dr. Hogan reached for a briefcase that sat on top of a stool at the back of the stage. She undid the clasp and lifted the lid, holding it up for the audience to see. Everyone shifted in their seats, straining to get a better view. A few rows away, a Renegade called Optico popped out one of his removable eyeballs and held it up to get a better look.

Inside the case were three rows of vials, each filled with a dark green liquid.

"This," said Joanna Hogan, "is Agent N. It is a neutralizing agent . . . hence the name. Here we have the substance in liquid form, which has a number of viable uses, but we have conducted successful experimentation with the agent in capsule form as well." She pulled one vial from the case and held it up. "This vial, containing just ten milliliters of the agent, has the ability to swiftly and permanently remove the powers from any prodigy on this planet."

A murmur of surprise swept through the audience, and a few of the Renegades seated closest to the stage scooted their chairs away.

Nova tried to disguise the shudder that worked its way through her shoulders. She felt Danna's scrutiny on her but didn't meet her gaze.

"Don't be alarmed," said Joanna. "In liquid form, the solution must be imbibed orally or intravenously in order to be effective. You're all quite safe." She lowered her hand, cradling the vial in her clasped palms. "We see Agent N as a humanitarian consequence for those who defy regulations put forth by our Council. After you have been trained on proper usage of Agent N, we will begin to equip all patrol units with release devices. Once this is in your hands, anyone with extraordinary abilities who chooses to conduct themselves in an unlawful manner will no longer be tolerated. They will forfeit the privilege of being a prodigy."

The audience's faces contorted in curiosity and subtle appreciation.

Nova felt queasy, remembering how horrified she had felt after going into Max's quarantine, when Adrian told her that Max could absorb the powers of others merely by being in their presence. When, for a moment, she thought she might no longer be a prodigy at all.

To have your power taken away, against your will . . . wasn't this a violation of prodigy rights, as much as any abuse they'd suffered before the Age of Anarchy? Ace had fought so hard to give all prodigies the freedom to reveal their powers without fear of persecution, but now the Renegades, the very people who should have been fighting on behalf of other prodigies, were determined to eradicate those who didn't follow their *code*. Even though none of their new laws had ever been put to a vote or officially accepted by the people. Even though the Renegades had made themselves judge and jury, lawmakers and enforcers.

Nova scanned the room, sure that she couldn't be the only one who saw the hypocrisy here. To change a prodigy on such a fundamental level, to alter the essence of *who they were*, merely because they broke a rule that they had never agreed to in the first place? What about fair trials? What about due process?

But all she saw around her were intrigued expressions.

Until her gaze landed on Adrian. He, at least, seemed troubled. At some point he'd taken out his marker and started bouncing it nervously against his fingers.

"Additionally," Joanna continued, "we are enthusiastic about the opportunity to use Agent N as an alternate sentence for some of the inmates incarcerated at Cragmoor Penitentiary. To date, seven inmates have been neutralized as part of our testing process, and we will be assigning a committee to look at all Cragmoor residents on a case-by-case basis. Their criminal behavior has never been tolerated by the Renegades, and now we will ensure that it can never happen again."

A murmur of approval swept through the audience, but her words left Nova cold. This was the first anyone was hearing about Agent N, and yet, seven inmates had already been neutralized? By whose order? Under whose approval? Had there been trials set up? Were the inmates given any choice in the matter?

Or had those seven victims been treated as nothing more than lab rats as the researchers perfected this new weapon? Had there been more inmates who had *not* been successfully neutralized and, if so, what had become of them?

It had to be a violation of human rights, but . . . who cared about the rights of villains?

Beside her, Adrian muttered something about Cragmoor beneath his breath. Nova cast him a curious look.

Leaning toward her, he whispered, "I saw a transport truck outside earlier. I think they brought one of the prisoners here."

Nova had only vague memories of Anarchists who had been captured and put in Cragmoor before the Battle for Gatlon, and she assumed they were still there. The other Anarchists never talked about their lost allies and she had paid them little thought over the years.

"I will now be giving a demonstration of Agent N. I think you'll be pleased to see how simple and efficient it is. Please bring the subject to the stage." Dr. Hogan gestured at the door the Captain had gone through. Blacklight stepped forward and pulled it open. Those in the front row craned their heads to see who would come through.

"Our subject has been convicted and found guilty of numerous attacks on our citizens. He has used his abilities to brainwash innocent children, which has resulted in injuries sustained by countless individuals over the years."

Nova inhaled a sharp breath.

She'd been wrong before. She did know someone who was being held at Cragmoor Penitentiary, after all.

"He is a criminal who once served beside Ace Anarchy himself," said Dr. Hogan, as Captain Chromium returned, hauling a prisoner at his side. "I introduce Winston Pratt . . . the Puppeteer."

# CHAPTER EIGHT

NOVA SLID LOWER into her seat as Winston was led onto the stage. He wore a black-and-white-striped prison jumper instead of his usual purple velvet suit, and there were chromium chains binding his ankles and wrists, but he was not fighting against his captor. His orange hair was matted and unbrushed, but his makeup remained—thick black liner around his eyes, rosy circles on the apples of his cheeks, and sharp lines drawn from the corners of his mouth down the sides of his jaw, reminiscent of a wooden mario-nette. It confirmed that, despite what Nova had assumed for all the years she'd known him, Winston did not wear makeup at all, but rather, his power had transformed his face into that of a puppet.

Or, a puppet master.

Nova tried to position herself so she would be hidden behind the Renegade in the next row while still being able to peer over his shoulder. The last thing she needed was for Winston to spot her in the crowd. She thought she could trust him, but she couldn't be sure, and she hadn't seen him since his interrogation months ago. He had not given her away then and had kept her secret since. Still, he might decide this was the perfect opportunity to give up her identity, perhaps in exchange for a pardon.

It would be no worse than what she had done to him. At the parade, Nova had tossed him out of his own hot-air balloon, landing him in the hands of their enemies. She wouldn't blame him if he decided to incriminate her now in order to save his own skin.

Her knee started to bounce with mounting energy. Adrenaline surged through her system, preparing her to run at the first sign of Winston's betrayal.

But Winston did not look vengeful. He seemed delighted to be the center of attention in a room full of Renegades, with everyone gawking at him like curious attendees at a superhero convention.

"What's wrong?" Danna whispered.

Nova started. "What?"

Danna slid down in her chair until she and Nova were shoulder to shoulder. Danna was so much taller than her that the effect was comical. "Are we hiding from something?"

Lips pursing, Nova scooted up again. "No," she said—too defensively, she knew. "My uncle is always saying I need to work on my posture."

On the stage, Simon Westwood had removed the briefcase of Agent N and brought the stool front and center. Hugh Everhart clapped a hand on Winston's shoulder and nudged him down onto the seat. Winston ignored them both, along with Dr. Hogan, who had recoiled when he passed by her. He was busy taking in the room with twinkling, merry eyes.

"Oh, my Captain," he said, in his squeaky, gleeful voice, "is this a party? For *me*?" He jingled his chains. "Is it my birthday?"

Casting the prisoner a withering look, the Captain didn't respond.

Nova swallowed.

To the side of the stage, Thunderbird whispered something into Blacklight's ear, and the hint of a smile lifted one corner of his mouth. Something about that look made Nova's blood run cold.

Did they even see Winston as a human being? Or had he become nothing more than a science experiment to them? Just like Max, and how many others?

Despite his easy prattle, Nova knew Winston well enough to tell that he was frightened. He was hiding it as well as he could, but buried deep behind his eyes was a bewildered, silent plea. For mercy. For rescue. For a way out of here.

He must have known it was useless. Surrounded by Renegades, trapped in their headquarters, without a single ally . . .

Nova shuddered.

*She* was his ally.

She was supposed to be his ally.

But Winston was a fool who had ruined their mission at the parade and gotten himself caught. He was a bully who preyed on *children*, which had always struck her as too despicable even for an Anarchist.

And yet, for all his faults, he had been loyal to Ace. He was on her team.

She should do something.

What could she do?

What would Ace want her to do?

*Nothing,* her mind whispered, and it sounded like Ace's steady wisdom burbling to the surface of her scattered thoughts. *He is not worth revealing your secret. Stay the course. Focus on your mission.*

Joanna Hogan took a syringe from the briefcase.

Winston was not paying her any attention. "I can't remember

how old I am," he said, tilting his head to one side. The chromium chains rattled as he brought his hands to his chest and drew an imaginary heart.

Dr. Hogan clicked a vial of Agent N into the syringe.

Nova gripped the seat beneath her thighs.

"By golly," said Winston, swinging his feet, "I am old, I think. And look at all of you Renegades, so sprightly and dewy-eyed. Why, you're practically children! In fact . . ." He tilted forward, peering at someone in the front row. His grin turned mischievous. "Methinks you *are* a child, you wee little defender of justice."

Winston launched himself from the stool. One outstretched finger released a sparkling golden thread. The puppet string wrapped around the throat of a young Renegade and the boy cried out. Winston's finger twitched and the boy charged for the stage.

Nova jumped to her feet, but so did the rest of the audience, disrupting her view. With a growl, she stepped up onto her seat to see over their heads. Captain Chromium charged toward the boy, whose screams of fury could barely be heard over the sudden din.

But onstage, Joanna Hogan was serene as she reached out and took hold of Winston's arm. He glowered at her. His fingers curled and the Renegade boy who was under his control ran at Dr. Hogan, teeth bared and fingers curled like claws—a wild animal, ready to tear her into bite-size pieces and devour each one. He released a banshee scream and threw himself at the doctor, but Captain Chromium caught him seconds before he struck her. He pinned the child's arms to his side, securing him tight.

Winston Pratt smiled.

Nova's mouth ran dry.

She spotted his second puppet before anyone else did—they were all so focused on the boy thrashing in the Captain's arms.

No one else noticed Magpie, the prodigy pickpocket. No one else saw her lift her palm. Two rows away from her, Stalagmight didn't notice his iron hatchet being wriggled free from its sheath and flying into Magpie's waiting hand. She raised the hatchet and charged at Tsunami. A Council member. Tsunami's back was to her. No one would notice until it was too late.

Nova stood frozen, unable to decide if she should try to stop Magpie or not. This was her objective too. Eliminate the Council. Destroy the Renegades. One less Council member would be a good thing—

*"No!"*

The scream was so close to Nova's ear that for a moment she thought maybe it had come from her own mouth, but then Danna dissolved into a swarm of butterflies and soared over the audience.

On the stage, surrounded by chaos, the doctor drove the needle into Winston's arm and pressed in the plunger.

Danna reformed just in time to grab Magpie's wrist and haul her away from the Councilwoman. Magpie screamed as Danna bent her arm back so far she was forced to drop the hatchet. Tsunami spun around, eyes wide.

Nova exhaled, but if it was relief she felt, it was short-lived. Danna, her arms locked around a flailing Magpie, was staring straight at her. Confused. And maybe, betrayed.

Shivering, Nova looked away, her cheeks flushing hot. Had Danna been watching her? Did she know that Nova had seen the whole thing and done nothing to stop it?

The uproar in the room suddenly changed as the screeching from Winston's first puppet fell silent. From her vantage point on the chair, Nova saw the thin golden strings that were connecting the two young Renegades to Winston's fingers snap and disintegrate.

Winston studied his hands, flexing his fingers in surprise. Small wrinkles formed in the dark paint around his eyes. His breath became erratic. His jaw began to tremble. A low, distressed wail crawled out from between his lips.

"N-no," he stammered, his voice coated in terror. "What is this? What have you done?"

The dark eyeliner began to bleed.

Nova clapped a hand to her mouth. It *was* makeup, or at least it appeared so now, its inky blackness dripping down his face in thick, gloppy tears. It mingled with the rosy splotches on his cheeks and soon all his features were melting black and red. Even his porcelain-pale whiteness began to fade, oozing down the sides of his face and onto the collar of his striped jumpsuit.

Winston let out another wail. Those who were onstage took a collective step back. Dr. Hogan seemed enthralled as she watched Winston's transformation. Everyone else seemed wary, even afraid.

Winston regarded his curled fingers, shivering. Nova wondered what he was seeing, or not seeing. Feeling, or not feeling.

He started to sob. Huge tears dripped down through the mess on his cheeks. He turned his head and rubbed his nose on his shoulder. The striped fabric came away stained with black and red smudges. When his head lifted again, Nova could see that the lines on his chin were gone. His skin was sallow and tinted faintly blue. He continued to cry, inspecting his hands in disbelief, and he must have known—whatever he felt, whatever he could sense occurring within his body—he must have known the truth.

He was no longer a prodigy. No longer a villain. No longer the Puppeteer.

And despite having never much liked Winston Pratt, Nova could not ignore the twinge of pity that ran through her.

What would become of him now?

As her thoughts roiled, someone in the audience began to clap. Then another joined in. And soon the room was applauding while Winston Pratt sobbed on the stage.

The experiment had been a success, and they were all beginning to realize what that meant. For the Renegades. For the world.

And for the Anarchists.

With a substance like this at the Renegades' disposal, how long before the Anarchists were annihilated? The Renegades wouldn't even have to compromise their own morals. They wouldn't be killing anyone, only taking away their powers.

The room began to right itself. With the villain neutralized, the Renegades returned to their seats. The two kids who had been taken over by the Puppeteer were led away from the room by one of the healers.

Nova started to step down from the chair, but then her gaze landed on Winston again and she froze.

He was staring at her—apparently more distressed than surprised to see her.

One knee buckled. She stumbled forward, but Adrian caught her by the elbow.

"Are you all right?"

She blinked. In all the commotion, she'd forgotten he was beside her. Yanking her arm away, she dropped into her seat, trying to hide herself from Winston's view.

"Just dandy," she muttered.

Winston was hauled from the stage by two security guards. Though he had been walking on his own feet when the Captain had brought him in before, now his entire body was limp, like a marionette whose strings had been cut.

Nova did not sit up again until the door shut between them. How would he be able to cope with such a change? They had stripped him not just of his power, but his identity. If he could no longer be the Puppeteer, who was he? *What* was he?

And those same questions would be forced upon everyone who became a victim of Agent N.

Did the Council truly believe they had the right to decide who should be allowed to be a prodigy, and who shouldn't?

Once the crowd had settled, Tamaya Rae stepped up to the microphone. "Thank you for that powerful demonstration, Joanna. Beginning next week, all active patrol units will be required to receive a minimum of thirty hours of dedicated Agent N training, where you will learn the most effective means of administering the substance, as well as how to protect yourself and your teammates from becoming victim to its effects yourselves. We are preparing a press release to inform the media about Agent N and how it will be used to further protect the people of this city and ensure justice. At that time, all units who have completed the necessary training will be equipped with an emergency supply of Agent N, to be used as a defensive measure against any prodigy who demonstrates an act of violence against a Renegade or civilian, or who demonstrates willful defiance of the code."

"Without a trial?" Nova whispered. "They're giving us the power to just . . . use this stuff, against anyone we feel like, no evidence of a crime required?" She shook her head. "How can *that* be within their code?"

Adrian was watching her. She dared to meet his gaze, unable to hide her disgust. Adrian said nothing, but she thought she saw her worries mirrored in his face.

"Additionally," Tamaya continued, "any prodigy who is currently wanted for recent transgressions is to be neutralized on sight, including all known members of the Anarchist villain group, and, as we have not yet found a body confirming his death, this includes the vigilante known as the Sentinel as well."

"Naturally," Adrian muttered, scratching the back of his neck.

Tamaya continued, "You will receive your training schedule—"

"Is it reversible?" shouted Nova.

Tamaya paused, irritated at the interruption. "Excuse me?"

Nova stood. "Is it reversible? Hypothetically, if a prodigy were ever neutralized by accident, or . . . without due cause, is there a way for their powers to be restored?"

Dr. Hogan stepped forward and took the microphone. "That's a good question, and I'm glad it's been asked, as we must relate the importance to all Renegades that this substance is to be treated with the utmost responsibility." She fixed her gaze on Nova. "No. The effects of Agent N are permanent and irreversible. Make no mistake, this is a dangerous substance, and going forward, we will expect that it be handled with utmost care at all times."

"Thank you, Dr. Hogan," said Tamaya. "I want to reiterate once more that what you have heard today is confidential until further notice. We will be available to answer immediate questions after this meeting and as you begin your training. You are excused."

The conference room filled with chatter. Nova and the others followed along with the crowd, but as soon as they had poured out into the wide hallway, Adrian pulled them to the side to wait for Danna to catch up.

"Well," said Oscar, "that was about a thousand times more intense than I expected it to be. Who else wants to decompress over some pizza?"

Ignoring him, Nova turned to Adrian. "It's from Max, right? This is why they've needed all those blood samples from him."

"It's got to be," said Adrian. A crease formed over the bridge of his glasses and Nova recognized his serious-contemplation face. "I'd always hoped they were trying to find a way to help him. To . . . you know, let him be with other prodigies. Although . . ." His lips pressed thin. "It's thanks to Max they were able to defeat Ace Anarchy. I suppose we shouldn't be surprised that they would try to find a way to . . . to . . ."

"Abuse his power?" Nova muttered.

Adrian frowned, but didn't disagree. "But he's a prodigy. A living, breathing person. While that stuff is . . . *synthetic*. To replicate his power like that . . . it doesn't seem possible."

"Possible?" said Ruby, chuckling. "Adrian, I've seen you create living, breathing creatures out of a pencil and a piece of paper. *I* sprout gemstones when I bleed. Danna turns into a bunch of butterflies. Are we really questioning what's possible?"

"What?" said Oscar. "You're not going to remark on all the mind-blowing things I can do?"

Ruby gestured halfheartedly in Oscar's direction. "Oscar can eat two extra-large pizzas in one sitting while quoting the entire third season of *Star Avengers* from memory."

Oscar nodded solemnly. "It's hard to believe I even exist."

Nova massaged her temple. "I just wonder if Max knows what they've been working on all this time."

"If he does," said Adrian, "he's never said anything to me about it."

"Maybe it was *confidential*." Nova couldn't keep the bitterness from her voice. Everything about Max was confidential. The truth of his ability, the reason behind the quarantine, and now this. As far as she knew, most people in the organization weren't even sure why Max was locked up in the first place. The general rumor seemed to be that his power weakened prodigies who came in contact with him, and he had to be kept separate for his safety and theirs—but few people seemed to realize the full extent of what he could do. How he could drain abilities from other prodigies and absorb them into himself. How he had taken power from Ace Anarchy himself.

When she had first met Max, she had been told that he was both valuable and dangerous. Only now was she beginning to realize exactly how true those words were.

"What worries me," said Adrian, "is how easy it would be to abuse this stuff."

Nova lifted an eyebrow. "What? You think a *Renegade* would abuse this sort of power?"

"Not everyone, of course, but even Renegades can have selfish motives sometimes." He paused, frowning at her. "Wait . . . you were being sarcastic, weren't you?"

"Good catch," she snapped.

Adrian peered at her, bewildered. "Are you mad at *me?*"

Nova took a step back and took some calming breaths. She was lashing out unfairly. Adrian had nothing to do with this, she reminded herself. And during the presentation, there had even been moments when he'd looked as appalled as she was.

"No," she said, quieter now. "I'm sorry. I'm just . . . worried about what Agent N could mean. You said yourself that people are going to abuse it."

"No, I said it would be *easy* to abuse it, not that I think someone will. We'll have to see how the training goes."

Nova shook her head. "This is a clear corruption of power. They can't just send patrol units out on the streets with this stuff and expect that mistakes won't be made. That people won't let their emotions get away from them. What about a fair trial? Evidence? What if someone makes a living using their ability, and then it gets taken away, without a second thought?" She thought of Cyanide, who, for all his illegal dealings, also made a lot of legitimate concoctions that he sold to legitimate customers, from insecticides to wart removers. "Or what if someone were to turn their life around and start using their power to help people? Agent N would take that choice away from them. You know, the Renegades talk an awful lot about human rights, but this is a violation of prodigy rights."

"Villains don't get *rights*."

Nova jumped. She hadn't heard Danna come up behind her, and the glare Danna was fixing on her made her immediately wary. "Agent N is going to be used on villains. On people who don't follow the code. Yet you seem awfully keen to defend them."

"Not everyone who disagrees with the code is a villain," said Adrian.

Danna stared at him, aghast, "Really? What would you call them?"

Adrian scratched his ear with his capped marker. "The code hasn't even been in place for ten years, and the Council is making changes to it all the time. Who knows what it will look like in another ten years, or fifty years? It's not all black and white, good and bad. People's actions . . . their motives . . . there are "—he circled his hands in the air—"gray areas."

"Exactly," said Nova, and she felt the knot in her chest begin to loosen. "And people deserve to have a chance to explain their actions and their motives before they have their abilities stripped away."

"I don't need to know what Hawthorn's motivation was," said

Danna, "to know that she is a thief and a danger to society. If I'd had Agent N the other day, I would have neutralized her without a second thought, and I certainly wouldn't be feeling guilty about it now. Can any of you say otherwise?" She glowered at Nova.

Nova clenched her jaw, annoyed to feel a snag in her own conviction. Even Hawthorn deserved a trial, surely. Even she deserved a chance to choose a different path.

But then Nova thought of Ingrid. She had shot her. *Killed* her. There had been no trial. No reasoning with her. It had been self-defense. It had been protecting innocent lives.

It had also been irreversible.

And she didn't regret it.

Would she have regretted seeing Hawthorn being neutralized by Agent N? A fate which, surely, had to be better than death?

"You know, Nova," said Adrian gently, before she could formulate a response, "you once said that the world would be better without any prodigies in it at all. So . . . maybe, in that way, Agent N can be a good thing?"

"No," she said, firmly. "This is different. I *do* think humanity would be better off without any prodigies at all. People would have control over their own world again and be forced to make their own decisions. Helping themselves for once rather than relying on superheroes all the time. It would level the playing field." She considered her own team and thought of the amazing powers surrounding her just in this small group, and then all the powers of all the prodigies all over the world. Normal humans, without any such abilities, could never compete with what the Renegades had become. "But that's not what's happening here. This is oppression, pure and simple. If they succeed, the Renegades will be putting themselves even higher above everyone else than they already have. There will be no one to challenge . . . us. No one to stand in our way or keep us from achieving total power, and then where will humanity be?"

"It will still be better off than it was in the hands of the villains," said Danna.

Scowling, Nova forced herself to meet her gaze and hold it this time. "And once they"—she paused—"once *we* have total power, what's to keep us from becoming villains ourselves?"

# CHAPTER NINE

A DRIAN WAS STILL waiting outside the meeting room, tapping his foot and listening to the rise and fall of conversations
beyond the door. The rest of his team had headed off to the
cafeteria, at Oscar's urging, of course, but he'd had an idea during
the meeting that kept him from joining them. He'd been waiting
to talk to Hugh or Simon for nearly twenty minutes now, but the
Council was taking forever to leave the room, stopping to talk to
every single person who accosted them. Finally, Hugh split off from
a group of patrol units, all evidently excited about the prospect of
starting Agent N training.

"Hey, Dad!" Adrian worked his way through the lingering
crowd.

Hugh turned to him, beaming. "Adrian! What'd you think?"

"Uh—great," he said quickly, though saying it felt like a betrayal,
of both Nova's hesitations and his own. He needed more time to
process Agent N and what it could mean for the organization and
society at large. What it could mean for the Sentinel. But that wasn't
what he wanted to talk about now. "I have a question."

"You and everyone else," said Hugh, dropping a hand onto Adrian's shoulder and steering him through the crowd. "We're going to have lots more information to impart over the coming weeks, and your training will clear up a lot of confusion——"

"Not about Agent N. I want to know what's happening with the Puppeteer."

"*Winston Pratt,*" said Hugh, holding up a finger. "He is no longer the Puppeteer, nor will he ever be again."

"Right," Adrian drawled. "I'm wondering—is he being sent back to Cragmoor today, or . . ."

"Cragmoor? Why would we send him back to Cragmoor?" Hugh's eyes were twinkling. Literally twinkling. "Cragmoor Penitentiary is for prodigy criminals, and Winston Pratt is no longer a prodigy."

"Okay . . . so . . . where are we sending him?"

"He'll be put in one of our temporary holding cells here in HQ until he has completed a series of psychological evaluations and his past crimes have been reassessed in light of his new status. He's no longer the threat that he once was, and that will be taken into account."

"The holding cells, great," said Adrian, clapping his hands together. "Is he on his way there now?"

For the first time, Hugh sent him an uncertain look. "Nooo," he said. "He'll be taken back to the laboratories first, so we can monitor him for potential side effects from the neutralization. We don't expect there to be any, but our researchers are adamant that we continue to collect as much information from our subjects as possible, to prevent future surprises, blah blah blah." He waved a hand through the air.

"The laboratories," repeated Adrian. "How long will he be there for?"

"I don't know, Adrian. A few days, maybe. What is this about?"

They had reached the elevator bank and Hugh jabbed the up button. Adrian stood straighter, trying to channel his dad's confidence. "I'd like to ask him some questions."

"You already asked him some questions."

"That was months ago, and it was a part of the Nightmare investigation. Things are different now."

"I'd say. One difference being that you're no longer an investigator." Hugh stepped into the elevator, and Adrian followed him in, scowling.

"I'm also no longer on patrols, at least until Danna is cleared," Adrian said. "So I have some free time and I thought—" He hesitated as Hyperspeed and Velocity stepped over the elevator's threshold. "Uh . . . would you mind waiting for the next one?" he said, gently nudging them back out again. Their gazes skipped between Adrian and the Captain, then they stepped away without argument.

The doors closed and Hugh made a disapproving sound as he pressed the floor for the Council's offices. "There's no call to be rude, Adrian."

"Listen," he said.

"I am listening," said Hugh, "but I can listen and be polite at the same time." He fixed Adrian with a look of adamant concentration that felt borderline mocking.

He plowed on. "Nightmare was confirmed an Anarchist, and I still believe that she knew something about my mother's murder."

Hugh's expression became a bit more doubtful, but Adrian ignored it.

"If she knew something, then it's reasonable that the other Anarchists might know something too. It's likely that the murderer *was* an Anarchist, right?"

"We have always regarded that as a strong possibility."

"So, just because Nightmare's dead doesn't mean the investigation is over. I want to talk to the Puppe—to Winston Pratt about it, see if he knows anything."

"You are aware that we've been questioning him off and on ever since the Detonator attacked Cloven Cross Library, aren't you?" said Hugh. "Some of our best detectives have interrogated him to try to find out where the remaining Anarchists might have gone, and as far as we can tell, he is completely oblivious. I'm not sure—"

"I don't care where the other Anarchists are," said Adrian. Then, realizing that he actually did care very much, he adjusted his glasses and continued, "Yes, obviously, I would love to catch them as much as anyone, but that's not what I want to ask him about. Somebody killed Lady Indomitable, and if Winston Pratt has any information on that case, I want to talk to him about it."

"And if he doesn't?"

Adrian shrugged. "Nothing lost, right?"

The elevator slowed and the doors opened onto an immaculate lobby. Behind a desk, Prism launched to her feet, holding up a folder. "Captain, sir, I've finished preparing that memo—"

Hugh held up a hand to her and she fell quiet. His attention was still fixed on Adrian, his mouth twisted into a frown.

"Please," said Adrian. "I know that I might not learn anything, but . . . I have to try."

Hugh let his hand fall as he stepped out of the elevator. "I'll approve temporary clearance to the labs for the sole purpose of speaking with Mr. Pratt."

A grin stretched across Adrian's mouth. "Thank you!"

"But, Adrian . . ." Hugh's brow tensed. "Don't get your hopes up, all right? He isn't exactly a reliable resource."

"Maybe not," said Adrian, stepping back as the doors started to close between them, "but he did lead me to Nightmare."

◇◇◆◇◇

CLEARANCE ARRIVED NINETY minutes later via a chime on his wristband. When it came, Adrian was in one of the patrol dormitories making a list of everything he knew about his mother's death, about the Anarchists, about Nightmare, and trying to come up with a strategy for questioning the ex-villain.

He thought about reaching out to Nova to see if she would go with him—he could have used her intuition—but then he remembered her saying that she was going home to check on her uncle after the meeting.

Though she'd never come out and said it, Adrian suspected there might be something wrong with her uncle. Perhaps he was sick, or just getting old. He never felt like it was his place to ask her about it, but he had noticed the way Nova's mouth pinched whenever she mentioned him. Part of Adrian was hurt that she wouldn't confide in him, but he knew it was hypocritical to think that way when there were so many secrets that he had yet to confide to her.

So he went to the labs alone. He scanned for Max as he passed by the quarantine walls, but the kid was nowhere to be seen in his glass city.

A portly man in a white lab coat was waiting for Adrian when he entered the laboratory. "Follow me, and don't touch anything," he said brusquely. "The patient is currently undergoing an important post-procedure evaluation and we expect him to be tired and agitated. I ask that you limit your meeting with him to no more than fifteen minutes today, though his assigned counselor might approve further questioning sessions in the weeks to come."

"Counselor?" asked Adrian.

The man tucked his hands into his coat pockets. "To assist with the transition from prodigy to civilian. We're still trying to understand the full extent of emotional struggles that arise from such a change, but we've found that offering counseling from the start severely lessens some of the psychological ramifications going forward."

Adrian followed the man through a maze of workstations, cubicles, and storage spaces. "How many people have received Agent N so far?" he asked, wondering if the seven that Dr. Hogan had mentioned was the extent of it.

The man's shoulders stiffened. "I'm afraid that is confidential, Mr. Everhart."

Of course it was.

Then the man's posture relaxed, and he slowed his pace so Adrian was walking alongside him. "Though I can say . . . ," he said, glancing around in a manner that suggested he really *wasn't* supposed to say, "that everyone here has been . . . surprisingly pleased at the reactions from many of our patients. It was an unexpected result, but it has not been uncommon for ex-prodigies to feel, well, a sense of relief, after the procedure. They often talk about their previous abilities as being a burden, as much as a gift."

Adrian tried to imagine feeling grateful to lose his powers but he couldn't. The loss would devastate him, and he couldn't help being suspicious at the man's words. Either the neutralized patients were just saying what they thought their counselors wanted to hear, or the people in this laboratory were skewing their words to justify using the patients for their tests . . . against their will, he assumed.

"Here we are," said the man, stopping outside an unmarked white door.

The door opened and a polished woman smiled out at them. "I'm just finishing up here. One moment." She stepped back into the room, leaving the door open. Adrian craned his head, watching her approach a simple cot against the wall, where Winston Pratt was lying flat on his back. She leaned over him and touched her fingers to his shoulder, whispering something.

Winston appeared to have no reaction.

The woman gathered up a purse and a notepad and stepped out into the hall. "I'll be back to see him in the morning," she said. Then, turning to Adrian, she added, "Try not to upset him if you can help it. It's been a difficult day."

"'Difficult day'?" said Adrian, appalled at the sympathy in her tone. This was the villain who had brainwashed countless innocent children, forcing them to attack their peers, their families, even themselves on occasion. And the people here were concerned that *he* might be having a *difficult day*?

Adrian bit back his thoughts and forced a wan smile.

The woman slipped away and Adrian turned back to the small room. A couple of chairs were stationed beside the cot, and a plate of sandwiches, apparently untouched, sat on a side table. The lighting was dim and warm, and the air smelled of a mix of chemical cleaners and lavender room spray.

"Um . . . shouldn't he be restrained . . . or something?" whispered Adrian.

The man chuckled. "He's not a villain anymore," he said, slapping Adrian on the shoulder. "What are you afraid of?" He started to walk away. "I'll be back to get you in fifteen minutes, but if you're done sooner, have them page me."

Adrian stood inside the doorway for a long moment, observing the villain on the cot. He knew that Winston must be aware of his presence, but he never took his eyes from the ceiling. He had been changed out of the striped prison uniform into light blue sweatpants and a white T-shirt, and he appeared so utterly disheartened that

Adrian felt a twinge of that sympathy he'd criticized the woman for.

"Mr. Pratt?" he said, shutting the door behind him. "I'm Adrian Everhart. We met once before . . . I'm not sure if they told you I was coming today or not . . . but I was hoping to ask you some questions."

Winston did not move, except for his eyelids closing and opening in slow motion.

"I know a lot of people have talked to you lately about the Anarchists, and where they might be hiding out, but there's a different mystery that I was hoping you could maybe shine some light on."

When Winston still didn't react, Adrian perched on the edge of the one of the chairs, resting his elbows on his knees. "Last time I spoke to you, the Anarchists had just abandoned the subway tunnels, and most of them have not been seen or heard from since. I'm told that you've been questioned at length on their whereabouts and I believe you when you say that you don't know where they are."

No response.

He looked so different from when Adrian had interrogated him before, without the permanent etchings of marionette lines on his jaw or the circles of rouge on his cheeks, without the sinister grin. He still had the ginger-red hair, but it now fell uninspired across his forehead.

He looked so . . . so *normal*. He could have been anyone. A math teacher. A truck driver. A shop owner.

Anyone but a villain.

Adrian lifted his chin and reminded himself that, despite his harmless appearance now, the man before him had done despicable things. Losing his powers didn't change that.

"However," Adrian continued, "you did give me some really useful information regarding Nightmare."

This, at last, provoked a twitch in Winston's cheek.

"I don't know how much they keep you informed around here, but we were able to track Nightmare down to her hiding spot at Cosmopolis Park."

Winston's eyes shifted toward him, then straight back to the ceiling.

"Have you heard about the fight that happened there between Nightmare and the Detonator?" pressed Adrian. "Did you know that they're both dead?"

He waited, and after a long silence, Winston's head listed to the side. He seemed to be considering Adrian.

"Both dead?" the villain said, feeling out the words. "Are you *sure?*"

Adrian's jaw tightened. He wasn't sure, of course, no matter how convinced of Nightmare's death the rest of the world seemed to be. But Winston didn't need to know that.

"The Detonator killed Nightmare with one of her explosives, and one of my teammates killed the Detonator. I saw it happen."

Winston made a sound that suggested he was unconvinced by Adrian's story.

"Here's the thing," said Adrian, leaning forward. "Before Nightmare was killed, she was overheard using a phrase. A . . . slogan, of sorts. She said, 'One cannot be brave who has no fear.' Do those words mean anything to you?"

Winston scowled. Then he sat up, without warning, and swung his legs over the side of the cot. He mimicked Adrian's stance, leaning over his knees, studying him.

A chill ran down Adrian's spine, but he refused to show his discomfort. Holding Winston's gaze, he squeezed his hands together until one of his joints popped.

"Lady Indomitable," Winston whispered. The name hung between them, filling up the silence, feeling like a shared secret somehow, until Winston leaned back and brought his knees up, crossing his legs on the cot. All signs of melancholy vanished and he sounded almost cheerful as he began to talk. "Did you know, she once got hold of my hot-air balloon and flew it all the way into the next county. I wasn't in it at the time. Was busy robbing a bank or something. . . ." He snapped. "No, no, a warehouse, that's right. The balloon was supposed to be our getaway vehicle. Didn't quite work out that way, obviously. Took me almost a month to track it down. She'd left the thing in a *cow pasture*, can you believe that? Meddling little *Renegade*." He stuck out his tongue.

Gaping at him, Adrian stammered, "She was my mother."

"Well, clearly. You look just like her, you know."

Adrian's mouth opened and closed for a minute, trying to determine the importance of this story, if there was any. Unless . . .

Unless.

Rage flared in his chest. "Did you do it?" he barked, jumping to his feet.

Winston pushed his back against the wall, startled.

"Did you kill her? Did you murder her because . . . because she stole your *balloon*?"

"Did I . . . ?" Winston let out a shriek of a laugh and clapped his hands to the sides of his face. "Did *I* kill Lady Indomitable? Goodness gracious, no." He paused, considering. "That is, I would have, had the opportunity ever presented itself."

Adrian snarled, his hands still clenched into fists.

"But I didn't!" he insisted.

"But you know who did, don't you? You know she was found with that note—those words on her. 'One cannot be brave'—"

"'Who has no fear,' yakkity-yak. Trying a bit too hard to be pro-found, isn't it?" Winston yawned exaggeratedly.

Adrian lowered himself back to the chair. "Who killed her? Was it an Anarchist? Are they still alive? Are they still out there?"

The look behind Winston's eyes changed then. No longer hollow and distressed as they had been when Adrian had first arrived, nor jovial and worry-free.

Now he appeared to be considering something.

To be . . . calculating.

For the first time since he'd entered the room, Adrian could see the villain this man had once been. Or was still, despite what everyone wanted to believe.

"I will give you information, but I ask for something in return."

Adrian tensed. "I'm not in a position to bargain with you."

"I don't ask for much. You can even run my request by that Council of yours if you'd like."

Adrian hesitated, but Winston kept talking without waiting for a response.

"When I was a child, my father gave me my first puppet—a wooden marionette with orange hair, like mine, and a sad face. I named it Hettie. Well, the last I saw of Hettie, he was fast asleep in his little bed right next to mine—on the subway platform at Blackmire Station." His expression turned pleading. "Bring me Hettie, Mr. Renegade, and I promise I will tell you something you want to know."

# CHAPTER TEN

"**A**DMIT IT. You had a bit of a thing for him."

Nova turned her face to Honey, her jaw dropping with disgust. They were crammed into Leroy's beloved yellow sports car, Nova straddling the center console between Honey and Leroy. "I did *not*."

Honey tittered, shooing Nova's comment away with the tips of her glossy gold nails. "Psh. What girl your age doesn't fawn over such golden-hearted righteousness, that boldness, that sheer . . . *heroism*." Despite her mocking tone, there was a dreaminess in her eyes as she watched the city pass by their window.

Nova gaped at her. "Gross."

Leroy snickered. "Believe me, it isn't the heroics that Honey finds attractive, it's the power."

A shrill giggle escaped Honey and she leaned forward to peer around Nova at him. "Oh, the Sentinel's obviously not for me, all those muscles and gratuitous masculinity." She stuck out her tongue. "But Leroy makes an excellent point. Power like that, it does make my heart pitter-patter. If you claim otherwise, you're lying."

Nova shook her head and peered down the line of red stoplights stretched out before them, knowing that Leroy would ignore most of them. Luckily, this neighborhood was a ghost town this time of night.

"Absolutely not. There was nothing attractive at all about that pompous, arrogant, attention-craving—"

"Renegade?"

"Wannabe."

Honey smirked. "Your protests speak volumes. But they haven't found the body yet, have they? Who knows, maybe your Sentinel survived."

Nova crossed her arms over her chest, sensing that she was fighting a losing battle. "I watched him get thrown in the river. That armor sank like it was made of concrete. No way he could have gotten out of it fast enough." She hesitated, before adding, with some annoyance, "Though he has surprised me before."

"Shame," Leroy mused. "I was beginning to enjoy your heated griping on his egotism and . . . how did you put it that one time? That his personality was as interesting as a bloated carp?"

"That might have been a little harsh, in hindsight," said Nova, "given the whole drowning thing."

Leroy shrugged, but the jerkiness of the movement sent the car careening into the opposite lane. He smiled impishly as he course-corrected. "Regardless of your personal feelings, *whatever* they might be"—he cast Honey a sideways smirk—"I'm saddened by the vigilante's death. He'd done more to benefit our cause than any underground villain these days."

"The Sentinel? He made it his personal mission to hunt me down!"

"When the world believed that Nightmare was alive, yes, he was problematic. But since you were proclaimed dead, he's been quite helpful, embarrassing the Renegades at every turn."

Nova shook her head. She didn't like to think of the Sentinel as being a benefit to their cause. She didn't like to think anything positive about that inflated action figure at all.

But maybe Leroy had a point. The Sentinel had been active since the attack on the carnival, frequently showing up at the scene of a crime before even the Renegade patrol units arrived, though no one knew how he was finding out about the crimes so fast. He'd captured more low-level criminals than some Renegades had in their entire careers, and his success was largely thanks to his refusal to adhere to the Gatlon code authority. In fact, something told her that *he* would have had no problem shooting that guy who had held the barista hostage, potential risks or not.

But there was still something about him that made her skin crawl. The way he talked—like all the world should stop to listen and be enraptured by his brilliance. The way he was always striking those silly poses in between battles, like he'd read far too many comic books. The way he had tried to intimidate her during the parade, and how he'd threatened Leroy in the tunnels. He acted like he was superior to the Renegades, but he was nothing more than a hero reject with a power complex.

But it no longer mattered. He'd been a nuisance both to the Renegades *and* Nova, and now he was gone. Soon his body would be dredged up from the river, his identity would be revealed, and his story used as a bulleted talking point for the Council to remind people why vigilantism was a bad idea. Prodigies needed to join the Renegades, or they needed to keep their powers to themselves—at least, that's what the Council wanted everyone to believe.

Annoyed with the conversation, Nova was glad when she finally spotted the cathedral looming at the top of its hill.

Or, what had once been a cathedral. Now it was merely a shell of a structure. The northeast side was relatively unscathed, but the rest had been demolished during the Battle for Gatlon. The nave and two elaborate towers that had stood at the west entrance had been reduced to rubble, along with the high altar, the choir, and both of the southern transepts. A handful of columns still stood around the open cloister, though they looked more like the ruins of an ancient civilization than destruction wrought only a decade ago.

Leroy parked outside the gate. The ruins stood in the midst of a dead neighborhood. The battle had destroyed the surrounding city blocks. On top of that, some people worried that dangerous radiation and various toxins had leached into the ground as a result of so many colliding superpowers, leaving the area uninhabitable and feared by most of the populace. There was no one to see them. No one to wonder about the yellow car parked outside the wreckage or the mysterious figures trudging through the wasteland.

The night was overcast. With the nearest street lamp four blocks away, it was almost pitch-black as they stepped over the DANGER—DO NOT ENTER sign strung between two metal posts. Honey dug an industrial-size flashlight from her industrial-size handbag and went on ahead of them.

It was no longer safe for them to enter Ace's catacombs through the subway tunnels, for fear they were being monitored by the Renegades, and it had taken a full day to clear away the rubble that had divided Ace's sanctuary from the fallen cathedral since the Day of Triumph. But now they had a new secret entrance for their visits—a narrow staircase tucked between a crumbling archway and a fallen stone column, hidden by a muddle of splintered pews and toppled organ pipes.

As soon as Nova descended the first set of steps, it felt like stepping into a different universe. There were no hints of the city down here. No sirens or angry voices coming from apartment windows or the rumble of delivery trucks ambling down the streets. This was not Gatlon City. This was a place forgotten. This was a place without Renegades, without law, without consequences.

She sighed.

That wasn't true. There were still consequences. There were always consequences, no matter which side she was on. No matter who she fought beside. There was always someone left disappointed.

Her hand went to her bare wrist. She'd gotten used to the feel of the Renegade wristband that she usually wore, and now felt strange without it. She had left it at the house, so that if anyone back at headquarters tracked her whereabouts, they wouldn't notice anything suspicious about her location.

They reached the first crypt, overcrowded with stone sarcophagi, and Nova sensed Phobia's presence, first by the shiver that coursed through her body and then by the way the shadows converged in one corner, solidifying into his tall, cloaked form.

Honey shone the flashlight straight into the overhang of his hood, where a face should have been but was, instead, only more darkness. Phobia shrank away slightly, blocking the light with the blade of his scythe.

"How nice to see you," said Honey. "I was beginning to think someone might have conducted an exorcism and sent you back to the underworld."

"You believe that's where I'm from?" said Phobia, his raspy voice eerier than usual in the dank chamber.

Honey hummed to herself. "Well, I don't think you're from the suburbs."

Phobia sauntered in their wake as they descended another stairwell, spiraling down into the earth. Faint light could be felt as much as seen, emanating from the deepest sublevel. Leaving the stairs behind, they passed through a chamber with vaulted stone ceilings and ancient pillars. The walls were lined with more coffins, many carved with the faces of knights and holy men, others chiseled with Latin proverbs. Beyond the chamber was an open door and the source of the light—a standing candelabra lit with nine taper candles. The ground beneath was covered in wax that had dripped into a series of small hillocks over the years, puddling and splattering across the stone floor.

Inside this final room, there was an old writing desk, teetering stacks of books, a stately four-poster bed, and bones. So many bones. Countless eye sockets watching from their hollow skulls. Femurs and rib cages stacked neatly across open shelves. Tiny finger and foot bones lined up side by side, as precisely as mosaic tiles.

And there was Ace, sitting in the room's only chair, drinking a cup of tea while a small book of poetry hovered in front of his face. He took a sip from the porcelain cup at the same time one of the brittle yellow pages turned.

Ace Anarchy. The catalyst of a revolution. The world's most feared villain. But also, Nova's uncle. The man who had saved her. Raised her. *Trusted* her.

His gaze moved slowly across the worn yellow page of the book, and only when he had reached the end of the poem did he look up.

"Acey, darling," Honey cooed, "you're skinnier than half the skeletons down here! Haven't you been eating?" She snapped her fingers. "Nova, there are a few jars of honey up in the car. Would you be a dear and go fetch them?"

"Thank you, Your Majesty," said Ace, his voice gravelly and tired, "but I have had enough honey to last several life times."

"Nonsense. It's food fit for gods."

"Alas, I am a mere mortal, and I am quite content with my tea."

Honey made a suit-yourself noise in her throat and sank onto the edge of a marble casket. She clicked off the flashlight, letting the warmth from the candelabras engulf them.

Nova never spoke outright about the state of Ace's health. Honey had embraced the role of both his doting nurse and apparent beautician, and though Ace often complained about being fussed over, they had both fallen comfortably into the routine. Honey would comment on his appearance, his health, how worried she was for him. Ace would rebuke all concerns. Everyone would move on.

Nova did not think she could get away with pointing out Ace's growing weakness like Honey did, but it didn't stop her from worrying. Ten years in the catacombs had made him as pale as his skeletal companions, and almost as gaunt. He seemed to move slower every time she visited, each movement matched with crackling joints and flinches of pain, which he couldn't always hide. And that was when he moved at all. Half the time he sat almost comatose in his chair, letting his mind fetch him his books and his food when his body refused to cooperate.

Nova did not want to think of it, but the truth couldn't be denied.

Ace was dying.

The most brilliant visionary of their time. The most powerful prodigy in history. The man who had carried her all the way to the cathedral after her family had been murdered. A growing six-year-old girl, and he had carried her for miles as if it were nothing.

The poetry book closed with a snap and returned itself to a stack of tomes in the corner. "It is a rare treat to be visited by all my brethren at once," said Ace. "Has something happened?"

Nova could feel the weight of everyone's focus attach to her. She hadn't told Leroy and Honey anything yet, only that something big had happened that day and she needed to call an emergency meeting—with Ace, too.

She squared her shoulders. "There was an organization-wide presentation today and . . . well, I have good news and bad news."

"Good first," said Leroy. Nova glanced at him and he shrugged. "Life is short."

Nova licked her lips. "All right. I received a public commendation for . . . um. For killing the Detonator."

A short silence was filled by Honey's guffaw. "Oh, sweetheart. We need to work on your delivery. You make the praise sound like a death sentence."

"Well, it wasn't exactly my proudest moment, was it?"

"And why not?" said Ace, and though he spoke quietly, he immediately had everyone's attention. Even Phobia's cloak seemed to flutter as he tilted his head toward their leader. "Ingrid might have been a great ally for many years, but she had grown impatient and selfish. She betrayed you, and in doing so, she betrayed us all." He smiled, the change stretching deep wrinkles across his cheeks. "I see her death as the worthiest sacrifice she could have made, particularly as it has earned you a great deal of respect from our enemies. That alone is worth a thousand of Ingrid's explosives."

The knot in Nova's chest loosened. "Thank you, Uncle."

"And your bad news?" said Leroy, rocking back on his heels.

The knot tightened right back up. "The main reason for the presentation today . . ." Nova took in a long breath and told them everything she had learned about Agent N. How long the Renegades had been developing it. What it could do. How all patrol units would be equipped after they finished their training.

Lastly, she told them about the Puppeteer.

"Well, if it had to be any of us," said Honey, tapping her nails against the coffin's lid, "I'm glad it was him."

Nova started, dismayed.

"Oh, come," said Leroy, noticing her reaction. "You always hated it when Winston used his powers."

Nova glared at him, her cheeks flaming. It felt like an accusation, and one that she didn't like being put forth right in front of Ace. Even if it was true. There was a part of her—and not a small part, either—that had not been sad to know that the Puppeteer was gone. That no children would ever be forced to suffer the mind control he could exact with his creepy glowing strings.

Did that make her as bad as the Renegades who were enthusiastic about Agent N and its possibilities? Did that make her a traitor to the Anarchists, her family?

"The Renegades don't get to decide who gets superpowers and who doesn't," she said, jaw tense.

"And who should we entrust with such a decision?" rasped Phobia. "Fate? The whims of chance? The Puppeteer was a fool and now he is suffering the consequences."

Nova was surprised to see that no one seemed particularly upset. Winston had been with them for so long. Could it be that, for all these years, they had only barely tolerated him?

For some reason, the thought made her sad.

"So we have lost the Detonator and the Puppeteer," said Ace. "Our numbers are dwindling."

"And we'll all be in trouble once this neutralizing agent is approved for use," said Nova.

"How could they have created such a poison?" said Leroy, rubbing his jaw. "It must be a marvel of chemical engineering."

"I suspect they are using the child," said Ace.

Nova spun back to him. She had avoided telling the Anarchists about Max, worried that one of them might try to target him specifically. But of course Ace knew of his existence. Max had been the one to drain away some of his powers during the Battle for Gatlon.

"What child?" said Honey.

"One whose mere presence can suck the power from our souls." Ace's eyelids fluttered shut and he leaned against the back of his chair. "I have no doubt that he has served a role in the development of this . . . this Agent N."

"Y-yes," Nova said. "They call him the Bandit." Saying it felt like a betrayal, but she tried to ignore it. Her loyalties were *here*, not in a quarantine at Renegade Headquarters.

But then Ace opened his eyes again and they were burning. "He is an abomination."

Nova took a step back, surprised by his vehemence and the unfairness of such a statement. She wanted to be sympathetic to Ace and the grudge he must have held against Max all these years. The baby who had weakened him, who had cost him everything.

But still . . . Ace had always fought for prodigy rights. For freedom and equality. To call Max an abomination for a power he couldn't control went against everything Ace had taught her.

She wanted to say as much, to defend the kid, but the words wouldn't form.

"We need to know more," said Leroy. "How the substance works, how they plan to administer it, what might be its limitations."

Nova nodded. "We start training with it next week. I'll find out more then. Do you think . . . if I could steal a sample or two, do you think you might be able to replicate it?"

He frowned, doubtful. "Unlikely, without the . . . source material."

Meaning the Bandit, she assumed.

"But I would still like to study it and see what can be learned."

"If you make me a decoy sample, I might be able to swap it out," said Nova.

"Our efforts must go beyond learning the properties of this substance," said Phobia, stepping into the halo of candlelight. "We must consider how it can be weaponized against our enemies."

"I agree," Ace murmured. "Our Nightmare presented this news to us as a problem to be overcome, and yet . . . I think you might have just told us of our salvation."

"Salvation?" barked Honey. "Those tyrants want to strip us of our powers!"

"Indeed," said Ace, "and their quest for power has led them to create what might be their own undoing. As Nova has said, they are as vulnerable to this weapon as we are. If we can find a way to weaponize it, as Phobia suggests, we can turn it against them."

"Hold on," said Nova. "Finding a way to protect ourselves is one thing, but even if we could get ahold of Agent N and find a way to use it against the Renegades . . . how is that any different from what they want to do to us?" She stared at Ace. "You started your revolution because you wanted autonomy and security for all prodigies, but this is just another form of persecution."

"What do you propose, little Nightmare?" said Ace. "We cannot defeat the Renegades in a battle of skill. There are so many of them, and so few of us. They must be weakened if they are to be overthrown."

"But if we neutralize the powers of all the prodigies who believe differently than we do . . ." She groaned, frustrated. "This can't be what you had in mind. This can't be what we've been fighting for. It would make us just like them."

"No, it would not." Ace's voice cut through the catacombs. "This is a means to an end. We end the Renegades, and we rebuild our world upon their ashes. Fairness. Justice. *Peace.* These are ideals worth sacrificing for."

"But you're talking about sacrificing *them*. Their powers, their livelihoods . . ."

"*They* are the enemy. *They* have made their choices—just as Ingrid and Winston. We all must take responsibility for our decisions. We all must suffer the consequences. That is the only way for true justice to prevail." Ace started to stand, bolstered by the strength of his beliefs, but he just as quickly slumped back into his chair. A fit of coughing overtook him and he buried his mouth into his sleeve.

Nova and Honey both started to move toward him, but Ace lifted a palm, signaling for them to stay back.

Nova wrung her hands, hating the sound of those wracking coughs. Her eyes began to tear at the sight of his fingers clawing the arm of the chair, fending off what pain she could only imagine.

He needed a doctor. He needed a hospital. He needed one of the Renegades' healers.

But of course, that wasn't an option.

"Perhaps you should lie down," murmured Honey, once the fit had passed.

"Soon, soon," said Ace, his voice rough. "Nova. Have you found anything more on my helmet?"

Nova stood straighter. This, at least, she had finally made progress on.

"Not yet, but my request to work in the artifact warehouse was approved. I start tomorrow. If the helmet is there, like the Dread Warden said, I'll find it."

And it had to be there. No artifact was more powerful than Ace's helmet, which he had used to amplify his telekinetic abilities.

Without the helmet, he could raise a book and a teacup easily enough, but he would struggle with lifting anything much heavier than a sofa.

*With* the helmet, however . . . he would be unstoppable. He could destroy the Renegades and everything they had built, almost single-handedly. The Renegades had gotten lucky when they defeated him last time using Max and his power absorption. The Anarchists wouldn't fall prey to such a trick again.

"Good, good." Ace exhaled. "Learn what you can about this Agent N, but do not lose sight of your main objective. Use the boy if you must."

Nova blinked. "The Bandit?"

Ace wheezed. The coughing fit had left his face splotchy and red, and though his breaths were still rattling, he looked almost energized. "Does *he* have my helmet?"

"Um . . . I don't think . . ." She trailed off.

Oh.

He meant the *other* boy.

"Your companionship with the Everhart boy remains one of the greatest assets you've acquired so far," he said. "His name and family alliances come with their own sort of power, one we may need to exploit."

"Yes, power," said Honey, her eyes laughing in the candlelight. "I told you it was attractive."

Nova glowered at her. "I'm not sure how much I'll be able to . . . *exploit* Adrian. He's the leader of my patrol unit, but we haven't really . . . spoken a whole lot lately."

It was a simple truth, but one that made her breath hitch.

Things had not been the same ever since the carnival, and Nova knew it was her fault. Adrian had tried to kiss her. For a moment, she had even thought that she might want him to kiss her. That she might *like* it.

But she'd blown it. She ran away. Literally *ran*. She couldn't even remember what excuse she gave at the time, but she could clearly recall the rejection that flashed across his features.

He hadn't made any attempts to kiss her since. He hadn't asked her on any more semi-dates. He hadn't tried to get her alone or bring her sandwiches in the middle of the night or stop by her house to see if she was okay. All those things that had seemed like such a nuisance before, but now . . .

Much as she hated to admit it, even to herself, she missed him. She missed the way he used to look at her. No one had ever looked at her quite the way that Adrian Everhart did.

"You are afraid . . . ," Phobia rasped. "Afraid to feel too deeply, afraid that the truth will—"

"Okay," Nova interrupted, almost shouting. "Don't need the evaluation right now, thank you."

"Is there a problem?" asked Leroy. "You're not fighting with your team, are you?"

She shook her head. "No, everything's fine. We've just been busy with patrols, and I . . . I'm so focused on finding the helmet, and uncovering the Council's weaknesses, and . . . lots of other really important reconnaissance-type things."

"Ah, but, child," said Ace, "we already know one of the Council's greatest weaknesses." He chuckled, and the sound made Nova squirm. "You have befriended the son of our enemies. Do not squander this gift. Earn his trust. Earn his respect." He paused, before adding, "Earn his affection. And when the time is right, we will use him to considerable advantage indeed."

Nova's skin prickled at the thought of earning Adrian's *affection*, but she forced herself to nod. "Of course. I'll do my best."

Her best. To find the helmet. To learn more about Agent N. To get close to Adrian Everhart. Her chest squeezed under the weight of their growing expectations.

She *was* doing her best, but at the moment, she was doing her best not to let her escalating panic show.

She could do this. She would not fail.

"I know, little Nightmare," said Ace. "I have faith in you. And when you succeed, we will rise again. We will all rise again."

# CHAPTER ELEVEN

Nova stepped off the elevator onto the fourteenth floor of headquarters. She had expected a space as modern and chic as the main lobby downstairs, or the Council's offices on the top floor, or the training halls in the sublevels. She'd expected glossy white furniture and industrial fixtures. She'd expected an elaborate request-and-retrieve system, automated with computers and machinery. She'd expected a bustling laboratory, where weapons were inspected and relics were preserved. Having worked in the weapons-cataloging system, she knew how expansive the collection was, and she'd imagined the actual storage facility would be as elaborate and heavily monitored as the research and development division, or the virtual-reality training rooms.

And so, from the moment she stepped onto the floor housing the weapons and artifacts storerooms, she found her lip curling with surprise—and disappointment.

The small reception area was unassuming in every way. Two mismatched wooden desks greeted her, though there was no one behind either desk. One held nothing but a computer, a jar of pens, and a clipboard. The second desk, on the other hand, was cluttered with snow globes and elephant figurines and an unhappy ivy plant in a garishly painted ceramic pot. A day-by-day paper calendar was almost a week behind schedule. A Blacklight-branded coffee mug held an array of scissors, hole punchers, and candy sticks, along with a variety of pens that sprouted fake flowers from their ends.

A small plaque read:

Tina Lawrence

"Snapshot"

Director, Weapons and Artifacts

Someone had drawn a smiley face next to Tina Lawrence's name in glittery ink.

The two desks were hemmed in by walls on all sides, though a large door stood cracked open to Nova's right, from which Nova heard upbeat whistling. She approached the door and nudged it open farther. The room beyond was filled with filing cabinets. A woman who must have been close to seventy was bent over a drawer, riffling through the files. She had a fringe of stark-white hair and spectacles with purple cat-eye frames. She paused at a file and dropped a small plastic baggie full of tiny stones into the folder, then slammed the drawer shut. She grabbed a clipboard from the top of the cabinet, checked something off, and turned.

Spotting Nova, she cried out in surprise and nearly toppled over, clutching the clipboard to her chest.

"Sorry," said Nova. "I wasn't trying to sneak up on you. I'm—"

"Nova McLain, yes, yes, of course," said the woman, sheepishly taking off her reading glasses and setting them on top of her head. "Is it ten o'clock already?"

"Not quite. I'm early." Nova glanced at the bin of plastic bags the woman had been sorting, but couldn't see what was inside them. "Should I come back?"

"Oh no, you're fine." The woman strode toward her and offered a hand. "I'm Tina."

Nova accepted the handshake. Though the offer of skin-to-skin contact had struck her as remarkably trusting when she first joined the Renegades, she'd gotten used to it. It was a small reminder that no one knew who she really was.

"Snapshot, right?" she said, withdrawing her hand. "I was curious about the alias."

Tina tapped a finger against her temple. "I can tell by inspecting an object whether or not it's been imbued with extraordinary powers. When my eyes land on a prodigious object, it is as though a shutter on a camera closes on my vision, forever storing that object in my memory. It's handy in my line of work here, but not much else."

Nova searched her tone for resentment, but couldn't find any.

Tina brushed past her into the small reception area. "Let's get you set up. You can start familiarizing yourself with the system. Callum will be in soon and he can show you around." She dropped her clipboard on the cluttered desk and walked behind the desk that was mostly empty. "He's in charge of stocking and maintenance. Once you're familiar with the system, we are going to need a lot of help back in the vault."

"Vault?" said Nova, ears perking.

Tina waved a hand absently toward the back wall. "That's just what we call it. There's been a surplus of new items coming in lately, what with the library and the Anarchist holdings. I've got an entire shelf back there full of confiscated hair accessories from Queen Bee herself, believe it or not."

Nova coughed. "Do you?"

"Left behind when the Anarchists abandoned their *lair*."

She said *lair* like it was an unmentionable word.

"But for now," Snapshot continued, her tone brightening, "I think we'll have you monitor the rentals. This is our checkout form." She nudged the clipboard with a mostly blank chart toward Nova. "Not the most high-tech system, but you know what they say. If it ain't broke . . ." She trailed off.

Nova smiled tightly. She'd always felt that, just because something wasn't broken, didn't mean there wasn't room for improvement. But it didn't seem wise to be contrary in the first five minutes of her new job.

There were half a dozen sheets of paper curled over the top of the clipboard. Nova flipped the front sheet down and scanned through the columns.

| NAME (ALIAS) | OBJECT (OBJ. NO.) | CHECKOUT DATE | RETURN DATE |
|---|---|---|---|
| Zak Ashmore (Flash Flood) | Serpent's Tooth (H-27) | June 14 | June 19 |
| Norma Podavin (Swamp Madame) | Startorch (P-14) | June 17 | |
| Glen Kane (Pulverizer) | Arcelia (J-60) | June 17 | July 2 |
| Fiona Lindala (Peregrine) | Clockwork Beetle (O-139) | June 25 | August 3 |

She didn't recognize any of the names or aliases on the chart, but she did recognize some of the objects they'd checked out. Nova turned the page again and her heartbeat sped up. *Suncloak. Key of Truth. Zenith's Pocket Watch.*

"I didn't know we could rent this stuff."

"Well, you haven't been here all that long, have you?" said Tina. "All new recruits require a ninety-day clearance before they're given access to the stacks."

Nova set the clipboard back on the desk. "How do we find out what's available to be rented? Is there a catalog or something?"

"Just the database," said Tina. "You do know about the database, don't you?"

Nova nodded. She had spent some time cataloging the new weapons that had been confiscated from the Librarian—a black-market arms dealer—so she was familiar with the system. But no one had said anything about the information being open to all Renegades or that they could *borrow* the stuff.

"But there are limitations on it, right? You wouldn't just let anyone come in here and take"—Nova hesitated, scanning her own words to make sure she wasn't overplaying her cards, before continuing—"I don't know. Ace Anarchy's helmet, or something."

Tina chuckled and started digging through a drawer. "Oh, sure. Lot of good it would do them in its current state."

Nova frowned. Was Tina referring to the lie that the Renegades had promoted to the public for the last ten years, that Ace Anarchy's helmet had been destroyed?

"But you're right," added Tina, handing Nova a three-ring binder. "Each object is coded based on its usability and danger levels. More hazardous objects require higher clearance. This has all the information you'll need. The code levels are explained on page four, and rental procedures on page seven. Why don't you start going through it while you wait for Callum?"

Nova took the binder and sat down at the desk. Tina busied herself shuffling around stacks of papers for a moment, then disappeared into the back room again.

Nova opened the cover on the binder. The first page was a short essay describing the importance of maintaining the historical integrity of the artifacts housed in the Renegade collection. Page two listed the expectations of any Renegade wanting to use a weapon or artifact. A sticky note on top of the page pointed out that each Renegade needed to sign a copy of the rules for their files before they could rent their first object.

Page three outlined the steps for searching and retrieval, followed by the procedure for restocking a returned object.

As Tina had said, page four listed the various codes and limitations on the artifacts, and how they were categorized in the larger system. There were types: hand-to-hand combat weaponry, long-distance weaponry, explosives, and the vague yet curious categorization of *unprecedented*. There were power sources: user-generated, opponent-generated, elemental, unknown, other. There were danger levels, on a point scale from zero to ten. Some objects were classified by their ease of use—some could be operated by anyone, even a non-prodigy, while others were tied to a specific user and would be useless in the hands of anyone else, such as the coronet that had once been worn by a prodigy called Kaleidoscope.

Nova glanced up to see that Tina had closed the door to the filing room behind her.

Chewing the inside of her cheek, she turned on the computer and pulled up the object database.

She had downloaded a record of the artifact collection weeks ago, but at the time, a search for Ace's helmet had been fruitless. She'd never taken the time to peruse the list further. Maybe this department kept a more complete record.

She typed a query into the search form.

Ace Anarchy

Two objects appeared on the list. A stone relic found in the debris of the cathedral that had served as a sanctuary for Ace Anarchy before his death (significance: historical; danger level: zero; applications: none). And also something called the Silver Spear.

Nova clicked on it and was astonished to learn that, despite its name, the Silver Spear was not silver at all, but chromium. It was the javelin the Captain had used to try to destroy the helmet, which was now stored among the rest of the prodigy-created weaponry in the warehouse.

She returned to the search field and tried *Alec Artino*, Ace's given name, and returned no matches.

She tried *Helmet*.

A list scrolled down the page. *Astro-Helm. Helmet of Cylon. Helm of Deception. Kabuto of Wisdom. Titan's Golden Headpiece.*

None of them were Ace's.

Despite her disappointment, she couldn't smother a spark of interest at the sheer breadth of the collection. She remembered reading about the Helmet of Cylon and how Phillip Reeves had confounded an entire enemy battalion with it during the Four-Decades War, even though he supposedly wasn't a prodigy. Or how Titan had survived being crushed in an avalanche, which many attributed to his famous headpiece. Some of these artifacts were so mythical, she had trouble believing they were real at all, much less being housed in a drab warehouse on the fourteenth floor.

And people could just . . . *borrow* this stuff?

The elevator dinged. Nova straightened, expecting a stranger—that Callum guy Tina had mentioned—but her polite expression fizzled when her eyes landed on a pale, scrawny girl with a bob of shiny black hair.

Magpie. A Renegade, and a thief, though the rest of the organization seemed willing to overlook that character flaw.

Nova wrapped a hand around the bracelet her father had made when she was a child—the last of his creations before he'd been murdered. Magpie had tried to steal it during the Renegade Parade. She would have gotten away with it, too, if Adrian hadn't seen it happen.

Nova still shivered when she thought of how Adrian had taken her wrist and redrawn the clasp on her skin.

Magpie froze when she saw Nova, and her flush of dislike must have mirrored Nova's exactly. The girl was carrying a small plastic bin, which she hefted over to Nova's desk and dropped to the floor with a loud *thunk*.

"Have fun," she said, scowling. She turned on her heel to head back to the elevator.

"Hold on." Nova pushed herself out of the chair and rounded the desk. "What is this?"

Magpie let out a melodramatic sigh, complete with drooping shoulders and rolling eyes. "You're new, aren't you?"

Nova's jaw clenched. Crouching, she peeled the lid off the bin. Inside she saw what appeared to be a lot of junk. A corkscrew. A metal ashtray. A stack of tattered postcards featuring photos of Gatlon City, pre–Age of Anarchy.

"I'm on cleanup duty," said Magpie, fisting her hands on her hips. "You know, after your patrol buddies make an enormous mess of things—*again*—they send us in to put things back together and scavenge anything useful." She nudged the bin with her toe. "Here's our latest findings. So you can catalog them, or whatever it is you do. It's a bunch of rubbish in this haul, if you ask me."

"Not surprising," said Nova, "given that anything you find of value is more likely to end up in your pockets than the Renegade system, right?"

Magpie returned her glare and they stood in mutual hate-filled silence for a moment, before the girl heaved another sigh of exasperation. "Whatever. I did my job. You do yours." She pivoted away.

Nova picked a doll off the top of the heap, and her attention caught on something metallic. "Wait," she said, reaching for it. Her fingers wrapped around the edge of the piece of curved metal and she pulled it from the bin.

Her pulse skipped.

It was Nightmare's mask. *Her* mask.

# CHAPTER TWELVE

"WHERE DID YOU get this?" said Nova.

Magpie pressed the elevator call button, then slowly turned around, her expression rife with disinterest. "Where do you think?" she said, with barely a glimpse at the mask. "Pulled it out of the rubble at Cosmopolis Park. You were there that day, weren't you?" She crossed her arms. "Superiors thought it should be filed away, but I don't care if you throw it in the trash. It's just a piece of banged-up aluminum. Even I could make one if I wanted to."

Nova's fingers curled defensively. "That was a long time ago. Why are you just bringing it in now?"

Magpie lifted an impetuous eyebrow. "Because for the last month we've been digging through all the junk down in the subway tunnels left behind by those pathetic Anarchists. I deserve a medal for how much of their trash I've had to sift through. Nothing of value and absolutely nothing to help the investigation. A waste of time—that *and* the funhouse. But"—she lifted her hands—"what's it to me? I'm just a laborer."

"Did you find anything else . . . interesting?"

"What, like body parts? My abilities don't translate to human flesh."

"And . . . nothing from the tunnels either?"

The elevator dinged and Magpie turned away. "You're the one who has to catalog it all, right? I guess you'll find out."

Nova glowered. She stood, still clutching the mask. "How *do* your powers work, anyway? Are you, like, a walking metal detector? Or a magnet? Or what?"

The doors opened, revealing a lanky boy with shaggy brown hair and a spattering of freckles. His face lit up when he spotted Magpie.

"Maggie Jo, say it ain't so! Bring us some new treasures today?" He went to give her a fist bump, but it was ignored as Magpie brushed past him into the elevator.

"That's not my name," she spat, jamming her thumb into one of the floor buttons. "And my *powers*," she said, returning her glare to Nova, "are none of your business."

The boy stepped back as the elevator shut.

Using his distraction, Nova tucked the metal mask into the back of her waistband. Anything that wasn't in the database had never been received, right?

"That kid needs to lighten up," the boy said, spinning toward Nova. "She does bring in cool stuff, though. Once dredged up an antique music box from the bottom of Harrow Bay. It didn't have any special powers, but still, how cool is that?" His grin brightened. "*You* must be the infamous Insomnia." He practically skipped to her side and thrust one palm toward her. "Callum Treadwell. A fine pleasure."

"Nova," she said, shaking his hand. "Tina said you'd be able to show me around?"

"I can, indeed." Callum picked up the plastic bin and tucked it behind the desk. "We have some of the coolest stuff here. You're gonna love it. Come on."

He marched toward the filing room without checking to see if Nova was behind him. Shoving open the door, he greeted Tina with the same zeal he'd greeted Nova and Magpie, then bypassed the rows of filing cabinets on his way to a larger metal door at the back of the room.

"This is the filing room," he said, with a general wave to the collection of filing cabinets. "Any paperwork or historical documentation we have on the artifacts gets stored here, along with items that are so small they could get lost on the bigger shelving units. You know, chunks of lightning-fused fulgurite, ion-enhanced meteor dust, magic beans, stuff like that."

"Magic beans?"

Callum paused at the door and shot her an eager look. "You never know."

He waved his wristband over a scanner, and Nova heard the locks clunking. Callum shoved the door open with his shoulder.

"And this," he said, lifting both arms like a circus director revealing a grand spectacle, "is the vault."

Nova stepped in beside him. The door slammed shut.

The vault was enormous, taking up the entire fourteenth floor of the building, and broken up only by structural support columns and row upon row of industrial shelving. It was cold concrete and steel and fluorescent overhead lights, one of which was flickering in the corner of Nova's vision.

Yet her breath caught all the same.

"Is that . . . the Shield of Serenity?" she asked, pointing.

"Oh, you're a fan!" Callum bounced toward the shelf and lifted the shield as tenderly as a priceless vase. "The one and only. Donated by Serenity herself. Almost pristine condition, except this dent back here." He flipped it over to show Nova. "An intern dropped it a few years ago. Not me, I swear!" He lowered his voice into a conspiratorial whisper. "But if anyone ever asks, the damage was totally incurred in battle."

Returning the shield to its spot, Callum began walking along the aisle. "The vault is organized by category. Did Tina show you the binder? It's all in there. Within each category, every object is given a number and shelved in order. Except weapon types, those are alphabetical, *then* by object number. So all the swords, scimitars, and spears are grouped together in the weapons section, but over here in artifacts, a chalice might be in a completely different aisle from, say, a chain-mail suit. Unless they were input into the system together, in which case, they would have back-to-back object numbers. Seems confusing, but you'll get the hang of it."

"Is there really a chalice?" said Nova.

Callum spun to her but kept walking backward as his arms flailed. "Yes! The Widow's Cup. Put a marriage band in it, and it automatically turns any wine into poison. *Awesome*, right? Don't be fooled by the gender-specific title, it works on wives too." He shook his head. "I would love to know how they figured some of this stuff out."

He headed down a central aisle, with rows of shelves stretching away from them, going so deep into the building Nova couldn't see where they ended. She followed in his footsteps, trying to ignore the mask digging into her spine.

Callum recited the various categories as they strolled. "Body armor here, and costumes on this side. You know, iconic capes, masks, color-coordinated belt-and-boots sets, stuff like that. Lots of nostalgia. When you have a chance, you should definitely check out Gamma Ray's jumpsuit. It is a work of art."

Nova spotted a mannequin wearing Boilerplate's unmistakable armor and another donning Blue Ninja's original costume, which was, Nova noted, actually more of a seafoam green.

Callum continued, "This way we have protective artifacts, most notably Magnetron's Shield. Behind those ominous doors," he said, pointing at a pair of fortified chromium doors in the far wall, "is the official armory. Sounds impressive, but it's mostly basic weaponry. A sword that's just a sword, a crossbow that's just a crossbow. No extra powers, but still useful for a lot of Renegades. That's also where we keep the heavier artillery, like guns and bombs, et cetera. *And . . .*" He swooped his arms up. ". . . what you've all been waiting for! Our supernatural, prodigy-specific, largely historic collection of fine artifacts. We've got power-bestowing earrings. Boxing gloves equipped with superstrength. A lightning-charged trident. And oh, so much more. It's a treasure trove of awe and amazement. Including my personal favorite—Sultan's Scimitar, said to be able to slice through absolutely any material on this planet, excepting only the invincible Captain Chromium."

He shot Nova a grin and she couldn't tell if he was being sarcastic or not, so she smiled wryly back. "Has anyone tried?"

His smile fizzled into uncertainty, and Nova turned away before he could decide if she was joking or not. She saw a pile of bones on a nearby shelf—though she couldn't tell the animal it came from—and a shallow bronze dish on another. Down one aisle she spotted a set of golden wrist cuffs. On the next, a stone wheel that was as tall as Nova.

Walking through the warehouse felt like walking through a comprehensive museum of prodigy history, and yet she couldn't help being annoyed by Callum's infatuation with the objects surrounding them. He wasn't even trying to hide how enamored he was with it all, and he seemed just as impressed with the silver shovel that held the power to liquefy solid earth as he was with a brush that painted secrets into portraits, and had gotten one unlucky artist burned at the stake in the seventeenth century.

She assumed, as they made their way through the vault, that Callum wasn't a prodigy. Only civilians were *this* excited by superpowers or supernatural objects. Plus, he wasn't wearing a uniform. She wondered if perhaps it had seemed safer to give the job of maintaining such powerful objects to someone who wouldn't be able to wield most of them, even if he tried.

"So, what do you do here?" asked Nova, once Callum had finished telling her about the fifteenth-century prodigy who had single-handedly defended an entire village from raiding conquerors using nothing but his powers of flora manipulation and a branch taken from a willow tree. (The branch could be found two aisles over.) "Prodigy historian?"

"Might as well be," he said, chuckling. "But no. I mostly do cataloging, cleaning, researching, sorting, filing . . . whatever Snapshot needs done."

"I'd like to help with all of that," Nova said, working up her enthusiasm. "I'm really fascinated by this stuff and I want to learn as much as I can. Snapshot said I'd start working the checkout counter, but eventually I'd like to do more back here. Cataloging, cleaning . . . I can do it all."

"That sounds great," said Callum, clapping his hands together. "Manning the checkout counter can get tedious. Except, sometimes, a Renegade might not know exactly what they're looking for, or what weapons are going to suit their specific abilities, and then we get to help them figure out the best options, and that can be really cool, too. You learn a lot about the superheroes we have here." His eyes shone as he gestured at Nova. "I'm glad you like artifacts, too, because it could seem a little slow down here after being on patrols, and ambushing the Librarian, and fighting the Detonator, and everything you've done. This is going to be a much more laid-back experience, though also really fulfilling."

"That sounds perfect."

"Cool." Callum lifted his thumb back toward the reception area. "Let's get you settled in, and maybe see what sort of stuff Magpie brought us."

"Wait," said Nova, scanning the back wall of the vault. "What's down there?"

"Ah, that's the restricted collection."

Nova's nerves hummed. "Restricted, how?"

"As in, not available to be checked out." Callum tucked his hands into his pockets. "Want to see?"

Nova spun back to him. "That's allowed?"

"Oh yeah. We can't loan this stuff out, but we still have to come back and dust it from time to time. Come on." He led her into the last aisle.

The shelves were sparser than the rest of the vault. Heart drumming, Nova scanned the objects as Callum started rambling on about the destructive qualities of Fury Fire, and how Dark Matter's ring could theoretically blow up the moon if put in the wrong hands, and how a prophetic pair of goggles had already caused more trouble than they were worth.

"This is . . . amazing," said Nova, and she meant it. "But why isn't all this under more security? So far I've just seen you, and Snapshot, and two locked doors, and"—she gestured at a camera on the ceiling—"a handful of security cameras. Where are the laser barricades? The motion triggers? The armed guards?"

"Please. We're in Renegade Headquarters." He spread his arms wide. "Who would try to break in here?"

She gawked at him. "Really? That's . . ."

*Arrogant*, she wanted to say. *Asinine. Completely, unrealistically overconfident.*

But she reeled in her thoughts just in time. "Uh . . . right," she stammered. "That's right. Renegade HQ." She laughed awkwardly. "Who would ever try to break in here?"

"And given that the vast majority of objects are available for rent—" Callum shrugged. "There's no need for the added protection. The folks up in the security center keep a close enough eye on us down here." He saluted the camera.

"I'm sure they do," said Nova, meandering away from him. She ran her fingers over the shelves that, frankly, didn't seem to have been dusted in recent history.

But there was no sign of Ace's helmet.

Her shoulders drooped.

"Is the restricted section not meeting expectations?"

She spun around. Callum was watching her, holding a pair of antique aviator goggles in one hand. "Prophetic goggles," he said emphatically. "Come on. How can that be disappointing?"

"Sorry," said Nova. "I was just . . ." Inhaling a sharp breath, she confessed, "I heard a rumor that Ace Anarchy's helmet was in here. I thought it would be cool to see it in person. And not, you know, on the Captain's pike half a block away."

"Oh," said Callum, setting down the goggles. "That's a replica, actually. The one he carries around at the parade? Total fake. The real one's down here, but if you weren't impressed by the goggles, you are going to be *really* disappointed by the helmet."

"What do you mean?"

"I'll show you." He breezed past her.

Nova's eyes widened. It could *not* be that easy.

Halfway down the aisle, Callum paused in front of a metal cube sitting on a shelf. "Ta-da," he said, thumping its top. The cube was roughly the size of a small microwave. "I give you Ace Anarchy's helmet."

Nova stared, horror and denial creeping into her thoughts. "I don't understand."

"Well, after the Battle for Gatlon," said Callum, leaning his elbow on the shelf as he prepared to go into another history spiel, "the Council tried to destroy the helmet, but were unsuccessful. So to keep it from falling into the wrong hands again, Captain Chromium made an indestructible chromium box to hold the helmet for the rest of time. And here she lies. Protected. Secure. Completely inaccessible." He patted the cube again. "And I get it. I mean, it caused so much destruction and that kind of power shouldn't be made available to anyone, you know? But at the same time, the historian in me is a little sad that such an important relic is going to sit here, unable to be seen or studied, forever."

Nova's mouth went dry as she stepped closer to the box.

There should have been some fanfare here. A spotlight streaming onto the shelf. A set of ropes keeping onlookers at bay. A pedestal. But there was nothing. Just a dusty box on a dusty shelf.

Why hadn't the Dread Warden told her this when he'd said the helmet hadn't been destroyed, when he said it was here, in the artifacts department?

*No one is ever going to use that helmet to torment the people of this city again.*

His words carried new meaning now. Nova had imagined a coded safe, a security system requiring retina scans and fingerprints, even armed guards keeping watch over the helmet.

She had never imagined this.

Imprisoned in a chromium cube. Forever.

She felt a light tug at her wrist. Her bracelet was straining against her skin, as if being pulled toward the box and the helmet inside.

Nova lifted her hand. The bracelet pulled harder, until the thin filigree dug into her skin. The empty prongs that had never received the gemstone they were intended to hold stretched outward toward the trapped helmet.

"Huh," said Callum. "Never seen that before."

Nova dropped her arm and took a hasty step back.

Callum's attention stayed on her wrist. "What's that bracelet made out of?"

"I don't know." She clapped a hand over the bracelet to hide it from view. It was the truth. She *didn't* know what the material was. As far as she was aware, it didn't have a name, and she wasn't about to tell Callum that it was made from solidified bands of ethereal energy only her father had been able to access.

Just like she wasn't about to tell him that it was made from the same stuff the helmet was.

"Copper, maybe?" said Callum, scratching his ear. "Can copper be magnetized? I'll have to look it up. Anyway." He swirled his hand toward the box again. "There you have it. The helmet that almost destroyed the world. Ready to head back?"

Callum led her out of the vault, chatting the whole time, though Nova didn't hear a word. She ignored the awe-inspiring objects they passed. She barely felt the mask digging into her back.

What was she going to tell Ace? What would she say to the other Anarchists? Ever since they'd learned that the helmet hadn't been destroyed, they'd been hinging their hopes on getting it back. On giving Ace back his strength, his power.

What were they going to do now?

There had to be some way to get inside that box. Captain Chromium wouldn't have made it *impossible* to access the helmet. What if the Renegades needed it someday?

She couldn't walk up to the Captain and ask him about it, but . . . she did know of one other person who might have an idea.

# CHAPTER THIRTEEN

B LACKMIRE STATION. The defunct entrance to the abandoned subway had a hole in it the size of a small car, strung across with yellow caution tape. The sidewalk was littered with rubble from the explosion and there were still visible scorch marks on the wall. This was where the Anarchists made their escape when the Renegades had gone after them, after the Detonator's attack at the library had made it clear that their group wasn't as dormant as they seemed. Though regular patrols had been set up to search the tunnels and monitor various access points, in case any of the villains tried to return to their sanctuary, there had been no sign of them. Other than Nightmare and the Detonator, of course.

The last time Adrian had gone into the tunnels, determined to find out what their connection to Nightmare was, he was wearing the Sentinel's armor. Even now, Adrian's fingers twitched, itching to unbutton the top of his shirt and peel open the zipper tattoo that would transform him into the vigilante. He craved the security that armor would afford him. But he ignored the urge, knowing it was little more than paranoia, and maybe a bit of habit.

The tunnels were abandoned. Wherever Cyanide, Queen Bee, and Phobia had gone, they had not been reckless enough to come back here.

He crouched in front of a DO NOT ENTER sign that had long ago been spray-painted over with a warning to anyone who might not know who was lurking down those stairs.

A circle drawn around an acid-green *A*.

Adrian took out his marker and drew himself a flashlight.

He stepped over the tape and flashed the beam of light over the graffitied walls and the bolts sticking up from the concrete where a turnstile had once been. The stairs beyond faded into blackness.

He listened, but if there were noises inside the subway, they were buried beneath the sounds of the city.

But there wouldn't be any noises, he told himself, other than the rats. There were no more villains down here. No more Anarchists.

He crept down the stairs, his sneakers thudding, the beam from his flashlight darting over old concert posters, broken wall tiles, and more graffiti, so much graffiti.

He passed a mezzanine with two offshoots—one set of stairs heading to the northbound rails, the other to the south. His wristband chimed quietly as he descended toward the lower platform, probably the last alert he would get before he lost reception so far underground. He ignored the sound, as he'd been doing ever since Hawthorn threw him into the river and Max pointed out that maybe, just maybe, this was the time to let the Sentinel go. The chime wasn't the notification he got when he was receiving a message from his teammates or a patrol assignment from the call center. Rather, it was the alarm he'd set for himself, to be notified when one of the other patrol squads was being called for an emergency situation.

Years ago, as part of an effort to ensure the safety of their recruits, it was decided that all dispatches to patrol units could be accessed in real time by all active Renegades, and that the movements of on-duty patrols could be tracked and monitored. The information was made available to any Renegade who wanted it, though they were usually kept so busy with their respective jobs that Adrian didn't know of anyone who actually took advantage of the information. Except for himself, and then, only since becoming the Sentinel.

It was part of how he had managed to be so effective. Whenever he heard that a patrol unit was being sent to handle a particularly high-profile crime, he only had to log in to the system to see where they were being sent. If there was a chase happening, he could easily follow their movements through the city. With the spring tattoos on the bottoms of his feet, Adrian could move faster than most Renegades, excepting only those with flight or superspeed powers. That advantage alone often allowed him to reach the scene of the crime and deal with the perpetrators before the assigned Renegades showed up.

Over the last week, he'd considered turning off the notifications every time the wristband chimed at him. He was caught in a constant battle with himself. The almost irresistible yearning to involve himself in the situations, to prove both his value and his good intentions. But on the other hand, he knew it was safer to let people go on believing the Sentinel was dead, especially with the reveal of Agent N. The Sentinel was a wanted man, and he knew that once patrols were equipped with the neutralizing agent, few of them would hesitate to use it on him.

Unable to fully resist the temptation, Adrian glanced at the most recent notification, just to make sure no one was being murdered or something. But no—a patrol unit had been summoned to deal with a car theft. Definitely something his peers could handle.

He sent the alert away and silenced all other incoming notifications.

Pausing at the base of the stairs, he shone the flashlight over the walls. There was an empty vessel where a fire extinguisher had once been, and an ancient pay phone with the receiver missing at the end of its curled cord. The platform itself was littered with the bodies of dead wasps, a few stray candy wrappers, and a handful of silhouettes drawn in red chalk and labeled with official Renegade signage.

He stepped closer and scanned the nearest signs: EXHIBIT 19: PUPPETEER TENT (1/3). EXHIBIT 20: MISC. PUPPETEER BELONG-INGS. EXHIBIT 21: SHELL CASING—POISON RELEASE DEVICE.

None of the objects mentioned were there anymore, only the chalk outlines and the signage to indicate what had been there before the Renegades' investigative teams and cleanup crew confis-cated it all.

Adrian's frown deepened. He should have guessed that all of the Anarchists' belongings would have been removed from the tun-nels by now. For some reason, he'd expected that only weapons or things that indicated criminal activity would have been taken back to headquarters, but clearly he was wrong. It seemed that nothing had been overlooked.

Pacing to the edge of the platform, he peered down onto the tracks, turning his head each way as they disappeared into the tun-nels. More signage. More chalk lines. And here, more evidence of the battle that had occurred. One tunnel was partially caved in as a result of the Detonator's bombs. More dead wasps were strewn across the tracks.

Adrian knew a lot of the Renegades who had been involved in that fight. Some of them he'd known almost his whole life. They'd been lucky that no one died, but there were countless injuries, from broken bones and severe burns to lungs and throats that had been scraped raw from Cyanide's poisons. Even now, Adrian could detect the tangy smell of chemicals hanging in the musty air.

The healers had worked overtime for weeks afterward.

And in the end, the Anarchists had gotten away. It was the proverbial salt in their extensive wounds.

Adrian sighed. He wasn't going to find Winston Pratt's puppet down here. He would have to talk to the cleanup crew, maybe call in a favor with the sort-and-tag team. He hoped they hadn't already shipped a bunch of the Anarchists' stuff to the junkyard. *That* wouldn't be any fun to wade through.

He was about to turn back when his flashlight caught on one of the tags posted beside the next tunnel.

EXHIBIT N/A: NIGHTMARE?

An arrow had been drawn, pointing into the tunnel.

Pushing up his glasses, Adrian hopped down onto the tracks. A quarter of a mile later he reached a wide chamber of arched ceilings, where multiple train lines intersected and diverged. A series of narrow platforms stood on either side of the tracks, not for passengers, but perhaps maintenance crews.

Adrian hadn't been in this part of the tunnels before. He had never been on one of the patrols sent to check that the Anarchists weren't hoarding weaponry or recruiting new members. He had only been to visit the villain gang once, when he caught Frostbite and her squad trying to bully the Anarchists into false confessions.

Though he still didn't agree with their tactics, he couldn't help thinking that if he had let Genissa and her crew handle things, probably the Anarchists would have been arrested that day, and the city would have been spared a lot of trauma.

It made his jaw twitch to think about.

An abandoned train car sat at one end of the chamber, still on its track as if it could roll away at any second, though the accumulation of dirt and grime on its windows made it clear that it hadn't moved for a long time.

Adrian approached the car and read the sign on one of its windows. EXHIBIT 47: TRAIN CAR—USED BY NIGHTMARE?

Flexing his fingers and tightening them back into fists, Adrian stepped around to the door on the side. He had been so close. All that time he had been searching for her, and if he had just questioned the Anarchists a little more, if he had dared to search their dwelling more thoroughly, he would have found this. He would have found her.

He stepped into the car, but if he'd hoped to find anything of use there, his hopes quickly evaporated. The interior was as stripped of belongings as Winston's platform had been. All that was left behind were the Renegades' tags—a hundred white squares pasted over the walls and floor indicating where evidence had been found. Here: a small suitcase of clothing. There: a workbench containing deconstructed weaponry in varying stages of completion. On that window: a magazine cover with a photo of Captain Chromium inundated with small puncture holes.

He tried to imagine her, a girl he had never met, who had never met him or his family, carrying so much hostility for his dad that she threw darts at magazine photos, practicing for the day when she would try to assassinate one of the most beloved superheroes of all time. What could possibly have driven her to such hatred?

Shaking his head, he turned away. The train car shifted under his weight as he descended back to the tracks. He tried to imagine living down here. The stale, damp air. The years of trash accumulated at the edges of the tracks. The cobwebs strung between the broken light fixtures. No breezes, no sunlight, no flowers or trees or animals or birds . . . other than the rats and the cockroaches, that is.

The only splotches of color were the graffiti tags and a line of advertising posters hung up on one wall, though their plastic covers were so dingy it was hard to make out what they were trying to sell. One promoted the opening of a new exhibit at the Gatlon Art Museum—Adrian couldn't help but wonder how much of that priceless art had gone missing during the Age of Anarchy. Another poster offered "wedding-day skin" after sixty days of using a newly patented night cream. Beside it was an ad for time shares at a tropical resort, though someone had drawn crude images over the bikini-clad model.

Adrian tilted his head, inspecting the last poster. A book was pictured, a thriller novel with a shadowy figure silhouetted between two pine trees. The book's tag line read, *It's not that he's back . . . it's that he never went away.*

And though Adrian couldn't be sure, it almost appeared as if the large poster was . . . crooked.

He stepped over the tracks, the flashlight trailing down the next tunnel. He could see no more Renegade signs that way. Perhaps this was the last platform that the Anarchists had claimed for themselves.

Approaching the poster, he saw that it definitely was askew. Not drastically, but enough to make his fingers twitch to straighten it. Probably the hardware that had held it up all these years had started to pull free of the wall. And yet—there was something about it that made the hair prickle on the back of Adrian's neck. A bit of dirt smudged on the corner, almost like a handprint. The way the tiled wall was chipped around its frame.

Adrian was about to reach for the poster when a shadow loomed in the corner of his eye.

Heart lurching, Adrian spun and sent the flashlight beam into the tunnel.

A rat squeaked angrily and scurried out from behind an empty milk jug before skittering off down the tracks.

Cold sweat dampened his forehead as Adrian flashed the light all around the tunnel, across the tracks, over the arched ceilings. Whatever had startled him had disappeared, or—more likely, he had to admit—had been nothing more than his own imagination.

Still, the feeling that he wasn't alone, that something was watching him from the shadows, was impossible to shake.

His heart rate was just beginning to slow when a musical ditty erupted from his wristband, making him jump all over again. He cursed and hurried to shut it off. Scowling, he peered at the message. There was no way he was getting reception down here, and he'd already turned off notifications from the call center . . .

*Oh.* Right.

Not a message, not an alert. It was the reminder he'd set for himself to be at City Park in an hour, or risk Ruby's wrath when he was late for her brothers' first competition.

He did a quick calculation of how long it would take to get there, cursed again, and started to run.

# CHAPTER FOURTEEN

T HE PARK WAS as crowded as Adrian had ever seen it, overrun
with children, almost all of whom were bedecked in sparkling
spandex, neon tights, and bedazzled capes. There were small
booths set up where vendors were selling miniature Renegade uniforms or costumes that mimicked the nostalgic superhero costumes
of the past. Others were selling custom T-shirts, handmade jewelry,
and even superhero costumes for cats and dogs. Beyond the shops,
there was a long line of food trucks, as promised, and a courtyard of
inflatable bounce houses, and even a temporary stage where a music
band was setting up their speakers and microphones.

But the main draw of the day, it was immediately clear, was on
the sports fields that were snuggled between native flower gardens
and duck ponds and running paths. There were more than a dozen
types of competitions kids could compete in, separated by age group
and skill level, in hopes of winning a medal and being dubbed an
(unofficial) superhero sidekick. There were track races and gym-
nastics courts, archery and long jumps, wrestling and martial arts.
A large tent near the playground even held intellectual-focused

contests, such as speed-reading tests and a spelling bee. Adrian wasn't entirely sure how being an excellent speller would translate to defending justice, but he liked that the Sidekick Olympics were so inclusive. Every kid deserved to feel like they could be a super-hero, even if only for a day.

He was worried he was already late by the time he arrived at the bleachers that surrounded the main event—an elaborate obstacle course that took up an entire soccer field. He found Ruby, Danna, and Nova near the front.

Ruby waved at him excitedly, indicating a seat they'd saved for him. "Come on, come on," she said. "The twins are in this next round."

"Where's Oscar?" he asked, sliding in beside Nova. Opposite to Ruby's enthusiasm, Nova looked vaguely bewildered as she observed the crowds of costumed children.

"Where do you think?" said Danna, cupping her chin in her hands.

Adrian didn't respond. Food, obviously.

"There they are!" Ruby jumped to her feet and started scream-ing her brothers' names, but either they couldn't hear her or they were too embarrassed to acknowledge their older sister. They were huddled with a group of kids, all around eleven or twelve years old, but their identical heads of light blond hair were easy to spot in the mix. Adrian had only met the twins once before, at a Renegade family picnic last summer, but he remembered how much their faces had been just like younger versions of Ruby's, freckles and all. He wondered if Ruby had had the same thick blond hair at their age, too, before she started dying it in layers of black and white.

"They look great," said Adrian, admiring their gray-and-red suits.

"Thanks, my mom and grandma made their costumes. Jade hasn't wanted to take it off all week. I'll be glad when today is over so maybe he'll actually let us wash it."

"Make way, coming through!" Oscar shuffled down the bench, one hand clutching a paper bag, the bottom of which was already soaked through with grease. Adrian and Nova both turned their legs toward each other to make room for him to pass, their knees knocking together. "Sorry," Adrian muttered, making eye contact with her for the first time since he'd arrived.

She smiled, the look oddly flustered. "Have you been to this before?"

"No, but I've heard a lot about it. Kind of fun, right?"

Nova pursed her lips. It took her a long moment to answer, and when she finally did, she sounded almost sad. "People sure do like their superheroes."

"I brought enough to share," said Oscar, who had plopped down beside Ruby and was handing out cardboard cartons overflowing with salty fries. "But pace yourselves, okay? There are also gyros and chicken wings out there, and I've got my eye on a strawberry shortcake cart for dessert." Propping his cane between his legs, he peered out at the field. "Which ones are—oh, never mind, I see them."

Ruby frowned at him. "You've never met my brothers."

"I know, but they look just like you." He pointed, then grabbed a fry from Ruby's carton and chomped it in half. "Except, you know, the hair. How long before they start?"

"Any minute now," said Ruby, eyeing Oscar speculatively. "Sterling's going to be great on this one, but Jade's more excited about archery later."

On the field, the kids were told to line up at the start of the course. A referee was giving them instructions. Ruby started to bounce her legs so quickly the whole bench was trembling. Without warning, she cupped her hands over her mouth and screamed, "*Come on, Sterling! You've got this!*"

Danna flinched, covering an ear.

A horn blared and the race started. The contestants bounded forward and started scaling a faux brick wall. Ruby leaped to her feet, screaming at the top of her lungs. Oscar joined her, hollering just as loud. One of the kids scampered to the top shockingly fast—a dark-skinned girl with a gold capelet on her shoulders, reminiscent of Lady Indomitable's costume.

Adrian's throat tightened at the sight of her. She would have been too young to remember his mom when she was still alive, and it warmed him to think that her legacy was living on. That she could still serve as an inspiration to today's kids.

He wanted that too. To be a role model. Like his mom and his dads and all the superheroes who had come before him.

But as the girl pulled into the lead, swinging across a series of monkey bars with Sterling trailing behind, he heard Oscar lean over and whisper to Ruby, "Do you want me to blind her with a smoke arrow?" He pointed his finger toward the course as a curl of smoke erupted from its tip. "Just a small one. No one would have to know."

"Don't you dare," Ruby hissed, pushing his hand down. "Sterling will catch up on the barrel roll, you'll see." Still squeezing Oscar's wrist, she set her carton of fries on the bench so she could lift her other fist in the air, cheering wildly.

Oscar looked down once at her hand, then over at Adrian with a giddy yet panicked expression.

Adrian flashed him a thumbs-up that he hoped was encouraging.

Leaning back on the bench, Adrian devoured a handful of fries. He offered his carton to Nova, but she shook her head.

"Are you okay?" he asked, noticing that her expression was as serious now as it had been when he arrived.

"Yeah, yeah," she muttered distractedly.

"Nova?"

She glanced at him, then back at the field. "I just . . . have a lot on my mind."

Adrian's mouth twitched. He didn't want to say *I know the feeling*, but . . . well, he totally knew the feeling. "You had your first day in the artifacts department, right? How'd it go?"

Her posture stiffened and she seemed to be debating something, watching as Ruby's brothers bounded down a long trampoline, then scurried through a maze of transparent pipes. All obstacles that were incredibly relevant to real-life heroics, Adrian noted.

Nova leaned toward him, her voice lowering. "Did you know that Ace Anarchy's helmet is down there?"

Adrian turned to her, startled. "Um . . . actually, I think it's on display up in the Council offices."

Nova shot him a clearly marked you're-not-fooling-anyone glare.

He smiled sheepishly. "Oooh. You mean the *real* helmet."

"Yes, the real one," she whispered emphatically. "How many people know about it?"

"I don't know. It's not a secret, exactly, but it's not something that gets talked about much either. It's simpler to let people believe the one upstairs is the real thing."

"And that it was destroyed," said Nova. "Except it *wasn't* destroyed."

"Not for lack of trying." He cocked his head to one side. "You seem concerned."

"Of course I'm concerned. It's dangerous!" Her voice dropped again and Adrian found himself tucking his head close to hers to listen, so close that a lock of her hair brushed against his shoulder. "And it's just sitting there, completely unprotected. Do you know who they have running that department? A seventy-year-old woman with minor psychometry, and this guy who's not even a prodigy. And *they* are supposed to provide security for one of the most powerful objects of all time? Anyone could just walk in there and take it."

Adrian held up both hands to pacify her. "It's not as bad as that."

Nova folded her arms. "Why? Because of a big metal cube?"

He laughed. "Yeah, exactly. You know who made that cube, right?"

"Yes, and while Captain Chromium himself might be invincible, I don't think we should rely on his handiwork alone to protect the helmet. In fact, I'd like to talk to your dad about it. If he could clarify any potential weaknesses, then I could work on setting up a more comprehensive security system."

"It's indestructible," said Adrian. "It doesn't have any weaknesses."

"Indestructible," Nova repeated, her gaze searing into him. "But not *unopenable*?"

Adrian hesitated. Could it be . . . ?

No. He shook his head. "Unopenable to anyone who would ever want to use it for evil again."

Something seemed to kindle in Nova's expression and she scooted closer to him, until their sides were pressed together from shoulder to knee. He gulped.

"So it *can* be opened," she said. "By who?"

"Uh—that's not what I—no one can open it. I mean, I'm sure my dad could, if he ever wanted to. But he wouldn't. Why would he?"

She licked her lips, drawing his gaze toward them. In that same moment, the crowd erupted in a cheer and Adrian lurched instinctively to his feet. The carton of fries toppled from his lap, spilling across his and Nova's shoes. "Ah—I'm sorry!"

Ignoring the fries, Nova stood, too, and then her hand was on his elbow. Adrian's heart palpitated in his chest. On Nova's other side, he heard Ruby screaming—*Go! Go! Go!*

His eyes darted toward the field where he saw that both Sterling and the girl in the Lady Indomitable cape were more than halfway through the course, neck and neck as they swung across a series of knotted ropes.

"Adrian."

He looked back at Nova, his cheeks burning.

"Are you sure he didn't leave it vulnerable somehow?" she prodded, and the intensity of her expression made him realize just how important this was to her. Her earnestness surprised him. He never would have thought to doubt the security of the helmet. If Captain Chromium said it was taken care of, then it was taken care of. But clearly, Nova didn't share that confidence. "I need to make sure there isn't some unknown vulnerability. Now that I'm working in the artifacts department, it's my job to keep the objects there safe, you know? And that helmet . . . we can't let it fall into the wrong hands."

"There's never going to be another Ace Anarchy, Nova. You're overthinking this."

"You don't know that. I just need to be *sure*. Maybe Captain Chromium installed some sort of backup—a way to get to the helmet, in case it was ever needed again and he wasn't able to open the box himself. A . . . key, of sorts. Or is there some other way that someone could open it? Even hypothetically?"

Adrian heaved a long breath and tried to take the question seriously. "I don't know. My dad could get into it easily enough by manipulating the chromium. And maybe . . ." He dropped one hand to his pocket and pulled out his marker. He turned it over in his fingers, considering. "Maybe I could?"

"You?" said Nova, and he tried not to be offended at her tone of disbelief.

"I don't know. I've never tried to draw anything using my dad's chromium before. But I don't see why it would be any different from drawing on glass or concrete or Ruby's gems."

Her grip tightened on his arm. "What would you draw to get into the box?"

His mouth quirked to one side. "A door?"

Nova's brow tensed, and Adrian's teasing smile faded. "But it's still safe, Nova. I would never open that box, and I don't even know for sure it would work. Besides, there are no other prodigies like me—at least, not that I've ever heard of."

Nova hummed thoughtfully and, to his disappointment, pulled her hands away. "You might be right, but there are new prodigies every day. We don't know what sort of powers will be uncovered next. Who knows? Maybe your dad's chromium won't always be invincible."

Ruby, Oscar, and Danna let out simultaneous groans. Adrian looked up. Sterling had reached the final obstacle—a large, above-ground swimming pool full of nets, buoys, and robotic sharks. Though Sterling was a fast swimmer, the girl was quickly pulling ahead.

"If you think of anything else," said Nova, "any possible weakness that box might have . . . will you let me know?"

"I will," he said, smiling. "I promise."

The girl climbed out of the pool and darted across the finish line. Sterling followed seconds later.

Jade, trailing a ways behind, came in seventh.

"Second place," said Ruby. "That's not bad."

"Are you kidding?" said Oscar. "Any Renegade worth their alter ego would be proud to have that kid as a sidekick. Jade too. In fact . . ." He rubbed his chin. "I could use a couple sidekicks. Think your brothers would be interested?"

"What, to make food runs for you?" said Ruby.

"Among other important sidekicky things. It would really help clear my schedule for more damsel-saving work."

Ruby snorted. "I helped save that barista too."

"Yeah, but she was clearly thanking me, and I plan on milking it forever and ever. It's like a constant reminder of the risks and rewards that come with true heroism."

"The struggle is real," said Danna, leaning across Ruby to steal one of Oscar's fries.

The bleachers began to clear as the obstacle course was reset for the next group.

"We have an hour before Jade's wrestling match, and then they both have archery," said Ruby, checking the schedule on a flyer. She lifted her head, beaming. "Anyone want to go get matching face paint?"

"You read my mind," said Oscar.

"Uh, you two go ahead," said Adrian, recalling Oscar's face when Ruby had grabbed his arm. "There was something I wanted to show Nova and Danna . . . uh . . . over there." He pointed toward a cluster of vendor booths by the lake. "But we'll meet you at the wrestling match, okay?"

Danna cocked her head at him, suspicious, but no one argued as Adrian headed toward the bottom of the bleachers and melded into the bustling crowd. When he glanced back, Nova and Danna were beside him, but Oscar and Ruby were nowhere to be seen.

"That was just a ploy to give them alone time, right?" said Danna.

"Yeah," he said, scratching the back of his neck. "Too obvious?"

"Subtlety doesn't seem to be making much progress, so . . ." Danna shrugged.

"Hey," said Adrian, snapping his fingers, "how was your medical exam?"

Danna beamed. "Cleared for duty. I'll file the paperwork for reinstatement on Monday."

"Don't worry, I'll take care of it," said Adrian. "And you feel good?"

"Great. The scratches didn't even leave scars." She cast a sideways glance at Nova, her tone taking on a new edge. "No random fainting spells either, so . . . I guess I'm good as new."

Nova seemed to pale, but covered it quickly with a look of concern. "That's great, Danna."

"Fainting spells?" said Adrian.

Danna shrugged at him. "Remember when Nova was in the med-wing, after the quarantine fiasco? I went to visit her and . . . weirdest thing, but I actually fainted. I mean . . . I *never* faint."

"Classic case of overexertion," said Nova. "You were still recovering from your burns, remember?"

Danna stared at her for what felt like a moment too long, before she smiled. "Right. Classic." It seemed as if she wanted to say more, but she thought better of it. "Anyway, I saw a booth back there I wanted to check out. See you at the wrestling match, okay?"

She disintegrated into her butterfly swarm. A gasp arose from the people around them, children squealing and pointing as the butterflies spun into the air and whirled away.

"Speaking of subtlety," Nova muttered as they started down a jogging trail. "I'd been wondering if she could do that in civilian clothing. I wasn't sure if there was something in the Renegade uniform that allowed her to switch between forms without losing her clothes, or if it was a part of her power."

"I wonder about those details sometimes too. Like, Simon can make his clothes disappear, and also small objects if he's holding them—but he can't touch a car or a building and make the whole thing disappear. It's interesting to figure out the extent of someone's abilities. Of course, that's what we have training sessions for."

"Could Danna carry an object around with her, do you think? Not just clothing?"

He pondered the question, trying to remember if he'd ever seen Danna disappear with a weapon, but she'd always been more comfortable in hand-to-hand combat. "I'm not sure. I'll have to ask her when we start Agent N training next week. Wouldn't make much sense to equip her with a neutralizer gun if she's just going to lose it the first time she transforms."

Nova grunted in agreement. "I suppose we've all got weaknesses," she said. "Even the magnificent Monarch."

# CHAPTER FIFTEEN

IT WAS A LITTLE BIT like being at the Renegade Parade again, with all the costumed kids and the booths full of cheesy memorabilia. The excited children all around her were adorable, even if their faith was misguided. Nova couldn't help but think of Evie, who would have been only a little younger than Ruby's brothers. If her family had lived, would she and Evie have been raised to love the Renegades as much as these kids did? Would Evie be among them now, wearing Thunderbird wings or a Dread Warden mask, preparing to run and tumble her way through a series of competitions to prove she could be a superhero . . . or at least a sidekick?

Or maybe Evie would have turned out to be a prodigy, like Nova and their dad. Like Uncle Ace. She'd shown no sign of powers when she was alive, but she was a baby, and a lot of prodigies didn't develop abilities until later in life. Nova tried not to dwell on questions that could never be answered, but thinking of it made her heart ache.

"Nova?"

She startled. Adrian was watching her, his brow creased.

"Are you still thinking about that helmet?"

*The helmet.*

For once—no, she hadn't been. A ghost of a smile touched her lips. "My sister, actually. I . . . I think she would have enjoyed something like this."

Sadness echoed in Adrian's expression. "I'm sorry. I forget that you had a little sister."

She didn't respond, though she knew what she was supposed to say. *It's okay . . . it was a long time ago . . .*

But she'd never understood why that should make any difference. The loss of Evie still hurt every day.

"I know it's not the same thing," said Adrian, "but . . . I think Max would enjoy something like this too."

Nova sighed. Adrian was right—Max would have liked the Sidekick Olympics, though the Bandit was far too powerful to be relegated to a mere sidekick role. Having experienced life in the tunnels for so long, she had some idea of how hard it must be for Max to be always inside his quarantine, watching the world pass by outside his prison. He missed out on so much. He missed out on the entire world.

"I wish he could be here," said Nova. "I wish they both could."

Their eyes met, mirrors of unfulfilled wishes, and Nova noticed a streak of gray dust on Adrian's cheek. She frowned and reached up to brush it off. Adrian stilled. "You're filthy," she said and, now that she was looking, she spotted cobwebs clinging to his shoulder, and smudges of dirt on his sleeves. "What were you doing today?"

"Eh—nothing worthwhile," he said. "Just a stroll through some defunct subway tunnels. You know, typical Saturday morning."

"Subway tunnels?"

"It's kind of a long story, but . . . I was given clearance to talk to Winston Pratt after the presentation the other day."

One of her toes clipped into the trail and Nova stumbled. Adrian reached out to steady her. "You what?"

"I thought maybe I could learn something about the Anarchists. Don't get excited; he didn't say anything useful. But he did say that if I could bring him this puppet of his, he would give up some information."

*A puppet of his. Hettie.* He had let Nova play with it occasionally when she was little and it had always felt like a great honor.

"So I went looking for the puppet, but of course, everything was gone. All that's down there now is a bunch of dead bees and some stray trash."

Nova scowled. She hated to think of the Renegades picking through her home, analyzing and inspecting everything they found.

"Speaking of bees," said Adrian, his tone lightening, "how's your uncle's beekeeping business?"

She laughed at the unexpected absurdity of the question. She'd nearly forgotten about the lie she'd told him in an effort to explain away Honey's hives in her backyard. "Uh . . . not great, to be honest. But he's not the type to give up."

Adrian grinned. "That must be where you get it from."

It was obviously a compliment and Nova felt her neck warming. "Oh yeah, stubbornness is definitely a family trait."

Unbidden, Ace's words turned through her head, reminding her that this was not a casual weekend outing. She had a mission, and Adrian was a part of it. *Earn his trust. Earn his respect. Earn his affection.*

It shouldn't be that hard, she had been telling herself all week. Adrian was handsome, talented, honorable, kind. So why did every nerve in her body rebel at the thought of faking attraction to him? Of flirting with him, merely for the sake of flirting? Of pretending to be interested?

The answer was thrown back in her face, and she fidgeted with her bracelet.

*Because maybe it wouldn't be fake.*

And to discover that she actually liked him, against all her better judgment, would cost far too much.

Still, if she was ever going to sneak useful information out of Adrian or use his loyalty to undermine his fathers, she had to get close to him.

She had to . . .

Her thoughts trailed off as her attention fell on a crop of trees around the north side of the lake. Her feet halted and she glanced around, spotting a small playground not far away. Her breath hitched. "Do you know where we are?"

"That seems like a trick question."

She grabbed his sleeve and started walking again. "The statue glen is this way."

"Statue glen?"

"Yeah, you know. You had that drawing of it in your sketchbook, the one you showed me when we were watching the library. The statue of the hooded figure?"

"Oh—right. You said you used to go there when you were a kid?"

"Only once." Nova couldn't quite explain the giddiness that was surging through her limbs. Her feet sped up almost of their own accord. They rounded a corner and the paved path turned one way, while a smaller gravel trail led into a strip of dense woodland. "My parents brought me to that playground, but I wandered off and found . . ." Nova pushed back a low-hanging branch and froze.

She stood at the top of a rough, moss-covered staircase. The steps curved down into a small ravine, surrounded by towering oak trees and dense shrubs. "This," she whispered.

She descended into the glen. The clearing was not much bigger than the bedroom she shared with Honey at the row house, with a short rock wall set in a circle around the edges. A wrought-iron bench on one side faced a solitary statue.

Nova felt like she'd stepped back in time. Nothing had changed, not since she was a little girl.

"This is silly, but . . . until I saw that drawing you'd done, there had been a part of me that thought maybe this place was my own little secret. Which makes no sense. Probably thousands of people come here every year. But . . . being so little when I found it, I guess I felt like it belonged to me. Like maybe I'd imagined it into existence." She chuckled and knew she would have been embarrassed to admit this to anyone else, at any other time. But being here again was so surreal she couldn't bring herself to care.

She circled the statue. It was exactly as she remembered, if maybe sporting a touch more moss than it had back then. A hooded figure dressed in loose robes, like a medieval monk. The face carved beneath the hood was amorphous, with closed eyes and a contented smile and rounded features. Its hands were stretched toward the sky, like it was trying to catch something.

She did not know how old the statue was, but it looked like it had stood there for a thousand years. Like it would stand there for a thousand more.

"I've only known about this place for a couple years," said Adrian. "Though I've been back to sketch a handful of times. How old were you when you found it?"

"Four or five," she said, trailing a finger along the statue's sleeve. "That night, I dreamed about it. This was before I stopped sleeping, obviously, and to this day it's the only dream I can remember in perfect detail." She surveyed the glen. The woods were so dense here the sounds from the festival could no longer be heard. Only bird melodies and rustling leaves. "I dreamed that I was walking through a jungle, with flowers bigger than my head, and a canopy so dense I couldn't see the sky. The whole place hummed with life . . . insects and birds . . . Except I kept coming across things that didn't belong there. Concrete steps that were covered in moss, and vines dangling from street lamps instead of trees . . ." She swirled her hand through the air, tracing the vines from memory. "It was Gatlon, but it was in ruins. Just a jungle now, all overgrown. And then . . . I found this clearing, and there was the statue. It was facing away from me at first, but even before I got close, I knew that it was holding something. So I walked around it, and I looked up, and . . ." She paused, feeling like she was back in that dream, drowning in the sense of wonder she'd almost forgotten.

"And then you woke up?" Adrian guessed.

She snapped her attention away from the vision and glared at him. "*No.* The statue was holding something." She hesitated, feeling childish now, and a little defensive.

"Are you going to make me guess?" said Adrian.

She shook her head and tried to temper the emotion she felt at the memory. "It was holding a . . . a star."

Only in saying it out loud did Nova realize how ridiculous it sounded. "Whatever that means," she finished lamely.

"Dream logic," said Adrian. "Or . . . possibly nightmare logic. I can't tell if this was a good dream or not."

Nova chuckled. "It was a good dream. I'm not sure why, given that all of civilization had collapsed, but . . . it was a really good dream." She rubbed the back of her neck. "My parents were furious when they finally found me, and they never brought me back to that playground. But I never forgot about that dream. I must have fantasized about finding that star for years afterward."

"Funny how some dreams stick with you," said Adrian, sitting down on the grass and stretching his long legs in front of him. "You're lucky. Most of the dreams I remember from childhood were nightmares. Or . . . a nightmare. I had a recurring one for years."

Nova sat down next to him. "About what?"

He squirmed. "Never mind. I shouldn't have said anything. It's not important."

"And mine was?"

"Yes," he insisted. "Yours was amazing. A jungle? Collapsed civilization? A statue holding a *star*? That's epic. Whereas mine was just . . ." He waved a hand carelessly. "You know. A nightmare. I don't even remember that much about it, other than how much it terrified me."

"Let me guess," said Nova, cupping her cheek in one hand. "You used to dream that you arrived at HQ only to realize you'd forgotten to put on clothes that morning."

He shot her an annoyed look. "I was, like, four. HQ didn't even exist yet."

"Oh."

"No, it was more like . . . there was this *thing*, watching me, all the time. I called it the monster, because I was original like that. Half the time I couldn't even see it, but I would know it was there, waiting to . . ."

"To what?"

"I'm not sure. Kill me, maybe. Or kill my mom or all the people I cared about. I don't think I ever had a dream where it actually did anything, other than lurk in the background, waiting to grab me or chase me." He shuddered. "In hindsight, it's probably not that surprising. I grew up surrounded by superheroes. Every time my mom left our apartment I didn't know if she would ever come back. And the news was always full of stories of people getting kidnapped or being found dead in gutters . . . What was my subconscious supposed to do with all that information?" He shot her a wistful smile. "I can see why your subconscious thought it would be better to just let the whole city collapse."

A surprised laugh escaped her, and though she knew Adrian was joking, she wondered if there was a hint of truth to his words.

"Nightmares," she mused. "I don't miss them."

Adrian's face softened, and she couldn't quite look away. Her nerves tingled.

"We should probably get back," he murmured, without breaking eye contact. Without moving at all.

"Probably," agreed Nova. But she couldn't move either. Anticipation mingled with nervousness. Her heart pounded like a mallet.

*Earn his affection.*

She glimpsed his hand resting in the grass and tried to work up the courage to touch him. She tried to channel Honey Harper, imagining what she would do. A brush of her shoulder, a graze of her fingertips?

The thought of it made her shiver.

What would Honey do?

Nova's gaze skipped down to Adrian's lips.

She gulped and leaned forward.

Adrian took in a sudden breath and, before Nova knew what was happening, he had jumped to his feet and started brushing himself off. "Yeah, wow, we need to hurry," he said, glancing at his wristband. "Don't want to be late for . . . uh . . . jousting or . . . whatever it was . . ."

Nova gaped up at him.

Sweet rot. She had tried to kiss him and . . . *he had rejected her.*

So, that's what that felt like.

Mortification overtook her, and she was grateful that he seemed determined not to look at her, as it gave her a moment to gather her wits and shove down her disappointment.

Shove it far, far down inside.

So far down that she could almost convince herself it wasn't there at all.

# CHAPTER SIXTEEN

OVA WASN'T SURE which riddle was more frustrating.

Adrian, who had gone from trying to kiss her at the amusement park to acting like she had a contagious, incurable disease.

Or Ace's helmet, which was trapped inside an unopenable box.

Nova wasn't fond of riddles in general, but of the two currently plaguing her, she found it far less uncomfortable to focus on the chromium box, and so she had spent all morning sitting at the front desk outside the artifacts warehouse contemplating just that.

How do you open an unopenable box?

How do you destroy an indestructible material?

What could be strong enough to safely get past the chromium and free Ace's helmet from its prison?

Nova still didn't have the answer, but she knew who did. Captain Chromium. He had made the box. He must know how to unmake it. And though Nova wasn't sure what she could say to him to get him to give up this secret, she knew she would have to try.

Before Ace faded away into nothing.

She was caught up in a very long, very clever, very imaginary conversation with the Captain when the elevator doors dinged and none other than her second riddle strolled into the reception area. Nova jerked upward. "Adrian?"

He was practically bouncing on his feet as he hurried to her desk. "It's *here*," he said, beaming.

She gaped at him, feeling like she should know what *it* was, but all she could think about was the helmet.

"Excuse me?"

"I was thinking that all that stuff from the tunnels had probably gotten thrown away after it was checked for evidence, but I talked to the head of crime-scene investigation this morning and she told me it's all been brought *here*. They don't throw anything away until an investigation is closed, so right now all the Anarchists' stuff is supposedly just sitting around in a stockpile somewhere, waiting to be tagged and categorized and"—he waved his hand absently toward the vault—"whatever it is that happens here, exactly."

Nova studied him, her stomach dropping. "Winston's puppet."

Settling his elbows onto the desk, Adrian leaned toward her. "Exactly. On top of that, I've gotten approval from both the Council and Winston's counselor. He can have the puppet in exchange for information, just as long as Snapshot checks it first to be sure it isn't hiding some secret magical power."

Winston's puppet. That he was willing to trade information for.

Nova swallowed. "Oh. That's . . . great."

"Is Snapshot in?"

The door to the filing room opened, but it was Callum, not Snapshot, that strolled out. He froze as soon as he saw Adrian. "No way! Sketch in the flesh! I'm a total fan."

"Oh, thanks," said Adrian, accepting a firm handshake with a bewildered expression.

Nova gestured between them. "Uh . . . Adrian, Callum. Callum, Adrian."

"Are you here to check something out?" said Callum. "We've got a feather quill that I think you'd really like."

"Oh yeah?" said Adrian, though he quickly shook away his interest. "No, thanks. Actually, I was told there's a place here where they're storing all the stuff that was confiscated from the Anarchist holdings in the subway tunnels?"

"Sure, there's a storeroom in the back. But I'm warning you, it's a mess back there. It's on my list to get cleaned up, but . . ." Callum shrugged. "Hey, maybe that'd be a good job for us to do together, yeah?"

It took Nova a moment to realize he was talking to her. She jerked upright. "Yeah. Great. Sounds like fun."

Callum pointed at Adrian. "You know, I should probably check that you've been given clearance, but . . . bah, who am I kidding? Of course you can see it. Come on back." He waved his arm.

Adrian flashed an excited grin at Nova and started to follow.

"Hey, wait," she said, jumping from her chair. "Can I come too, or . . . ?"

Callum laughed. "This girl! Her curiosity is insatiable!"

Taking that as a yes, Nova flipped over a BE RIGHT BACK sign on the desk and darted after them. Callum weaved through the front section of the warehouse, giving Adrian much the same orientation he'd given her on her first day, until they arrived at a freestanding room near the back corner, with walls that didn't quite stretch all the way to the ceiling.

Callum thrust open the door. "All right, you two have fun. I'll let Snapshot know you're back here."

Nova hovered beside Adrian in the doorway, her jaw dropping. She half expected to be overcome with sadness to see all of her things and the belongings of her family, now in the hands of the Renegades—unappreciated and unloved.

But instead, she felt overwhelmed.

And a little relieved.

The chances of Adrian finding anything amid this clutter were slim.

Squaring his shoulders, Adrian angled his body to fit between two towering shelves and squeezed into the room. "He wasn't kidding, was he?"

Nova followed after him. It was as if the Renegades had filled cart after cart with all the random things they had found down in the tunnels and just . . . dumped it here, without care or ceremony. Though, as her eyes adjusted to the chaos, she began to notice at least some half-hearted attempts at organization. She spotted Honey's beloved wardrobe against one wall, piled over with her sequined dresses and silk scarves, but also Leroy's bathrobe, and a trash bag from which Nova's own street clothes were bursting through. Other accessories—jewelry, shoes, and the like, almost all Honey's—were strewn across a cart nearby. The furniture was mostly lumped into a teetering stack in the middle, including Leroy's beloved moth-eaten armchair. Practical household items were grouped erratically across a series of shelves, from electric teakettles to can openers and even a broom, though Nova couldn't recall anyone ever using a broom down in the tunnels.

Wait, no, there had been that time when she'd seen Ingrid chasing a rat with one . . .

Adrian weaved through the narrow pathway, and Nova saw what had caught his attention. A bright-colored play tent, crumpled beneath a long table. "Looks like there's some Puppeteer stuff over here," Adrian said, crouching to dig through the rumpled nylon fabric.

"Great," said Nova, unable to muster even a hint of enthusiasm. The smell of the subway was all around her, and she hated being reminded of it after so many weeks of life aboveground. Though there were things that had been taken from her that day that she would like to have back, she had to admit that she wasn't sad to have left their underground prison.

Sad to leave Ace behind, yes, but not sad to be gone.

"I've been doing some research on the Anarchists lately," said Adrian. He found a plastic toy kitchenette behind the tents and started yanking open its mildew-covered cupboards. "Did you know Winston Pratt's dad was a toymaker?"

Nova blinked at the back of his head. "No," she said, and it was the truth. She knew little about Winston or who he had been before he was the Puppeteer.

"I don't know this for sure, but something tells me this puppet he wants might have been made by his dad. Makes sense it would be something he's attached to, right?"

Nova didn't respond. She had spied a desk tucked behind a series of shelves.

*Her* desk.

"Couldn't find anything about his origin story, though," Adrian continued. "Or Phobia's. Actually couldn't find *anything* about Phobia."

Nova pushed aside a rack hung with more of Honey's dresses, making her way to the desk. "That's odd," she said half-heartedly, though, in truth, she knew hardly anything about Phobia either. With a power like his, so immersed in humanity's greatest terrors, she wasn't sure she wanted to know his origin. She did know there were times when Phobia seemed halfway normal. Like there could be just a regular guy under that cloak—quiet and solitary, with an odd sense of humor and subtle ambition.

Who had he been before? How had he become this?

If Phobia had ever given up these secrets, she didn't know about it.

"But there's lots out there on Honey Harper," said Adrian with a chuckle. Nova glanced over to see him digging through a cardboard box labeled, simply, JUNK FOOD. "She grew up on a farm about fifty miles south of here. Claims that when she was twelve years old she stepped on a hornet's nest. The stings sent her into anaphylactic shock and she passed out. When she woke up hours later, she was swollen up like a balloon."

"Wait—*she* said this?" asked Nova.

"Uh-huh. It was in a newspaper interview, back near the start of the Anarchist revolution."

Nova frowned. It was difficult to imagine Honey ever admitting to being swollen up like a balloon.

"But," Adrian continued, "she survived, obviously, and she found the hive's queen crushed under her shoe. After that, the whole hive was under her control." He looked up at Nova. "Now, *that's* an origin story."

"Why are they always so traumatic?" she murmured. She reached the desk and pulled open the top drawer. Her heart surged. A set of screwdrivers greeted her, rolling around in the drawer. They were her first tools, scavenged by Ace when she was just four years old. She stroked one of the handles lovingly, not having realized she'd missed them until that moment.

"Cyanide has a sad story, too," said Adrian.

Nova bit the inside of her cheek. She had heard Leroy tell his story before. A victim of bullying in high school, he had been accosted by some of his peers after a chemistry lab. Things got out of hand and soon they started to attack him—not just with their fists, but by dousing him with random chemicals and acids, too.

Although, when Leroy told the story, he liked to jump ahead to the part where he cornered his lab partner in a restroom and ensured his face would be forever even more hideously scarred than Leroy's own. Nova remembered Leroy chuckling about it, but she hadn't thought it was funny, not for either of them.

"Sometimes," said Adrian, his voice sounding hollow, "it's impossible for me to fathom why anyone would ever have joined Ace Anarchy. Why would anyone do such horrible things like the Anarchists did?"

Nova's jaw clenched.

"But then I hear the stories and . . . I don't know. Sometimes you can see how it makes sense, you know?"

Gathering the screwdrivers in her hand, Nova turned to face Adrian, checking that he was preoccupied before tucking them into a pouch on her belt. "Any luck?"

"No puppet, but . . . do you know what these are?" Adrian held up a shoe box full of jagged metal disks.

Nova's eyes widened.

Adrian didn't wait for her to answer. "Nightmare's throwing stars. Heat-tracking, I think . . . or maybe motion-detecting? I don't know, but they have caused us a world of trouble. Vicious little weapons." He lifted one from the box, turning it over to inspect it from both sides. "I always wondered how they worked. We should probably take these up to research and development."

"I'll do it," she said quickly. "That's part of my job here, you know. Sorting through things . . . figuring out what could be useful . . . making sure it gets to the right people. I'll run it over to them after my shift today."

Adrian put the throwing star back into the box and slid it up onto a table.

Nova exhaled. "At least we don't have to worry about her anymore, right? The other Anarchists are scary enough, but I sure am glad Nightmare's been taken care of."

"I suppose . . . ," Adrian said.

Nova frowned at him. "What do you mean, you suppose?"

He shrugged. "We haven't really proven that she's dead."

Goose bumps raced down her arms. "What?"

Adrian started pawing through a trunk, mostly filled with cheap magic tricks and plastic party favors. "They never found a body, or . . . any evidence at all that she was killed."

"Because she was *obliterated*," said Nova, more forceful than she'd intended to be. "The Detonator's bomb destroyed her. No wonder there was nothing left!"

"Maybe. I mean, it definitely caused a lot of damage, but . . . shouldn't there have been something? Body parts? Blood?"

Nova gawked at him. All this time, all these weeks, she'd felt sure about this *one* thing, at least. This one thing that had actually gone right. She had faked her own death. The Renegades believed that Nightmare was gone. They had called off the investigation. It was one less thing for her to worry about, and she'd embraced it heartily.

And Adrian didn't believe it?

"But . . . but no one could have survived that explosion."

"You did."

She froze.

"You were in the fun house when the bomb hit."

"I . . . I was on the opposite side of the fun house," she whispered. "And I was protected by a giant metal cylinder."

Adrian's lips tilted upward again, but she could tell he was humoring her. "I know. You're probably right. She's probably dead. I just . . . wonder about it, sometimes."

"Well, don't."

He chuckled, but quickly became serious again. Sliding the cardboard box beneath the table, he stood. "You know, we never talked about what happened that day."

Nova's pulse jumped, and just like that, she was back in the neglected corner of Cosmopolis Park, and Adrian was telling her how worried he'd been when he thought she was dead, and he was stepping closer, and her breaths were coming quicker—

"*Do* you want to talk about it?" His eyes were on her, unsure.

Heat climbed her neck and blossomed across her cheeks. Did she want to talk about it?

No, not really.

She wanted to pretend like it hadn't happened. She wanted to start over.

She wanted him to try to kiss her again, because this time, she wouldn't run away.

"I . . . I'm sorry," she said, wetting her lips. "I think I just . . . I just got scared."

It was true. It was *still* true. She was scared. Scared that she felt this way for Adrian Everhart, a Renegade. Scared that she couldn't quite escape it, no matter how many times she reminded herself that he was the enemy.

Scared that even now, she knew that she wasn't trying to get close to him *only* because Ace had suggested it. If anything, that was just a convenient excuse to do exactly what she'd wanted to do all along.

"Of course you were scared," he said. "*I* was terrified."

"You were?"

"But you were braver than I was. I completely froze up, and you . . ." He trailed off.

Nova stared at him, perplexed. *She* was brave? *He* froze up?

"But still, even if the Detonator was a monster, I know it couldn't have been easy. You killed someone, and—" He lifted both hands like he was trying to calm her, but Nova wasn't upset. She was baffled. "You did what you had to do, but it couldn't have been easy, and . . . I just . . . if you want to talk about it, you can talk to me."

"About . . . killing the Detonator," she said, as her thoughts reshuffled and fell back into place.

Here she was, dwelling on an almost-kiss, and Adrian wanted to talk about the time she'd killed someone.

"I'm sorry," Adrian said. "Maybe I shouldn't have said anything. I just thought—"

"No, it's fine. I mean . . . I was offered trauma counseling, if I wanted it, but I don't really feel like I need it." And she wasn't about to spill her innermost thoughts to a Renegade psychiatrist, even if she did need it. "The thing is, killing the Detonator wasn't hard." She exhaled, and wanted to move closer to Adrian, but there was so much stuff between them. So much baggage. Her entire past life laid out at their feet, and she couldn't bring herself to wade through it. "It wasn't hard at all. She was hurting all those people, and she would have hurt so many more." Her palms were becoming damp, but she forced herself to hold Adrian's gaze and tell him the truth, what she had known even then was the truth. "She would have hurt *you*."

Surprise warmed his features. "Nova . . ."

She turned away, her heart fluttering with the way he was looking at her.

Then—"*Nova.*"

She glanced up again, and Adrian was suddenly grinning. He pointed to something behind her.

Nova peered up. Her shoulders fell.

Winston's puppet, Hettie, was perched on the topmost shelf over Nova's old desk, its wooden legs dangling over the side, its sad eyes watching them as though it had been listening in on the whole conversation and found it severely disheartening.

She bit back a groan. "Brilliant."

AFTER ADRIAN RETRIEVED the doll, they made their way back through the warehouse and found Snapshot talking to Callum in the section devoted to artifacts with healing properties.

"It should clearly go in defense," Callum was saying, holding up a thick black pendant attached to a slender chain.

"I disagree," said Snapshot, punching something into a handheld label maker. "It belongs here, with the other healing objects."

"It doesn't *heal*," Callum said.

"It protects from disease," said Snapshot.

"Yeah, it protects you from getting sick, but it won't do anything if you're already sick. It's preventative. It's a defensive measure. *Defense.*"

"Excuse me?" said Adrian, drawing their attention.

Callum opened his arms wide. "Nova, tell her! Vitality Charm, healing or defense?" He held up the necklace. The large round pendant swung from the chain. It appeared old—ancient even—with a rudimentary symbol impressed into what might have been iron, showing an open palm with a serpent curled up inside it.

Nova shook her head. "Sorry, Callum. Never heard of it."

His shoulders sank. "Okay, well . . . mostly it's used to protect against poison and disease, but there was also one account of it fending off a strength-draining attack from a prodigy."

"Cool," said Adrian. "Can I see?"

Callum handed the pendant to him. "They've had it in healing for years, but that doesn't make sense."

"Fine, Callum, fine," said Snapshot, pressing a label onto the edge of a shelf. "Shelve it wherever you want. Hello, Adrian—I heard you were going through the Anarchist room. Did you find what you were looking for?"

"As a matter of fact . . ." Adrian held up the puppet. "Can I get it cleared to be taken out?"

She set down the label maker and took the puppet from him. She brought her cat-eye glasses down from her head and inspected the doll from every angle. After a long, quiet moment, she handed Hettie back to Adrian. "Just a puppet," she confirmed. "Nothing extraordinary about it. You have my permission to take it from the warehouse. Callum, maybe you can make a note in the database?"

"Great, thanks," said Adrian. He went to return the medallion to Callum, but hesitated. He looked closer at the design, his brow creasing.

Nova inched closer, trying to see what had caught his interest, but it was just a big, ugly pendant so far as she could tell. Albeit one that could protect from disease. She wondered to what extent. The common cold? The plague? Everything in between? And why wasn't it at the hospital, rather than gathering dust in here?

"Actually, is this available to be checked out too?" asked Adrian.

"Sure," said Callum. "But once you bring it back"—he cut a sharp look at Snapshot—"I'm putting it in defense."

She shooed them away. "Just make sure you fill out the form, Mr. Everhart," she said. "Nova can help you with that."

Nova smiled tightly. "Right this way."

# CHAPTER SEVENTEEN

WINSTON PRATT HELD the puppet in both hands, peering into its sad face with apparent indifference. Adrian had not known what to expect when he brought the doll to him. The counselor had insisted on being there, pointing out that objects that were significant and sentimental to a patient could result in strong outbursts of emotion—positive *and* negative. So Adrian had been prepared for delighted squeals, or wretched sobs. But had not been prepared for total apathy.

Even confusion, as Winston tilted his head from side to side. He seemed to be inspecting the doll's face, but for what, Adrian couldn't begin to guess.

"Well?" Adrian said finally, his patience reaching its end. The counselor shot him a disgruntled look, which he ignored. "That is Hettie, isn't it?"

"Yes," said Winston Pratt. "This is Hettie." He rubbed the pad of his thumb across the black teardrop on the puppet's cheek, as if trying to scrub the paint away. It didn't work. Holding the doll in both hands, he lifted it to eye level and whispered, "*You* did this to me."

Adrian cast a glance at the counselor. She looked worried, like she was ready to step in and divert Winston's attention to more cheerful subjects at the first sign of trouble. Clearing her throat, she took a subtle step forward. "What did Hettie do to you, Mr. Pratt?"

Winston looked up, startled, as if he'd forgotten they were there. Then his lip curled in annoyance. "Hettie is a puppet," he said, shaking the doll so that the wooden head bobbed back and forth. "It can't do anything it isn't made to do."

The counselor blinked. "Yes," she said slowly, "but you said—"

"It's what he symbolizes," Winston said. His indifference vanished, and suddenly, his face was carved with emotion. His brow creased, his eyes burned. His breaths turned ragged. "It's what he did!" With a scream, he pulled back his arm and threw the puppet. It clacked hollowly against the wall and fell to the floor, its limbs splayed at odd angles.

Adrian watched, frozen, and wondered distantly if he should come back in an hour or two.

But then Winston took in a long breath and giggled, almost sheepish. "I didn't mean to do that." He looked at Adrian. "Could you hand him back to me, pretty please?"

When the counselor didn't object, Adrian scooped the doll from the floor. Winston snatched it from his hand and spent another moment trying to scratch off the teardrop with his thumbnail, before huffing with irritation and tucking Hettie against his side.

He met Adrian's eyes again and shrugged, a little sadly. "I shouldn't have taken my anger out on poor Hettie," he said, petting the doll's fluffy orange hair. "It really isn't his fault."

Adrian forced a smile, not sure how else to respond. He waited a full ten seconds before lifting his eyebrows. "So?"

"So?" said Winston.

His fist started to tighten and Adrian shoved it into his pocket in an attempt to make it less obvious. "We had a deal. The puppet, in exchange for information. You promised to tell me who killed my mother."

Winston clicked his tongue. "No, no. I promised to tell you something you would want to know."

Adrian's hand squeezed tighter, until he could feel his nails digging into his palm. He'd known better than to trust an Anarchist. He'd known.

He was seconds away from leaping forward and snatching the puppet away from the villain when Winston started to smile. Teasing and sly.

"And I *will* tell you something you want to know. More than you realize."

Adrian held his breath.

"You told me that you watched the Detonator kill Nightmare," said Winston. "That you were *there*. But . . . I'm afraid, young Master Everhart, you were mistaken." His eyes twinkled. "Our precious little Nightmare is very much alive."

HE WENT TO the Council's offices first, but only Blacklight was available. Adrian supposed he could have told him, as he was as high-ranking as any of the others. But no—he needed to talk to his dads first. They knew the whole story of his search for Nightmare. They knew why it was so important to him.

But according to Prism, Captain Chromium and the Dread Warden were out to dinner with the commissioner of Gatlon City food security and they were not expected back in the office until tomorrow. Though Adrian pressed, she refused to tell him where they had gone—it would not be appropriate to divulge that information, even to *him,* she said, forcefully apologetic.

So he headed home, teeth grinding the whole way.

Winston Pratt had refused to say more, no matter how Adrian cajoled, or how many of the Anarchists' belongings he offered as bribes, to the growing annoyance of his counselor. Pratt was not swayed. He had given the information he intended to give, and his lips were now sealed. He'd even made a zipper motion across them to prove his point.

It was so *infuriating.* To know that he had more information, but was refusing to share it. Adrian definitely would have smacked Pratt on the side of the head a few times if he'd thought the counselor would allow it.

*Nightmare was alive.*

He had known. Somehow, he had *known.* She hadn't been killed by that explosion. She'd sneaked away while they were distracted by the bombs going off in the park. She was still at large.

And there was a chance that he could find her. There was a chance he could find out her connection to his mother's murderer.

He had been pacing inside the dining room for nearly two hours when the front door finally opened and Hugh's boisterous laugh echoed through the house. Adrian charged into the foyer. Both of his dads were grinning, but the looks faded when their eyes landed on him.

"Nightmare is alive," he blurted. "Winston Pratt confirmed it. She wasn't killed by the Detonator. She's still out there!"

"Whoa, whoa, whoa," said Hugh, holding up his hands. "Slow down."

Adrian paused to take a deep breath. His dads shrugged out of their jackets as he started again. "When I spoke to Winston Pratt the other day, we made a deal. If I brought him this puppet of his, he would answer one of my questions."

"Yes, we know," said Simon. "We had to approve the incentive."

"Right," said Adrian. "Well, I got the puppet and today he told me that Nightmare isn't dead. She tricked us!"

They both stared at him, wool jackets draped over their arms.

"And," Simon started, "how, exactly, does he know that?"

Adrian rubbed a hand over his hair. "I don't know. He wouldn't say anything else, but he seemed certain."

"He's been in jail for months," said Hugh, "with no outside contact. He couldn't possibly know whether or not Nightmare is alive."

"I'm sorry, Adrian, but Hugh's right. He's just trying to distract you—to distract us. Classic villain technique. Get us looking for one thing over here, while they make plans to attack us over there. We need to stay focused on finding Hawthorn and the remaining Anarchists, not chasing after a ghost."

"No, but . . ." Adrian trailed off. His eyes darted between them, and he felt the sudden sting of pity. He rocked back on his heels. He didn't want to believe them, but he couldn't explain why he was convinced that Winston Pratt was telling the truth.

*Because you want it to be the truth*, a voice whispered. His own annoying subconscious.

If it wasn't true, then the trail to find his mother's killer was cold again, nothing more than a vague hope that maybe, maybe, one of the other Anarchists might know something. If they were ever found again.

And it would mean that he'd been fooled by a lousy villain. He'd gone to the tunnels, he'd searched through the artifacts warehouse. Could it have been a staged mission, with no prize to gain at all?

"I'm sorry," Hugh started, but Adrian cut him off with a wave of his hand.

"Don't be. I . . . I probably should have thought of all that before I let him get to me. I just . . ."

"You wanted it to be true," Hugh said. "We get it."

"Yeah, well——" Adrian cleared his throat. "How was your dinner?"

Hugh thumped Adrian on the back as he headed for the staircase. "Long."

"But . . . ," said Simon, revealing a cardboard to-go box that had been invisible in his hand, "we brought you cheesecake."

It felt like a small consolation, but Adrian took it.

He trudged down to his bedroom in the mansion's basement, fork in one hand and dessert in the other. The basement was huge, though still mostly unfinished, as his dads' efforts to restore the home had been focused on the upper floors. Adrian had dominion over what happened down here, which so far meant he'd put up a few shelves of old action figures and some of his favorite comic drawings, mostly from artists who had been prolific before the Age of Anarchy. There was also his bed, a small sofa, his desk, and an entertainment console with video games and a TV. It wasn't luxurious, but it was his.

He threw himself onto the sofa. He didn't know who he was more frustrated with. His dads, for not being willing to even consider that Nightmare might still be alive. Or Winston Pratt, for revealing a potentially fake and almost certainly useless bit of information. Or himself, for believing him. For *still* believing him, despite the logic of his dads' words.

He shoveled a few bites of cheesecake into his mouth, but he wasn't tasting it. His mind was going over the fight at the theme park again. The moment when the Detonator had thrown the bomb at Nightmare and Adrian had seen her try to dodge the blast.

Try—and fail? He wasn't sure then, and he wasn't sure now. What he did know was that they hadn't found her body, or even bits of it, gruesome as the thought was.

Only her mask.

But what did it matter? Even if Winston was right and she was alive, Adrian was no closer to finding her. He had no more clues to investigate. No more leads to follow. He supposed he could dig through all that stuff from the subway tunnels, but just thinking about that gave him a headache. And if the investigators hadn't found anything useful, why did he think he would do any better?

After tearing through half the slice of cake, Adrian stood up and marched to his desk. He rummaged around until he found a charcoal pencil.

He would sketch for a while. It always helped focus his thoughts, or at least quiet them.

Grabbing a spiral-bound book from the shelf, he sat down and found a blank page. He let the charcoal guide his fingers, scrawling hasty shapes and messy shadows across the paper, until an image began to take shape.

Overgrown ferns. A moss-covered staircase. A cloaked figure haunting the background.

A shiver shook Adrian so hard, the charcoal scratched a sharp line through the landscape, disrupting the vision. Adrian sat up straighter. The figure was turned away and for a moment, his subconscious returned images of the monster that had haunted his nightmares as a child. It had been years since he'd thought of those terrors, but telling Nova about them had stirred up feelings of powerlessness that he would have preferred to keep buried.

But when he took in the drawing in its entirety, he realized that it wasn't the monster that he'd been drawing. It was the statue.

The statue at City Park.

This wasn't *his* dream, it was Nova's.

Adrian lowered the sketchbook, an idea sharpening in his thoughts. He stared at the closed door that divided his bedroom from the only other finished room in the basement, though "finished" was a subjective term. It had four walls and a ceiling, all covered with drywall, though not much else. No trim, no texture, not even windows.

He stood, clutching the sketchbook as he opened the door. Striding into the darkness, he waved his arm until his hand collided with a thin chain. With a tug, he turned on the bare light bulb in the center of the ceiling.

When they'd first moved in, Adrian had dubbed this space his "art studio," somewhat ironically. He had drawn himself an easel and a second worktable and a bookshelf for storing his sketchbooks, which was, admittedly, a little crooked. Otherwise, the space remained barren and a bit on the forlorn side.

He turned in a full circle, inspecting the bare white walls.

His eyes returned to the drawing.

Then back up. White space. Emptiness. A canvas waiting to be filled.

He regarded the meager stash of art supplies he'd been hoarding for years, a vision filling his thoughts.

Turning, he strode back through his bedroom and up the creaky stairs. He found Hugh in front of the TV in the living room, having changed into sweats and an old triathlon T-shirt. (He had served as a commentator, not a contestant, which would have been supremely unfair.)

"No more talk about Nightmare tonight," said Hugh, without

looking up from the TV. "Please." He clicked through channels until he landed on the news.

Adrian scowled. "I wasn't going to."

Hugh shot him a disbelieving look.

"I just wanted to ask if it's okay for me to paint my studio."

"What studio?"

"You know, my art studio. That empty room downstairs, next to my bedroom."

"The storage room?"

Adrian pushed up his glasses. "If *storage* is code for 'Adrian's random drawing stuff,' then yes."

"I think he means the room we planned on using for storage," said Simon, appearing behind Adrian with a bowl of popcorn, "but we didn't end up needing it."

"Yep, that's the one. So, can I paint it?"

Simon flopped onto the sofa, propping his feet on the coffee table. "Fine by me."

"Cool. Any idea where I can find acrylic paint by the gallon?" As soon as he had asked it, he held up his hand. "You know what? Never mind. I have an old box of pastels down there. I can make my own paint."

"Why do I get the feeling we're not talking about a neutral beige in an eggshell finish?" said Hugh.

Adrian grinned. "Does it make a difference?"

"Well, no, not really."

"That's what I thought. Thanks!"

"Whoa, whoa, whoa," said Hugh, muting the television. "This conversation is not over."

Adrian paused, one foot already out the door. "It's not?"

Hugh sighed. "Fifteen minutes ago you were ready to lead a full-scale manhunt for Nightmare, and now you're painting a room? Why don't you take twenty seconds and tell us what it is you're doing?"

Adrian bristled. "Well, I'm *not* going after Nightmare, or Hawthorn, for that matter, or even running off for patrol duty, given that my team is still waiting for our reinstatement request to be approved. So I have to keep myself busy somehow, right?"

"Adrian," said Simon, the word a warning. Hugh appeared equally irritated, and for some reason, Adrian had a flashback to his mom, all those years ago, giving him that stern look and a pointed finger and insisting that he *drop that attitude, young man.*

He deflated fast. "I'm painting a mural."

Hugh's eyebrows rose with interest. "A mural?"

"Yeah. It's still a pretty new idea. So can I . . . ?" He gestured toward the foyer.

Simon cast Hugh an exasperated glance. "When did he become such a teenager?"

"Adrian," Hugh said, digging a handful of popcorn from Simon's bowl, "we just want you to talk to us for a minute. You've seemed distant since . . . well, since Cosmopolis Park."

Though it wasn't said like an accusation, Adrian couldn't help feeling defensive. *He'd* been distant? They were the ones always busy trying to govern the entirety of the civilized world.

But he knew better than to say that. "You guys have been busy. With the fallout from the Detonator and the big Agent N announcement and everything, I didn't want to bother you."

"You never bother us," said Simon. "You're always our top priority, no matter what else we're dealing with. I know we haven't been giving you much attention lately, but it doesn't mean we haven't noticed how you've changed."

Adrian felt the prickle of tattoos imprinted on his body. "I haven't changed," he insisted.

The comment earned a snort from *both* dads. He scowled at them.

"How are things going with you and Nova?" said Hugh.

Adrian gawked at him and, for the first time, began to regret coming up here. He should have just gone ahead and done the painting. It's not like they ever went down there. He probably would have grown up and moved out before they discovered it. But no—he was trying to be responsible, and this is what he got. "What do you mean?"

"Are you two . . . dating?"

When Adrian returned his question with a somewhat horrified stare, Hugh raised his palms. "We are allowed to ask that, aren't we?"

"Nova's a friend," Adrian said quickly, to get it over with. "We're fine. I don't want to talk about it."

Simon grunted and sang under his breath, "Told you so . . . ," leaving Adrian to wonder what, exactly, he had told Hugh, and for how long his love life, or lack thereof, had been a topic of conversation.

"Fine," said Hugh. "I'm sorry I said anything. I just . . . I just hope you know that you can always talk to us." He smiled awkwardly, like he couldn't quite believe how much of a dad thing that was to say.

"About anything," Simon reinforced.

Adrian nodded. Even though suffering through this conversation was about the last thing he wanted to be doing at the moment, he had to admit, it was nice to be reminded that his dads cared about him, even if he didn't fully believe that he was their top priority like they claimed. Which, usually, was okay with him. They were the world's greatest superheroes. What did he expect?

"Of course, Dad." He glanced at Simon. "Pops. I swear, I'm fine. So . . ." Adrian inched back into the door frame. "Can I go now?"

Hugh huffed and waved a hand at Adrian. "Fine. Return to your solitude. Go make your masterpiece."

Adrian cast them both a quick salute, then darted into the hallway before they could think of more touchy-feely, father-son stuff to talk about.

He was downstairs again in a heartbeat, digging through a box of old art supplies. A lot of them had been collected by his mom, way back when he was still a kid, first learning to draw. There were broken crayons and paintbrushes with their bristles long ago cemented together and a watercolor set where all the colors had bled together into a murky greenish-brown.

He found the pastels tossed together in a plastic bag. Though many were broken and partly melted, he was overjoyed to see the vast array of colors that greeted him.

Sitting cross-legged in front of the wall, he started to draw a new collection of supplies. A series of quart-size paint cans, each filled with rich, earthy tones and tropical bright hues.

Within minutes, he had the paint cans scattered across the concrete floor, along with a set of brand-new brushes.

He considered the blank walls one more time and began to paint.

# CHAPTER EIGHTEEN

ORMALLY, THE TRAINING HALLS located in the sublevels of Renegade HQ were a hive of activity. This was where Renegades practiced running through the various obstacles or tested out new techniques with their powers. But when Nova arrived for the first day of Agent N training, the vast hall buzzed with a strange, nervous hush.

For once, there was no one lifting weights or throwing punches, no one manipulating the giant pool of water or doing cartwheels through flaming hoops, no one traversing zip lines or scaling walls. The entire hall had been reserved for the patrol units who would be working with their new chemical weapon for the first time, and the effect made the hall feel lifeless and ordinary.

Nova's skin prickled as she made her way along the catwalk that spanned the length of the training floor. She was early, and only a dozen Renegades were waiting by the projectile targets, including Adrian, though there was no sign of Oscar, Ruby, or Danna yet. Adrian was talking to Eclipse, the leader of one of the other patrols.

Nova let out a slow breath.

All morning her mind ticked down the growing list of priorities.

First: damage control. She needed to know what Winston had told him and ensure that her secret was still safe.

After that, her goals were a little more vague. Get close to Adrian. Earn the Council's trust. Find out more about Agent N. Figure out how to weaponize Agent N against the Renegades.

And of course, above all else . . . get Ace his helmet. Everything would fall into place, she knew, if only she could restore that helmet to its rightful owner.

As far as she could tell, Adrian Everhart was her best hope. He thought his powers could get into that box. Then Nova would find a way to make it happen. She would not be rejected again. Something had passed between them at the park. She knew she wasn't imagining the way his breathing had shallowed. The way his gaze had seared into her.

There was still something there. Maybe she had hurt him at the carnival, and maybe all the walls he'd put up these past weeks were a result of her rejection, and maybe it was going to take time and persistence to bring those walls down.

But Nova liked a challenge.

Squaring her shoulders, she started down one of the narrow staircases toward the training area. Adrian glanced up and noticed her. He started to smile, a reflex, she knew. He smiled at everyone.

And yet—

With her focus on Adrian, Nova lost track of how many steps she had taken. She misjudged the last stair and started to fall forward, barely catching herself on the rail.

She jolted upright, cheeks already burning.

Startled, Adrian jogged toward her. "You okay?"

"Fine," she spat, tugging down the wrists of her uniform. "I'm fine."

Adrian's grin broadened and he looked like he wanted to tease her, but he refrained.

Standing up again, Nova plastered a brilliant smile to her own face, freezing him in place. "So—how did it go with the Puppeteer?"

Adrian blinked, and immediately Nova could tell she had to reel in the enthusiasm. She toned down her cheer and wrapped a hand around Adrian's elbow. He tensed, but didn't resist as she pulled him into the shadow of the catwalk, away from the waiting patrol units. "Did he say anything . . . useful?"

He was contemplating her hand, still on his elbow, and then he was pulling away. It was a subtle shift, but not subtle enough. Nova's heart squeezed.

"Not . . . exactly," he said.

"Oh?"

His attention fixated on her, and Nova realized he hadn't planned on telling her how the meeting with Winston had gone. Her gut clenched. What did that mean? What had Winston said?

"Actually . . . ," he said, slowly, "remember when I said that I wasn't *entirely* convinced that Nightmare is dead?"

Her skin went cold. "Y-yeah?"

"Well." He rubbed the back of his neck. "Winston Pratt agrees."

Her mouth moved, but no words came out.

"He told me that Nightmare isn't dead. He seemed *really* sure about it. But . . . after I brought it up to my dads, they pointed out that he's been in prison since before her death and there's no way that he could know whether or not she's still alive. So . . . it seems that I've been duped."

She blinked. "Oh . . . really?"

He shrugged. "I don't know. He was so convincing. But obviously, he knew that Nightmare being alive would distract me, given our interrogation last time. The more I think about it, the more likely it seems that he was just toying with me. Like"—he rolled his eyes—"a *puppet*."

"Wow," mused Nova, pressing a hand to his forearm. "Adrian, I'm . . . I'm so sorry."

*And so, so relieved,* she thought.

Adrian peered at her, and this time, he didn't immediately pull away from her touch. "It's not a complete loss. If I hadn't come to the artifacts department, I never would have known about that Vitality Charm. I've done some research, and it's amazing what it can do."

"Oh yeah? You should come spend a day with me in the vault sometime. There's a *lot* of neat stuff in there. I'm not an expert on it all like Callum is, but . . . I could point out some of the highlights."

Adrian's smile widened, and there it was again. The faintly drooping eyelashes. The current of electricity that seemed to spark where her hand rested on his arm.

"I'd like that," he said.

Nova grinned. "Me, too."

"Uh-oh," came Oscar's voice.

Nova jerked away. She spun around to see Oscar, Ruby, and Danna standing beside the staircase. Oscar wriggled a finger in Nova and Adrian's direction. "Is this a moment? It looks like a moment."

"Seeking privacy under the catwalk?" said Danna, smirking. "Definitely a moment."

"We should give them some space." Ruby swooped her arms around Oscar and Danna, turning them away.

"Very funny, guys," said Adrian, jogging after them. "We were just talking."

"That's not what it looked—" Oscar started, but then stopped. "Actually, that is what it looked like."

Sighing, Nova followed.

"Are you excited?" asked Danna. Though her expression was neutral, Nova immediately felt her body attuned to her, as if assessing a threat. Ever since the meeting when Agent N had been revealed, she had sensed a change in Danna. A suspicion, a distance, an entrapment in her words. The way her eyes seemed to follow Nova whenever they were together.

"Excited?" said Nova, aiming for the same level of nonchalance that Danna displayed.

"For Agent N training." Danna nodded toward a station where dozens of handguns had been set up before an array of targets. "I'm curious to see what they have us doing today."

Nova swallowed, unsure what Danna wanted her to say. Nova hadn't been shy about voicing her disapproval of Agent N, though she knew she would have to play along if she wanted to avoid raising any more alarms.

She unclenched her jaw to respond. "I just want to be the best Renegade I can be."

Danna's eye twitched, and though she said nothing, Nova could tell she was unconvinced.

Nova was grateful when Thunderbird strode into the midst of the waiting patrol units, her black wings folded behind her. "Good morning, Renegades. Today marks the beginning of our official Agent N training period. You are our second group of patrols and I am pleased to say that, thus far, training has gone quite smoothly. I don't doubt that you will exceed expectations as well." She turned a cool gaze upon the gathered units. It almost seemed like a threat.

Danna took a small step back, and Nova remembered her once saying that she was a little afraid of Thunderbird. At the time she'd made a joke of it—birds were natural predators of butterflies, she'd pointed out. But now Nova felt the Councilwoman's intimidation for herself.

She scanned the other patrol units that were gathered in the hall. There were six teams total, and though Nova had met most of them by now, her attention fixed on Frostbite and company, who looked more eager than anyone to get started.

Gargoyle caught her staring and sneered, flashing jagged black-rock teeth.

Thunderbird set a briefcase on a table and Nova's heart danced, recognizing it as the same that Dr. Hogan had shown them during the meeting. Sure enough, as Thunderbird unlatched and lifted the lid, they were greeted with nineteen vials of green liquid. The twentieth was missing, having not been replaced from when they had neutralized Winston.

Nova licked her lips, practically salivating over those vials. She barely refrained from touching the pouch on her belt where a vial exactly like those was sequestered away, filled with the concoction Leroy had made to her specifications—a mixture of ink, acrylic paint, and corn starch for thickening. Nova had worried her memory might not have replicated the substance well enough, but studying the rows of vials, she could tell it was nearly identical.

Her fingers twitched, but she urged herself to be patient.

An opportunity would present itself. She just had to wait.

Thunderbird pulled one of the vials out and held it toward the gathered patrols. "Today, we will be running through a series of exercises designed to get you more comfortable with the different methods you might find yourself using on the field to neutralize a prodigy with the Agent N serum. We will be practicing with a false serum, of course. But first, we arc going to discuss some logistics and precautions when it comes to using Agent N." As she turned the vial from side to side, the liquid oozed like honey. "As you can see, the serum is quite thick. It must enter a prodigy's bloodstream and be delivered to the brain in order to take effect. Our scientists have found that once the serum reaches the brain, the transformation begins instantaneously and is completed within seconds, as you witnessed with the Puppeteer. How long it takes for the serum to reach the brain depends on how and where in the body it is administered. When injected intravenously, it will reach the brain in less than a minute for most prodigies, depending on their heart rate."

Nova dug her fingers into her elbows. *Our scientists have found . . .*

She thought again of the criminals locked away in Cragmoor Penitentiary. How many had been used as lab rats while the scientists perfected this weapon?

Stingray lifted a finger. "What if a prodigy is cold-blooded?"

"Or doesn't have blood at all?" added Gargoyle.

Nova squinted at him. Trevor Dunn's— Gargoyle's—skin might be able to mutate into rock, but she was still fairly certain he had blood. Maybe a day would come when she could test that theory . . .

Beside her, Danna muttered, "Or what if they don't have a brain?"

Nova's cheek twitched and she momentarily forgot that she was supposed to be wary of Danna.

"Those are good questions," said Thunderbird. "There are many exceptions and unusual circumstances in the wide array of prodigies, and we will be covering those during your second training session. For today's purposes, know that more than ninety-five percent of all prodigies will be neutralized within one minute of having the serum administered. As I said, it must enter the bloodstream, and due to its density, it will be ineffective if applied topically. You do, however, have a few options. The most obvious is through an injection directly into a vein or artery. A shot into the heart will be particularly fast-acting. You can also administer the serum through an open wound, though this may slow the process. Additionally, the serum can be taken orally, to then be absorbed into the bloodstream through the lining of the stomach. However, as we don't expect many prodigies to willingly imbibe the serum, we don't expect that to be a viable option in most cases."

"What if it's inhaled?" a girl called Silver Comet said. "Can it be made into a gas?"

"In theory, yes," said Thunderbird. "The liquid can be vaporized and, if inhaled, will eventually reach the brain. However, it's important to remember that we are all susceptible to the effects of Agent N as much as our enemies, and at this time we don't have any way of protecting ourselves. Attempting to weaponize the serum with something such as, say, a gas bomb, would be too risky."

Thunderbird put the vial of Agent N back in the case, then drew a small dart from a pouch. Nova swallowed. The dart was almost identical to the poisoned projectile she had once used to try to kill Captain Chromium. Nova's hand went to the pen she always wore on her weaponry belt, the one she had designed a long time ago with a secret blow-dart compartment inside. She couldn't be sure without closer inspection, but she suspected one of the Agent N darts would fit inside just right.

"Once your training is complete," said Thunderbird, "and we have publicly unveiled Agent N, you will be outfitted with special handguns and darts like this one. Today, the darts are empty, and the guns by the practice boards"—she gestured to the firing range—"have been preloaded. Now, I'll have everyone pick a—"

"I have a question," said Nova.

Thunderbird nodded at her. "Go ahead."

"Will there be consequences for Renegades who abuse Agent N?"

"Abuse?"

"This is an enormous responsibility," she said. "I'm not convinced that we, as individuals, are qualified to make the life-changing decision of whether or not a prodigy should be allowed to keep their powers, even those who have been found breaking the law."

Thunderbird gave a smile, but it was close-lipped. "There is no greater responsibility than protecting and serving the citizens of this city, and the rest of the Council and I fully trust the judgment of our patrol units."

"Yes, but shouldn't there be some sort of limitation? A way to counter anyone who might decide to use Agent N as a punishment, or for their own gain, or in a situation where it was unwarranted? What if a Renegade neutralizes someone for, say, stealing a candy bar? That's an abuse of power, isn't it? So I just want to know what the consequence for something like that would be."

Thunderbird held her gaze for a long time. "Your concerns are relevant. I'll discuss potential consequences with the rest of the Council and we'll make sure to have a memo distributed with our decisions."

"A memo?" said Nova, with a guffaw. "Oh, good. Because those are always taken seriously."

"What is this, Ethics 101?" Genissa Clark muttered, just loud enough to make sure everyone heard.

"*Also*," said Thunderbird, her tone stern, "during your next training session we will discuss what factors we expect will be considered during an altercation before Agent N is administered. We do trust your judgment, but we will offer some guidelines to follow when considering whether neutralizing an opponent is the best course of action to take." She regarded Nova, as if waiting to see if this answer was adequate.

It wasn't, of course, but sensing Danna's eyes on her, Nova held her tongue.

"Now then." Thunderbird gestured to the firing range. "Everyone, please take a weapon."

The teams started to drift toward the firing range, claiming their positions in front of an array of targets.

Everyone except Genissa Clark. Nova's eyes narrowed as she left her group and approached Thunderbird. The tips of Thunderbird's massive feathered wings dragged on the floor as she and Genissa peeled off toward the side of the training hall. The two tilted their heads together, and Genissa began to whisper something, gesturing occasionally at the briefcase full of Agent N.

Thunderbird was frowning, but in a way that suggested contemplation more than disapproval.

Ruby strode toward a cluster of open stands by the range and the others followed, but Nova lingered behind. Her fingers delved into the pouch on her belt and wrapped around the vial inside. Her attention latched on to the open briefcase, left unattended.

The Renegades were focused on their new weapons and the targets before them.

Lifting her chin, she sauntered toward the drinking fountain on the far side of the hall. She bent over it, taking a long draft of water. When she turned back she saw Genissa and Thunderbird still deep in conversation, and the rest of the patrol units focused on their training.

She made her way to the target range. As she brushed past the case, her hand darted out and snatched a single vial from the case, just as quickly replacing it with the decoy.

Her pulse thrummed as the sample of Agent N disappeared into the pouch on her belt.

Nova smiled, and in that moment, Adrian glanced around at her. He noticed her expression and smiled back.

# CHAPTER NINETEEN

ADRIAN INSPECTED THE GUN, turning it over in his palm. He wasn't a total ignoramus when it came to projectile weaponry, but for all the time he'd spent training and even drawing his fair share of pistols, he had never been comfortable holding one in his hand.

It hadn't bothered him until recently. Maybe his frustration had started at the carnival, when Nova had killed the Detonator with a single shot to the head, while he had hesitated. Or maybe it was because now, with Agent N becoming a part of their regular practices, patrol units would be expected to be accomplished shooters, and he knew he was far behind the curve on that particular skill.

Not that he was the only prodigy who was less than impressive when it came to modern weaponry. Lots of Renegades preferred to use their own powers in lieu of handheld weapons. He knew plenty of patrol members who had *never* fired a gun. So he couldn't be that terrible, he told himself. He couldn't be the worst.

But then Nova appeared at the station next to him and he couldn't help sneaking glimpses at her while she checked the cartridge and the safety mechanism as efficiently as if she used tranquilizer guns every day.

Once she was finished with her inspection, Nova raised the gun, gripping it in both hands, and fired. It was so fast Adrian wondered if she'd even bothered to take aim at anything, but a glance at the targets showed her dart dead center in a distant bull's-eye.

On Nova's other side, Danna gave a low whistle. "Nice one, Insomnia. I sure am glad you're on our side."

Nova seemed to tense at the comment, but didn't respond.

Exhaling, Adrian lifted his own gun and assessed the range before him. There were bull's-eyes of all sizes, some near and some far. And there were other targets, too—from cardboard cutouts of known villains from the Age of Anarchy to an assortment of bottles, cans, and ceramic pots. He noticed that there was even a framed WANTED poster of Hawthorn.

Bracing for the recoil, he aimed at the poster and fired.

His dart sailed over the poster and struck the distant wall.

"Psst, Nova."

Adrian turned. Oscar was peering around at Nova from the last station.

Nova fired another dart, knocking down a glass bottle, then lowered her gun. "Yeah?"

"Do you think you could make me a cane gun, like one those fancy gentlemen in the Victorian era had? Because I'm thinking, if we're all going to be carrying guns now, I might as well keep it classy, right?"

Before Nova could answer, Thunderbird came by, pacing behind the line of firing stations. "While you're familiarizing yourselves with your weapons, I want each of you to consider how you and your teammates can make use of your unique abilities in conjunction with the Agent N projectiles. Being able to think fast on your feet and use the resources available to you during an altercation is often what separates the victorious from the defeated."

The sounds of darts peppering the targets thumped in Adrian's ears.

"Try to think outside the box. How can your abilities make more efficient use of Agent N?"

"I could dip my tail in the serum," said a nasally voice. Raymond Stern, or Stingray—one of Genissa's team members. "It would pierce an enemy as easily as a dart would."

"Good, good," said Thunderbird. "That's an excellent point. Though I think it will be most prudent to stick with the darts for now as, of course, if you happened to have even a small cut on your tail it could become infected with the serum, and we wouldn't want that."

"Wouldn't we?" Nova muttered.

Adrian shot her a knowing smile.

"Anyone else have any thoughts on using Agent N cohesively with your powers?"

"I could tip an ice spear with it," said Frostbite. She pulled her gun's trigger and sent a projectile into the face of the Rat—a long-dead Anarchist. "Or freeze an enemy's feet to the floor, holding them immobile while we administer the shot."

"Very good," said Thunderbird.

Nova lowered her gun and spun away from the targets. "Except," she said, practically yelling, "if you can freeze someone's feet to the floor and render them immobile, then they're no longer a threat and there's no longer any need to administer Agent N. In that case, the prodigy should be arrested and put under trial." She turned fiery eyes on the Councilwoman. "*Right?*"

Thunderbird nodded calmly, unfazed. "You are correct,

Insomnia. But for the purposes of this exercise, I only want ideas for how one *might* use their powers with relation to this new tool. I would rather not edit our suggestions quite yet."

"And how will your power be utilized?" said Frostbite, smirking at Nova. "Maybe you can invite your opponent over for a slumber party and wait for them to fall asleep before injecting them? It's a bit time-consuming, but we all have to play to our strengths."

Beside her, Trevor snickered. "Maybe her boyfriend can draw her a slingshot."

"Good idea," snapped Ruby. "That way we can all watch Nova slingshot one of the darts straight into your eye."

"That's enough," said Thunderbird, her glare slicing through them. "I want each of you to spend the next few days considering the question, and we'll discuss it further at the next session. In the meantime, let's keep practicing with the targets."

As the teams returned their attention to the shooting range, Adrian stared at Genissa's group, puzzled. He knew they were just trying to get a reaction out of Nova, who had humiliated Trevor during the trials, but still. Everyone here knew that Nova was one of the best shots of all the patrol units. Her talent with weaponry was unmatched, and her inventions had helped them time and again. Hell, she'd been the one to take out the Detonator! Were they really still under the impression that Nova, of all people, wasn't worthy of being a Renegade?

Shaking his head, he lifted his gun and again focused on the poster of Hawthorn. He tried to call on his angry feelings—how frustrated he had been when she got away with those drugs, how embarrassed he'd felt when she dumped him into the river, and right in front of Nova too.

Not that Nova knew it was him. But a small part of him still hoped that someday he would be able to tell her the truth.

He was imagining Hawthorn's smug face and preparing to pull the trigger when a dart struck the board just above Hawthorn's shoulder.

Ruby huffed. "So close."

Adrian smiled. Clearly he wasn't the only one holding a grudge.

"Hey, you guys know about that gala that's coming up?" said Oscar. He was perched on the short wall that divided the range from the shooters, passing the handgun from palm to palm, apparently uninterested in actually shooting it.

"Of course," said Ruby, without lowering her gun. She took another shot. "It's like the whole organization is going."

Oscar scratched his ear. "Yeah, I heard it's turning out to be this real swanky affair. And now, with the fund-raiser auction, it's like . . . for a good cause and stuff." Oscar took out the magazine from his gun, flipped it over a few times, then clipped it back in. "I was thinking it might be fun if we all went together. I heard we can bring family, too, so I thought I'd mention it to my mom, and . . ." He glanced up, quickly, then back down. Ruby's attention was glued to the targets, but Adrian caught the look. The fidgeting, the nerves. "I thought maybe you could bring your brothers too, Ruby."

This, finally, brought Ruby's head swiveling toward him. "My brothers?"

"Yeah," said Oscar. "You've said how much they wish they were Renegades, right? They might think it's cool to rub elbows with some of the patrols. Adrian could introduce them to his dads, they could listen to us all talk shop for a while." He shrugged. "It could be fun for them."

Ruby studied him for a long time before saying, carefully, "You're talking about going to a swanky gala . . . and you think I should bring my *brothers*?"

Oscar blinked at her. "I like being inclusive?"

Ruby turned to the targets and went to take another shot, but her gun clicked, empty.

"And maybe Nova could invite her uncle?" suggested Oscar.

Nova let out a peal of laughter. "He's not the gala type."

"Oh. But . . . you'll go?" asked Oscar.

Nova pulled back and Adrian could sense the emphatic *no* building on her tongue, but then she hesitated. Their eyes met and he saw indecision there. A question. A . . . hope?

"I'll think about it," said Nova.

"Okay," said Oscar, checking his wristband. "Does anyone know when we get to break for lunch?"

"Maybe," said Ruby, "after we've actually practiced."

Oscar inspected the gun. He seemed about as enthusiastic about learning to use a new weapon as Adrian was.

"Come on," said Adrian, raising his gun again. "I'll buy you a pizza if you hit a bull's-eye before I do."

Ten seconds later, he owed Oscar a pizza.

Adrian groaned.

"Okay, I can't take it," said Nova, setting her gun down. "I'm teaching you how to do this."

Adrian chuckled and shook his head at her. "Honestly, Nova, I've had some of the best Renegade trainers here try to teach me. It's just not in my skill set."

"Oh, please. It's not that hard." She came to stand beside him and took the gun from his hand. "You know what the sights are?"

He gave her an annoyed look.

"It's a legitimate question, given that you apparently don't *use* them," she said. "We're starting with the basics here."

"Do you know how many times I've drawn a handgun?" he said. "I must have practiced it a thousand times when I first started on patrols. So, yes, I know what the sights are. And the hammer, the barrel, the cylinder . . . all of it. I understand how gunpowder works and the physics of propulsion. I know how guns *work*. I'm just not very good at getting the bullet to hit what I'm trying to hit."

"Okay, smart guy." Nova returned the gun to him, handle first. "Show me what you're doing."

He groaned. "You really don't have to do this."

"So you're okay being mediocre?" She clicked her tongue, disappointed.

He scowled at her, but it was competing with a smile. "What am I aiming at, oh wise teacher?"

"That bull's-eye," she said. "The close one."

"Oh, the close one," he said. "You're already setting your expectations low."

"No, *you* already set my expectations low. Now stop talking and shoot."

His lips twisted, but he conceded her point. He lifted the gun and fired.

He heard the dart hit something, but whatever it was, it surely wasn't the bull's-eye.

"Okay, for starters," said Nova, "you need to relax. You tense up when you shoot."

"Of course I tense up. It's loud and . . . loud."

"You need to relax," she repeated. "And hold the gun like this, straight up and down. You're not a cowboy." She folded her hands around his, locking the gun's handle between them.

Adrian swallowed. Her hands were smaller than his, but there was a confidence in her touch that surprised him. She'd always seemed so unsure when it came to physical contact . . . but maybe that was one more thing he'd only imagined.

"Like this," Nova said, lifting his arms so they were parallel to the floor. Her cheek was against his shoulder now. "And widen your stance. You want strong, stable legs."

He planted his feet, though his legs didn't feel strong and stable. If anything, the closer she was, the weaker his limbs became.

"Do you ever think about aiming?" she asked.

"Of course I aim."

"Could have fooled me."

His eyes skipped toward hers.

She was smiling, teasing him. Then her lashes fluttered in surprise and she backed away, putting a couple of inches between them.

"I think that's your problem," she said, turning toward the targets. "You like to take in the whole world. But you need to stop and focus. In the moment you squeeze the trigger, nothing should exist except you and your target. Here, try again. This time, ignore everything else. Just focus on that one target."

As he lined up the target in his sights, Nova moved behind him, pressing one hand to his back while the other wrapped around his on the grip. "It's an extension of your arm," she said. "Like . . . like your marker."

He chuckled. "It's nothing like my marker."

"Don't argue with me."

His smile broadened.

"Imagine your arms absorbing the kickback," Nova continued, "and sending all that energy through your feet and into the ground. That will help keep your body loose so you don't tense up every time you fire."

But he couldn't think of anything beyond the closeness of her. Her hand between his shoulder blades. Her arm grazing his. He found himself wanting to stall. Wanting to draw out this moment just a little longer. He inhaled and it carried a bit of a shiver with it.

He felt her go still.

"Whenever—" Her voice scratched and she cleared her throat. "Whenever you're ready."

"Am I supposed to be shooting something?" Adrian whispered, startling her.

"The target," she said dryly. "Ignore everything else."

He turned his head enough that he could meet her eyes again. "You want me to ignore *everything* else?"

She held his gaze, but her confidence was swept away. He watched as color bloomed across her cheeks. *Great skies*, she was beautiful.

Adrian gulped and looked away. He gripped the gun even tighter, found the target, and fired. But he forgot to set up his stance. Forgot to relax his shoulders. Forgot to focus.

The dart went wide.

He grinned sheepishly, stepping back until they were no longer touching. "Like I said, I'm hopeless."

# CHAPTER TWENTY

Nova stomped down the back alley behind the dilapidated row houses, hands clenched at her sides.

What was *wrong* with Adrian? She was doing her best to flirt with him, and making a complete fool of herself in the process. She couldn't possibly be any more obvious. But either Adrian was the most oblivious boy this side of the Stockton Bridge, or—

Her teeth gritted.

She really hated that *or*, and she found herself growing more livid every time she thought of it.

*Or* . . . Adrian just wasn't interested in her anymore. Maybe Nova had lost her chance when she'd run away from him at the carnival.

Ace had told her to stay close to Adrian Everhart, and she was doing her best. She understood the reasons behind it. She knew that Adrian's trust could lead to a weakness in his fathers. Which was precisely why it was so infuriating every time he turned away from her, or avoided eye contact, or dodged her touch. Again and again.

It was making her mission more difficult. She hated that.

Her annoyance had nothing to do with the sting she felt in her chest every time Adrian proved that what he'd once felt for her was over.

And, apparently, her best efforts weren't going to bring it back.

A flash of gold fluttered in the corner of her vision and Nova froze. A monarch butterfly was flitting around a patch of ironweed that had gone rampant in one of the neighbors' neglected yards.

Nova's pulse thrummed as she watched the insect dither over one purple bloom before moving to another, methodical in its hunt for nectar. Her feet, still sporting her Renegade-issued boots, were cemented to the alley's cracked asphalt. She told herself that she wasn't afraid—*her*, Nova Artino, afraid of a *butterfly*? But the goose-flesh on her arms suggested otherwise. What if Danna had been watching her today when Nova had taken the vial of Agent N? She'd been careful, but had she been careful enough?

The butterfly moved to the stand of plants on the other side of the garden. A swallow trilled from a power line overhead. Nova almost hoped the bird would soar down and snatch the butterfly into its beak, because then she wouldn't have to worry about whether or not the creature was really one of Danna's spies.

She wouldn't have to spend the rest of the day wondering whether Danna was following her.

She wouldn't be terrified that Danna had already discovered her secret.

She was beginning to contemplate the odds of the butterfly staying put long enough for her to run into the house and find something to capture it with when the creature finished its meal and took off, flittering up and over the row house and toward the next road.

At least it was flying away from headquarters.

It was probably just an ordinary butterfly, she told herself. Nothing to worry about.

Nova trudged the rest of the way toward her own weed-infested yard, ignoring the deafening buzz of Honey's beehives as she stomped into the shadow of the crumbling row house. Her hands shook as she yanked open the sliding glass door and trudged into the dingy kitchen. They continued to tremble as she unclasped the buckle of her utility belt. She dropped it onto the counter beside a coffeepot half full of long-cold coffee and an assortment of vials and beakers, remnants of Leroy's latest work.

She tore off the wristband next and tossed it onto the table where a plain gray vase sat forgotten. A bouquet of flowers that had once flourished at the tip of Adrian's marker now stood shriveled, the dead, papery heads hanging forlornly from their stems.

Her heart jolted even now, but this time it wasn't with sorrow, but resentment.

Damn Adrian Everhart.

It had been more than a month since he had come to this house and drawn her those flowers. When he asked her to go to the carnival with him, on a date that wasn't a date. Weeks in which her heart had jolted a tiny bit every time she passed that bouquet, every day draining the color from their petals, until they formed one more sad, dejected still-life in this sad, dejected house.

Though, to be fair, the house had become a lot less dejected under Honey Harper's ministrations. She had embraced their new home with singular devotion, giving Nova the impression that Honey was actually living out some fantasy of homemaking she'd held on to for years, but had kept deeply buried. It was always clear how much Honey hated living in the tunnels, away from flowers and sunshine and breezes. They had been trapped for years, unable to abandon Ace as his health failed him, or to risk making the Renegades suspicious of their activities by moving somewhere closer to civilization.

But since they were forced from their home—away from the tunnels and the cathedral and Ace—it had become clear that Honey, at least, was flourishing with the change. She had spent her weeks merrily toiling away at their new abode, often singing show tunes at the top of her lungs as she worked. Their furniture had been aired out, the floors had been scrubbed, and while the offensive paisley wallpaper still hung in the living room, at least the cobwebs had been swept away. Nova had been surprised at the vigilance with which Honey had attacked the grime throughout the house, and how she hadn't once heard her complain about a broken nail or calloused fingers. When she'd mentioned that to Honey, she received a knowing wink in return and the sage observation that "A true queen is made not in times of prosperity, but in times of hardship."

Nova kicked off her boots into a corner of the front room. Leroy was reading a newspaper by the window, where he had hung a mustard-yellow blanket for privacy. Honey despised that blanket and had tried multiple times to replace it with lightweight sheers, but on this, Leroy was firm, insisting that they needed privacy more than beauty. The daylight that filtered through the blanket made the room feel sickly, as if the walls themselves were suffering from late-stage jaundice.

It was Honey's least favorite room in the house.

A headline at the top of Leroy's paper read PRODIGY DRUG-THIEF "HAWTHORN" STILL AT LARGE.

But when Leroy lowered the paper, Nova could see he'd been reading the comics pages.

"Rough day, Insomnia?" His reading glasses dropped to the end of his scarred nose, revealing the ring of discolored skin around one eye.

The other Anarchists had all taken to calling her this lately. Insomnia—her Renegade alias. At first it had irked her, but now she didn't think they were using the name to be mocking. Rather, it was a reminder, always, of what she was doing with the Renegades. She was a spy. A detective. A weapon.

"I don't want to talk about it." Reaching into her sleeve, Nova retrieved the vial of Agent N she had taken from the training hall and tossed it to Leroy. He made no effort to catch it, letting it bounce off his chest and land in his lap. He folded the paper and picked up the vial, inspecting the liquid. The solution sloshed thickly as he tipped the vial from side to side. "Terrifying stuff."

"Most patrol units will have finished their training by the end of next week. They'll start equipping us with it then. We'll need to be extra careful."

He turned over the vial and watched as a single air bubble rose through the elixir. "This is for me to keep?"

"For now. Like Ace said, we need to see if we can weaponize it against the Renegades, before they use it against us. Or if we can even replicate it. I might be able to steal more in the coming weeks, but not enough to use against the whole organization."

"I'll see what I can do."

"Also, there was talk of it being effective in gas form. I wonder if that might be a possibility. A gas could be used against more than one Renegade at a time, at least."

"It will be easy enough to figure out its properties and what sort of combustion would be required for vaporization," said Leroy. "We'll also need to determine its reduction in potency as the molecules are diffused, so that we can predict its range of effectiveness. I can get started on all that, but unless you're also going to obtain some deconstructed hand grenades for the substance, there won't be much we can do with the knowledge."

"You figure out how to turn it into a gas, and I'll start working on a dispersal device," said Nova. "I have my eye on some explosives I saw in the Renegades' collection that I think could be altered for something like this. Plus, they'd be easy to steal."

"Shame that our only reliable contact for explosives is no longer among us."

Nova ground her teeth. "I'm not sure I would call Ingrid *reliable*."

Leroy lifted an eyebrow at her—or what would have been an eyebrow, if the hair hadn't long ago been singed off. "I was referring to the Librarian."

Nova curled her nose, almost embarrassed. "There's been some debate around headquarters about whether or not Captain Chromium would be affected by Agent N. He couldn't be injected, given that no needle could puncture his skin, but it's unclear whether or not the liquid would harm him if he swallowed it, or the gas if he breathed it in. If you come up with any theories one way or the other, I'd love to hear them."

He tapped a finger against his chin. "I'll see what I can find, though I'm not sure how much I can accomplish with such a small test sample. And without access to the Renegade labs, their tests, their supplies . . . and, of course, the boy."

A shiver traipsed down her spine. Max had been brought up several times in their conversations lately, ever since she'd told them about Agent N. Nova couldn't help feeling like telling the Anarchists about him had left Max vulnerable somehow, and she hated it.

"Do your best for now," she said, turning away. "I'll try to bring you more samples after my next training session."

She plodded up the stairway to the bedroom she shared with Honey. It was a relief to peel the Renegade uniform off her skin and change into her own clothes. She had just finished pulling a T-shirt over her head when Honey threw open the door and sauntered into the room, her hair in a towel and a silk bathrobe tied at her waist. The smell of oat-and-honey soap wafted after her into the room, mingling with the cloying scents of Honey's perfumes, body creams, and cosmetics.

"Oh, sweetheart!" Honey cooed. She pulled the towel from her hair and began squeezing water from her curls. "You're back early today. Isn't there enough murder and mayhem happening on the streets to keep the Renegades busy?" Dropping the towel onto the floor, she stretched one pale arm toward the mattress in the corner of the room. A handful of black wasps that had been crawling over her bed linens zipped toward her, alighting on her shoulder and knuckles. Nova watched one disappear into the opening of Honey's sleeve.

"Our schedules were adjusted for Agent N training."

"Oh? Does that mean you saw that darling Everhart boy today?"

Nova's gut clenched. "I pretty much see him all the time."

"Good." Honey sat in front of her vanity mirror and began picking a wide-toothed comb through her damp hair. "I went to see Ace this morning. He wanted to be sure you're staying close to him like he asked, and keeping your ears open for anything that might be useful regarding the Council."

Nova's skin prickled. It made her uncomfortable to think of the other Anarchists, Ace especially, talking about her when she wasn't there. "You can tell Ace that I see him plenty," she said, pacing to the window. She pried open two of the cheap plastic blinds and peered into the alley. A plump bumblebee was wandering over the glass, trying to figure out how to get inside.

"And? How are things going?"

Nova's mouth dried as she tracked the bee's movements.

How were things with Adrian?

"Fine," she spat.

It was true. They were fine. Always fine. He was as friendly toward her as he had ever been. Always welcoming. Always ready with an encouraging smile and a kind word. Always so damned nice.

"That doesn't sound fine," Honey mused.

Nova thrust open the window and waited for the bee to zip inside. She turned away, enjoying the cool air on the back of her neck. She expected Honey to be watching her, but no. Honey Harper was fully involved with her vanity mirror, tracing thick black eyeliner along her lower lash line. It was a daily ritual for her, and one that Nova found as baffling now as she had in the tunnels.

It wasn't like Honey could leave the house, and Nova doubted she cared much about getting dolled up for Leroy or Phobia.

"How was Ace when you saw him?" she asked.

Honey dipped her lashes suspiciously. "You're dodging."

"I've been thinking," Nova went on, ignoring the accusation, "maybe we can start taking him out for walks. No one ever goes to the cathedral ruins. If he could get out in the sunshine, get some fresh air—even just for a few minutes a day—it could help him, right?"

Honey stiffened. "Take him for walks? He's not a dog."

"I'm serious." Nova gestured at Honey. "Being out of the tunnels has been so good for you, for all of us. Maybe if we could get him out of those catacombs, let him *breathe* again—"

Honey rose from her chair. "He is *Ace Anarchy*. Have you forgotten? If anyone were to see him—"

"We'll be careful."

"He would be murdered on sight or locked away in that horrible prison."

"He's already in prison!"

"Absolutely not. It isn't worth the risk."

Nova huffed and peered out the window again. It was a beautiful day—crisp and breezy, with flashes of sun streaming through the clouds. Sometimes she worried that Ace's weakness was as much in his mind as his body. To be locked away from the very society he had tried to help . . .

He never complained. He had Nova and the others, he would say. He had his books and his teapot and that was all he needed.

But Nova knew it wasn't enough. He was dying. Soon he would be just one more forgotten skeleton beneath those hallowed ruins.

"I understand," Honey said, her voice gentler now. "I truly do. Ace is like a father to me, too, you know. I hate seeing him this way. But you know how to help him, and it isn't with a little bit of fresh air."

Nova pursed her lips. *The helmet.* "I know," she whispered. Then a thought occurred to her and she glanced back at Honey. "Aren't you *older* than Ace?"

Honey gasped in dismay. She snatched a jar from the vanity and tossed it at Nova's head. Nova ducked and the jar crashed against the wall, exploding in a cloud of talcum powder.

"Never let me hear those words from your mouth again, do you hear me?"

Nova laughed. "I'm sorry, I'm sorry. Clearly I was mistaken." She stooped and picked up the near-empty jar and returned it to the vanity. Her mouth dried as she scanned the array of cosmetics and perfumes, most of them crawling with curious wasps. "Actually, Honey? I . . . I could maybe use your help with something."

Honey crossed her arms, still irate.

"It's about Adrian."

Her expression quickly turned to intrigue. "Oh?"

"I'm not sure if he's . . . interested in me anymore. At least not like . . . like that." At Honey's skeptical look, Nova attempted to gather what dignity she could in the stiffening of her shoulders. "So, maybe you could help me figure out . . . how to get him interested. Again."

An eagerness brightened Honey's face. "Oh, my sweet girl," she said, placing her fingers against her chest. "I've been waiting for you to ask."

*WE ALREADY KNOW one of the Council's greatest weaknesses . . . and when the time is right, we will use him to great advantage indeed.*

That's what Ace had said, and he was right. If Captain Chromium and the Dread Warden had a weakness, it was their adopted sons— Adrian and Max. Nova could use Adrian's trust to her advantage, especially if that trust also came with his *affection.*

But why did earning his affection have to seem so horrifically awkward?

"I can't do that," said Nova, arms folded tight over her chest.

"You can, and you will. Here, like this." Honey crossed one long leg over her knee and scooted a hair closer to Nova on the mattress. Her bare toes nudged Nova's shin, so tenderly she would have thought she was imagining it, except Honey had just outlined this exact flirtation technique in painful detail. "Then you angle your shoulders, like this." Honey flipped her hair to one side and shifted her body closer. "Give him your undivided attention. Like there is nothing else in the room half as interesting to you as *this* conversation. He needs to believe you are mesmerized by every-thing he's saying." Honey settled an elbow on her knee and her chin on her knuckles. Her smoky eyes locked on to Nova's. The look was so intense, Nova found herself starting to blush.

"Now, this is the clincher," said Honey. "Whatever he says next, you laugh. Not too robustly, but just enough to let him know you think he's charming, and you could listen to him speak all day. Ready?"

"What if he doesn't say anything funny?"

Honey giggled and tapped Nova on the knee. It was a sweet chirp of a laugh that sent a tingle of pride through Nova's chest, until she realized that Honey wasn't laughing because she was amused, but was only trying to demonstrate what she was talking about.

Nova flushed. It was uncanny, the way Honey could pull some-one into her orbit. Make them feel so important, so witty, so *worthy*, all with a few well-timed laughs and the faintest of touches.

She shook her head and stood up, kicking some of Honey's dis-carded shoes to the side of the room.

"This is never going to work," she said. "He'll see right through me."

"You worry too much," said Honey, settling back on her palms. "If he can tell you're trying to flirt with him, even if you're terrible at it, he'll be charmed by your attempts, and flattered all the same. Just like that, the flame will be rekindled and you'll be back to your angst-riddled un-relationship before you can bat those pretty lashes at him."

Nova scowled. "I think you're underestimating his intelligence."

"And I think you're overestimating the egos of teenage boys everywhere. Trust me, little Nightmare. You can handle this. It isn't chemical gastronomy or . . . whatever it is Leroy does."

Nova scoffed. "I'd rather take my chances with the chemicals." She rubbed her palms down the sides of her pants. They had started to sweat as she mulled over the possibility of looking at Adrian like Honey had looked at her. Touching him. Suggesting with every gesture, every glance, that she wanted him to try to kiss her again.

Her heart thumped as a bewildering thought occurred to her. Sweet rot. What if it actually *worked*?

# CHAPTER TWENTY-ONE

DRIAN WAS BOTH nervous and exhausted as he reached the mezzanine floor over the main lobby of headquarters. He knew he should be catching up on sleep, as he had stayed awake painting the last few nights. The mural was starting to take shape, even if only in underlayers of shadows and light, general outlines and suggestions of the work still to come. The details still needed to be filled in, all those little highlights that would bring it to life.

He'd finally put the paintbrush down when his alarm reminded him that there was something else he wanted to do today, something far more important than his new art project. Even more important than his hunt for Nightmare or the Anarchists. An idea that had been growing in the back of his head since he'd left the artifacts warehouse, filled with equal parts intrigue and hope.

He crossed the sky bridge and paced around the glass wall of the quarantine. He could feel the weight of the Vitality Charm pressing against his chest, warm even through the fabric of his uniform.

He had spent hours reading about the medallion in the database and doing what research he could do on his own, though the charm's history was not as well documented as some artifacts in the Renegades' collection. It had been forged by a prodigy blacksmith during the Middle Ages. The blacksmith's abilities were questionable, but he was evidently a healer of some sort, and the charm soon earned a reputation for being able to ward off the plague. *That* plague. Naturally, such a coveted object was eventually stolen and the blacksmith was hanged for crimes of witchcraft not long after, and so a duplicate was never made, so far as anyone knew.

The charm disappeared from the history books for a few centuries after that, eventually resurfacing during late 1700s, where it was purchased at auction by a superstitious and perhaps paranoid prince who would claim for the rest of his life that the charm protected him from the enemies who were always trying to poison him. That prince eventually died of (apparently) natural causes in old age, and the charm was passed down through generations of duchesses and barons until it was sold off to pay for a large amount of debt many years later. It disappeared from the public eye again, until eventually it was donated to a small prodigy-themed museum, the entire collection of which was given to the Renegades after the Day of Triumph.

*Given to* or *confiscated* . . . the details on how the Renegades had obtained many of the artifacts in the vault were rather vague.

It was believed that the charm could protect a person from poisoning, illness, and "any threats that would sap the physical strength or otherwise weaken the prodigious abilities of the wearer," according to its description in the database. It was unclear how much this theory had been tested, but it gave Adrian an idea that he couldn't shake.

*Any* threats.

That's what the description said.

And what, or who, was more of a threat than Max?

Adrian wasn't a fool. He knew that whoever had worn the Vitality Charm over the years had likely never encountered a threat quite like Max. He suspected his theory was untested, and it would be putting his powers at great risk to be the first.

Immunity from the Bandit *wasn't* impossible. Captain Chromium was proof of that. And with every step Adrian took toward the quarantine, a voice whispered louder in the back of his head: *What if it worked?*

What if this small, unassuming medallion could actually protect him from Max's power? What if it could allow him to get close to his little brother, maybe even give him an actual hug, for the first time in his life?

Though it was late, the massive lobby of HQ was still faintly lit by the flickering blue television screens stationed throughout the space, illuminating Max's miniature glass city. It had mostly been put right since Max's telekinetic attack—when he'd been practicing levitation and lost his concentration, putting a glass spire through his palm. His wound was healing, though prodigy healers were unable to work on him due to the nature of his powers. A civilian doctor had had to replace a tendon in Max's finger with one taken from his forearm—a procedure that struck them all as vaguely antiquated. But it went well, and the doctor had promised that the only permanent side effect would be a gnarly scar.

Since recovering from the incident, Max had kept busy fitting the broken glass buildings back into place, using his own power of matter fusing for most of the repairs.

The glass city always looked so different at night. Usually the daylight that streamed in from the surplus of windows set the city aglow, reflecting off the glass spires in shades of orange and yellow.

But now it appeared that twilight was falling over the structures, as if even this model city were preparing for a peaceful night's sleep.

Not that the real Gatlon City was ever peaceful. In a lot of ways, Adrian sometimes thought he preferred this small glass city, closed off from the world. There was no crime, no destruction, no pain. No villains and no heroes.

Other than Max himself. The only prodigy in his small universe.

Except, as Adrian stopped beside the curved glass wall, he saw that Max wasn't alone.

"Well, speak of a villain," he said.

Inside the quarantine, Hugh peered up from a hand of cards. His face lit up. "Who are you calling a villain?"

"Just a phrase, Dad."

Hugh tipped his head. "Nice to see you, Adrian."

Adrian waved, trying to disguise his disappointment. It wasn't unusual for Hugh to visit Max, and he knew it was good for the kid to have some human interaction that didn't involve syringes and hazmat suits.

Still. The medallion was heavy around his neck and he was eager to test his theory.

"Hold on," said Max, lifting a finger in Adrian's direction. "I'm about to kick his ass."

Hugh looked back at him, aghast. "Don't say *ass*."

"Fine. I'm about to kick your *donkey*." Max laid down one card, then shook out his shaggy hair. They were sitting cross-legged in the middle of City Park, and Max, who was already small for his age, looked downright infinitesimal next to the Captain, whose effortless muscles had long served as inspiration for superhero comic artists everywhere.

Hugh laid down two cards. "You know, you're not supposed to let your opponent know that you have a good hand."

"Maybe I'm bluffing," said Max.

Hugh eyed him. "That's not really how bluffing works."

"Are you sure?" said Max, taking the new card he was dealt.

Hugh met Max's bet, throwing a couple pieces of candy into a pile that sat between them. They showed their cards—Max won with two pairs. Hugh had nothing at all.

Max sighed, almost as if disappointed in the exchange as he pushed the pile of candy toward the park's carousel. He looked up at Adrian, shaking his head. "He can't resist seeing a good hand, even if he knows he can't beat it. I think it could be a diagnosable disorder. Like a psychological need for closure, along with an aversion to ambiguity and an authoritarian demeanor."

Hugh scowled. "What? I'm not like that. Am I?"

"Eh," said Adrian, avoiding comment.

Hugh scoffed and gathered up the cards. "Maybe I just like seeing my younger son winning at life." He pointed at the pile of candy as he stood. "Can I take one Choco-Malt for the road?"

"No," said Max, sweeping the pile out of reach. "But you can go to the corner store and buy some more." He pointed toward a small glass strip mall. "I'm pretty sure the nearest one is on Broad Street."

"Fair enough." Bending down, Hugh gave Max a squeeze around his shoulders. "Thanks for making some time for your old man. I'll see you later."

Max leaned into the embrace. "Night, Dad."

Hugh grinned at Adrian as he emerged from the quarantine. "Are you back on patrols tonight?" he asked, giving Adrian a quick sideways hug.

"Yeah, but we're only supposed to be called out for minor dis-putes for the next few days."

"How are Danna and Ruby?"

"Fully recovered," said Adrian. "Ready to get back work."

"Well, I know you're all young and eager, but I think this break might have been good for them, for all of you." He yawned, though Adrian could tell it was fake. "I'm taking off. Been another long day on the Council. You boys stay out of trouble now."

As soon as he had gone, Max groaned. "Sometimes I think he really does believe he lives in a comic book."

"If anyone did, it would be Captain Chromium," said Adrian. He watched as Max lifted up the roof of Merchant Tower and started loading the stash of candy into it. "Listen, Max, I have something to show you. Something kind of huge. At least, if it works it will be kind of huge."

Max turned to him, interest piqued. "Are you drawing me a dragon? Because Turbo is cool, but a *dragon* . . ."

As if recognizing his name, the tiny velociraptor crept out from beneath the Stockton Bridge, where Max had made him a small nest out of shredded newspaper.

"Uh, no," said Adrian.

Max wrinkled his nose. Popping open a bag of gummy worms, he fed one to the dinosaur. Adrian noticed the white bandages crossed over the back of his hand.

A prodigy doctor would have had that wound fully healed weeks ago . . .

He sighed. Max was fine. It didn't matter.

"Go stand over there," he said.

Max looked at where Adrian was pointing, but didn't move. "Why?"

"Don't argue, okay? If this works, it's going to be the best thing that's happened in headquarters since . . ." Adrian trailed off, stumped.

"Since they upgraded the virtual reality simulators with flight capabilities?" suggested Max.

Adrian cocked his head. "How'd you know about that?"

Max just shrugged and went to stand where Adrian had pointed. He picked up a tiny street sign as he passed Burnside.

"Okay," said Adrian. "You have your emergency call button?"

Max's thick brows furrowed with suspicion, but he lifted his arm, revealing the wristband he had worn ever since he'd crashed onto the city and driven the glass spire through his palm. He'd had it before, but until that night it never seemed important for him to wear it.

"Good. Wait there."

"Where are you going?"

Jumpy with anticipation, and a bit of pride at his own intrepidness, Adrian headed toward the antechambers that separated the quarantine from the laboratories where Max's blood and DNA had been studied, tested, and altered to make Agent N.

Through the glass, he noticed Max frowning. Adrian flashed him a thumbs-up that went unreturned, then pulled the door open to the tertiary chamber. In the next room, he bypassed the racks hung with protective suits, each one outfitted with chromium cuffs to offer some protection to the prodigy scientists and researchers who had to get close to Max on a regular basis.

Adrian approached the sealed door to the quarantine, where new signage had been added since the fiasco when Nova entered the quarantine in an attempt to help Max, the placards warning prodigies to stay away unless they had followed all required security measures. Adrian took a moment to reflect on whether or not this was a horrible idea. He was hopeful, but it was still a risk. A huge risk, if he was being honest.

What if the nature of Max's power rendered prodigy artifacts useless?

Lifting a hand, Adrian pressed his fingers over the charm, tracing the symbol of the open palm and the curled serpent.

"Please let this work," he whispered, then yanked open the door.

Max's eyes went wide. He pushed himself off the wall, as if he were preparing to dive out of Adrian's path, but there was nowhere for him to go that wouldn't bring them closer together.

"What are you doing?" he yelled. "Get out of here!"

"Trust me," said Adrian, taking a cautious step. Then another over the Scatter Creek bus terminal, which set him on a straight path down Drury Avenue. "I'm testing a theory."

"A theory?" Max barked. "What theory? That you've lost your mind?" He reached for the call button on his wrist.

"Hold on! Don't push it yet. I think . . . I think I might be immune to your power."

Max laughed, but it lacked amusement. He pressed his back against the glass as Adrian took another step forward. "We *know* you're not immune. So, come on, get out of here. This isn't funny."

"No, see this?" He lifted the charm. "It was in the artifacts warehouse. I think it might protect against powers like yours."

Max gawked at him. "*What?*"

Adrian was a quarter of the way into the quarantine. He tried to recall at what point he had started feeling the effects of Max's power when he'd rushed in to rescue Nova, but that night was a blur in his memory.

He kept walking. Slow, hesitant step after slow, hesitant step.

He was barely breathing, waiting for the slightest warning sign that the pendant might be failing. He distinctly remembered the numbness that had entered his hands before. The way his body had felt like it was moving through molasses. The sensation of a plug being pulled up from his navel, and all his strength draining out through it.

How close had he been to Max when it started? Surely he was closer now, and yet he felt completely normal. Twitchy and nervous, but still normal.

He was more than halfway. He passed Merchant Tower. Strode the length of City Park.

Max's eyes narrowed, fearful, but curious too. His focus was glued to Adrian's feet, watching him pace through the city they'd built over the years.

Adrian reached the place where Nova had collapsed. The nearby block of buildings still bore signs of the fall, though the shards of broken glass had been removed.

The forgotten street sign dropped from Max's hand, clattering to the floor.

"If you lose your powers because of this," Max whispered, "I'm not taking any responsibility for it."

"You shouldn't take responsibility for it anyway," said Adrian. He was constantly working to dispel Max's beliefs that he had done anything wrong. It wasn't his fault he was this way. It wasn't any prodigy's fault.

Three-quarters of the way into the quarantine, Adrian began to smile.

Still petrified, Max didn't return it.

"I feel fine," said Adrian, unable to keep some of the disbelief from his own tone.

He came to a stop three paces away from Max. Close enough that he could reach out and put his hands on his shoulders.

And so he did.

Max flinched, at first ducking from the touch, but then froze. His eyes went wide.

Starting to laugh, Adrian pulled Max into a hug, crushing him in one exuberant embrace before letting go. "I feel fine!" he said again, ruffling Max's unruly hair. "Great, even. I can't believe it worked!" His laugh got louder. "Except . . . I *can* believe it. Because of course it worked. I totally knew it would work. By the way, you need a haircut."

"Draw something," Max demanded, ignoring his glee. "Quick."

Adrian took out his marker, still beaming. "Sure thing, Bandit. Any requests?"

Max shook his head, and Adrian stepped closer to the window and drew the first thing that came to mind—a Renegade pin, like the one he gave Nova at the trials.

When he pulled it fully formed from the glass, Max gave a little squeak of shock. "How?"

Adrian met his eye, and beneath the stunned disbelief, he could see the start of possibilities filtering into the kid's mind.

For almost Max's entire life, he had been kept separate from the ones who loved him, everyone but Hugh, anyway. And Hugh may have loved Max, but he was so busy, trying to squeeze his fatherly responsibilities in between Council meetings and public appearances and the occasional heroics. When was the last time Max had sat next to someone and played video games and ate snacks into the wee hours of the morning?

Never. That was when. He had never experienced anything like that before.

"I have the best idea," said Adrian. "Tomorrow, I'm going to bring some chips and soda and a super-greasy pizza and I'm going to completely slaughter you in an all-night *Crash Course III* marathon. Unless you'd rather, I don't know, learn to play backgammon or something, and then we'll do that. Doesn't matter. It's up to you. You let me know."

Max shook his head, bewildered. "Adrian, *how?*" he repeated, more forcefully this time. He grabbed the medallion and flipped it over, examining the back, which contained a mirror image of the protective hand. "What is this? How does it work?"

"I don't know!" said Adrian, still beaming. "It protects from diseases and poisons and stuff, so I just thought——"

"I'm not poison! I'm not a disease!"

"I didn't mean it like that."

"It shouldn't work!" Max dropped the pendant. "It shouldn't."

"But it does. And next, I'm going to give myself a tattoo of this symbol," said Adrian, pointing. "That will make me permanently immune, and then I can give this charm to anyone who wants to visit you. Can you imagine the look on Ruby's face? And Oscar, and Danna? They'll be so excited to come see you. And Simon, of course." He gasped, leaning forward. "Dude. Simon. He'll be . . . I don't even know. I bet he'll cry."

"The Dread Warden crying?" said Max. "Let's get it on film." He said it jokingly, but Adrian could tell he was overwhelmed, and on the verge of tears himself. "Did you say tattoo?"

"Oh. Yeah. That's how I do . . . you know. All that other stuff I do."

Scanning Adrian's shirt, Max stammered, "You give yourself *tattoos?* And that's how you——"

Adrian held up his hands. "That's not important right now." He swooped his arms around Max's waist and lifted him off his feet, letting out an excited whoop. "Vitality Charm! Visitors! Think of the possi"—his voice hiccupped as he glimpsed a figure in the lobby beyond the glass—"bilities."

"Put me down!"

He set Max down and took a step back, clearing his throat. "Visitors like . . . Nova?"

Max spun around.

Nova was standing not far from the lobby's information desk, staring up into the quarantine with her mouth hanging open.

"Act normal," Adrian whispered, his glee quickly overcoming his surprise. He elbowed Max in the side and they both raised their hands and waved.

# CHAPTER TWENTY-TWO

"EXPLAIN," SAID NOVA the second she stomped onto the sky bridge. Her arms were folded tight over her chest, her brain churning through a hundred explanations, each more absurd than the last. Adrian was inside the quarantine. And smiling. And apparently fine.

Then the pendant around his neck caught the light and Nova gasped, launching herself forward. She pushed her finger into the glass wall. "*That?*" she barked in disbelief. "Really?"

"Really," Adrian confirmed, flashing more teeth than she had ever seen him flash before. He was practically luminescent with joy.

He started to explain his theory and the research he had done on the Vitality Charm and why he'd guessed it would protect him from Max's power, but there were so many pauses and jumps in his story that Nova struggled to follow it all.

Plus, he couldn't seem to stop laughing. It was partly the laugh of a mad scientist who hadn't fully expected his latest experiment to be successful, and partly the laugh of a guy who could finally hang out with his little brother, without a glass wall dividing them.

He kept reaching out to ruffle Max's hair, or punch him lightly in the shoulder, or wrap his elbow around Max's neck and put him in a pretend chokehold. Max didn't seem to know quite how to respond to this outpouring of brotherly affection, but he kept smiling. A smile as full of disbelief as Nova felt, but a smile all the same.

There was something endearing about the way Max was watching Adrian. A bit of awe, coupled with an abundance of hope.

Yesterday, Max was a prisoner and an outcast. Valuable and loved, yes, but also an anomaly. A science experiment. A lab rat. He knew it as much as anyone.

"What about Agent N?" said Nova.

Adrian turned to her, startled. "What about it?"

"It was created using Max's blood. Will the charm protect people from it too?"

Adrian's eyebrows knit together over his glasses. He peeked at Max, but Max just shrugged and said, "Don't look at me."

"I don't know," said Adrian. "It might." He opened his mouth to say more, but hesitated. He studied Max again, then looked back up at Nova. "Yes. I'm pretty sure it would."

"And does the Council know about this? They've put so many resources into developing Agent N . . . and there was this necklace in the vault the whole time, able to protect someone from it? There could be other things too. First the Captain is immune to Max, and now this?" She bit her tongue to stop herself from talking, worried that her eagerness would show.

Protection from Max. Protection from Agent N.

Maybe the Anarchists didn't need to be quite so worried about this new weapon after all.

"I'm convinced no one knew about the medallion and what it could do," said Adrian, "otherwise someone else would have taken it out of the vault as soon as Agent N was revealed. And you heard them at the presentation. There are no known antidotes. And invincibility, like my dad has, is just about the rarest superpower ever documented. No one else is like him. There's no reason to think his powers can be replicated, at least not where Max is concerned. There might be other things that could act as a ward against Max's power, but as far as I could find, this is the only artifact of its kind."

Maybe Adrian was right, but even so, the existence of this charm gave her hope that Agent N wasn't the death knell for the Anarchists.

She wondered if such a charm could protect others from a power like hers, too. As an Anarchist, Nova most often used her ability to put people to sleep as a weapon, but sleep in itself didn't *weaken* a person, beyond making them vulnerable. If anything, sleep helped to restore them. It was an interesting puzzle, and one she would have to consider at length if Adrian shared the discovery of the Vitality Charm with any more Renegades.

"Could I use the charm sometime?" she said, plastering a smile to her face. "It would be easier to help Max reconstruct the broken parts of his city if I could go in there."

"Sure!" they said in unison, and the way Max's eyes brightened made Nova's heart surge.

"But," said Adrian, "I think we should give it to Simon first." He grimaced apologetically. "It's just symbolic, but . . . I know it would mean a lot to him."

She refused to let her smile fade. "Of course. I understand."

Adrian's expression was so endearing Nova felt a little guilty for contemplating how the charm could serve *her* purposes over Max's.

"I know it doesn't change everything," said Adrian. "You're still stuck in the quarantine. You still can't go out into the world. But . . . it's something, right?"

"It's a lot," said Max. "Even just . . ." As he gestured between himself and Adrian, his control over his emotions started to crumble. "This has been . . . This is . . ."

Adrian wrapped an arm around Max's shoulders and pulled the kid against his side.

Nova turned away. She felt like she was intruding. Not just because she wasn't a part of their family, but because she wasn't even really a Renegade. She didn't deserve to enjoy this moment with them.

The velociraptor, who had disappeared into his nest, emerged and made a melancholy cooing sound, poking at Max's ankle with its needlelike talons. Wiping his eyes, Max stooped and picked it up, pointedly avoiding Nova's gaze.

"Max," she said, hesitantly, "why . . . why don't you just live with a non-prodigy family?"

Adrian flinched. "I've thought that, too, but . . ." His face was tight with pain, but Max only shrugged.

"It's okay," he said, resigned. "I'm fine here."

"No, you're not," said Nova. Her fists clenched. "You're a prisoner! You're a—a—"

Adrian shot her a warning look and she bit back the words on the tip of her tongue.

*You're a science project to these people.*

"It's not safe for me to be out in the world," said Max, letting the tiny dinosaur nibble at the tip of his thumb. "I could cross paths with a prodigy at any time, and it wouldn't be fair to them. And also, if news ever got out about who I am and what I can do . . . it would make me a target. There are still villains out there who would want to use me for their own purposes—"

"Or anti-prodigy zealots who would love to get their hands on a kid who can wipe out superpowers," added Adrian.

"And also . . . ," Max said, his voice distant. "I'm needed here."

Nova ground her teeth. Though there might be some truth to what Max was saying, she couldn't help but feel that it was also a whole lot of fear propaganda, intended to keep him a compliant prisoner.

"For Agent N?" she asked.

Max nodded.

"How long have you known about it?" said Nova. "Did you know what they were doing with your DNA samples all this time?"

"Not . . . exactly," Max said, tucking Turbo into his pocket. "For a long time I thought they were trying to find a way to neutralize *me*. So they wouldn't have to be keep me separate from everyone anymore. Eventually, I realized it was more than that, though. I figured it was something like Agent N, but I didn't know for sure."

"Skies, Max, maybe it *would* work on you," said Adrian, eyes brightening again. "I can't believe I didn't think of it until now. I was so excited about the charm, but . . . why couldn't we just inject you with Agent N? You wouldn't be a prodigy anymore! You could . . ." His words dwindled off as Max shook his head.

"They tried that already," he said. "It doesn't work on me."

"They tried to take away your powers?" Nova gasped. "Why? Because you're a threat?"

Max laughed at her obvious disgust. "No, because I asked them to. After they had their first few successes on prodigies at Cragmoor and it didn't, you know, turn them into big piles of radioactive sludge or anything, I asked them to use it on me. I wanted it to work. It's not really that much fun to be a prodigy when you're trapped in a place like this." He gestured around at his glass prison.

"Oh," said Nova. Her vehement anger on Max's behalf faded. "I guess I can understand that."

"Nova is concerned with prodigy rights," explained Adrian. "She's worried we're going to start abusing the power of Agent N."

"If I recall correctly," said Nova, "you weren't exactly convinced that it would be handled with the utmost responsibility either."

"Why?" asked Max. "It's only for bad guys. They would never neutralize a Renegade."

Every muscle in Nova's body tightened, eager to argue the distinction between *Renegade* and *bad guys*. "They're planning to dole it out to every patrol unit, to be used however we see fit. I guarantee mistakes will be made and this power will be mishandled. How long before innocent prodigies are being threatened or blackmailed, just because they haven't been conscripted into the Renegades yet? This life isn't for everyone, you know."

"Threatened and blackmailed?" said Max. "By who?"

"I don't know, how about Frostbite and her goons?" said Nova, remembering a time, not long ago, when she had witnessed Frostbite trying to bully Ingrid into making a false confession. "Or thieves like Magpie? Not every Renegade is as chivalrous and upstanding as Adrian."

She made the mistake of glancing at Adrian as she said it and saw surprised flattery flash across his face. She jutted a finger at him. "Don't take that the wrong way."

"Is there a wrong way to take that?"

She glowered and Adrian lifted his hands, still beaming from the compliment. "All right, I agree that restrictions need to be in place, and I don't like the idea that they're going to start injecting every questionable prodigy out there with it either. In my opinion, someone like the Sentinel definitely doesn't deserve that sort of punishment, without even being given a chance to explain himself, first."

"Oh, please," said Nova. "He's the least of my concerns."

Max's expression brightened into an odd, goofy grin. "Of course you're not concerned about him, now that he's fish food and all. Right, Adrian?"

Adrian's lips pinched. "Right. My point is, there are still some kinks that need working out with the Agent N thing, but it has potential. I'm glad we never have to worry about the Puppeteer anymore, and we would have saved ourselves a lot of headache if the Detonator had been neutralized before Cosmopolis Park happened." He turned to Max. "And now that they have Agent N figured out, they don't still need you and your blood samples, right? You're done with testing?"

"I think so," said Max. "They haven't taken any in a while, and . . . I don't think they would have agreed to try to neutralize me if they still needed my powers to work."

"Right. See? No more testing, no more samples, and now this." Adrian tapped the Vitality Charm. He pulled Max in for another exuberant squeeze. "It's like the Bandit hit a jackpot."

Max groaned loudly and squirmed out of the embrace. "You know, you like to make fun of Hugh for being so corny, but sometimes you're just as bad."

Nova felt again like she was intruding on something. "I need to get ready for my shift in artifacts. See you both later, okay?"

"Your shift?" said Adrian. "It's the middle of the night."

"Prime work hours," agreed Nova, with a carefree smile. "I like the peace and quiet."

She waved and headed toward the elevator, her grin fading as soon as her back was turned. There was a charm that could protect Max. A charm that could maybe protect from Agent N.

Her nerves vibrated with the possibility.

She wanted that charm.

But not as much as she wanted Ace's helmet. And tonight, that was exactly what she planned to get.

# CHAPTER TWENTY-THREE

T WAS JUST past one in the morning when Nova scanned her wrist-band against the digital lock and entered the vault. A handful of sparse lights flickered on down the rows of shelving units, one after another, lighting the corridor with a dull, eerie glow. Nova shut the door behind her and settled the large plastic tub she'd brought on a waiting cart.

She ignored the security cameras, though she could feel the lens watching her as she pushed the cart down the main aisle. Looking at the cameras always garnered suspicion, so she kept her expression neutral. Her pace casual.

Snapshot wouldn't arrive for hours. Until then, she had the vault all to herself.

She hoped it would be enough time.

A brilliant idea had come to Nova the day before. She was never going to magic her way into the chromium box that held Ace's helmet. The box would never be chopped open with a mystical ax or smashed with an indestructible hammer. Adrian would never draw an opening into it for her, no matter how much awkward flirting she suffered through.

But Nova had forgotten what *she* was capable of. She may not have superstrength or psychic powers or control over the natural elements, but she had science, and she had persistence, and she was going to get into that box.

She didn't hurry, knowing there was someone in the security room right now who could be watching her slow progress down the aisles. They might be curious why she was there in the middle of the night. They might even be suspicious. But they would lose interest by the time she got to the helmet. Nova kept her actions slow and trivial. She and the cart ambled from row to row, its squeaking wheels grating on her nerves. She made frequent stops, checking the clipboard that hung off the side of the cart, pretending to make notations from time to time. She pulled mundane items from the cart and spent time organizing them neatly on the shelves.

Nova had never been in the vault when she didn't have Callum's constant jabbering in her ear, and she noticed for the first time how a number of the relics seemed to hum, as if with a quiet electrical current. Some even emitted a subtle coppery glow, not unlike Ace's helmet.

The similarities made her hesitate as she was passing the Infinite Hourglass, where the glittering white sand was being pulled upward into the top half of the container. Stepping closer, Nova placed her finger against the ebony wood base. *That glow.* It was familiar. The exact shade and vibrancy of all the wonderful things she'd watched her father create when she was little.

She peered down the length of the aisle. Now that she was searching for them, she could easily spot the glimmering artifacts. She knew there were probably things in the vault that had in fact been made by her father, but not *all* of these. Not the Ravenlore Quill, which had been around for centuries. Not the Arctic Saber, which had been forged on the other side of the world.

She shook her head and turned the cart back into the main aisle.

"Stay focused," she whispered to herself. She would have time to dwell on the many mysteries of the artifacts department later. For now, all she cared about was Ace's helmet and how she was going to free it.

Nova turned into the last aisle, past the RESTRICTED sign posted at the end of the shelf. Halfway down the row, she positioned the cart a few feet away from the chromium box, keeping her back to the camera at the far end of the aisle. She opened her plastic crate and pulled out her equipment—a battery and connector clips, a large bucket full of an electrolyte solution that Leroy had mixed up for her earlier, and a steel wheel she'd found in the gutter on Wallowridge, which she'd painstakingly cleaned in a bath of sodium chloride and acetic acid.

She checked the clipboard again, pretending to be dutifully following orders from above. Then, opening the bucket, she dumped the solution into the bin. The smell of chemicals wafted up, making her nose wrinkle. Smothering a cough, Nova grabbed the wheel and submerged it inside the vat.

Taking a deep breath, she wrapped her hands around the chromium box. The metal was cool to the touch, and though it was heavy, she managed to lift it into the bin with only mild straining. The solution sloshed up its sides. She wasn't sure how thick the walls of the box were, but she hoped the solution was deep enough to corrode the entire base. She hoped there would be enough time to complete the process. She hoped no one bothered to come to the restricted section while the experiment was underway.

She hoped a lot of things.

*Electrolysis.* The idea had struck her like one of the Sentinel's laser beams. It was the process that was used for metal plating, and chromium was used to plate other metals all the time. Using a battery, she could alter the charge of the neutral atoms at the box's base. The atoms would lose electrons, turning them into positively charged ions, which would dissolve right off the box. Over time, the positive chromium ions would move through the solution, attracted by the electrons that were being pushed out from the other side of battery, and be turned back into solid metal on the surface of the wheel.

The result: no more chromium box.

Or, at least, a big hole in the chromium box.

As an added bonus, she might even have a newly indestructible chromium-plated wheel once the process was complete.

It was so simple, so obvious, she couldn't believe she hadn't thought of it before. She'd even begun to wonder whether the Captain himself could be weakened this way, although it would be considerably more difficult to hook *him* up to a battery or dunk him into a vat of chemicals.

She attached the conductors.

Crossing her fingers, Nova switched on the battery.

And hoped.

She half expected the battery to flare to life with sparks and the sizzle of energy, but of course it didn't. Only the digital readings on its side indicated that amps were flowing through the system. Nova adjusted the dials, increasing the voltage.

She inspected the wheel, not really expecting to see any visible change. The process would take time.

"A watched cathode never plates," she muttered to herself, then pushed the entire electrolysis cell back into the shadows of the shelving unit.

She would let it run for an hour, she decided, before coming to check on it. She knew it could take all day before there would be visible signs of the chromium eroding. Which was fine. Ace had gone without his helmet for a decade. If he could be so patient, then so could she.

As long as it worked in the end. And as long as she kept Callum or Snapshot from coming to check on the restricted collection while the process was underway. She wasn't entirely sure how she would accomplish that, but she was considering a toxic chemical spill in the next row. Or maybe she could orchestrate a diversion on the other side of the vault. A few broken jars of radioactive rocks would keep them busy for a while . . .

Brushing off her hands, Nova set the bucket on the cart and started to wheel it away, leaving the chromium box and her experiment behind.

She was nearly to the end of the aisle when a sound made her ears prickle. It sounded like something was . . . boiling.

Frowning, Nova slowly turned around.

A cloud of steam was drifting up from the shelf where she'd left her experiment.

Her pulse skipped. "What now?" she murmured, abandoning the cart. The sound of bubbling got louder. The steam grew thicker. The air stung her throat with the tang of chemicals.

Nearing the plastic vat, she saw that the electrolyte solution was boiling—great, rolling bubbles popping at the surface and splattering the sides.

"How is that even—"

It exploded.

Nova gasped, jumping backward as the solution splattered everywhere, coating the underside of the next shelf. It flowed over the edges of the bin and splashed across the floor. One of the conductor cables snapped off the battery and was flung from the cell, nearly taking out Nova's eye before it crashed into the wall.

With the circuit severed, what was left of the liquid quieted to a simmer and soon became still, but for the last dregs still dripping down the sides.

The chromium box sat unaffected, looking infuriatingly innocent inside the bin.

Nova gawked at the mess of chemicals. Her destroyed battery. The wheel that she had scrubbed for a solid hour to make sure it was clean enough for the chromium atoms to adhere to.

A guttural scream tore from her mouth. She grabbed the nearest thing in reach—a gemstone-encrusted brooch—and flung it down the aisle. When it struck the concrete floor, it emitted a blinding white flash. Nova threw her arms in front of her face and stumbled back, but the light disappeared as fast as it had come and the brooch clacked and skittered a few more feet. As the ghost of the flash faded from Nova's vision, the brooch appeared, luckily, unharmed.

"Okay," she said, rubbing her eyelids. "I probably shouldn't have done that."

"McLain?"

She jumped and spun in a full circle before realizing that the stern voice had been coming from her wristband.

Gulping, she lifted her hand. "Uh . . . yes?"

"This is Recoil in security. We just saw what appeared to be a small explosion there in the artifacts department. Is everything all right?"

Nova willed her nerve to stop trembling. "Uh—yeah. Sorry. Everything's fine. I was just"—she cleared her throat—"cleaning a few of the objects here, and, um . . . must have mis-measured the . . . cleaning . . . solution. Sorry to worry you."

"Would you like us to send down a cleaning crew?"

"No," she said, adding a lighthearted laugh. "No, no. I'll take care of it. You know the things in here can be . . . temperamental. I think it's best if I handle it."

"You're sure?"

"Positive."

The communication faded out, and Nova inspected the results of her failed—oh, so very failed—experiment.

She ran her hands through her hair and cursed.

So much for science and persistence.

Shoulders slumped, she picked up the brooch and set it gently back in its place, then went off to find a mop.

# CHAPTER TWENTY-FOUR

ADRIAN'S CHEST ACHED from his newest tattoo, still sore from a thousand tiny pricks of the needle. Of all his tattoos, this had been the easiest to persuade himself to go through with. He'd known he would do it the moment the Vitality Charm had successfully admitted him into Max's presence.

The charm worked, and this tattoo would too. After this, he would be able to come and go from the quarantine as he pleased.

With so much importance resting on this design, he had not simply copied the symbol onto his skin. He had spent hours poring through dictionaries, encyclopedias, and tomes on symbolism and ancient healing practices. The symbols that the blacksmith had long ago stamped into the medallion were found across multiple religions and cultures, often carrying messages of protection and health.

The open right hand was said to be a ward against evil, and snakes had been associated with healing and medicine for eons. The more he read, the more he understood how this design could protect someone from forces that would seek to weaken him or her.

Protection. Health. Strength.

The words came up again and again in his research, and had repeated like a mantra in Adrian's mind as he'd worked on the tattoo.

A serpent curled inside the palm of an open hand.

The hand held up in defiance—Stop. You may not pass.

The serpent, ready to devour any affliction that dared to ignore the hand's warning.

Together—*immunity.*

The tattoo, inked directly over his heart, would work. Adrian had already accomplished remarkable things by inking new designs into his skin. He had stretched the limits of his power beyond anything he would have previously thought possible. He had made himself into the Sentinel, and the scope of his abilities seemed endless, limited only by his imagination.

So who was to say that he couldn't give himself this ability too? Not complete invincibility, like the Captain had. The only way he could think to accomplish *that* would have been with a tattoo that spanned the full length of his body, and he wasn't ready for that sort of commitment.

But invincibility from Max? It could be done. It was possible. He had never been so sure of anything in his life.

He went to the mirror to inspect his work. The design looked good. Clean and sharp. Despite having had to work upside down on himself, he was pleased to see how balanced he'd gotten the overall shape. It had turned out exactly how he'd envisioned. A perfect replica of the symbol on the Vitality Charm.

Relaxing his shoulders, Adrian pressed his palm over the tattoo and let his power seep into his body. He felt the same warm, stinging sensation he had every time he did this, as the design sank through his skin and into his muscles, through his ribcage, into his steadily beating heart. As it became a part of him.

When he pulled his hand away, the ink was glowing orange, like melted gold inlaid on his skin. But it faded fast, leaving only the tattoo behind, no different than it had been when he first pulled off the bandage. Unlike his other drawings, the tattoos didn't disappear after he willed them into reality. Maybe because they were intended to be permanent. Maybe because he wasn't creating a physical manifestation of the drawing, but rather, using it to change himself.

Adrian was as confident in his tattoos and his new abilities as he'd ever been about anything. As he put away his tattooing kit, he found himself wishing that he could have been even half as sure about Nova and the mixed signals she'd been sending lately.

He was sure . . . well, pretty sure . . . a solid 83% sure that Nova had been flirting with him in the training hall. And at the park too. A dozen small moments kept flashing through his memory. A smile that was a bit too bright. Eyes lingering on his a second too long. The way she sat just a little closer to him than she had to. The way her fingers brushed against his back when she'd been teaching him how to shoot.

That was flirting. Wasn't it?

And flirting meant interest. Didn't it?

But then he remembered the carnival, and how she had pulled away so hastily when he'd tried to kiss her, and how everything had been awkward between them since, and he figured he had to be imagining things.

The biggest problem was that their time at the carnival had made Adrian painfully aware of how much he had started to like Nova.

Really *like* her.

He liked how brave she was—that dauntless courage she'd had

when she faced off against Gargoyle at the trials. The lack of hesitation to chase after Hawthorn or take out the Detonator. The bravery that veered just a bit toward recklessness. Sometimes he wished he could be more like her, always so confident in her own motivations that she didn't mind bending the rules from time to time. That's how Adrian felt when he was the Sentinel. His conviction that he knew what was right gave him the courage to act, even when he would have hesitated as Adrian or Sketch. But Nova never hesitated. Her compass never seemed to falter.

He liked that she defied the rules of their society—refusing to bend for the Council, when so many others would have been falling over themselves to impress them. Refusing to apologize for their decision to go after the Librarian, despite the protocols, because she believed wholeheartedly that they made the right choice with the options they'd been given.

He liked that she'd destroyed him at every one of those carnival games. He liked that she hadn't flinched when he brought a dinosaur to life in the palm of her hand. He liked that she'd raced into the quarantine to help Max, despite having no clue what she was going to do when she got there, only that she had to do *something*. He liked that she showed compassion for Max, sometimes even indignation for the way his ability was being used—but never pity. He even liked the way she feigned enthusiasm for things like the Sidekick Olympics, when it was clear she would have rather been doing just about anything else.

But no matter how long the growing list of things that attracted him to Nova McLain had become, he still found her feelings toward him to be a mystery, with an annoying shortage of evidence to support the theory that maybe, just maybe, she sort of liked him too.

A smile here.

A blush there.

It was an infuriatingly short list.

He was probably reading into things.

It didn't matter, he told himself again and again. He couldn't risk getting too close to anyone right now. If Nova found out about his tattoos or noticed how his disappearances coincided with the Sentinel's actions, or if she ever stumbled onto one of his notepads detailing the Sentinel's armor or abilities, she would figure it out. She was so observant. So quick. She would know in a heartbeat, and then how long would it be before she told the rest of the team, or his dads, or the entire organization? Nova had made her feelings for the Sentinel quite clear, and they were anything but tender.

At least his life had taken on a quieter pace since he'd put the Sentinel's armor aside. His supposed death had been accepted as fact, even though there had been no success in dredging up his body from the bottom of the river. Adrian knew it would be easier to go on this way. To let the Sentinel die with the public's belief.

He didn't regret anything he had done while wearing the armored suit, and he couldn't comprehend why the Council and the Renegades were so determined to stop him, even after all the criminals he'd captured, all the people he'd helped. They were so focused on their *code,* they couldn't appreciate the good that could be accomplished when someone stepped outside of their rules.

But regrets or not, the Sentinel was considered an enemy of the Renegades, and he couldn't stomach the thought of having to explain his secret identity to his dads, or the rest of his team. Including Nova. *Especially* Nova. The best way to keep his secret was to keep distance between them.

Even if she had been flirting.

Which she most definitely had been.

He knew, with a solid 87% certainty.

His thoughts spiraled.

With the tattoo finished, he needed another distraction.

Stretching the kinks from his shoulders, he went into his art studio. What had started out as a flash of random inspiration had grown into something . . . well, kind of spectacular, if Adrian did say so himself. What before had been a dark, windowless room, with drab white walls and concrete floors, was now a sight that would have stolen anyone's breath.

The painting, inspired by the dream Nova had told him about from her childhood, had become a tropical paradise, spanning every wall from floor to ceiling. As the kapok trees had grown, their branches stretched outward into a tangle of leaves and vines, forming a jungle canopy that devoured every inch of the ceiling above. Down below, the floor had been overtaken with thick, tangled roots, stones and ferns, and patches of bright-colored flowers. There were also remnants of the abandoned ruins Nova had described, including a series of steps leading toward the corner where the statue could be seen, surrounded by a crumbling stone wall and encroaching plants. The statue itself was turned away, so that its hooded face and outstretched hands could not be seen, adding an air of mystery to the image. Spotted with moss and chipped with age, the statue was a lone, steadfast figure, the last remnant of a lost civilization.

It was just paint, but Adrian couldn't recall ever being so proud of any of his art. When he stepped into the room, he imagined he could smell the heady fragrance of wildflowers. He could hear the squawks of native birds and the thrum of a thousand insects. He could feel the humidity on his skin.

He had just opened a can of paint, intending to finish some of the highlights on a cluster of ferns, when a brusque voice echoed through the house.

*"ADRIAN!"*

He froze.

It had been a long, *long* time since he'd heard Hugh yell like that.

Setting down his paintbrush, he made his way hesitantly up the stairs.

He found his dads in their office on the second floor, huddled around a shared tablet on the large mahogany desk.

"You called?"

They both looked up at him, momentarily speechless.

Hugh launched to his feet and jabbed a finger at the tablet. "What were you *thinking*?"

Adrian took a step back. "Excuse me?"

Simon held up the tablet for Adrian to see. "Would you care to explain this to us?"

Adrian approached them hesitantly, watching the screen. It was security footage of Max's quarantine, and—

"I . . . was going to tell you about that."

"I should hope so," said Hugh, still on the verge of yelling. He spread his arms wide, a gesture of frustration that Adrian hadn't seen from him in a long time. "How could you just . . . ? Why would you . . . What were you *thinking*?"

"Adrian," said Simon, with much more patience, "did you . . ." He trailed off. Squared his shoulders. Started again. "Did you sacrifice your powers . . . so you could be closer to Max?"

Adrian gaped at him. The way he said it, Adrian could tell that he thought the idea was both ludicrous and also enviable. Like maybe he'd considered doing exactly that more times than he would admit.

"No," Adrian said. "I didn't sacrifice my powers."

"Then what is happening in this video?" said Hugh. "The poor security guard on duty nearly had a heart attack when he saw this."

Adrian rubbed a hand over his hair. "I'm sorry. I . . . I was going to talk to you about that—"

"We're talking about it now," snapped Hugh.

"Would you stop yelling?" Adrian said.

Hugh glowered, but then deflated, at least a little. "Sorry."

Adrian sighed. "I . . . figured out a way to be immune to Max."

"No one is immune to Max," said Hugh.

Adrian frowned. "*You're* immune to Max."

His voice rose again. "And I'm the only one. Now, try again. The truth this time."

"I found this thing in the vaults," Adrian said, more forcefully now. "It's called the Vitality Charm. It's this old medallion that's said to protect against pretty much anything that weakens a person, like poison or disease. And I thought . . . well, maybe it would work against Max's powers too. And it did. It does."

Hugh and Simon exchanged doubtful looks.

"It's the truth." He gestured at the tablet. "I'm wearing the charm in the video. You can see it."

"What do you mean you *found* it?" said Simon.

"I was getting that puppet for Winston Pratt, and Snapshot was there, talking about it with that guy, um, Callum. I did some research and learned what it could do, and I just . . . I figured it would work." He focused on Simon. "I have the charm downstairs. I was going to give it to you. You can wear it and you'll be able to see Max, just like I did. You can get close to him and nothing will happen to you."

"Adrian, that's . . . that's impossible," said Simon.

"It's in the video!" He gestured at the tablet. "I wouldn't lie about this."

"But how did you know?" started Hugh.

"It was a hunch I had. And it worked."

Hugh rocked back on his heels and a silence filled the office.

"Immunity," Simon finally murmured. "From Max?"

Adrian hooked his thumbs on his pockets. "And . . . other things too."

"Poisons and diseases," said Hugh, "and *Max*."

Adrian scratched behind his neck. "I don't know this for sure, but . . . I think it might also protect from . . . something like . . . Agent N."

Their expressions mirrored each other. Disbelief, but also intrigue.

"How did we not know about this?" said Hugh.

Adrian shrugged. "I figured since we have so many prodigy healers, no one really worries that much about fending off poisons and diseases. The medallion had never been checked out by any Renegade, not since the database was created. It just must not have seemed important."

"Well, it will now," said Hugh. "Something like this . . . I never thought . . ."

For a moment, Simon looked almost proud. And . . . hopeful. "That was really brave, Adrian."

"Thanks," Adrian muttered, even as his heart swelled.

Hugh leaned against the windowsill. "We need to talk about this. About what it could mean, for Max and for Agent N. For now, don't tell anyone else about this . . . Vitality Charm, okay?"

"Yeah, sure, of course," said Adrian. "Except I already told Nova."

Hugh rolled his eyes. "Of course you did. Well, tell *her* not to tell anyone else, all right?"

Adrian nodded, even though there was a tinge of disappointment that came with the words. He'd been excited to tell Oscar and the others. He tucked his hands into his pockets and swayed impatiently. "So, was that all?"

His dads traded another look, and Adrian bristled on the inside. What was with all the silent *looks* these days? Didn't they know he could see them?

Then they both sighed, practically in unison.

"Yes," said Hugh. "That was all."

# CHAPTER TWENTY-FIVE

NOVA WAS NEARLY finished cleaning up the disaster when a chime echoed through the vault. She cocked her head, frowning. It sounded like the alert from the reception desk, but . . . it was far too early for someone to be there, wasn't it?

She waited until she heard the chime a second time, then sighed and headed to the front of the warehouse.

A girl was standing at the checkout desk, drumming her fingers on the counter.

Nova's feet stalled.

Genissa Clark's ice-blue eyes met Nova's, then swept down the length of the mop. Her lips curled, just a tiny bit. "First you go from patrols to administration duty, and now they've demoted you all the way down to janitorial? Your family must be so proud."

Nova's teeth ground—more at Genissa's flippant mention of her *family* than the pretentious attempt at an insult.

During her time masquerading as a Renegade, Nova had been forced to admit that many Renegades had good intentions, even if they were part of a harmful social hierarchy. But she had also become even more aware that many Renegades craved author-ity over those they deemed inferior, and Frostbite was among the worst. Back when the Anarchists had lived in the subway tunnels, Frostbite's team paid frequent visits—mocking the Anarchists, destroying their property, wasting their resources . . . all in the name of "keeping the peace." Nova despised her and her team more than she despised most Renegades.

"There are no unimportant jobs," said Nova, leaning the mop against Snapshot's desk, "only pretentious, small-minded individuals who seek to inflate their own importance by demoralizing every-one else." Plastering on a brilliant smile, she rounded the desk and booted up the computer. "Can I help you with something?"

Genissa picked up the clipboard with the checkout information on it and tossed it at Nova. "I need Turmoil's Deadener."

Nova scanned the top sheet on the clipboard and saw that Genissa had already begun to fill out the information for her request.

"Turmoil's Deadener?" she said skeptically. "What's that?"

Genissa stared at her, silently, for a long moment.

Nova stared back. Having cultivated a lifetime's supply of patience, she was quite good at staring contests.

Finally, Genissa sighed with mild exasperation. "His *Sound* Deadener? I thought the people in this department were supposed to be useful."

The Sound Deadener was familiar, now that Nova thought of it—a metronome that, as the pendulum swung back and forth, would create a soundproof perimeter beyond the area where the ticking could be heard.

"What do you need that for?" said Nova, setting down the clipboard.

Genissa grunted. "I'm sorry. Are you supposed to ask questions, or bring me what I ask for?"

Nova's saccharine smile returned. "Actually, I'm *supposed* to defend the innocent and uphold justice. So, again. What do you need it for?"

Small ice crystals were forming around Genissa's fingertips, crackling against the sleeves of her uniform, and Nova could tell she thought this conversation was the biggest waste of her time. It sort of made Nova enjoy it.

"My unit has a busy night ahead," Genissa said, her voice flat and annoyed. "And unlike some patrol units, we actually make an effort to keep from disturbing the peace." Leaning forward, she pressed a finger down on the checkout sheet, sending a ripple of ice crackling against the paper. "Oh, wait—I'm sorry, how very inconsiderate of me. I should have realized how our assignment would be upsetting to you. But I'm sure your team was passed up with good reason."

Nova narrowed her eyes. "Excuse me?"

"We've been assigned to the Hawthorn case," Genissa gloated. "And we finally have a lead. We should have her in custody within the next forty-eight hours. But don't worry." She leaned over the counter. "We'll be sure to tell everyone what a *difficult* opponent she was, just to save you further embarrassment. Now, are you going to get that thing for me, or do I need to go find someone who actually knows how to do their job?"

Nova's blood curdled, to think that Hawthorn might be found and captured, and Frostbite of all people would get the credit for it.

But she gripped her smile like a weapon. "Have you already signed the rental agreement?"

"Of course."

"Well, then." Nova shoved away from the desk. "I guess I'll be right back with your . . . Deadener."

It wasn't hard to find Turmoil's Sound Deadener, stocked in the power-imbued tools section between a pewter-surfaced mirror and a collection of small red spheres. Nova snatched the wooden metronome from the shelf and turned away, her jaw still clenched.

She froze, then slowly turned back to the spheres.

There were six of them, all nestled into a tray not much bigger than a shoe box. Nova picked one up and inspected it. The device reminded her of a pomegranate—shiny and smooth, with a plugged crown on one side.

"Hello, mist-missiles," she whispered, reading the label beneath the box. These were some of the explosive devices she had mentioned to Leroy that she thought could be altered to work with a gaseous form of Agent N, but she hadn't been able to inspect them yet. The infamous mist-missiles were an invention from Fatalia, who could release an acidic vapor through her breath that would pulverize the lungs of any opponent who breathed it in. Her power was only effective at close range, though, which her enemies eventually caught on to. And so she created her missiles, similar to a hand grenade, that she could breathe her acid into. Upon impact, the acid would be released into the air. Nova could see a thin line around the device's circumference where it would have split open to emit the noxious vapor.

She wondered if there was any of Fatalia's breath still inside these bombs.

And she wondered how difficult it would be to fill them with something like Agent N. Seeing them in real life, she was already picturing how she could make it work.

If the Anarchists were really going to try to weaken the Renegades with their own weapon, a dispersal device like this would be far more effective than trying to take out every opponent with an injection dart. Besides, not everyone could be shot. The darts wouldn't puncture Captain Chromium's skin or Gargoyle's.

The Renegades wouldn't use Agent N in gas form because it was too risky. But if she had that Vitality Charm . . .

The chime from the front clanged through the vault.

Cheek twitching, Nova settled the mist-missile back into the box.

She returned to the reception area and tossed the metronome at Genissa without fanfare. Genissa stumbled and barely caught the device on a rising bed of ice crystals. She scowled at Nova.

"There you go! Enjoy!" Nova chirped.

With a sound of disgust, Genissa grabbed the Deadener and marched back to the elevator.

"You're welcome!" Nova shouted after her.

Once she was gone, Nova sank into the desk chair and tapped her fingers against the clipboard. Steal the missiles, or rent them? If she got caught stealing them, it would send off all sorts of alarms. But if she was able to turn them into Agent N bombs, then later they could be traced back to the rental agreement. By that point, though, the Anarchists would be in full attack mode, and this charade would be over anyway.

Her lips twisted. Maybe she should wait and discuss it with Leroy and Ace first.

The elevator dinged again and Callum swept into the room, his expression giddy. "Was there really an explosion?"

Nova tensed. "What?"

"I got paged from security. What happened?"

Panic seized Nova's gut, but Callum didn't look concerned so much as curious. And eager, of course. Always so eager.

"N-nothing," she said. "I was just . . . um . . . cleaning some stuff. I think maybe I mixed some bad chemicals."

Callum deflated. "That's it? I was thinking maybe you'd uncovered a new magical function for something."

She shook her head, feigning disappointment. "I don't think so. Sorry."

"Meh." He waved a hand through the air, his expression clearing. "It's probably a good thing. Spontaneous combustion is cool and all, but not great for the workplace." He bent over the desk and swiveled the checkout sheet toward him. Nova had noticed that he always checked who was renting the equipment and what they had taken—an argument in favor of stealing the missiles, now that she thought of it. He grimaced. "Frostbite came in? She terrifies me."

"You're not completely infatuated with her super snowflake skills?"

He chuckled. "Are you kidding? She's totally using her power wrong. If I had ice manipulation, I would wear ice skates all the time and make a constant path of ice in front of me everywhere I went." He pushed the clipboard away. "What did she want the Sound Deadener for?"

"Not sure," she muttered, refusing to admit that her team had been passed over for the Hawthorn case. "It's not my job to ask questions." She paused. "I mean, it's not, is it? Are we allowed to say no to someone if they want to check out something we don't think they should have?"

He grunted. "Typically, no. Not if they've passed clearance and signed the agreement. But if you're really hesitant about something, you can ask Snapshot to bring it up to the Council. I only had to do it once, when I was pretty sure that one of the new recruits was using a skeleton key to break into people's apartments. I'm sad to say that I was right."

Nova gawked. "What happened?"

"He was taken off patrols and spent a lot of time doing community service after that. He works in the food court now."

"Lucky for him. If he pulled a stunt like that today, he'd probably be stuck with Agent N."

"I don't think so." Callum rubbed the pale fuzz on his chin. "He was breaking the law, but he wasn't particularly dangerous. The punishment seemed fitting."

Nova grunted, but she wasn't sure if she agreed. Once the public knew about Agent N, they'd be crying for it to be applied to every case of prodigy wrongdoing. And the Council was so eager to hold on to their reputation, she suspected they would acquiesce easily.

And with every prodigy who was neutralized, the Renegades' power would grow and grow.

"You don't like Agent N either, do you?"

She started. "What?"

Callum leaned against the desk. "I think it's tragic. For someone to be given these incredible abilities, only to have them stripped away? It's so wasteful. To know what this world could look like, what humanity could be, if only we all chose to do our best, to help others, to . . . to be, well, heroes. I don't like to think of that chance being taken away from someone before they've lived up to their potential."

"Right," said Nova. "Except, having superpowers doesn't automatically turn you into some selfless hero. People are greedy and cruel, and . . . for some, having superpowers just makes them even *more* greedy and cruel." Her jaw tightened. "Genissa Clark is proof of that."

"Yes . . . ," Callum said, speaking slowly, as if he were forming his thoughts as he spoke. "But I think that when given the choice to do good or to do harm, most people choose good."

"And I think," Nova countered, "that nothing is as black and white as people want to pretend. Doing good and doing harm aren't mutually exclusive."

He listed his head. "Example?"

Nova pulled the chair toward her and dropped into it. "I don't know. Ace Anarchy?"

Callum's expression turned to delight. "I'm listening. Go on."

Nova frowned at him. Sweet rot, he was a strange guy. "Well, he's a villain, right? Everyone knows that. Unquestionable. He killed people. He destroyed half the city."

"But?"

"But if it weren't for him, prodigies would still be living in fear. Persecuted, victimized, abused . . . *He* created a world where prodigies could stand up for themselves. To declare what we are and not be afraid that we'll be punished for it. He fought for the rights of all prodigies. Whereas the Renegades only seem interested in defending prodigies who agree to their code."

"But people were still afraid," said Callum. "The Age of Anarchy was not a nice time—not for anyone. It was the Renegades who made people feel safe again. So really, it was the Renegades who showed the world that prodigies deserved rights."

"The Renegades wouldn't have existed without Ace Anarchy."

"Do the ends justify the means?"

"Sometimes."

"Then Ace Anarchy was a hero."

She peered at him suspiciously. "I didn't say that."

His grin returned, and Nova had the impression that this conversation was little more than a fun debate to him. She wondered if he was one of those devil's advocate types—who could argue on either side, regardless of his actual opinion.

"Follow me," he said, turning his back on her.

"What? Where are we going?"

"I want to show you something."

Nova didn't move. As Callum waited for the elevator to arrive, he shot her an impatient look.

Nova stood. "Fine. But I'd better not get fired over this."

Callum chuckled. "You and I are the only ones in this whole organization who think that working in the artifacts department is fascinating. Trust me. They're not going to fire you."

The elevator arrived and Nova followed him inside. She felt compelled to deny his assumption—she wasn't working here because the artifacts were *fascinating*. She was here because she had a job to do. She had a helmet to retrieve.

But then she realized that Callum wasn't altogether wrong. She did think the job was interesting. As an inventor, she could appreciate the innovation that had gone into a lot of things in the collection.

Still, though. She wasn't about to nerd out about it like Callum did.

The elevator began to rise, and Nova glanced at the panel of numbers. With a start, she pushed herself away from the wall.

Callum was taking her to the topmost floor, where the Council's private offices were located.

Tension wrapped around her limbs.

Why was he taking her to the Council? Had he figured her out? Did he know?

She shouldn't have defended Ace Anarchy. She shouldn't have been so careless with the electrolysis experiment. She shouldn't have criticized the Renegades and Agent N.

Nova curled her fingers, feeling the familiar sensation of her power warming her skin. She targeted the back of Callum's neck. Half a second and he would be unconscious.

Her attention skipped to the camera attached to the elevator ceiling and she hesitated.

"Have you been up here before?" said Callum, watching the numbers flash above the metal doors. "They keep some of the coolest things from the collection on display outside the Council offices, though between you and me, their choices are questionable. I mean, everything has its place, but people are way too obsessed with weapons and warfare. If it were up to me, I'd display something like the Legacy Torch. It may not be flashy, but it played a huge role in early prodigy history."

As he rattled on, Nova allowed herself to relax.

He wasn't turning her over to the Council. He was just showing her more of his beloved memorabilia.

Figured.

Prism was seated at an imposing desk when they stepped off the elevator, her crystal skin glinting in the light from a blown-glass chandelier. She beamed when she saw Callum, her teeth sending a dazzling array of rainbows across the glossy white floor.

"Hey there, Wonder Boy," she said. "Is it already time to change out the exhibits?"

"Not today. I just wanted to show Insomnia the scenery. Have you met?"

Prism's smile alighted on Nova. "Just once. So nice to see you again." She stretched out a hand. When Nova shook, she found her skin was as hard and cold to the touch as glass. Here, she realized, was yet another prodigy who might not be vulnerable to Agent N darts.

Though she couldn't imagine why anyone would care to neutralize Prism. As far as she could tell, the woman was made of some sort of crystal, and . . . that was it. Her only "power" was a pretty show when light struck her skin the right way.

"Go on," said Prism, gesturing toward a door. "The Council isn't in yet, so you'll have plenty of peace and quiet."

They passed through a circular lobby with various display cases and prominent paintings, but Callum didn't comment on the prized artifacts. Not even the enormous painting that depicted the defeat of Ace Anarchy on the Day of Triumph—a painting that infuriated Nova as much now as it had the first time she'd seen it. Instead, Callum showed her through a wide door, down a short corridor that passed Tsunami's office, and out onto the headquarter building's observation deck.

Nova stepped outside and felt the temperature drop. They were surrounded by glass and steel—beneath their feet and curving upward to form a transparent shelter over their heads. Callum went ahead of her, placing his hands on a rail that wrapped around the deck.

Nova followed.

Her breath hitched.

The view wasn't like anything she'd ever seen before. She had spent plenty of time on the rooftops of buildings, even skyscrapers, but never had she been so high up. Never had she seen Gatlon City laid out like a dream. There was the bay in the distance, where the morning sun was dancing on the waves like molten gold. She could see both the Sentry and the Stockton Bridges spanning the river, majestic with their towering pylons and the graceful arcs of their suspension cables. There was the landmark Merchant Tower, with its recognizable glass spire, and the centuries-old Woodrow Hotel, still sporting a ghost sign on its brick. Things she had seen a thousand times before, but never like this. From so far away, she could no longer see the scars of time left on the city. The buildings that were crumbling to the elements. The abandoned neighborhoods. The drifts of garbage and debris piled up on sidewalks and in alleyways. There was no noise up here to compete with the tranquility. No sirens, no shouting, no car horns. No yowling of stray cats or squawking of territorial crows.

It was breathtaking.

"You know what's amazing?" said Callum. He pointed, and she followed the angle of his finger down to City Park—its lush green fields and autumn-painted forests like an unexpected oasis in the sea of concrete and glass. "You see that tree, near the southeast corner of the park? The evergreen, that kind of stands up over all those little deciduous ones? That's a queen cypress tree. Do you know how slow those things grow?"

Nova blinked at him, unable to discern where he was going with this. "I don't."

"Slow," Callum said. "*Really* slow. So whoever planted that tree, they must have known that they were going to have to wait years—*decades*—before they could sit under it and enjoy its shade. Maybe they never got to. Maybe they planted it, hoping that their kids or their grandkids, or even complete strangers, generations away, would be able to sit under the boughs of that tree and that maybe someone would spare a moment of gratitude for the person who had the foresight to plant a little sapling in the first place."

He fell silent and Nova's brow furrowed. *This* was the important thing he had to show her?

"Also," said Callum, "trains. Trains are so cool."

Nova hummed to herself and began plotting what she could say to politely remove herself from this conversation and go back to work.

"Think of the early steam trains. All that engineering, all those resources . . . It must have been faith at first, right? A confidence that this was the future—travel and industry and trade. There was no guarantee that those tracks would be laid, connecting all these cities and ports, but someone had enough conviction to go ahead with it anyway."

"Callum—"

"And the alphabet!" he said, turning to her. "Have you ever stopped to consider the alphabet?"

"Uh . . ."

"Think about it. These symbols, they're just lines on paper. But someone, at some point, had the idea to assign them a meaning. And not just that, but then to teach those meanings to other people! To envision a way for ideas and thoughts to be recorded and shared . . . it must have seemed like an impossible task at first, but they persisted, and think of all that's led to. Isn't that fantastic?"

"Callum," Nova said, more firmly now. "Do you have a point?"

He blinked the excitement from his eyes, and peered at Nova, almost sadly for a moment. "My point is that Ace Anarchy, whatever his motives might have been, was ultimately a destructive force. He *destroyed* things. But we are so much stronger and better when we put our energy into creating things, not destroying them."

"Of course," she said sourly. "And the Renegades are the ones that create."

Callum shrugged. "They're trying, but no one's perfect. Like you said, even Ace Anarchy was fighting for a cause he believed in—a cause that was worth fighting for. But he didn't build anything. Instead, he killed and he destroyed and he left the world in shambles. The result wasn't freedom for prodigies. It was twenty years of fear. Twenty years in which people weren't thinking about writing books or planting trees or building skyscrapers. It was an accomplishment just to survive another day." He smiled wryly. "But then . . . Agent N is a destructive force too. It depletes, but it doesn't replenish. I'm worried it's a step backward, for all of us."

They were silent for a moment, then Callum groaned and ruffled his own hair. "I'm sorry. People have told me I'm boring when I talk about this stuff, but sometimes it's so frustrating to go through life seeing all of this." He spread his arms wide, as if he could embrace the city below. "There are so many things to marvel at. How could anyone want to hurt it? How can people wake up every morning and not think—look, the sun is still there! And I'm still here! This is incredible!" He laughed and turned to Nova again. "If I could just make everyone see . . . I mean, for more than just a minute, then . . . I don't know. I can't help but think that then we could all start working to create things. Together, for once."

Nova regarded the city again. She saw fishing boats cutting through the waves, heading toward the sea. Cars making their way through the streets, almost as if they were part of a choreographed dance. Teams of cranes and construction workers repairing fallen buildings and erecting new structures over the skeletons of the old.

Hundreds of thousands of people, going about their lives. Day after day. Year after year. Generation after generation. Somehow, humanity had managed to build *all of this*. Despite everything that had tried to get in its way. Somehow, they prevailed. They continued on.

It *was* incredible. How had she never considered it before? Maybe because she'd never had a chance to see it like this. She had spent so much of her life underground. Squirreled away in the dark, lifeless tunnels. She had never paid much thought to exactly how much that secrecy was costing her and the Anarchists. The lives they could never live.

Or maybe she was seeing it now, because . . .

Because.

"Wonder Boy?" she whispered.

Callum groaned. "Just Wonder. Prism thinks adding the Boy turns it into a cute nickname, which would have been fine when I was seven."

She turned to him, shaking her head. "I didn't think you were a prodigy."

"Yeah, it doesn't come up often. Being able to temporarily reveal all the great wonders of this world"— he swooped his arm toward the horizon again—"doesn't seem like much when compared to chrome biceps or volcanic eruptions coming out of your fingertips." He snapped to prove his point, but rather than seem disappointed, his face took on that captivated expression again. "Did you know that in the seventeenth century, a prodigy held back the lava flow of an erupting volcano so their village could be—"

"*Callum.*"

He drew up short.

Nova stared at him. "You were manipulating me. I thought . . . there was a second when I . . . You can't just mess around with people's emotions like that!"

"Ah, common misconception," he said, unperturbed. "I can't

do anything to people's emotions. I can only show them their true feelings . . . or what they would see, if they bothered to look close enough. And when people see the truth—that they really are surrounded by a lot of amazing things—they tend to naturally experience an overwhelming sense of awe. I mean, why wouldn't you?"

She frowned, not sure if she was buying his explanation. She felt toyed with, like she'd had a moment of blinding clarity, only to discover it was an illusion.

Except now, she wasn't so sure what was real and what wasn't.

It was, she had to admit, kind of a neat gift, to bestow a sense of wonder on those around you. It wasn't flashy, but she suspected he was right. Maybe the world would be different if everyone could see it the way he did.

"Why don't they have you on patrols?" she said. "With a power like that, you'd be able to defuse a lot of dangerous situations."

"Eh, not as easily as you might think. People have to take a second to notice the world around them, and when someone's in the middle of a brawl or committing a crime, they're not going to stop and smell the hypothetical roses. I can have more of an impact here. Helping other Renegades change their perspective, reminding people what it is we're trying to accomplish. If we are going to rebuild the world, I'd like it to be built on a foundation of gratitude and appreciation, not greed or pride."

"If that's your goal," said Nova, rubbing her forehead, "then I'm not sure you're succeeding."

"It's a slow process, but I'm patient."

Nova paced along the edges of the observation deck, sliding her fingers across the rail. She reached the edge of the balcony and paused. Gatlon City was mostly built on a series of slopes that descended toward the bay, and from this angle she could see Ace's cathedral, situated at the top of a tall hill, the crumbling bell tower jutting above the wasteland.

She could hear Ace's voice in her head, telling her that sometimes you needed to destroy the old in order to make way for the new.

Progress was often built on sacrifice.

She hated to think of the Renegades having access to something like Agent N, but her reasons weren't the same as Callum's. He hated the idea of obliterating the potential of superpowers, but Nova hated the imbalance of power it would cause more than anything. Yes, superpowers could be used to accomplish great things, but they could also be used for cruelty and domination. And the fewer prodigies there were, the more likely those who remained would become all powerful tyrants.

If it were up to her . . . if she could change the future of the world . . . she would make it so there were no superpowers at all. No more heroes. No more villains.

Just humanity, powerless and vulnerable, all struggling through life together.

Something told her Callum wouldn't agree with that position.

"Why did you bring me up here?" she asked.

It took Callum a moment to answer. When he did, his voice was quiet. "I like you, Nova. I don't know what you've been through, but I can tell you've been hurt. And you're still hurting."

She flinched.

"I know that some prodigies become Renegades because they like the idea of having power," Callum continued, fixing his gaze on her. "And some want the prestige and the fame. But a lot of us are here because we want to make a difference. We want to change things for the better." He paused, his gaze slipping to the horizon. "I don't know what your story is, but I think you want to change things for the better, too. I thought that maybe seeing this would be a good reminder of what we're all doing here. What it is we're fighting for."

Nova studied the city beneath her. It *was* a good reminder of what she was fighting for.

But Callum was wrong about one thing.

Sometimes, things did have to be destroyed before something better could be built.

# CHAPTER TWENTY-SIX

"**H**AVE I MENTIONED that you look ridiculous?" Max whispered, hiding behind Adrian as he peered around the corner.

"Do I?" Adrian looked down at the white hazmat suit. "To be honest, I sort of feel like an astronaut."

"Well, you look like a walking air mattress."

Adrian cast a smirk over his shoulder. He could tell Max was nervous. The kid always got irritable when he was nervous. "You ready?"

"No," Max answered, his brow drawing tight. "This feels like breaking the rules. What if I run into someone? What if I . . . hurt them?"

"It's four o'clock in the morning," said Adrian.

"So, there could be security personnel and late-night patrol units coming and going and sometimes the healers come in early, and you know Nova is always around at weird hours and—"

"Max." Adrian fixed him with his sternest look. "We just have to get to the elevator. It's literally"—he estimated the distance—"fifty feet away, and the coast is completely clear. We're not going to run into anyone."

"But what if the coast isn't clear when we're getting off the elevator? We could be blindsided. Or—we could blindside someone else, I guess, would be more accurate—"

"No one's getting blindsided. We've got the floor staked out, with blockades on the stairwells. It's going to be fine."

"What would Hugh and Simon say?"

The corners of Adrian's mouth twitched, but not wanting to give away the surprise, he only said, "I'm fairly sure they would understand."

Adrian fidgeted with one of the chromium cuffs on his wrist. He wanted to reach out and rumple Max's hair—he had quickly grown accustomed to being able to show outward affection—but the thick gloves prevented it. It was doubly frustrating given that he didn't believe he needed the hazmat suit. He had the tattoo now. He should be able to get close to Max without any trouble.

But the tattoos were still a secret that needed to be kept, and the last thing he wanted was for certain people to start asking questions about them. So, for now, the hazmat suit would have to do.

"Come on," he said, opening the quarantine door.

With worried eyes, Max started to follow Adrian, but then paused. Turbo was gnawing on the strap of his sandals. "No. Stay here, Turbo," he said, nudging the creature back toward the miniature shore of the bay.

Adrian checked each direction one more time, and ushered Max through. Turbo didn't follow, just cocked his head and watched them go for a second, before skittering off toward his food bowl. The creature ate so much, Adrian was beginning to think they should have named him Oscar, Jr.

Their shoes thumped on the sky bridge as they passed over the lobby. Adrian could see the security booth inside the main entrance.

The personnel had been given clear instructions, though, and no one called out to stop them as they made their way toward the elevator bank.

"That's all they've talked about today," said Max.

"Hm?"

Max pointed and Adrian followed the gesture toward one of the television monitors hung around the lobby. A news story was playing, and though the sound was muted, an icon of a pill bottle over the news anchor's shoulder gave away the story.

A fourteen-year-old girl had died of a drug overdose two nights ago, a result of the illegal substance that was pervading the city's drug market. The drug that was concocted, in part, from medications like those Hawthorn had stolen from the hospital. It was the eighth overdose that week. In addition to the rampant drug usage, the growing popularity of the substance was also being linked to increases in street violence, trafficking, and prostitution.

Perhaps most troubling was that the Renegades had done little to counter the growing epidemic of drug abuse or the flourishing black market. If anything, they seemed at a loss as to how to fight an enemy that couldn't be knocked out with punches and laser beams.

On the screen, the most recent victim's family was being interviewed, their eyes swollen with mourning. Adrian turned away and jabbed the elevator button. There was no way for him to know if the drugs that took that girl's life had been developed from the same drugs Hawthorn had stolen, but he couldn't help feeling the weight of his failure.

The elevator arrived, and they both shuffled in. He could feel Max's anxiety every time the boy glanced up at the camera on the ceiling or the numbers above the door. His nervousness seemed to increase as the elevator rose. One foot was tapping rapidly against the floor. One hand kept brushing back an imaginary lock of hair from his forehead. He kept pursing his lips and shaking out his hands in an attempt to calm himself.

"I know this is weird for you," said Adrian, his breath fogging up the inside of the suit's face shield in a way that reminded him vaguely of being inside the Sentinel's armor. "But it's really not as risky as it seems. I swear. I wouldn't do anything to put you in danger—or any of the Renegades."

"But where are we going?" asked Max with a slight whine in his voice.

"Floor thirty-nine." Adrian gestured at the highlighted button.

Max glowered at him. "And what's on floor thirty-nine?"

Adrian's secretive smile returned, unbidden, and Max scoffed in annoyance.

The elevator reached the floor and the doors parted. Adrian gestured for Max to go first and the kid crept out uncertainly, but paused on the landing.

"Hey . . . Dad?"

Hugh stood a few dozen paces in front of the elevator. "Hello, Max."

Max glanced back at Adrian, eyes round with panic, but Adrian was already grinning. "I told you they would understand." He poked Max between the shoulder blades, urging him into the vast open space.

The thirty-ninth floor was one of the many floors of headquarters that were vacant, waiting to be filled with cubicles or VR rooms or an expanded call center or medical rooms or laboratories . . . whatever they needed as the organization grew. But for now, it was just a plain concrete floor, exposed ceiling pipes, and row after row of support columns spanning from one end of the building to the other.

Empty but for Hugh Everhart, Adrian, and Max.

"I'm . . . not in trouble?" Max said, hesitantly approaching their father. "For leaving the quarantine?"

"No, you're not in trouble." Hugh's face got stern. "We can't go around making a habit of it, but it was easy enough to secure a space for one night. This is, after all, a special occasion."

"It is?" said Max.

Hugh nodded. His focus turned to the wall behind Max and Adrian and there was a hint of concern, but also hope. "Assuming it worked?"

Max turned around and Simon flickered out of invisibility. Max gasped, then smacked Adrian on the arm. "You should have told me."

Simon was standing beside the elevator, the Vitality Charm around his neck. He would have been close enough to touch Max's shoulder as they'd walked by.

"I . . . don't feel any different," said Simon. He was tense, which wasn't like him.

For a long second, no one moved. Simon was standing only five or six paces away from Max, close enough that he should have felt the effects of Max's power immediately. He would feel weak, first, and then the draining away of his abilities. When it had happened to Adrian, he had felt it most in his hands. His fingers had gone numb, threatening to never be able to bring his drawings to life again. He wasn't sure what the Dread Warden would feel. Vulnerable? Exposed?

"Anything?" said Hugh.

Simon shook his head. "I feel normal." He vanished, his whole body disappearing like a light being turned off.

Max grabbed Adrian's forearm and squeezed. The suit hissed around the cuffs.

Simon appeared a second later, a couple of steps closer and beaming. He reached for the medallion around his neck. "It's working." He laughed. "Adrian, this is incredible. Max, I—"

Before he could finish, Max launched himself forward, wrapping his arms around Simon's waist.

Simon's face crumpled with the unexpected embrace, and he bent forward, locking his arms around Max's shoulder.

"Does this mean I can kick your butt at cards too, now?" Max said into Simon's shirt.

Simon chuckled. "You'll be disappointed to know that I am a *much* better card player than he is."

Hugh cleared his throat, dragging Adrian's attention toward him. He jerked his head to the side, indicating for Adrian to follow him. "Let's give them a minute."

Adrian's cheeks were beginning to hurt from his grin, but he couldn't smother it as they made their way across the dusty floor.

"Simon's right," Hugh said, keeping his voice low to avoid an echo. "The Vitality Charm is amazing, and I'm mortified to know it's been sitting in our vault all this time and neither of us knew about it. Max's life could have been so different . . ." His voice trembled, but he covered it up with another clearing of his throat.

"Better late than never," said Adrian. "I'm glad I found it when I did."

"Me too. And we're going to assign some people to look more closely at the objects we have in the collection, see what other things of value might have been missed."

"You should talk to Nova about it," said Adrian. "She's been really invested in her artifacts work lately."

"I will," said Hugh. "It will be fascinating for us all to hear what else we might have been neglecting down there."

Once they reached the far wall of windows, Adrian checked the distance between them and Max and unlatched the face shield. Hugh tensed as he watched Adrian pull off the hood, but Adrian flashed him a grin. "We're far enough away."

When Adrian showed no sign of having his powers drained, Hugh conceded with a nod. "Listen, Adrian, there's something I thought you should know. Sooner than later."

Adrian's eyebrow shot upward. "Oh?"

"There's been a breakthrough in the Hawthorn case."

Adrian stood straighter. "What? When?"

"Early yesterday morning. After . . . that unfortunate fatality."

"The girl that overdosed?"

"Yes. We told Hawthorn's allies that if we're able to trace the drugs she bought to the ones that were stolen, they could be charged with aiding in involuntary manslaughter. One of them started talking. Gave us a few leads on where Hawthorn might be hiding out."

"That's great," said Adrian. "I'll notify my team immediately. We can . . ." He trailed off as Hugh started to shake his head. Adrian's enthusiasm waned. "You're not giving us the case, are you?"

"We've already put Clark's team on it."

It felt like being punched in the stomach. Adrian groaned. "Frostbite? Seriously?"

"I know you don't get along with her, and I don't blame you. They're . . . a frosty bunch." Hugh quirked a grin at his pun. Adrian did not return it. "But they're a good team, one of the most effective we have. I trust them to handle it."

Adrian scowled, knowing it made him look like a petulant child. He was tempted to say that the only reason Frostbite brought in so many criminals was because her team didn't play by the code—he'd witnessed as much when he'd seen them bullying the Anarchists in the subway tunnels and trying to frame them with a false confession.

But he resisted the urge, not only because he had no evidence of Frostbite's transgressions, but also because he felt the shame of his own hypocrisy. The Sentinel didn't follow the code either, and it was a part of the reason that he, like Frostbite's team, was so good at bringing criminals to justice. Catching bad guys was easy when you didn't have to deal with the inconvenience of evidence and trials.

Maybe that was part of why he disliked Genissa Clark so much. Maybe he was jealous that she could get away with what she did, whereas he was treated like a pest to be eradicated.

"I wanted you to hear it from me, before word gets around," said Hugh. "This choice isn't because we don't trust you and the others, Adrian. But this is a high-profile case, as you know, and—"

"You need the best," Adrian muttered.

Hugh frowned, but didn't disagree.

Adrian sighed. "The important thing is that Hawthorn is caught and brought to justice. It doesn't matter who brings her in. After all"—he glanced back at Simon, remembering what he had been told after the hospital heist—"there is no I in hero."

# CHAPTER TWENTY-SEVEN

I T WAS NEAR DAWN by the time Adrian got home and trudged down the stairs into his bedroom. He knew he shouldn't be so cranky after the night they'd had. After he managed to give Max something he had given up on wanting—quality time with Simon, and soon, quality time with his friends too. After his dads gave the okay for Adrian to tell people about the medallion, at least.

But all of Max's joy couldn't overcome Adrian's irritation, to know that Frostbite's team—of *all* the patrol units in the whole organization—had been chosen to go after Hawthorn. His jaw ached from grinding his teeth all the way home.

Pacing back and forth across his worn carpet, he held up his wristband. He had finally turned off the notifications from the call center, removing some of the temptation to put the Sentinel's suit back on. He was trying to trust the system, to put his faith in the code, just like his dads wanted him to. He was trying to give the Renegades the benefit of the doubt—to believe that they *were* enough to protect the city, to bring justice to the wrongdoers of their world.

But today, he couldn't resist.

He pulled up the map of the city and did a quick search for Frostbite.

His jaw clenched as a small signal blinked on the map. She was on active duty, moving down Raikes Avenue. As he watched, she turned north on Scatter Creek Row, moving fast, so she had to be in a patrol car.

He tried to puzzle out her destination based on the direction she was heading. Maybe Hawthorn was camped out in an old boathouse by the docks, or in one of the warehouses near the port, or in an abandoned train car by the defunct tracks.

Screwing up his face, Adrian forced himself to take off the wristband. He tossed it onto his bed, then flopped down beside it, burying his face into his pillow with a frustrated groan.

He told himself to let them deal with it.

He tried to persuade himself that going after them, after Hawthorn, wasn't worth the risk.

His fingers dug into his blankets.

Hawthorn would be captured. She would be brought into custody. The stolen drugs that hadn't yet made their way to the black market would be confiscated.

Frostbite would get the glory, but that shouldn't matter to Adrian. The point was that justice would be served, and a wrong would be made right. As right as could be at this point, anyway.

But for every logical reason to stay put, his brain threw back an excuse to go after them.

*What if Frostbite's team failed? What if Hawthorn got away again? They could use an extra hand. A backup, just in case.*

He turned his head to the side. The light on his wristband was still blinking.

Adrian gnawed on the inside of his cheek, feeling the strain of the internal debate tugging at him.

*Stay safe. Stay hidden. Let the Sentinel rest in peace.*

But somewhere deep inside, he knew it wasn't going to happen. He knew from the moment his dad had confessed that her team had been chosen over Adrian's.

He would go after Hawthorn. He had to.

"Just to make sure," he said, snatching up the wristband and bending it around his wrist again. "You won't reveal yourself unless it's absolutely, positively necessary."

It wasn't because he had something to prove. Not to himself or his dads or . . . or even Nova.

No, this wasn't about him. This wasn't about the Sentinel.

This was about justice being served.

It was almost noon when Adrian reached the port, the signals from his wristband guiding him from rooftop to rooftop. His heavy boots thumped loudly as he landed on the cabin of an old crane that years ago would have been used to lift the shipping containers from arriving barges. Judging from the film of dirt on the cabin's windows, he doubted anyone had used it for years. Frostbite's tracking signal was coming from a stack of shipping containers that had long ago been left to rust once international trading had been halted. The industry had picked up significantly over the past decade, but a lot of the infrastructure that was in place before the rise of Ace Anarchy had been left to slowly deteriorate.

Beyond a fence on the other side of the storage yard, he spotted the patrol vehicle with the red *R* painted on its hood—a van large enough that even Gargoyle would have been able to fit inside.

Adrian climbed halfway down the crane's tower before dropping to the ground. He landed hard, sending up a thick cloud of dust. He approached the shipping containers from behind, making his way through the rusting labyrinth in the storage yard.

A crash made him freeze. It was followed by the roar of splitting earth. The ground trembled beneath Adrian's feet, and dust was knocked from the towering containers, raining onto his helmet.

That had to be Mack Baxter—*Aftershock.*

A second later, he heard an enraged scream, and then the back of a container was blown across the path, not thirty paces in front of him. Hawthorn's brambled tentacles emerged first, slithering out from the container like a giant octopus.

Adrian crouched, then launched himself into the air before Hawthorn could spot him. He landed on the roof of the nearest container with a tooth-rattling clang, but the sound was disguised beneath Frostbite's shrill scream. "Stingray! Gargoyle!"

Hawthorn roped her extra limbs around the nearest stack of crates and hauled herself up them, lithe and quick. Seconds later, she was speeding across their rooftops, heading toward the water.

She was getting away.

Again.

Growling, Adrian fisted his right hand and thrust his arm toward her. The cylinder on the forearm of the armor rose out of his skin and began to glow white-hot as the laser prepared to fire. He was a better shot with the laser than he'd ever been with a gun, and she wasn't too far away yet. He could hit her. He could—

Somewhere below, he heard Gargoyle roar, then Hawthorn screamed in surprise as the tower of crates she was running across swayed and toppled to one side. She yelped and reached out with two of the tentacles, grappling for the next container. The extra limbs caught, the thorns puncturing the metal with a shriek that made Adrian wince.

Hawthorn dangled for a moment, caught her breath, then with a loud groan hauled herself up to the roof.

She had just flopped onto her stomach when Stingray appeared at the other end of her crate, smirking. He said something Adrian couldn't hear, and Hawthorn looked up, her expression frenzied.

One tentacle pulled back, preparing to lash out at Stingray, but she was too slow.

His tail whipped toward her, the barbed point jabbing her on the shoulder.

Hawthorn grunted and collapsed forward, sprawling face-first across the ridged top of the shipping container.

Swallowing, Adrian ducked into the shadows and dismissed the laser. The suit clunked as it sank back beneath its paneling.

The venom from Stingray's tail acted quickly, immobilizing Hawthorn's body and her extra limbs. Stingray jerked her arms behind her back and cuffed her wrists. He wasn't particularly gentle as he shoved her body back over the side. Adrian expected her to smash hard onto the ground below—but Gargoyle was there, waiting for her. He caught her limp body, but dropped it just as fast.

Frostbite strode out from behind a container, and Aftershock appeared on the far side of the path, the ground rippling as he approached them.

"Nice work," said Frostbite, tapping her palm against Hawthorn's cheek. A glaze of frost was left behind when she pulled away. "Between arresting the mastermind behind the hospital theft and bringing in all the drugs from that laboratory, I'd say we're nearly due for a promotion."

Adrian shut his eyes, his heart sinking. He had come all this way for nothing. The fight had lasted only a couple of minutes, and the Sentinel clearly wasn't needed. Maybe his fathers had been right to assign Frostbite to the case after all.

He sulked along the crate to avoid the telltale thumps of his footsteps on the metal. One of the containers he passed had windows roughly cut into the sides and covered with netting. He paused to peer inside and saw that the interior had been completely altered. From the outside it looked like an unassuming stack of abandoned shipping crates, but inside was an entire laboratory's worth of tools and equipment. Bunsen burners and measuring cups, flasks and gallon-size buckets sporting various tubes and labels, and shelf after shelf of stolen pharmaceuticals.

They hadn't just found Hawthorn. They had found her laboratory, the drugs, and the proof that they would need to not only show that she had stolen that medicine from the hospital, but also that she was using it to formulate illegal substances for sale on the black market.

Her trial would be a quick one.

Adrian backed away from the window. The disappointment he felt at having missed his chance to capture Hawthorn made it obvious that this really had been about wanting to prove himself. About wanting people to view the Sentinel differently. About wanting praise and admiration—from the public, yes, but from the Renegades too. From his peers and his dads.

Sighing, he prepared to jump down from the container when an odd noise made him hesitate.

He cocked his head, listening.

It was ticking.

Slow, steady ticking.

His pulse jumped and he swung around, his memory launching

him straight back to the carnival and the Detonator's glowing blue explosives set around the park.

A bomb. *Hawthorn has a bomb.*

He crept back to the window and peered inside, searching the laboratory. From his vantage point, he could see Frostbite standing just outside the far opening, and though the ticking must have been loud enough that they all heard it, she seemed as relaxed as ever.

Frostbite stooped and set something down on the ground. A triangular box of some sort.

Was *that* the bomb? Had Frostbite brought an explosive with them?

But . . . why?

Moving to the edge of the crate again, Adrian peered down into the valley between the containers. Frostbite, Gargoyle, Stingray, and Aftershock were standing around Hawthorn, who was on her knees, her hands latched behind her back and her six spiky limbs pooling beside her.

Adrian could see the device on the ground more clearly now, and the needle that swung steadily back and forth. Back and forth.

It was a metronome.

He was fairly certain it was Turmoil's metronome. The Sound Deadener, which would keep any noise, no matter how loud, from traveling beyond the area in which the ticking of the metronome could be heard.

But what possible use could they have for—

"No," Hawthorn whimpered, her voice slurred from the effects of Stingray's poison, as Aftershock and Stingray grabbed the ends of her tentacles and stretched them away from her. "What are you doing?"

Frostbite spread her fingers and six streams of ice shot toward the appendages, freezing them to the ground and locking them in place. Hawthorn grunted and Adrian could see the muscles beneath her shirt undulating as she tried to retract the limbs into her body, but the ice held them as tight as handcuffs.

Adrian's fingers curled around the edges of the crate.

"Here's what's going to happen," said Frostbite. "I'm going to ask you some questions, and you're going to answer them. If you don't . . ." She tipped her head.

Gargoyle raised one fist, and it hardened into gray stone. His smile was hideous as he crouched beside one of Hawthorn's tentacles and slammed the fist on top of it.

Adrian recoiled. Hawthorn's scream tore through him, echoing shrilly across the shipyard.

Nausea roiled in his stomach as Gargoyle lifted his fist and Adrian could see the place where the limb had been crushed from its weight. One of the thorns had splintered and was oozing yellow-tinted blood.

"So," said Frostbite, once Hawthorn's scream had died into a trembling whimper. "Are you ready to begin?"

# CHAPTER TWENTY-EIGHT

"You—you can't—" Hawthorn stammered through her clenched teeth. "I'm unarmed . . . immobilized . . . Your code doesn't allow . . ."

"Oh, so you're an expert on our code, are you?" Frostbite guffawed. "A thief, a producer, a dealer . . . I really don't think anyone will be upset about what happens to you."

Hawthorn snarled, tears wetting her face. "And when your precious Council sees that you *tortured* me?"

Frostbite laughed and unlatched a holster on her belt. "Oh, they're not going to see anything."

It was a handgun, exactly like those they had been training with lately. Adrian's pulse thumped.

They had Agent N. *That's* how Frostbite planned to get away with this. They could do whatever they wanted to Hawthorn's extra limbs, because once she was neutralized, those limbs would no longer exist. All evidence of the Renegades' abuse would disappear. And with the metronome steadily ticking away, no one would hear her screams beyond the shipyard.

It would be their word against hers—a known criminal and one that no one would be sorry to see stripped of her powers. Adrian wasn't sure how or why Frostbite's team had been allowed to arm themselves with the neutralizing agent, maybe they'd been given special permission for this high-profile case, but he did know it would be easy for them to claim they had neutralized Hawthorn out of self-defense.

Who would the Council believe?

His stomach was in knots.

"I know you've been selling your product on the black market," said Frostbite, her voice haughty and cold. The sound of it made Adrian's teeth grind. "I want the names and aliases of the dealers you've been selling to."

There was a moment of silence, punctuated only with the *tick-tick-tick* of the metronome. Swallowing the bile in his mouth, Adrian peered over the ledge again.

"I don't know any names," Hawthorn growled. "They tell me where to drop the stuff and pick up the payment, and I do it."

Frostbite signaled to Gargoyle.

He brought another fist down, crushing a second limb.

Hawthorn's scream tore through Adrian like a physical assault.

He didn't want to pity her. Hawthorn was a criminal. She had stolen medicine, used it to produce illegal substances. She had dealt it to teenagers. Her actions had likely resulted in numerous deaths.

He wouldn't even have been sad to see her shot with Agent N right now.

But he also knew that this was wrong. To beat her when she was helpless. To torture her unnecessarily. They were supposed to take her to headquarters, let her be interrogated there. Any information spoken under duress was likely to be fallible, anyway.

*But what if she says something useful?* his brain countered. *What if she gives up more names, or gives evidence that could lead to more arrests? What if they bring down a whole chain of dealers because of this . . . or an entire drug syndicate?*

He turned his head away from the scene below, face screwed up tight. He could walk away. Pretend he never saw any of this. He could allow Frostbite and her team to break the rules and hope that it lead to further justice.

"I'll ask the question again," said Frostbite. "What are the names of your associates?"

Hawthorn's voice was breaking, her gumption already buried beneath the pain. "I told you, I don't know. We don't share names."

Frostbite made a doubtful sound. She surveyed her companions, and Adrian could picture her smug expression.

He may not always act within the confines of the Gatlon code authority, but *this* was beyond vigilantism and justice. This was abuse of power, pure and simple.

He couldn't stand for it.

Adrian thrust his arm forward. The laser diode rose from his forearm plate and began to glow.

Gargoyle raised his fist.

Adrian fired. The bolt of light struck Gargoyle in his chest, blowing him back against the nearest crate. He hit the ground with a thud that shook the entire stack and left a sizable dent in the metal side.

Adrian leaped to the ground, centering himself between Hawthorn and Frostbite. "That's enough. She's captured. You've done your job. Now take this criminal back to headquarters and let the Council deal with her."

Frostbite's expression quickly turned from surprise to loathing. "Well, well. I had a feeling your death was too good to be true."

Long icicles began to form in her left hand. Her right still held the gun. "Are you going to try to tell me that the Council sent you? That your orders are to bring Hawthorn back too?" She spat into the dirt. "Sorry, but that lie's not going to work a second time."

"I don't have to lie about anything. You're acting outside of the code, and the Council is going to know about it. Now, are you going to arrest this criminal and confess your own crimes, or do I have to do it for you?"

"Better idea," said Frostbite, one side of her mouth lifting. "I think we're about to bring in two wanted criminals—already neutralized. Oh, won't the Council be pleased."

Something struck Adrian's shoulder. He felt a tug on his armor. The barb of Stingray's tail was latched beneath the shoulder plate, trying to rip it off him. Growling, Adrian grabbed the tail and yanked, pulling Stingray off his feet.

Frostbite yelled and hurled the icicle. Adrian blocked it with his forearm and the ice shattered, its shards skittering through the dust. He lifted his left palm toward Frostbite and a ball of fire began to curl around his hand, crackling orange and white.

Frostbite took a step back.

"No," said Adrian. "I'm taking Hawthorn into my custody. I'll deliver her to headquarters myself."

He said it without really thinking about what a terrible idea it would be for him to stroll into headquarters in full Sentinel armor, with Hawthorn draped across his shoulders—but he would figure out the details later.

Turning, he aimed the fire at the mounds of ice that had cemented Hawthorn's limbs to the ground. She was watching him, wary and bleary-eyed, her cheeks wet with tears and her shattered limbs coated with yellow blood.

"Cute," said Frostbite, "but that's really not how this is going to play out. Aftershock!"

Adrian looked up in time to see Aftershock stomp one foot into the ground. A crack splintered the compact dirt, shooting straight between Adrian's legs. He yelped in surprise and was thrown off balance, landing on his side. In the same moment, Stingray's tail wrapped around Adrian's neck, pinning him to the ground. Adrian tried to dig his fingers in between the tail and his armor but he couldn't gain purchase.

"That was a nice try, with your gallant speech and everything," said Frostbite. She stood over Adrian, one hand on her hip while the other tapped the gun against her thigh.

He glanced over at Hawthorn, who was still on her knees, her head hanging low. He had only managed to free one of her limbs from the ice and it was one of the broken ones.

"You know, I'm glad we had this meeting," Frostbite continued. "You are a perfect reminder of everything it is we Renegades are fighting against."

He glared up at her, though he knew his hatred couldn't be seen through the visor. "I think you're confused."

"No, *you're* confused," she spat. "With your vigilante act, your claim to *fight for justice*. But there's a reason you're not a Renegade, and everyone knows it. If you really cared about the people of this world, if you really wanted to help the weak and the innocent, then you would have joined us a long time ago. But no—you think you can go it on your own. There's a lot more glory that way, isn't there? The fame, the publicity . . . You talk a good game, but we both know you're in it for your own agenda. And here's the problem with prodigies who go around flaunting their own agendas." She crouched in front of Adrian, her gaze piercing the shield of his helmet. "It starts to give other prodigies all sorts of ideas. They start to think—who needs to become a Renegade? I can be more without them. Pretty soon, they're more concerned with their own reputation than helping people. They don't care about protecting the innocent. They don't care about stopping crime. They're above all that. And before you know it . . . there's another villain in the world that *we* have to deal with." She stood up again and aimed the barrel of the gun at Adrian's face. He narrowed his eyes, though he knew an Agent N dart wouldn't make it through his helmet. "Either you're a Renegade, or you're a villain. And yeah, we might bend the rules from time to time. We might even ignore the code completely when we can see a better way of doing things—a way that really *will* make this world a better place. But to go around pretending that you can be against us, and still be a hero?" She shook her head. "That just can't be tolerated."

A shadow fell over Adrian. Gargoyle reached down and grasped the sides of his helmet, preparing to pull it off.

With a roar, Adrian bent his arm and fired a beam into Stingray's tail. He gasped and jerked back, releasing his hold around Adrian's throat enough that Adrian could slam his helmet back into Gargoyle's stomach. Gargoyle grunted from the impact, his grip loosening. Adrian jumped to his feet and spun around, aiming a punch at the side of Gargoyle's head. His cheek morphed moments before impact, and the clang of metal on stone reverberated through Adrian's bones. He drew back and lifted his leg, instead, planting the bottom of his foot flat against Gargoyle's chest and shoving him to the ground.

Adrian barely kept from falling again as Aftershock rumbled toward him. All around, the towers of shipping containers trembled and swayed, threatening to collapse on top of their entire group.

Adrian sprinted away from Aftershock. He was preparing to vault up to the top of one of the container stacks when a wall of icy spears shot upward from the ground, angled toward him. Adrian yelped. He couldn't stop in time. He tripped and fell, smashing three of the spears beneath his weight.

A fourth pinioned up between the armored plates that protected his side and abdomen. The sharp point punctured him just beneath the ribs, and Adrian cried out, as much from surprise as the pain. Grunting, he wrapped both hands around the ice and levered himself off it.

He stumbled, panting. He was sweating and bleeding inside the suit, drops of it tracing the length of his spine, soaking through his shirt.

"So the suit isn't invincible," said Aftershock, lumbering closer to him. "That's good to know." He lifted his knee, prepared to send another earthquake ricocheting toward Adrian.

Bracing himself, Adrian gathered up his energy and launched upward. He landed on a stack of containers, four crates high. Clenching his fist, he started to prepare another concussive beam.

"Let Mack deal with him," Frostbite yelled. "Gargoyle, we have a job to finish."

Adrian climbed to his feet and aimed his glowing arm toward the group below. "Like I said, I'll be finishing the job for you. Consider Hawthorn my prisoner now."

Aftershock snarled and made to slam his foot down again, when Frostbite held up a hand, halting him. "Hold on. I think he should see this."

Stingray snickered, though the sound was tired. He hadn't fully recovered from the concussive beam yet. "Yeah, he should know what Agent N can do . . . because he'll be next."

But Frostbite shook her head. She was peering up at Adrian, her expression calculating. "No . . . I've changed my mind. We're not going to neutralize Hawthorn. That would be a waste of resources, given that we *found* her this way."

Adrian frowned. "What are you—"

"Aftershock, bring him down. Gargoyle . . . kill her."

"What?" Adrian barked. He swiveled his arm toward Gargoyle, then heard the rumble of earth below. The stack shook beneath him and he fired, but the bolt of energy went wide, striking a crate behind them.

Adrian yelped and grabbed the edge of the container to keep from sliding off as it lurched to one side.

The metronome could barely be heard over the grating of clay and dirt, the splintering of buried rock.

He spotted Gargoyle and his eyes widened. In horror. In disbelief.

"No!" he yelled, as Gargoyle wrapped both hands around Hawthorn's head. She started to scream. "You can't—"

In one merciless motion, Gargoyle crushed her skull between his palms, silencing her.

The air left Adrian. White spots shimmered at the edges of his vision.

"Don't be sad, Sentinel," Frostbite yelled up toward him. "No one is going to miss her . . . just like no one will miss you."

The earthquake reached a crescendo. The precarious stack under his feet began to topple.

Adrian forced himself to get up, urged on by adrenaline and rage. He ran. Down the full length of the container, leaping from it seconds before it collapsed under his feet. He landed hard on the roof of Hawthorn's laboratory and kept running, racing from stack to stack. The whole world was trembling now. The shipyard was a shamble of falling containers, groaning metal, shuddering earth. Every time Adrian landed on a new stack, it immediately began to sway and buck beneath his feet.

He kept going, pounding his legs as hard and fast as he could force them to go, and as the last stack of crates began to fall, he sprang upward, stretching.

He barely caught the hook of one of the enormous cranes. His momentum swung him forward, over the docks of the port. Letting go, he rolled in the air and crashed down inside a fenced graveyard for rusted tractors. He ducked behind a large forklift and hunkered low, gulping for breath, his heart racing.

He could no longer hear the ticking of the metronome.

He could no longer hear Frostbite or her allies.

He didn't move for a long time, waiting to see whether Aftershock would continue his pursuit. His skin was hot and sticky from sweat. Every muscle was shaking.

And every time he shut his eyes, he saw Gargoyle's stone hands wrapped around Hawthorn's head, and heard Frostbite's ominous words.

*Just like no one will miss you.*

# CHAPTER TWENTY-NINE

◇◇◆◇◇

THE VITALITY CHARM.

Nova had not been able to stop thinking about it since she had seen Adrian inside the quarantine, at least when she wasn't ranting about her failure to obtain the helmet. Max's ability to absorb other superpowers had not affected Adrian, and it was all because of a pendant on a necklace.

But it wasn't in the vault—she had checked the rental paperwork several times over the last few days and Adrian had yet to return the medallion.

She needed it. Not to protect from Max, but to protect herself against Agent N. Specifically—Agent N in gas form. Leroy was on the verge of a breakthrough, she knew, and with the mist-missiles she'd since taken from the vault, she now knew exactly how to convert the weapons into a delivery system for the toxic vapor. Any prodigy who entered a five-foot radius of the device within the first three and a half minutes of its release (the time it would take for the vapor molecules to disperse to the point of ineffectiveness, according to Leroy's calculations) would be neutralized. Their powers sapped away as surely as if the sludgy green concoction had been plunged straight into their hearts.

Finally, the Anarchists had a weapon they could use against the Renegades. Multiple Renegades at once, even.

But Nova did not want to risk her own ability, and no one else would want to take the chance either. In order to protect herself in the fight she knew was coming, a fight she expected sooner than later, she needed that medallion.

These were the thoughts churning in her head as she marked the six-mile path between the dingy row house she shared with the Anarchists and the nicest suburban neighborhood in Gatlon City limits.

She had known for years that Captain Chromium and the Dread Warden had taken up residence inside the old mayor's mansion on Pickering Grove. When the Anarchists were suffering their existence in the subway tunnels, she had heard Honey gripe incessantly about the unfairness of it all. That their enemies should be surrounded by luxury, while *she*, a queen, was stuck in those grubby, smelly caves. Once Nova asked, if they knew where two of their greatest enemies lived, why didn't they go there and attack? Leroy could fill it with poisonous fumes through the ductwork, or Ingrid could have simply blown the place up. Or Nova—thirteen years old and full of hubris at the time—could sneak in through a window and murder them both in their sleep, never mind that she'd never killed anyone at that point.

But Honey had sighed wistfully, while Leroy told Nova everything they knew about the mansion's security systems, both technological and superpowered protective devices.

No. Captain Chromium and the Dread Warden would not be so easy to kill.

But Nova wasn't planning on killing anyone tonight.

She just wanted to chat. And maybe have a peek around.

That wasn't a crime, was it?

Her footfalls began to slow from their determined pace as the homes surrounding her grew larger, the driveways leading to them stretched longer, and the trees lining the road became so old and established that in places their branches created a canopy over the whole street.

This neighborhood still bore the signs of destruction from the Age of Anarchy that had been felt by the rest of the city, and the number of boarded windows and unkempt yards suggested that many of these glorious homes remained abandoned. Nova wondered why so many of the apartments downtown were cramped and crowded to an almost unhealthy degree while such estates stood empty. Surely there was a better use for them than to let them rot and collapse from disrepair.

She couldn't help but picture what life might have been like here, before the Age of Anarchy. How different to peer out your window and see a neatly manicured garden and children riding bikes down the street. How unlike anything she had ever known, to have neighborhood barbecues in the backyard and to spend the evening helping young Evie with her schoolwork while Mom and Papà made dinner in the kitchen—

Nova had to forcefully shake the fantasy away before she could risk tears coming into her eyes.

Thanks to whatever Callum did to her mind, thoughts like these had been creeping up all day. Little daydreams about the what-ifs that surrounded her. What if there was more to life than revenge and lies? What if the Anarchists and the Renegades didn't have to be in constant war? What if Adrian Everhart wasn't her enemy and his fathers hadn't failed her, and her life could revolve around gossiping with Ruby and laughing at Oscar's jokes and not being afraid of every butterfly she passed, and every time she felt her heart patter at the sight of Adrian it wouldn't feel like a betrayal of everyone she cared about?

But that life would never come to pass. Not for her. Thanks to the Roaches, who had murdered her family, and the Renegades, who had failed to protect them. Thanks to all the people who had hated and abused prodigies for all those centuries. Thanks to the villain gangs who had taken advantage of Ace's beautiful vision.

And thanks to Nova, herself. She knew she had a choice. She had seen goodness among the Renegades, no matter how much she wanted to pretend it wasn't there. She could try to ignore their false promises, forget the lies they told the world. She could simply give up.

But Callum had wanted to remind Nova what it was she was fighting for, and it worked.

She was fighting to rid the world of the Renegades, so that no kid would ever again put their faith in superheroes who wouldn't come. So no one else would have to suffer the heartbreak that she had.

And also, of course, for Ace. He had taken her in, protected her, cared for her.

She would not let him die without a fight.

Exhaling a steadying breath, she checked the faded numbers on the nearest mailbox. Her heart lurched. She'd been so caught up in her own head she'd almost walked right past it.

Her attention jumped from the mailbox to the wrought-iron gate to the long flagstone walkway to . . . the house.

The mansion.

The . . . *palace,* at least in comparison to every home Nova had ever had.

"You can't be serious," she muttered.

The entry gate was connected to an old brick wall that lined the estate. The walkway curved around a tiered fountain, which either no longer worked or had been turned off for the coming winter. The large arched windows were trimmed in pristine white moldings. A Greek-style portico framed the front porch and the grand double doors, which were painted a welcoming butter yellow. A series of chimneys erupted from various gables around the roof and the occasional bay window added visual interest to the brick.

Awe and disgust mingled together as she took it in, and she wasn't sure which was more prominent. She wanted to jeer at how pretentious it all was, but she had to admit that wasn't entirely true.

The home was . . . stately, to be sure. It had a subtle classicism to it, like it could have been built at any point in the past two hundred years.

Still, it was far more square footage than three people could possibly use.

Maybe she was just feeling defensive, though. She couldn't help wondering what Adrian must have thought when he saw the decrepit row house on Wallowridge, when he was accustomed to *this.*

Gulping, Nova approached the gate. She reached for the handle, when a red light flickered on a device built into the nearest pillar. The light cascaded over Nova from head to foot, then came to rest on her wristband.

"*Renegade credentials detected,*" said a computerized voice from a speaker disguised in a lamppost. "*You may approach the main entrance and present yourself. Warning: Straying from the path could result in loss of life or limb. Welcome to the Gatlon City Mayor's Mansion!*"

The red light blinked out at the same time a lock clunked inside the gate.

Nova pushed on the gate and it groaned and creaked, but once she was through, it swung back of its own accord. She heard the locking mechanism bolt again and buried a shudder.

"Stay on the path," she said, scanning the flagstone. The vast green lawns to either side were tidy and quaint, like they were waiting for someone to roll out a game of croquet. "Duly noted."

She made her way to the door and stepped into the shadow of the portico. Two topiaries stood on the steps, taking up residence in ancient stone urns. A knocker on the middle of the yellow door was shaped like a tusked elephant, with the knocker held in its looped trunk.

A small bronze plaque beside the door read:

GATLON CITY HISTORICAL MARKER
MAYOR'S MANSION

*This house served as the home for Gatlon City mayors for*
*more than a century prior to the twenty-year period known*
*as the Age of Anarchy, during which Mayor Robert Hayes*
*and his family and staff were murdered in this location.*

Beneath this stoic plaque was a smaller, wooden one, with hand-painted words that read, EVERHART-WESTWOOD RESIDENCE: ALL SOLICITING, PICKETING, AND VILLAINOUS ANTICS STRICTLY PROHIBITED!

Before Nova could determine if she thought this was funny or not, one of the double doors swung open.

She jumped back. Her hand reached for her belt before she remembered she hadn't brought it with her.

"Nova?" said Adrian, haloed by the light of the foyer behind him. "I thought the security system might be pulling a joke on me." He almost, but not quite, smiled. "What are you doing here?"

A hundred little observations rushed into Nova's mind at once, rendering her speechless. That the smell of cinnamon wafted from the doorway. That Adrian's long-sleeved T-shirt seemed tighter than normal, and he was wearing paint-splattered jeans with tears in the knees. That there was a charcoal drawing on the wall behind him depicting the Stockton Bridge at night. That he was pressing a hand beneath his ribs in an odd way, and as soon as he noticed her noticing, the hand dropped to his side.

She picked what seemed to be the least problematic of her thoughts, and said, "You live in a mansion."

Adrian blinked, then considered the entryway, as if it had been a long time since he'd stopped to really take in his surroundings. "The Mayor's Mansion, yeah. You didn't know that?"

"No, I did," she said. "But I didn't expect . . . I mean, it's an actual, literal mansion." She gestured at the lawn. "You have a fountain in your yard."

A slow grin crept over Adrian's face. "Don't freak out, but there's a carriage house in the back. Oh, and the attic used to be servant's quarters. There's even a bell system that connects to all these little buttons throughout the house, so if the mayor's wife wanted a cup of tea, she'd just have to push one of the buttons and a servant would come and take her order." His eyes twinkled. "Classy stuff, right?"

Nova gaped at him. "Tell me you don't have servants."

Laughing, Adrian stepped back. "No servants. Do you want to come in? I was warming up cinnamon rolls for dinner."

"What, you don't eat seven-course meals every night?"

"Only on Sundays. Is that a yes?"

"That's a yes." Nova held her breath as she crossed the threshold, her focus roving from the intricate crown moldings to the crystals dripping from the chandelier. She glanced at Adrian's abdomen and could detect a squarish lump beneath his shirt. "What happened?"

"Nothing," Adrian said quickly, pressing a hand to the spot again, then waving the question away. "I was, uh . . . unpacking some boxes with a box cutter and it slipped and got me. You know how they always say to cut *away* from yourself? I finally understand why."

He turned and she followed after him, frowning. Adrian was a lot of things, but clumsy wasn't one of them. It was difficult to imagine him making such a mistake.

They passed an oak staircase that curved upward to the second floor and an arched doorway through which she could see a grouping of chairs and sofas and a piano in the corner, though even from here she could see a layer of dust on it.

"Is that a *parlor?*" said Nova.

"No, it's a *formal* parlor," said Adrian. "My dads hired a fancy interior designer to put it together a few years ago, and I don't think we've used it since. They insist it will come in handy, though, once we start inviting foreign dignitaries to visit and they need a place to 'host' them." He made quotes in the air.

Nova expected to be taken to a kitchen, but instead Adrian led her down a narrow staircase into some sort of basement. The aroma of cinnamon grew thicker around them.

Nova realized with a start, as her foot landed on plush carpet, that she was in his room.

His bedroom.

She must have hesitated in the doorway a second too long, because when Adrian turned back and noticed her expression, he tensed himself. "We can take these back upstairs, if you want," he said, lifting an aluminum tin full of sticky-sweet cinnamon buns. "I was just going to . . . um"—he gestured toward a shut door on the other side of the room—"work on this project . . . thing. But we could go watch a movie or something . . ." He hesitated, a crease forming between his brows. "What are you doing here, anyway?"

"I just . . . wanted to see you," said Nova. Adrian's eyes widened behind his glasses, almost imperceptibly. She had been practicing those words the entire walk, trying to find a way she could say them without blushing. She was not entirely successful. "Are your dads home?"

He shook his head. "Still at headquarters."

*Good.* She would have full access to search the house, though she hoped the medallion would be found here, in his room. She just had to knock Adrian out first.

"Is everything okay?" Adrian asked.

"Yeah. Yeah," she said. "Just . . . curious. A movie sounds nice." She meant it. A movie was easy. Comfortable. Completely without pressure.

Not to mention that people fell asleep during movies all the time, and there was nothing at all suspicious about it. All she needed was an excuse to put her hand on his. A brush of a finger against his knuckle. That was all she needed.

"Okay. Cool. There's a TV upstairs."

Nova nudged her chin toward the TV set on top of a small enter-tainment console. "That one doesn't work?"

"Uh . . . it does. I just . . . didn't want to assume . . . I mean, whatever you want to do."

For the first time in what felt like days, Nova felt the tension in her chest start to loosen. She had been frustrated over her failed attempts to flirt with Adrian, to get *close* to him. But she'd just gotten here, and it was obvious that her presence flustered him.

The thought of it sent a satisfying surge through her veins. That must be what Honey felt like, to know the sort of power she wielded over people. Nova even dared a small, teasing smile, and thought Honey might have been proud.

She took a step closer to Adrian. "Are you not allowed to have girls in your room?"

He chuckled. Then he took a step back, though it was subtle. "Wouldn't know. I've never had one."

Nova flushed, that moment of confidence gone as quickly as it had come. "Well. I trust you not to try anything . . . *inappropriate*."

He chuckled, but it was as awkward as Nova felt, and Nova was suddenly reminded of all the times she'd practically thrown herself at him these past weeks, and how he'd ignored every one of her advances.

She tucked her hands into her pockets. She would wait until they were sitting down. It would be easier to find an excuse to touch him then. It would be easier to be bold when she wasn't looking him in the eye.

Adrian grabbed the remote and the TV flickered to life. Nova started to pace around the room. It was a lot more casual than the house above. His bed; the blankets tussled and half draped across the floor; a small, worn couch; a painting easel and a desk; the entertainment center; and a bookshelf in the corner overflowing with comics, drawing guides, and an assortment of sketchbooks. A handful of drawings and video game posters were tacked to the walls.

"This whole huge house, and they make you sleep in the basement?"

"It was better than one of the upstairs rooms. That's where the murders happened." He glanced at her. "You know about the murders?"

"I read about them. On the plaque." *And I'm pretty sure Ace was here that night.*

Adrian nodded. "Besides, this way I get twelve hundred square feet to myself."

"This," said Nova, gesturing, "is not twelve hundred square feet."

Adrian pointed at a door. "Bathroom through there, then a bunch of unfinished basement space. And"—he gestured at a second door on the far wall—"that's my art studio."

"You have an *art studio*?"

"It's a big house."

"Can I see it?"

Adrian opened his mouth, but shut it again, hesitant.

"What?" said Nova. "Have you been practicing nude portraits or something?"

He cringed. "Nothing that scandalous."

"Then what?"

He sighed. "Okay. This might be weird. I hope it's not weird, but it might be." He cleared his throat. "Remember that dream you told me about? With the ruins, and the statue at the park?"

Nova blinked. "Yeah . . . ?"

"So, I had this idea, and I got really inspired, and . . . I thought it might be neat to . . ."

He trailed off.

Nova waited.

"To . . . create it?"

She continued to wait, but Adrian had nothing more to offer.

"I'm not following."

"I know." He set the tray of untouched cinnamon rolls down on the table. "It's hard to explain. Come on. Just—if it turns out this is more creepy than artistically flattering, blame it on sleep deprivation, okay?" He hesitated, then sent her a chagrined look. "Not that you know much about that."

She smiled. "I'm familiar with the concept," she said, as intrigued by how uncomfortable Adrian had become as by the mystery in the next room.

He cleared his throat and opened the door to his studio. Nova followed him inside.

Her feet stumbled. She caught herself on the door.

"Sweet rot," she whispered.

A jungle greeted her. Towering trees and lush greenery had been painted on every inch of every wall, the ceiling, the floor. Though the room smelled of toxic paint and clearly received little ventilation, the mural was so detailed and lush that Nova almost imagined she could smell exotic flowers and warm breeze instead.

Adrian stood in the center of the room. His expression was critical as he inspected his work. "I'm not really sure where the impulse came from, but . . . once I had the idea, it felt like something I had to do. The way you described that dream really inspired me, I guess. I've been working on it in my spare time."

Nova forced herself away from the door. Noticing that the back of the door itself had been painted, too, even down to the doorknob, she shut it to complete the vision. She felt dizzy as she drifted from wall to wall, but she knew it wasn't from the paint fumes.

Her fingers traced the painting as she went. Mostly there were plants. Exotic purple flowers spreading their giant petals like wind sails. Ancient gnarled tree trunks covered in fungi and moss, with long, looping vines trailing from their branches. Grasses and ferns sprouting from between the trees' uneven roots, their lacy fronds bowing over little clusters of white star-shaped blossoms and fiery orange buds. A toppled tree trunk formed a lichen-covered bridge over a family of broad-leafed shrubs.

But it wasn't just a jungle. Adrian had included hints of the ruins too. The city that the jungle had claimed. What might have been a boulder was, upon closer inspection, the corner of a building's concrete foundation. Those ascending plateaus of plant life were thriving on an ancient staircase. Beyond those trees—the subtle arch of a doorway, leading to nothing. The beams of sunlight that filtered through the thick canopy struck the hooded torso of a long forgotten statue, its back to them, concealing what treasure might have been cradled in its hands. A startling memory of her dream came back to her. *It was holding a star.*

"Adrian," she whispered, afraid to break the spell of this place, "this is amazing."

"Did I get it right? From the dream?"

"You . . . *yes.* It's exactly . . ." She realized with a start that her eyes were watering. She turned away, pressing a hand to her mouth to collect herself. As her shaking breaths evened, she dared to face him again. "You didn't do this for me . . . did you?"

Adrian glanced sideways at the statue. "No . . . ," he began. "Although, I didn't *not* do it for you either. If that makes sense. I mean, I had to do it for me too." He shrugged. "It just seemed like a really good idea at the time."

"It was a good idea. This is . . . magical."

Adrian started to grin, and Nova braced herself. She had become familiar with that particular look. The one that said he was about to do something that would impress her, whether she liked it or not.

"I guess I figured you deserve to have good dreams once in a while," he said. "Even if you never sleep."

Then he pressed his hand against the nearest wall and exhaled.

The mural started to come alive, emerging around his fingers. Fronds unfolded, engulfing his wrist, and the effect spread like the ripple in a pond, outward across the wall. Tree trunks sprouted from the concrete. Grasses curled against their knees. Lazy vines trailed over their heads.

Nova moved closer to him, pressing her side against his. The hard ground under their feet transformed into squishy moss. Flowers bloomed. Mushrooms sprouted. The smell of paint was replaced with the earthiness of dark soil and a heady perfume. Though Nova hadn't seen any birds or insects in the painting, it was easy to imagine birdsong disrupting the silence. The hum of cicadas, the clicking of beetles.

The tree canopy crowded in overhead, but sunlight was filtering down, spotlighting the statue.

Adrian lowered his hand. Nova stared at where he had touched and could no longer see the wall. Was it buried behind the panel of foliage? Were they still in his basement? The plants were so dense, the air so humid and sweet, it was almost impossible to imagine they were inside at all.

Adrian shuffled his feet and Nova realized he'd been watching her, but she couldn't strike the disbelief from her face.

"Cool trick?" he ventured.

Nova's heart thumped loudly.

"All of this," she said, speaking slowly, "and the best alias you could come up with was *Sketch*?"

His lips curled upward, and it was clear how much this small comment pleased him. "Better to under-promise and over-deliver."

"Well, you succeeded." Her cheeks were warm as she turned in a slow circle. "Where did the room go? Where are we?"

"We haven't left. If you pull some of these leaves aside, you'll be able to see the walls, but they'll be plain white again. I made sure to cover them with paint so they wouldn't be visible when you were standing in the middle like this." He gestured around at their mystical patch of jungle. "You can walk around, if you want. Nothing here will hurt you."

Nova kept her hands close to her body, in part to avoid taking Adrian's hand. She couldn't imagine putting him to sleep *now*, and without that singular purpose, the thought of touching him terrified her.

She paced herself, reveling in every step. Her fingers danced along each flower petal, glided across the blades of willowy grass, twined around a series of low-hung vines. It was uncanny how much it reminded her of the dream, or what she could remember of it. She was sure she hadn't gone into that much detail when she described it to Adrian, yet he'd captured it down to the smallest element.

She paused as her attention landed on the statue. It was turned away, so she could see only the back of its hooded cloak, its narrow stone shoulders green with moss, patches of stone having chipped off with age.

Nova dared to approach it, feeling the squishy ground give beneath her footsteps. She braced herself as she walked around the statue. Its outstretched hands came into view.

Her breath hitched, even though, somehow, she had expected it.

She could feel Adrian watching her, and she wondered if he knew. If this had been a part of his plan as he'd painted the mural.

"How?" she whispered.

To his credit, Adrian frowned in confusion. "How what?"

"Adrian . . . how did you make a *star*?"

# CHAPTER THIRTY

"Huh," said Adrian, coming to stand beside her. "Would you look at that."

He sounded as astonished as Nova felt, but that couldn't be. This was her dream, but it was *his* painting. His vision. His magic.

His star?

Nova frowned.

It *was* a star too. At least, she thought it must be. A single bright orb hovering between the figure's grasping hands. It was no larger than a marble, and no more difficult to stare at than the brightest star in the night sky. Its light subtly illuminated the fantastical world around them.

It was magnificent, and it was exactly like Nova's dream. As a child, in her delirious subconscious state, she had known it was a star, and she felt it just as strongly now, though everything she knew about astrophysics told her it wasn't possible.

But then, a lot of what Adrian could do didn't seem possible.

*A star.*

Neither she nor Adrian spoke for a long time. The room was silent, but there was something about the jungle he had created—*the jungle*, Nova thought with bewilderment, *the jungle he created*—that gave the impression of life and noise, of warmth and growth, of thriving permanence.

Finally, Adrian cleared his throat. "That wasn't in the mural."

"I know," said Nova, remembering the statue in the painting, and how Adrian had drawn it so that they could only see its back, not its hands. After another thoughtful moment, she said, "Intention?"

"Maybe," said Adrian. "I was thinking about your dream when I did it."

"What does it do?" said Nova, which might have been a strange question. What did any star do?

But Adrian merely shrugged. "It's your star. You tell me."

She bit the inside of her cheek. Was it her star?

"I don't know. I woke up before anything happened."

A part of Nova wanted to reach out and touch it. The star emanated a comforting warmth, and she didn't think it would burn her, like a real sun out in the real universe. But she was worried that she would ruin the spell if she touched it. Maybe it would fade away. Or, perhaps worse, maybe nothing would happen at all. She didn't know which of them was more responsible for dreaming this star into existence—her or Adrian—and she didn't want to tempt disappointment by finding it was nothing more than a pretty visual effect.

She breathed in the aroma of dew-soaked leaves and intoxicating flowers. Shutting her eyes, Nova sank down, sitting cross-legged on the soft moss. It was easy to fall into the tranquility of this place. To believe this was the real world, hundreds of years in the future. The city had fallen, and there were no more villains and no more superheroes. No more Anarchists, no more Renegades, no more Council. No more struggles for power.

Just, no more.

She opened her eyes as Adrian lowered himself to the ground beside her, a little stiffly, she noticed, as he tried not to bend around the wound on his side.

"Is it terrible," she said, "that it might take the fall of humanity to make me feel this relaxed?"

It took Adrian a moment to respond, but he sounded serious when he said, "A little."

Nova laughed, a real one this time. He chuckled too.

"Why?" he asked. "Why is it so hard to relax?"

She dared to look at him. She knew he wasn't prying, and that he wouldn't push her, despite his curiosity.

She braced herself.

She thought it would be hard to form the words, but it wasn't. Not really. They'd been perched in the back of her throat for ten years, waiting for her to speak them. She thought back to the first night she had sat and talked with Adrian, really *talked* to him, when they were running surveillance on Gene Cronin and the Cloven Cross Library. She hadn't told Adrian about her family then. She hadn't confessed her complete origin story. But somehow, she felt like she'd always known that she would tell him, eventually.

"When I was six years old, I once fell asleep holding my baby sister. Evie." Her voice was low, barely a murmur. "When I woke up, I could hear my mother crying. I went to our door and I looked out into the hallway and a man was there, holding a gun. I later found out my dad was being blackmailed by one of the villain gangs, and when he didn't fulfill part of their bargain, they hired this guy to . . . punish him." She frowned, her gaze lost in the shadows between ferns and fallen tree trunks, her memory trapped in that apartment. She scrunched her shoulders against her neck, once again paralyzed with fear. "He shot my mom," she whispered, "and then he shot my dad. I watched it happen."

Adrian's hand twitched, drawing her focus out of the shadows and down to his graceful fingers, his dark skin. He didn't reach for her, though she thought he would hold her hand if she moved first.

She didn't.

"I ran to my bedroom and hid in the closet. I heard him come inside, and . . . then I heard . . ." Tears began to fill her eyes. "I heard Evie. She woke up and she started to cry, and . . . and he shot her too."

Adrian jerked involuntarily, a flinch that shuddered through his whole body.

"She wasn't even a year old yet. And when he found me in the closet, I looked in his eyes and I could tell, I could just tell that he didn't feel an ounce of remorse. He'd just murdered a *baby*, and he didn't feel anything."

This time, Adrian did reach for her hand, slipping his fingers between hers.

"He aimed the gun at me, and . . ."

Nova hesitated, realizing at the last moment that she couldn't tell Adrian this part of the story. The shock of being on the verge of speaking an unspeakable secret startled her from the memory.

"And my uncle showed up," she said, swiping at her nose with her sleeve. "He killed the man. He saved me."

Adrian's shoulders fell. He cursed quietly beneath his breath.

Nova lowered her head. The pain that came with the memories was coupled with guilt. She had relived that night countless times in her thoughts, all the while knowing—she could have stopped it. If she had been brave. If she hadn't run. If she hadn't hid.

She could have put the man to sleep. Saved Evie, at least, if not her parents.

But she'd been a coward, and . . .

And she'd been so sure. *So sure* that the Renegades would come. It was her faith in them that had destroyed her family, almost as much as the hitman himself.

"After that, every time I closed my eyes, I would hear those gunshots in my head. I couldn't sleep. After a while, I stopped trying."

Even recently, when she had briefly fallen asleep inside Max's quarantine, the nightmare had plagued her. The hitman looming over her. The cold press of the gun to her forehead. The gunshots echoing through her skull.

*BANG BANG-BANG!*

She shuddered.

Adrian rubbed the back of his neck with his free hand. "Nova," he whispered, shaking his head. "I'm so sorry. I knew they were killed during the Age of Anarchy, but I never thought—"

"That I witnessed it? I know. It wasn't something I thought belonged in my Renegades application."

He nodded in understanding, his expression heavy with sorrow.

And though telling the story brought her sadness, it also brought anger. The resentment that had crowded out her own sorrow for the last ten years.

*Where were the Renegades?* She wanted to shout. *Where was the Council? Where were your dads?*

She clenched her teeth and peered down at their entwined hands. His was warm and solid, while her hand had gone limp.

"My mom was murdered too," he whispered.

She swallowed. "I know." Everyone knew. Lady Indomitable had been as much a legend as any superhero.

"I didn't see it happen, of course. No child should have to go through that. But I did"—his brow scrunched in pain as he spoke— "for a long time, I wondered if maybe it was my fault. At least, in part."

She jerked, startled at how his words mirrored her own guilt. "How could it have been your fault?"

"I don't know. It doesn't make sense, but . . ." He grimaced. "Remember how I said I used to have really vivid nightmares? The ones with the monster? Well, part of that recurring dream I had was where my mom would leave our apartment, flying out through the window to go save the day somewhere in the city, and I would be watching her go, when . . . this shadow would come over her and she wouldn't be able to fly anymore. I would watch her fall. I would hear her scream. And I would look up and the monster would be on the rooftop, just . . . staring at me."

Nova shivered.

"I had that dream more times than I could count. It got to where I would throw tantrums every time my mom put on her costume. I didn't want her to go. I was so terrified that she wouldn't come back. And then, one night, she didn't." He met Nova's gaze. "When they found her body, it was clear the fall had killed her, and there was a look of . . . of terror on her face. For a long time I thought that my dreams had made it come true. Like maybe they were prophetic or something."

"It wasn't your fault," said Nova, squeezing his hand. "They were dreams, Adrian. It was just a coincidence."

"I know," he said, though Nova wasn't sure if she believed him, or if he believed himself. "But she could *fly*. How could she have fallen so far without being able to . . ." He lowered his head. "No villain ever took credit for her death, as far as I know. Which is unlike them—a lot of the villain gangs liked to brag about their victories.

And killing Lady Indomitable . . . that would have been a victory worth bragging about." His voice turned sour, and it was clear that this mystery had haunted and frustrated him nearly as long as Nova's past had tormented her.

"You want to find out who did it," she said slowly, "so you can have revenge."

"Not revenge," said Adrian. "Justice."

She shivered. He said it with conviction, though she wasn't sure he would recognize the difference in his own heart.

And what of her own heart, she wondered.

Did she want revenge against the Council, or justice?

Her whole body felt heavy thinking about it.

This wasn't for her. This moment of peace. This sense of safety. This world with no heroes and no villains, where she and Adrian Everhart could sit holding hands inside a childhood dream.

This world didn't exist.

Rubbing his forehead, Adrian let out a sigh. "I'm sorry. *This*," he said, gesturing around, "is supposed to be a dream, not a nightmare."

A faint smile twitched at the sides of her mouth. "It is a dream, Adrian. The first I've had in a long time."

His eyes shone at her words. Then he fished his marker from his jeans pocket and glanced around. "I have an idea," he said, turning to a crumbling stone wall. He began to sketch. It amazed Nova that he could create something real and tangible out of nothing. He could go on like this forever, creating a dream within a dream within a dream.

He drew a set of large headphones and pulled them from the stone. He held them out to Nova. "Noise-canceling headphones," he explained. "Not even gunshots can get through." He nudged her shoulder with the headband.

Nose wrinkling with doubt, Nova took the headphones and

slipped the padded cuffs over her ears. Instantly the world, which had already been quiet, dimmed to impenetrable silence, fed only by the thundering of her own pulse, the drum of her own heartbeat.

Adrian's lips moved. A question, she thought, but Nova shook her head at him.

Adrian grinned. He lay down, extending his arm over the patch of moss. An invitation.

Nova hesitated for far less time than she should have, then sank down and settled her head into the crook between his shoulder and his chest. It took a moment for her to get comfortable with the headphones on, but when she did, she realized that there were two heartbeats now drumming against each other. Though the aromas from the jungle had filled the room, this close to Adrian she could smell the chemical tang of paint mixed with an undercurrent of pine-scented soap.

Her attention landed on the star. It never dimmed. Never brightened. Never changed at all. Just hovered, peaceful and constant.

And this boy, this amazing boy, had made all of this.

She remembered why she had come there that night. To find the Vitality Charm. To protect herself in the upcoming fight with Agent N. To fulfill her duty.

It could wait. Just one more hour. Maybe two. Then she would put Adrian to sleep and she would continue with her plan.

For now, in this strange, impossible dream, it could wait.

Steadily, slowly, their heartbeats fell into sync. Nova listened to them thumping in tandem for what might have been an eternity. She was still staring at the star when, unexpectedly, it winked out and Nova fell into a quiet, dreamless sleep.

# CHAPTER THIRTY-ONE

S HE AWOKE TO THE SOUND of birds. In that hazy place between sleeping and waking, it seemed entirely normal that the city's cooing pigeons and squawking crows had been exchanged for the trill and chatter of far more exotic creatures.

The tranquility lasted for only a moment. Eyes snapping open, Nova jolted upward, one hand sinking into moss and the other landing on a discarded pair of headphones. A blanket tumbled around her hips.

"Great skies," said Adrian. He sat a few feet away, his back against the statue. A large sketchbook rested beside him, a pencil settled in its gutter. From her vantage point she could make out an upside-down, half-completed toucan.

He smiled. "For someone who never, ever, *ever* sleeps, you sleep like a pro when you want to."

Nova palmed her eyes, trying to rub away her drowsiness. "Time is it?"

"Almost five," he said. "*At night.* You've been sleeping for nearly twenty-four hours straight. Which, by my estimate, still means you're nowhere near caught up." His expression turned serious, that little wrinkle forming over the bridge of his glasses. "I tried calling the number in your file, to let your uncle know where you are, but it said it's been disconnected. Is there another number I should try? He must be worried."

She blinked at him in bewilderment, unable at first to distinguish between the pretend "uncle" mentioned in her official paperwork and Ace. Her head felt like it was filled with fog and she wondered if everyone woke up this . . . this *groggy*. That was the word for it, right? *Groggy?*

How did people stand it?

"No, it's fine," she said, shaking her head. "He's used to me disappearing at night and not coming back for days. Hard to be cooped up inside while everyone else is sleeping. Plus, now, with patrol duty . . ." She raked her fingers through her hair, working out a few snags. "Anyway, I'll . . . uh . . . check my file. The number probably got entered wrong." She rubbed her lashes again and was surprised to find flecks of white caught in them. "Have I really been sleeping for . . ." She froze, a sting of panic coursing through her limbs. "Do you think it's because of Max? Is this some sort of aftereffect?"

"What, we can't give credit to my magically efficient, noise-canceling headphones?"

Nova frowned, even as her fingers fell on the headset.

But then she realized he was joking. "Actually, the thought crossed my mind too. It could be related. Max mentioned having some mild insomnia since you were in the quarantine that day. We know he got a small portion of your power. So maybe now you're *capable* of sleeping, but you can sleep by choice, not out of necessity? Or maybe the . . . conditions have to be right." He cast a wistful look at the headphones.

Nova curled her fingers around them. Even now, all these years later, she could hear the gunshots inside her head, deafeningly loud. She wasn't convinced that a set of headphones would allow her mind to rest, after ten years of terrors.

Or perhaps it didn't have much to do with the headphones at all. She flushed, remembering how it had felt to lay her head against Adrian's chest. To listen to his heartbeat. There had been a feeling she couldn't recall having experienced since she was a child.

The uncanny sensation of being *safe*.

Adrian was watching her, his expression serious. "It's all right, Nova," he said, leaning toward her. "It's been weeks since you came in contact with Max, and this is the first time you've slept since then. I'm ninety-nine percent sure that still makes you a prodigy."

She blinked, realizing how drastically Adrian had misinterpreted whatever he was seeing on her face. He thought she was worried about her powers, but that was a long way from the truth. She knew her true power—Nightmare's ability to put people to sleep—was intact. She wasn't afraid of that.

No, what she feared was something far, far worse, and had much more to do with the way she had sunk so easily into oblivion while in the arms of Adrian Everhart.

She was afraid, even now, of the way her fingers were twitching to reach out and touch him, when she never felt compelled to touch *anyone*, unless it was to disarm them.

And she might have been terrified of how hard it was to keep her gaze from straying to his mouth, or how her own traitorous lips had started to tingle, or how her own heartbeat had become an entire percussion section inside her chest.

Adrian's eyes narrowed, just slightly. "What's wrong?" he asked. A little suspicious, a little uncertain.

"Nothing," she whispered.

*Everything*, her mind retorted.

What was she here for?

Not to sleep. Not to tell Adrian all the secrets she'd kept locked up her entire life. Not to be reminded for the umpteenth time how things might be different, if only . . .

Well. If only things were different.

*What was she doing here?*

Her gaze darted up to the boughs of the surrounding trees, where she spotted an all-white parrot. "The birds are new," she said, eager to change the subject. To think about something else, before her mind tracked to kissing again.

Adrian didn't respond for a moment, and she desperately wanted to know what was going through his head.

Had he thought about kissing too?

Her fingers curled around the blanket that had been tucked around her while she slept. *Twenty-four hours.* He must have been awake for ages now. How long had he been sitting there while she slept? Had he been watching her? And why was it that the possibility normally would have been annoying, if not downright creepy, but now all it did was make her worry that she might have said something incriminating in her sleep? Or, worse . . . drooled.

No. No, that wasn't worse. She mentally shook herself, telling her thoughts to get themselves in order.

This was why sleep was dangerous. It addled her senses, and she needed to be on full alert. It made her vulnerable, regardless of how safe she had felt in Adrian's arms.

"It felt like it needed wildlife," said Adrian, "and I had some free time. And now I know that I can only draw so many parrots before losing interest."

She shook her head warily. If Callum ever got ahold of Adrian's sketchbooks, he would be beside himself. "You're incredible, you know that, right? I mean . . . you can create *life*. First that dinosaur, and now an entire ecosystem?"

Adrian laughed, and though his skin was too dark to be sure, she was almost certain he was blushing. "I don't think of it like that. I can create . . . the illusion of life." He tracked the blue wings of a bird as it hopped across the canopy overhead. "I have a vague idea of how birds fly, and I know they eat bugs, and if they were chased by a falcon they would run away. But they'll never learn or grow beyond what they are now. They won't build nests or hatch eggs. They're more like . . . like automatons, than real birds."

Nova peered at him and tried to feel like his humble comments were warranted, but she knew he was underselling himself.

Typical Adrian.

Before she could respond, someone shouted from what seemed like miles away—

"Adrian! Dinner's done!"

Nova tensed, surveying their jungle sanctuary.

She had forgotten, completely forgotten they were indoors at all, and not in the overgrown ruins of a long-dead city.

They were at his house. His *mansion*. The one he shared with the Dread Warden and Captain Chromium.

*And his dads were here.*

Adrian, too, seemed momentarily shaken. "Right," he said, closing the sketchbook over the pencil. "Are you hungry?"

Her lips parted. Suddenly her breaths were coming in short, uncomfortable bursts.

Dinner. An everyday family dinner.

With *them*.

Shutting her mouth again, she forced herself to nod. "Yeah. Actually, I'm famished."

"Me too." Adrian stood and offered a hand, which she pretended not to notice as she pulled herself up using the crumbled stone wall. She wasn't ready to touch him again. She didn't want to know how much she would enjoy it.

By the time she turned back, his hand had slipped into his pocket. In addition to the long-sleeved tee, he had changed out of his jeans into gray sweatpants, and there was something so intimate and relaxed about it that she almost found him even more handsome this way.

And he was handsome.

She'd noticed it before. A million different times, it seemed. The high cut of his cheekbones. The full lips that so easily gave way to that subtle smile. Even the glasses, thickly framing his dark eyes, added an air of ease and sensitivity to his features that made her mouth run dry when she stopped to think about it.

She was beginning to think she might really be in trouble.

She followed Adrian through the lush foliage and drooping vines. He pushed aside the leaves of some prehistoric-looking plant, and there was a plain wooden door set into a plain white wall.

Nova glanced back one time, wishing she had taken the time to admire the statue, and the star—what she was beginning to think of as *her* star—before she crossed over the door's threshold and returned to reality.

# CHAPTER THIRTY-TWO

NOVA FOLLOWED ADRIAN out of the basement and back up the narrow staircase, her mind churning as she tried to determine the likelihood of this being a trap.

Not much, she thought. She had been asleep for an entire night and day, and as uncomfortable as that made her, she had to admit that nothing had happened. She had not been attacked or captured.

And yet, her hackles wouldn't lower, not completely. There was always a chance. A chance that Winston had finally revealed Nova's identity, or that some incriminating evidence had been dredged up on her while she slept. Twenty-four hours was more than enough time for something to go wrong.

Adrian nudged open the door at the top of the stairs and Nova braced herself as she stepped into the imposing foyer again. The mansion, though, seemed as quiet and orderly as before.

She followed Adrian into a formal dining room, with wainscoting on the walls and a crystal chandelier dangling over a cherry wood table, which was large enough to seat twelve or more. Rather than being set with fine china and silver cutlery, the table was littered with newspapers, many still wrapped in rubber bands, and piles of junk mail, and two issues of *Heroes Today* magazine.

Adrian nudged his way through another door and the sounds of life engulfed Nova. Dishes clinking. A fan whirring. The steady beat of a knife against a cutting board.

The moment she stepped into the open-concept kitchen, her eyes darted not to the two men who were cooking, but to the large arched windows surrounding a casual breakfast nook, and a door that might have led to an exit . . . or maybe a pantry. To the block of kitchen knives on the granite countertop, and the cast-iron skillet simmering on the stove, and the row of bar stools that would shatter against Captain Chromium, but might be able to stun the Dread Warden if swung with sufficient force.

Once she had mapped out all possible exits and deduced enough potential weapons that she could feel confident she wasn't powerless, not even here, she dared to greet her hosts.

Hugh Everhart extended a hand toward her, the other clutching a wooden spoon. "Nova, it was a nice surprise to hear you'd be joining us."

She held her breath as she shook his hand, wondering first if her power would work against the invincible Captain Chromium.

Wondering second at what point Adrian had come up to inform his dads he had a guest. Was that before or after she had unofficially stayed the night?

Hugh gestured toward the bar, where Simon Westwood was chopping carrots into thin sticks.

"It's just about done," said Hugh, "but feel free to grab a snack while you wait."

Simon nudged a plate in her direction, loaded with cherry tomatoes and strips of raw bell pepper. Nova's attention, however, went to the massive chef's knife in his hand. Then she took in his blue-checkered apron, which was so opposite of anything she'd ever imagined the Dread Warden would wear that for a moment she thought she might be dreaming. This was what dreams were like, right? Ridiculous and absurd and utterly implausible?

When she thought of these two superheroes, she always pictured them in the midst of a battle, usually one in which she was discovering some clever way to kill them both at once. Never had she pictured them at home, doing something as mundane as cooking dinner together.

"Adrian," said Hugh, dumping the carrots onto the tray, "could you run down and grab another can of tomatoes from the pantry?"

"Sure," said Adrian. Picking up a carrot stick, he crunched it in half as he pushed himself away from the bar. He shot Nova a quick, encouraging smile before he disappeared back through the door.

"The pantry is at the far end of the hall," Simon said, arranging the vegetables on the plate. It took Nova a moment to realize he was talking to her. "Kind of a pain when you forget something halfway through a recipe. We keep meaning to clean out the broom closet"—he jutted his chin toward a narrow closed door—"and convert it into the new pantry, but somehow it always gets filled back up with superhero stuff."

Nova's thoughts were racing so fast she could barely understand him. Pantry? Canned tomatoes?

She tried to relax her shoulders. To even her breathing. To admit to herself that an attack was not imminent.

But she took a subtle side step to be closer to the block of knives, anyway. Just in case.

"I'm afraid this meal isn't going to be up to our usual standards, at least for when we have a special guest," said Hugh. He was standing over the stove, stirring a bubbling red sauce. "But it's been a long day for us both, and we weren't expecting to come home to company." He looked sideways at Nova, his eyes twinkling almost mischievously.

"I wasn't expecting to be served a homemade meal at all," Nova said, her attention skipping from the tomato sauce to the colander of steaming spaghetti noodles in the sink to a skillet full of cooked ground beef.

"I hope you like Italian," said Hugh. "You're not vegetarian, are you?"

She shook her head and watched as he scraped the meat into the sauce.

"I love Italian food," she said, trying to match their unprecedented normalcy. "My dad was Italian, and my mom used to cook pasta for us all the time because he liked it so much. It was never her specialty, though. Not as good as her lumpia."

"Oh, I love lumpia," said Hugh, more enthusiastically than the comment warranted.

Nova bit the inside of her cheek, almost willing him to read her thoughts. *My dad, my mom—who aren't here anymore. Who believed so strongly that you would come, that you would protect them. Who taught* me *to believe you would protect us.*

But Hugh just went on stirring the pot, his expression serene.

"Where did McLain come from?" said Simon, startling her. "If your dad was Italian."

Her heart hammered. She'd forgotten. She was not Nova Artino, not here. She was Nova Jean McLain. "Uh . . . my . . . grandfather," she stammered. "Paternal grandfather. He was Scottish, but . . . lived in Italy. For a while."

Simon made a noise of mild interest. A polite noise. A noise for trivial small talk.

Had she fooled them? Or were they trying to lure her off her guard?

Despite how cheerful they were both acting, she could see that Hugh had bruise-tinged shadows beneath his eyes and the start of stubble on his usually clean-shaven jaw. Simon, too, seemed less spirited than usual.

"Are you both okay?" she said.

Simon chuckled and he and Hugh shared a commiserating look. "Adrian told us you slept for a long time last night," he said, sweeping the carrot tops into his palm and dumping them into the sink on the other side of the bar. "I suppose he didn't tell you the news?"

"News?"

The door behind her swung open and Adrian emerged, holding a can of diced tomatoes like a trophy. "Mission accomplished."

"Thanks, Adrian," said Hugh, taking the can from Adrian. Instead of using a can opener, he dug his fingernails into the edge of the can and peeled back the aluminum top. He dumped the contents into the sauce. "Simon was just telling Nova about the Sentinel."

She and Adrian both stilled.

"The Sentinel?" she asked.

"Yep," Simon said darkly. "He's alive."

Adrian scowled. It surprised Nova. For all the times he'd heard *her* complain about the Sentinel, he'd never said anything negative about the vigilante himself. At least, not that she could recall. She'd had a sneaking suspicion that he sort of admired the guy.

"Right," said Adrian. "I guess I should have mentioned something. It's all over the news right now."

Nova blinked at him. His tone was odd—evasive.

Simon slid off his stool and came around the bar, passing in front of Nova. She caught sight of the knife in his hand and every muscle tightened. She clawed her fingers, targeting the exact patch of skin she would use to knock him unconscious.

He grabbed a towel from the counter and started to wipe off the blade.

"Excuse me," he said, turning back to her.

Nova started in surprise. "Right, sorry," she said, easing away from him.

He dropped the knife into the block with the others.

She tried to disentangle the knot in her stomach, irritated with her own overreaction. "So . . . how do we know he's alive?"

"He had a run-in with one of our patrol units. Do you know Frostbite and her team?" Simon caught himself and chuckled, but without much humor. "Of course you do. The trials. Anyway— they were sent after Hawthorn. We finally had some solid leads about where to find her, and . . . well. They found her." A muscle twitched beneath his beard.

"And?" said Nova.

"They got there in time to see the Sentinel torturing her— crushing some of her limbs."

Nova reeled back. *"What?"*

Beside her, Adrian picked up a carrot stick and jabbed it hard into a bowl of dip.

"When he realized the Renegades were there, he murdered Hawthorn, right before their eyes. Then he attacked them."

Nova peered at Adrian, in part for confirmation, but he was glowering at the counter.

"Let me guess," she said. "He got away. Again."

"It's one more reminder that he is not to be underestimated," said Simon.

Nova exhaled. "But why would he attack Hawthorn like that?

Why not tie her up and leave her for the Renegades, like all those criminals he's caught before?"

"We think it might have been a revenge killing," said Hugh. "Because she embarrassed him on that barge."

"Are we sure we can take Frostbite's word for all of this?" said Adrian, snapping another carrot between his fingers. "It seems a little far-fetched if you ask me."

"We've recovered Hawthorn's body," said Simon. "We've seen the destruction from the battle with the Sentinel. The story checks out."

Adrian opened his mouth to say something more, but hesitated. Still glaring, he chomped down on the carrot.

Nova crossed her arms over her chest. The Sentinel being alive drummed up a whole parade of feelings she'd forgotten about since she'd watched him sink in the river. He had been determined to find Nightmare. More determined than anyone.

Hopefully he believed she was dead as much as the Renegades did.

They carried the food to a breakfast nook. Nova let Adrian sit down first before sliding in beside him, so she wouldn't be trapped against the wall. But even that small bit of strategy made her feel just a little ridiculous and she was beginning to forget why she had been so concerned before.

She had slept under this roof for hours. *Twenty-four hours.* And nothing had happened to her. They did not know she was Nightmare. They did not know she was an Anarchist, or Ace's niece. To them, she was a Renegade, through and through.

*What was she doing here?*

Ace was wasting away in his catacombs and she was having dinner with his enemies.

For a short time, she'd felt comfortable. Safe, even. She'd been swept away by a mural and a dream. She'd imagined what it might be like to touch Adrian again, maybe even to kiss him. She'd admired *his glasses,* for all that was trite and pathetic.

But none of that was why she was here.

She should probably congratulate herself. She had started this charade intending to spend a few weeks inside headquarters and learn what she could from her fellow drones, but instead, here she was. In the private home of her two biggest targets. They trusted her. Maybe even liked her.

She paused.

Did they like her?

She scowled at the tongs as Hugh lifted spaghetti onto her plate, forcing herself not to be curious, not to care. She could use this to her advantage. All of it. Their trust, their unguarded routine. This was her chance to needle information from them. She couldn't waste it.

"So," said Adrian, taking a sip of water, "did the big crime scene at the shipyard turn up new evidence about the Sentinel? Do we have any clues about his identity yet?"

"They're still going over it," said Hugh. "So far, I think the only solid clue we have is that he just might be the most overconfident prodigy this city has ever seen."

Simon laughed. "The most overconfident? Surely no one can surpass you in that regard."

Hugh grinned. To Nova's surprise, he looked at *her* when he said, "They're always giving me a tough time, but they don't know how hard it is to be this charming. It takes real dedication."

Not sure what to say, Nova smiled back and shoveled a forkful of pasta into her mouth.

Adrian broke into a loaf of bread, releasing a cloud of steam.

His expression was distant as he said, "It seems to me like he's been trying to help people. What about what *you* guys did, back in the Age of Anarchy?"

Hugh and Simon both tensed and Nova sensed this was not the first time they'd had this conversation.

"There were no rules to follow back then," said Simon. "The code authority didn't exist. We did what we had to do to stop the villains who were running the city. But imagine if we still operated that way. If every prodigy out there went around doing whatever they wanted, whenever they wanted, all in the name of justice. It wouldn't take long for everything to fall apart. Society simply doesn't function that way, and neither can we."

Nova bit the inside of her cheek. She agreed on some level— society did need rules and consequences.

But who had elected the Council to make those rules?

Who got to decide what punishments should be doled out for breaking them?

"We know there's been a lot of controversy over the Sentinel's actions," said Hugh. "Good or bad, helpful or harmful. But the fight at the shipyard shows that he's not . . . entirely stable. He needs to be found and stopped."

"Neutralized, you mean," Adrian said, his jaw tight.

"If it comes to that," said Hugh. "The rise of the Sentinel is a good example of how important it is to keep the prodigy population under control. We need to ensure that the villains of this world will never be able to rise to power again. I know there's some . . . uncertainty about Agent N going around the ranks, but we can't have prodigies wielding their power without any restrictions."

"Speaking of, you know who that Sentinel guy reminds me of?"

said Simon, and Nova had the distinct impression he was changing the subject to avoid an argument. He gestured toward Adrian with his fork and Adrian sucked in a quick breath. "That comic you wrote when you were a kid. What was it called? Rebel X? Rebel . . ."

"Rebel Z!" said Hugh, his expression brightening. "I'd forgotten all about that. You're right, the Sentinel does sort of look like him, doesn't it?"

Adrian's fork hung a few inches from his mouth. "You know about that?"

"Of course we do. There was that one summer when you hardly worked on anything else."

"Yeah, but . . . I didn't think you'd actually seen it. I . . . I'm pretty sure I never showed anyone . . ."

Hugh and Simon had the decency to appear embarrassed. Hugh shrugged. "We may have peeked through them when you weren't looking. We couldn't help it! You were so focused and you wouldn't tell us anything. We were dying to know what it was."

"And they were great!" Simon said, as if his enthusiasm would soothe over the little issue of privacy invasion. "Did you ever finish them?"

Adrian lowered his fork and twirled it through the spaghetti again, his shoulders tight. "I got through three issues, then lost interest. It definitely *wasn't* great. I'm surprised you even remember it."

"I thought it was fantastic," said Simon.

"I was eleven, and you're my dad. You have to say that."

"I always wondered if Rebel Z might have been partly inspired by yours truly," Hugh said with a wink.

"He wasn't," Adrian deadpanned.

"Ah, well. Can't blame your old man for hoping."

"What are we talking about?" Nova interjected.

"Nothing," said Adrian, at the same time Simon answered, "A

comic book Adrian started years ago. About this superhero who had . . . some sort of biological tampering done, wasn't it?"

Heaving a sigh, Adrian explained, without much zeal, "It was about a group of twenty-six kids who were abducted by an evil scientist and subjected to a bunch of tests trying to turn them into prodigies, but only the twenty-sixth kid survived the testing. He turned himself into a superhero and made it his mission to seek revenge against the scientist and all his cronies. And later there was going to be a big government conspiracy involved, but I never got that far."

"Sounds good," said Nova, only partly teasing, because it was clear how uncomfortable this conversation had made him. She wanted to sympathize, even if it didn't seem like anything to be upset about. A comic book made years ago—who cared? But then, she'd always hated when Leroy wanted to see her inventions before they were ready to be shared, so maybe she understood after all. "Can I read it?"

"No," he said. "I'm pretty sure it got thrown away."

"I don't think so," said Hugh. "I think it's in a box in the office somewhere, or maybe in storage."

Adrian cast him a look even colder than Frostbite's icicles.

"Well, if you ever stumble across it, I'd love to see," she said.

Simon cleared his throat, and Nova could sense him about to change the subject again before Adrian decided to never bring another girl to dinner. "Nova," he started, dabbing his mustache with a napkin, "how are things going in weapons and artifacts? Did you ever find . . . what you were looking for?"

Nova aimed for innocence as she said, "What do you mean?"

"I figured part of your motive for applying to the department had something to do with your interest in Ace Anarchy's helmet."

Though Nova's heart felt like it would jump out of her skin,

Simon seemed nothing but jovial as he turned to Hugh. "You should have seen her with the replica. She took one look at it and knew it was a fake. I was impressed." He grinned at her. "Have they shown you the real one yet?"

Pushing her food around, she said, "They showed me the box it's in."

Simon nodded. "I hope seeing it for yourself was a relief. You didn't seem convinced when I said we had it well protected."

Nova glanced at Adrian, and she knew they were both thinking of the conversation they'd had during the Sidekick Olympics. She kept her face neutral as she prompted, "Are you sure?"

Hugh guffawed.

"Now, don't you go getting me into trouble," Adrian muttered.

"What?" said Hugh. "What are you talking about?"

"Just that Adrian thinks he *might* be able to get into it, if he tried."

"Ha! Adrian? No. Nice thought." Hugh stuck a forkful of pasta into his mouth, as if the conversation were over.

"I obviously haven't tried," said Adrian. "But I think it's possible."

"How would you do it?" said Simon.

"Draw a door on it?"

"A door!" Hugh chuckled. "Please. That's . . ." He hesitated, his brow creasing just slightly. "That would never work. Would it?"

They all exchanged uncertain looks.

Nova took a drink of water, avoiding eye contact so they wouldn't see her budding urgency. "It doesn't really matter. Adrian is never going to try to get that helmet. But it does bring up an interesting point. There are so many prodigies, with so many abilities. How do you know the box is infallible if you've never challenged anyone to get inside? It's just a box."

"Just a box." Hugh huffed, and his momentary concern seemed to have passed. "It's an interesting theory, but there's no point in speculating. I know myself and I know how my powers work. There's only one prodigy who can break into that thing, and it's not Adrian"—he gave Adrian a pointed scowl—"or anyone else we need to worry about."

"Really?" Nova's spine tingled. "Who is it?"

Hugh tossed up a hand, exasperated. "Me!"

Nova lifted an eyebrow. "Because you could . . . manipulate the chromium some more?"

"Well, sure. Or I could make a sledgehammer to take to it, if I was feeling destructive. But the helmet is safe. No one's gotten to it yet, and no one ever will."

Nova's pulse quickened, the start of an idea whispering deep in her thoughts.

*Chromium sledgehammer?*

Would that work? Would a weapon made of the same material be strong enough to destroy the box?

Only if it was made by the Captain himself, she suspected. As her electrolysis experiment had suggested, that box wasn't made out of *normal* chromium. Just like the Captain himself, his weapons were . . . well, extraordinary.

"Are you going to the gala tomorrow night?" asked Simon, and Nova was so lost in her speculations it took her a moment to realize he was asking her.

"Gala?" she said, trying to remember what day it was. "Is that tomorrow already?"

"I had that exact thought a few hours ago," said Hugh. "We've gotten a lot of last-minute sponsors and it's pulling together to be a nice event. Live music, fully catered. It'll be fun. Anyway, you have to come. You know, Nova, a lot of the people in the organization are starting to look up to you—the young ones especially. It would mean a lot if you were there."

Nova forced a close-lipped smile, though her heart was sinking from the implications of his words, and what she had become in the eyes of the Renegades. Someone to admire, to respect, to emulate.

She was Nova McLain. The superhero, and the fraud.

# CHAPTER THIRTY-THREE

NOVA REMEMBERED LITTLE ELSE about the conversation over dinner, most of which revolved around the Council's plans for ongoing community outreach programs. Finally, Hugh and Simon got up from the table and starting loading the dishwasher, moving like a well-rehearsed team. Nova watched them for a minute, unable to fully align this simple domestic chore with the superheroes who had defeated Ace Anarchy.

"So," started Adrian, pulling her attention back to him. He seemed more relaxed now and she suspected he was relieved that the meal was over. "You probably need to get home?"

She blinked at him and nearly started laughing.

Home.

*Right.*

Smiling tightly, she said, "How about that movie we never got to?"

Which is how Nova found herself back in Adrian's den, seated on the worn sofa. The entertainment industry was one that had ground to a halt during the Age of Anarchy and had been slow to get started again in the years since, so Adrian's entire movie collection consisted of thirty-year-old "classics." Nova hadn't seen any of them.

Adrian selected a martial arts film, but it didn't really matter to Nova what he picked. She wouldn't be watching it anyway.

Adrian settled down on the couch. Not touching her, but close enough to suggest there could be touching, if she wanted there to be. Or maybe there was no ulterior motive and he just had a favorite spot, a preferred cushion.

Nova chastised her heartbeat for increasing. It almost felt like a stranger had hijacked her body. Someone who had forgotten who she was and where she came from. Or more important, who *Adrian* was.

This attraction had to stop. She was an Anarchist. She was *Nightmare.*

What exactly did she think would happen when he found out? Because he would find out eventually. It was inevitable. Once she had the helmet, and that Vitality Charm, and she no longer had to play this game anymore.

Drawing in a stabilizing breath, Nova inched closer to Adrian and settled her head on his shoulder. He tensed, but it was brief. Then he slid his arm around her and she sank against his side. She urged her body not to get comfortable. Not to enjoy his warmth or the subtle strength in that arm, or the smell of pine that might have been soap or aftershave.

This time, her own calculating thoughts were louder than his heartbeat. The ticking clock in her mind was faster than her pulse.

The movie scrolled through the opening credits. A man appeared on the screen trudging through a blizzard. High on a mountain stood a foreboding temple.

Adrian's hand was resting on his leg. Nova, as casually as she could, started to reach for it. She was moments away from lacing their fingers together when Adrian pulled away, shifting his body so fast that Nova nearly sank into the dip between the cushions.

She straightened.

Adrian had turned to face her, lifting one knee onto the couch. His expression was worried, but his shoulders were set. Nova withdrew from him, her defenses rising like castle walls.

"The gala tomorrow night," he blurted, the words spoken so fast they blurred into one unwieldy statement.

Nova gaped. "Excuse me?"

"The gala. If you're going and I'm going and . . . Would you like to go together? As a date, I mean. Officially, this time." His Adam's apple bobbed in his throat. "I know I wasn't clear with the whole carnival thing, so I'll just put it out there from the start. I would like you to be my date. I would really like that a lot, actually . . ." He paused before adding, somewhat self-consciously, "If you want to."

Nova's mouth hung open. Her mind had gone blank and she was trying to formulate a response based on logic and strategy, and what would Ace want her to do, and would this be good for her cause or not, and how would this change anything, but all she could think about was how adorable Adrian was when he was nervous.

And also . . .

*He still likes me.*

Despite all the rejected advances, all the awkward silences. She'd been so sure he had moved on after the painful end to their non-date at the carnival, and yet . . . this. Not just to ask her to be his date, but to look so downright *eager* about it.

"Okay," she whispered.

She would figure out the strategy later.

Adrian's face brightened. "Okay?" With a confirming nod, he settled against the back of the couch again, returning his arm to her shoulders. He exhaled. "Okay."

Nova settled against him again, and a part of her wanted to be happy, but all she felt was dread.

She was going to get that helmet, and Ace Anarchy would return to power. The Renegades would fall. Society would be responsible for teaching its own children, planting its own vegetables, and they would be stronger for it. Better for it.

And Nova would be stronger and better too.

Soon, she would be done with lying. She would be done with secrets.

And Adrian would be done with her.

On the screen, the man had just entered the temple. His body was silhouetted in the massive doors as the snow gusted around him.

She tried to quiet her thoughts. She tried to reorient herself on what had to be done.

She had come here for the Vitality Charm. The thought crossed her mind that she could just ask Adrian about it, and she knew he would probably loan it to her, especially if she told him she wanted to visit Max.

But, no, if all went well, she would be wearing that charm as Nightmare, not Insomnia, and the fewer clues that connected her to her alter ego, the better.

"Nova?" he said, so quietly she almost thought she imagined it.

She turned her head up.

Adrian held her gaze for all of half a second, before he leaned down and kissed her.

Nova gasped against his mouth, overcome not just with surprise, but also by the current that jolted through every nerve.

Adrian pulled away, worried again. His eyes were a question. His lips an invitation.

Nova's mouth felt abandoned. The kiss had been too short and already her hands were itching to touch him, her entire body aching to move closer.

Though she knew what she had to do and she knew this was a terrible idea, she reached her hand behind his neck and pulled his mouth back to hers.

The kiss escalated fast. Hesitant curiosity and then, from nowhere, a desperate, unfulfilled need. To be closer. To kiss deeper. To touch his face, his neck, his hair. Adrian's arms circled her waist and he pulled her across him, turning Nova's body so she was cocooned in his arms.

He hissed suddenly and jerked away.

Nova's eyes snapped open, her heart catapulting into her throat. Adrian's features were contorted in pain. "Adrian?"

"Nothing," he said through his teeth, one hand pressing against his side. His face softened again as he peered at her.

"What—"

"Nothing," he repeated, and then he was kissing her again, and concerns about whatever had hurt him dissolved. Nova was shaking, overwhelmed by so much physical contact all at once. His lips. A hand in her hair, another against her ribs. Her body half draped across his lap, his heartbeat drumming against her chest, and his lips, *great skies, his lips* . . .

And still, that voice whispered in the back of her mind, reminding her why she was there despite how she wanted to ignore it.

Adrian's fingers curled against the back of her head. She was reclined so far now that she felt the arm of the couch beneath her shoulders. Nova squeezed her eyes shut, wanting to believe that this was the whole world. Just Adrian Everhart and every one of his magical touches.

But still, that relentless voice persisted, reminding her that this *wasn't* real. This could never be where she belonged. Adrian Everhart was not meant for her and she was certainly not meant for him.

Except—that voice faded into background noise, replaced with the heat from his mouth and the press of his arms, and another, quieter voice made itself known. A voice that could have been trying to catch her attention ever since the first moment she had met Adrian and her heart had lurched at the sight of his open smile.

*Why not?*

Why couldn't she belong here? Why couldn't she have this? She would simply never go back. She would go on pretending to be Nova McLain, Renegade, for the rest of her life. No one would ever have to know. *This could be real.*

She kissed Adrian harder, and he moaned in response. If she could just hold him tight enough . . . If she could just make this moment last . . .

*Bang. Bang.*

Her eyes shot open. Adrian didn't seem to notice, his fingers having discovered at that moment the bared skin of her waist. Nova trembled from the sensation, from the overwhelming convergence of too many desires crashing into her all at once.

The quiet voice of dissent was buried fast beneath her rising guilt. No, no, *no.* To choose Adrian would be to abandon the Anarchists, to abandon Ace.

*BANG.*

Choosing Adrian would be to abandon any chance of retribution for Evie and her parents.

Nova squeezed her eyes shut, tighter than before, hoping to

block out the noise of the gunshots as her purpose became clear again. As she remembered why she was there. Why she was *really* there.

She had failed her family once when they needed her. She would not do it again.

Nova held herself against Adrian, her fingers gathering fistfuls of his shirt. Tears were building behind her eyelids. She had to do this. She had to.

And if she didn't do it now, she might forget *why.*

As her body flamed in Adrian's hold, Nova released her power into the place where their lips met. It rolled through her, gentle as she could make it. It had been a long time since she'd been kind with her power. Not since putting her sister to sleep all those years ago.

Still, the effect happened just as fast.

Adrian's fingers loosened from her hair. His arms sagged. His head lolled to one side, breaking the kiss, and his body collapsed across the back of the couch, pinning Nova against the cushions. His breaths, which had been as erratic as hers moments ago, were already slowing.

Nova exhaled.

She stared up at the ceiling, her vision blurred with unshed tears. She spent a moment memorizing the weight of him and the warmth seeping through her clothes. They were tangled together— her knees curled around his hip, his arms trapped beneath her back. Her own fingers were resting on his neck and it was so easy to imagine how perfect this moment would be, if only it were real. Just a girl and a boy, cuddling, stealing kisses, falling asleep in each other's arms. Everything so simple and uncomplicated.

If only.

She started to extract herself. She moved slowly, even though she knew he wasn't going to wake up. As she shifted her weight off the couch and slid to the floor, Adrian readjusted himself, sinking into the sofa. The side of his face rubbed against the cushion, knocking his glasses askew.

Nova reached for his temples and pulled the glasses off his face. She folded down the sides and set them on the coffee table, then went and gathered a blanket from his tousled bed. She draped it over him, thinking of how he'd done this same thing while she'd been asleep. Had he paused to inspect her peaceful face, like she was doing now? Had he considered kissing her while she slept, like Nova found herself tempted to do? Her lips were still tingling, having been interrupted before the craving was satisfied.

But Nova knew that Adrian would never steal a kiss from her like that, and neither could she.

Instead, she stood and straightened her clothes, then scanned the room. She couldn't be sure how much time she had. Using her power gently like that tended to shorten the duration of sleep, and her powers had seemed different lately too. Weakened slightly, ever since she'd been caught in the quarantine with Max.

But she should have an hour at least, maybe two. It would have to be enough.

Where was he keeping that pendant?

She peeked under his bed first, then through the drawers of a small desk, but all she found were old electronics, broken colored pencils, and an entire kit for tattooing, which she figured must be related to yet another one of his artistic endeavors. She flipped through his collection of video games, and through a chest of drawers full of T-shirts and socks and underpants, after which the visual of Adrian in black cotton boxers became nearly impossible to shake from her thoughts.

Cheeks burning, she approached a bookshelf in the corner, where a stack of worn sketchbooks was sandwiched between a collection of comics and a set of Disastrous Duo action figures. As a kid, she had once kept an entire chemistry set inside the carved-out pages of a geographical dictionary, so she figured it was as good a hiding place as any.

She pulled out a stack of sketchbooks and started flipping through them, but one after another, she was met with actual pages of actual books, with actual, *amazing* drawings on them. Cityscapes and portraits and pages upon pages of odd symbols—a series of tightly wound curls, like springs, and others resembling small flames—but there was no context for what Adrian had been thinking when he drew them. They were followed by some preliminary concept art for the mural in the next room.

Nova slammed the last sketchbook shut and crammed it back onto the shelf.

The medallion was somewhere in this house. It had to be. Adrian wouldn't have given it—

Her breath caught.

*Of course.* He would give it away, but only to one person. He had told her as much. *We should give it to Simon first.*

Huffing, she stepped away from the bookshelf and sneaked around the sofa. She didn't dare look at Adrian again, afraid the temptation to curl up beside him and forget her task would be too strong to resist a second time.

Squaring her shoulders, she made her way up the stairs.

# CHAPTER THIRTY-FOUR

OVA STOPPED TO LISTEN when she reached the foyer. She could still hear dramatic music coming from the movie, and after a long while of standing with her head cocked, she thought she heard a shower running somewhere upstairs.

Squaring her shoulders, she began to climb the oak staircase. The old steps groaned and creaked beneath her.

At the top, a pair of double doors stood to her left. The master bedroom, she assumed. Someone inside was shuffling around, whistling to themselves. Also the direction of the running water, she noted, though the whole house seemed to hum as the water rushed through the pipes.

Opposite the landing was another hallway. Nova slinked forward.

The first door she checked turned out to be a linen closet.

The second brought a smile to her lips.

A home office.

Nova slipped inside, leaving the door open just a crack so she would hear if anyone came down the hall.

She was sure that Simon hadn't been wearing the Vitality Charm at dinner. If Adrian had given it to him, then maybe it was in their bedroom, or in his office back at headquarters. But she couldn't very well search either of those places at the moment.

At least, searching their home office might turn up something useful while she waited, hoping the two Councilmen would fall asleep without her assistance.

She approached the large desk, which was overflowing with stacks of papers and files, one of which had toppled over onto a keyboard. Nova grabbed the top file and scanned the label, then the next, making her way through the stacks, searching for anything useful. But these all seemed to be drafts of laws the Council was considering or had already put into effect. Ongoing social projects throughout the city. Plans for future construction. Trade deals with foreign nations.

She turned to the drawers, finding one full of statistics and reports on crime rates of various countries. Near the top of the drawer was a list of the cities around the globe that had Renegade syndicates in operation.

It was a very long list.

Nova set the list aside and turned to a filing cabinet beside the wall. Inside were fat folders outlining plans and blueprints for headquarters and other Renegade-operated properties, from alarm system details to elevator permits. Nothing about the helmet. Nothing about Agent N. But still, it wasn't bad information to have access to.

She pulled out a few documents to review later and set them beside the list of international syndicates.

She kept searching, though she sensed her luck, and time, were dwindling.

Turning toward the room's built-in bookcases, she scanned the spines of enormous volumes of legal guides and political manifestos, all published before the Age of Anarchy. On the bottom shelf were a handful of photo albums, and she ignored the curiosity spiked by the chance of seeing adorable kid pictures of Adrian and grabbed a box instead. She pulled off the lid and froze.

A monster was leering up at her from the box.

Breath hitching, she set the lid aside and picked up the top sheet of paper, where a creature had been drawn in frenzied scribbles of black crayon. The creature itself was a formless shadow that stretched to the edges of the paper, leaving only the hollow whiteness to show through where its eyes should have been.

Empty, haunting eyes.

Adrian's monster.

Nova picked up the drawing that had been beneath it. Another illustration of the creature—a floating mass of blackness. Two outstretched arms almost resembled wings. A bulbous head, the only detail of which was those eerie, watchful eyes.

She flipped through a few more drawings, though they were more of the same. Same, yet each with small differences. Some she could tell were made when he was very young, when his scribbles were more emotion than skill. But some of the later drawings developed details. Sometimes the wing-like arms ended in bony fingers or sharp talons. Sometimes it was a shapeless shadow, other times it was tall and thin. Sometimes its eyes were red, sometimes they were yellow, and sometimes they were slit like a cat's. Occasionally the monster would be holding a weapon. A jagged sword. A javelin. Iron shackles.

How long had his dreams been wrought with this creature? It was almost a wonder he hadn't developed insomnia himself.

At the bottom of the stack of drawings, she found a collection of pages stapled together. Nova lifted them from the box and a small, surprised laugh escaped her.

On the front page—in much more skilled artistic style than the images of the nightmare monster—was a drawing of a young, dark-skinned boy wearing a white straitjacket, with a patch on his chest that read *Patient Z*. He was strapped to a chair and a collection of electrodes and wires were plugged all around his shaved head, each one connecting to various machines. A stereotypical mad scientist hovered over him, scribbling onto a clipboard.

A title was printed boldly across the top: *Rebel Z: Issue 1*.

Her mouth twitching around an amused smile, Nova turned to the first page. It showed the kid from the cover trying to buy a candy bar at a convenience store, but being turned away when he didn't have enough coins in his pocket. Newspapers on a stand by the register sported headlines warning about missing children and government conspiracies.

A caption read, "I was the doctor's twenty-sixth victim."

Holding the stapled pages by their spine, Nova flipped through the rest of the book. Images of the boy flashed by, along with a bunch of other children, being locked in jail cells and subjected to various tests by the scientist and his minion nurses. The last page showed the boy crying over the body of a girl—Patient Y. The final dialogue bubble read, "I will find a way out of this, and I *will* avenge you. I will avenge you all!"

At the bottom: *To be continued . . .*

Shaking her head, smiling openly now at this glimpse into Adrian's eleven-year-old imagination, Nova reached for Issue 2 in the box. Her fingers had just closed around it when she heard a door open at the end of the hallway.

She froze.

Footsteps.

Immediately her brain clamored for an excuse. *Adrian decided he wanted me to see these old comics after all. I was just going to bring them downstairs to look at and . . .*

But her excuse went unneeded. The footsteps thumped down the stairs.

Nova listened, motionless. At some point during her search, the water had stopped running through the pipes.

She stuffed the comics into the box and closed it, pushing it back onto the shelf. She grabbed the folder detailing headquarters plans and the list of international dignitaries.

She approached the door and peered out. The double doors across the landing were cracked open, blue light spilling out along with the sound of the evening news.

She frowned. She had only heard one of them go downstairs, so the other was still in there.

Options: wait for them both to fall asleep, then slip in to search the room. Or create a diversion to lure them out.

The first option seemed the least risky.

She would wait. And if Adrian woke up in the meantime, well, she would just put him to sleep again.

She had all night.

When she was sure the coast was clear, she slid into the hallway and scurried back down the stairs, keeping close to the wall where there was less chance of making the old nails squeal beneath her feet. She reached the foyer and was rounding the column when she heard whistling again.

It was coming from the hallway. She would have to walk right by it to get back to the basement.

Flinching, she turned the other way and darted through the

door into the dining room, closing it quietly behind her. Pulse thrumming, she took in the room with its fancy wood paneling and glittering chandelier and the scattered piles of junk mail. She considered diving under the table, but that would appear far too suspicious if she was caught. Instead, she slipped the file beneath a particularly chaotic stack of mail and rushed into the kitchen, where the dishwasher was running and the smell of garlic hung heavy in the air.

She could no longer hear the whistling.

She held her breath.

Then the door to the dining room opened, and the whistling started up again.

Cursing, Nova ran for the best hiding place she saw—the closet that Simon had said would be turned into a pantry someday.

She ripped it open. Her feet halted. She reeled back in surprise.

A wooden rod across the top might normally have held coats and jackets, but she found herself staring, unbelievably, at the Dread Warden's black cape and Captain Chromium's shiny blue bodysuit. Both were tucked into plastic bags with dry cleaner tags dangling from the hangers. Lumped together on the floor beneath them were six sets of Renegade-issued boots, and a utility belt, not unlike Nova's own, hung from a peg on the back of the door.

Her jaw fell.

*There it was.*

The Vitality Charm, hanging around the neck of the Dread Warden costume, glinting in the kitchen's light.

What was it doing in a *broom closet*?

Swallowing hard, she reached in and unhooked the chain from the hanger. It was heavier than she expected, roughly the size of a silver dollar, with the hand and serpent engraved into its dark surface.

She almost laughed. She couldn't believe she had found it—actually found it, actually *succeeded.*

She clasped it behind her neck and tucked the medallion beneath the collar of her shirt. The iron was warm against her skin.

The kitchen door opened and Nova spun around.

Simon Westwood yelped in surprise and, ever so briefly, flickered invisible. Then he was back, clutching his chest.

"I'm sorry," Nova sputtered. "I was . . . um. Looking for . . . a snack! I just remembered that the pantry was"—she pointed toward the dining room door—"that way, right? At the end of the hall. I'm so sorry. I didn't mean to pry."

Simon waved her apologies away. "No, no, it's fine. It's a big house. Easy to get confused." Having recovered from his surprise, he meandered to a tall cupboard and pulled it open. "We keep most of the snack foods in here. Where's Adrian?"

"He fell asleep," she said, shrugging sheepishly. "He seemed so tired at dinner. I didn't want to wake him."

"Ah." He gestured at the open cupboard, stocked with a variety of cookies and chips. "Well, take whatever you want."

"Thanks."

Simon grabbed a candy bar for himself, which surprised Nova. She wouldn't have pictured Simon Westwood as having a sweet tooth. Shaking herself into movement, she shut the closet door and went to peruse the snacks.

Simon was halfway back to the door when he glanced back at Nova. "I know I probably shouldn't say anything, but . . . you know, you're the first girl Adrian's ever brought home to meet us."

She flushed. "Actually, I came here to see him, so . . . I'm not sure we can count it as him *bringing me home.*"

With a chuckle, Simon nodded, his wavy hair tumbling over

his forehead. "Fair enough. Though . . . I think he would have eventually."

Her blush deepened, which she hated. Were all parents so awkward?

The thought brought a twinge of pain to her chest. She would never know what it was like to be embarrassed by her father, and she would never invite a boy over to meet *Uncle Ace.*

"Good night, Nova," said Simon, walking out of the kitchen.

Her shoulders fell, releasing the built-up tension, and she cast her gaze toward the ceiling in relief.

Deciding to come back for the hidden folder before she left, Nova headed back downstairs.

Adrian was still sound asleep. She took a moment to inspect his face, telling herself she wanted to make sure he was still in deep. The planes of his cheeks, the cut of his jaw, the lips that were no longer such a mystery, yet were more enticing than ever.

"I'm so sorry you had to be the enemy," she whispered.

Then she crept back into the mural room. There was one last thing she needed from this house.

The jungle assaulted her senses even more strongly now that she could compare it to the real world. The birds were still up in the boughs, squawking and tittering, and the intoxicating perfume of the flowers engulfed her.

From the doorway, she could only see a glimpse of the statue's shoulder and a sliver of its hood. Nova made her way through the brush until she was standing before it again.

In her childhood dream, this was as far as she'd gotten. She could clearly remember the sensation of awe she'd had when she stood before this statue, caught up in that whimsical, unconscious state. Even now, she felt swept away by the impossibility of it. The sheer miracle of this tiny star brought into being.

She had wanted to touch it in the dream, but she never had the chance. She woke up too soon.

Her hands trembled as she lifted them, fingers outstretched. Some quiet instinct told her that she had to sneak up on the star. Like if she moved too fast, she would frighten it away.

It glowed, as if it were aware of her presence. When she was mere inches away, she realized that the star had begun to shift in color, from vibrant white to something mellow and rich. A copper gold, just like the material that her father used to cull from the air.

Nova brought her hands together, cupping them around the star. Its warmth pulsed against her palms.

Exhaling, she brought her cupped hands back to her chest. As her heart tapped a furious beat, she dared to part her thumbs. Just enough. Just enough to see the star clasped within.

It flashed suddenly, blinding her. Nova stumbled back, turning her head away.

The flash left a glaring spot against her eyelids that refused to fade for a long time, as she blinked and squinted into her hands. The imprint of light in her vision started to disperse and she looked around in awe, seeing flickers of thin, golden veins pulsing in the air all around her.

Nova squeezed her eyes shut, rubbing her knuckles into them.

When she opened them again, the strange patterns of light were gone, and so was the star.

Nova's chest tightened with disappointment, but it was followed by a self-deprecating laugh.

What had she expected? That she could take it with her? That she could keep this star forever, to remember this one blissful night? A night that had been built on lies and deception?

Sighing, Nova trudged back through the foliage. She was nearly to the door when a glow caught her eye.

She froze. A shadow had flickered across a fallen tree trunk. She turned, searching for the source of light, and the shadows shifted again. There was nothing behind her.

She turned in a full circle, and the play of light and shadow spun with her.

Nova looked down. Gasping, she extended her arm in front of her, staring at the filigree bracelet that her father had left to her, unfinished.

Now, where those prongs had sat empty for so many years without a precious stone to fill them, there emanated the light from a single golden star.

"Oh, for all the skies," she grumbled. She spent a minute trying to dig her fingers beneath the stone and wrench it free of the prongs, but it wouldn't budge.

She heard the crescendo of dramatic music coming from the television in Adrian's room. Gritting her teeth, she pulled her sleeve down over the bracelet and went back to him. The credits were rolling on the film and Adrian was still asleep on the sofa, but she knew he wouldn't sleep much longer.

Nova nudged Adrian's body up and nestled herself beside him. She had barely sunk into the cushions when Adrian groaned and stretched, his eyelids flittering.

He started when he saw her, quickly withdrawing the arm that she'd draped surreptitiously over her own shoulders. "Nova? I . . ." He scrunched his drowsy face. "What . . ."

She beamed, as bright as she could manage. "All that painting must have made you tired. I think you missed the whole movie."

"I fell asleep?" He glanced at the TV, rubbing his eyes. "I . . . I'm so sorry."

"Don't be. I slept for twenty-four hours, remember?"

"Yeah, but . . . we were . . ." His brow was crinkled as he reached for his glasses on the table and slipped them on. "Weren't we . . . ?" His voice trailed off.

"I need to head home," said Nova, flushing when she thought of the kiss. "I'll see you at the gala, okay? Try to get some more rest."

He gaped at her, his confusion beginning to clear. "The gala. Right. I'll see you there."

Before she could talk herself out of it, Nova leaned over and kissed him lightly on the cheek. "Good night, Adrian."

Then she hurried back up the stairs, a star on her wrist, a medallion tucked beneath her shirt, and a cruel twinge of giddiness fluttering inside her chest.

# CHAPTER THIRTY-FIVE

"AND THIS SILVER SPEAR will work?" said Ace, his voice thick with disdain as they discussed the chromium pike that most of the world believed had destroyed his helmet.

"I don't know for sure," said Nova. "But Captain Chromium definitely implied that one of his chromium weapons would be strong enough to damage the box. If I can wield it with enough force, that is." She frowned, letting her gaze travel between each of her companions. "I'm taking that helmet, one way or the other. If I can't get into the box, then I'll bring the whole thing back, and we'll figure out a solution later."

"Yes," said Ace, one lip curling. "We will."

Nova could see resentment in the shadows of his eyes, and though she didn't think Ace's telekinesis would be able to peel open the Captain's box, she could tell he was keen to try.

"Maybe Leroy can concoct a solution that can burn through the chromium," she said. "Or . . . or maybe there will be something else in the vault that can help. I've been through the database twice now and nothing seemed obvious but I'll look again—"

A hand fell on her shoulder. Leroy was grinning at her, the scars of his face stretched taut around his lopsided mouth. "We'll figure it out, Nova. You've crafted a fine plan here. Let's take it one step at a time."

"What are we supposed to do while you're doing . . . *every-thing*?" said Honey. She pressed a hand over her mouth to cover a yawn and the flickering candlelight caught on metallic gold varnish across her nails. "We're villains too, you know. We can handle some responsibility."

"We are not villains," said Ace, one hand tightening into a fist. "That may be the portrait that our enemies have painted of us, but we will not let it define us. We are freethinkers. Revolutionaries. We are the future of—"

"Oh, I know, I know," said Honey, shooing her hand at him. "But sometimes it's fun to meet expectations. It doesn't mean we have to take it all so literally."

Ace was about to say more, but then he bent over his knees in a fit of coughing. Nova jumped up from her place on the floor, but Phobia was already kneeling at Ace's side, his skeletal fingers pressed between Ace's shoulder blades.

No one spoke until the fit passed. The tension was palpable as Ace collapsed against the back of his chair, wheezing. "Just . . . bring me my helmet," he said, fixing his eyes on Nova. "*Please.*"

"I will," she whispered. "I promise I will."

"Your fears will not come to pass," Phobia hissed, and with his face shrouded in darkness, Nova couldn't tell who he was speaking to. "Your great vision will not be devoured by the passing of time. All will not be for nothing."

*Ace, then*, she thought, as her uncle gave an appreciative nod at the cloaked figure.

"I hope you are right, my friend," he said. He stood, leaning on Phobia's shoulder for a moment. "I am proud of you, my little Nightmare. I know this has not been easy, but your trials are nearing an end. Soon, I will be strong again, and I will take the torch that you have lit and lead us into a new era."

He stooped over Nova and cupped her face. His skin was as cold as the tomb itself.

"Thank you, Uncle," she said. "Now, please, go rest."

He made no argument as he limped toward the once-lavish four-poster bed. A curtain of bones fell, dividing the room in a melody of hollow clatters, hiding him from view.

"After all these years," said Honey, "you'd think he would have learned to talk like a normal human being."

Nova cut a glare toward her, relatively certain that they could still be heard through the bone curtain.

"He spends his days reading ancient philosophy," said Leroy, gesturing at an extensive collection of leather-bound tomes stacked against one of the marble sarcophagi. "What do you expect?"

Honey made an unimpressed face, then turned her attention to Nova. "So, what is it you expect us to do while you're off gallivanting with the *artiste*?"

"Leroy's already done his job," said Nova, forcefully ignoring the suggestive look Honey was giving her.

"Made easier by those devices you found." Leroy gestured at the cardboard box that held six pomegranate-like spheres.

Fatalia's mist-missiles had provided a perfect framework for Nova's newest invention—a dispersal device intended to release Agent N in a gaseous cloud upon detonation. Nova had managed to sneak out a handful of additional vials of the substance during the most recent training session, and with a few alterations based on Leroy's experiments, she was confident the devices were ready to go.

"I'll need a getaway driver," said Nova. "Someone to take me to and from headquarters."

"Naturally," said Leroy.

"And someone will have to take my wristband back to the house after I leave the gala, so if they track it later I'll have an alibi."

Honey sneered with disinterest, but then rolled her eyes. "Fine."

"Thanks," Nova deadpanned. "Couldn't do it without you. Phobia, at first I was thinking you could act as emergency backup for me, in case something goes wrong, but now . . ." She considered the wall of skulls dividing them from Ace. "Maybe it's best if someone stays here?"

"I could be your emergency backup," said Honey.

Nova cringed. "Well . . . thanks, but . . . I'm sort of going for stealth and subtlety?"

Honey stared at her, and for a moment Nova expected her to be insulted, but then she said, "You're right, that won't work for me."

"But," said Nova, swallowing, "there is one other thing I could use your help with. I . . . I'm going to need a dress."

Finally, Honey brightened.

"Something practical," Nova added quickly.

"Oh, sweetheart. I'm a supervillain. I am nothing if not practical." She winked.

"Yeah, I've noticed that," Nova muttered.

"We'll pick out something when we get back to the house," said Honey, bobbing her toes. "I have a sexy little sequined number that might work—"

"Not sexy," said Nova.

Honey scoffed. "Not sexy is *not* an option."

Her nose curled. "Well . . . not . . . not too sexy, then."

"We'll see," said Honey, lifting one shoulder in a half shrug. "You know, I used to be invited to galas and parties every week. Oh, the cocktails, and the *dancing* . . ." She sighed longingly. "The Harbingers, you know. They always threw the best parties. Anyone who was anyone would be there."

Nova peered at Phobia, who was as still as one of the creepy saint statues in the corner. "Let me guess—Honey has an acute fear of missing out?"

Leroy chuckled and even Phobia made a hissing sound that might have been a laugh.

"Among other devastating insecurities," Phobia said.

"What?" Honey barked. "I am not insecure!" She grabbed a stray skull and threw it at Phobia, who blocked it with a swipe of his scythe. The skull clunked against the floor and Nova flinched, unable to ignore that it had once belonged to a real person.

Phobia upturned his scythe and stuck the tip of the blade through one of the skull's eye sockets, lifting it from the floor. He took hold of the cranium with his own bony fingers and set it neatly, almost tenderly, back on one of the stone shelves that lined the catacombs.

"You just wait," said Honey, drawing Nova's attention back to her. "You're going to enjoy yourself tonight. Undermining those arrogant tyrants. Risking everything to achieve your goals. Taking back what's rightfully ours. Trust me, darling. It will be fun." She nudged Leroy with the toe of her pointed shoe. "Don't you agree?"

"All this planning does bring back memories," said Leroy, though the look he shot Nova was more mocking of Honey than agreeing with her.

Nova didn't respond to either of them. She wasn't excited for tonight. Eager to have it over and done with, perhaps. Determined not to fail. But there was also dread churning in her gut, and she couldn't quite pinpoint what was causing it.

Though she was sure it had a lot to do with Adrian.

"I'll be glad when the gala is over," she said. "I'll only be there for an hour—two at the most. And then—"

Honey grinned wickedly. "And then."

Nova's eye caught a flutter of movement over Honey's shoulder, and she frowned. At first she thought it was one of the wasps, but . . .

She stepped closer. Honey glanced around.

A butterfly, its wings splattered in orange and black, shot out from one of the skulls. It sped straight for the stairwell at the end of the catacombs.

Nova gasped. "No! Catch it!"

Phobia vanished in a drift of black smoke and reappeared, blocking the doorway. The butterfly turned, narrowly avoiding his chest, and dived toward the crate that hid the entrance to the subway tunnels. Honey jumped, having removed one of her shoes, and swung it at the creature.

Nova and Leroy launched forward at the same time, both slamming into the crate and shoving it against the wall. The butterfly smacked into its side, then soared frantically upward. Leroy jumped onto the crate, swiping at the creature with his palm.

"Don't hurt it!" Nova cried, her pulse thundering.

"Why ever not?" said Honey.

The butterfly darted around the ceiling, searching for another escape. But there was nowhere else for it to go.

It alighted on a marble tomb, and Nova could picture Danna trying to catch her breath. Its wings stilled, folding together to reveal their intricate pattern, like a golden stained-glass window.

"Just trust me," said Nova. "We need to catch it in something."

Nova had learned enough about her allies, and their weaknesses, to know how Danna operated. If they captured the butterfly, then Danna would be stuck in swarm mode. But if it got away . . .

Danna would know everything.

Spotting a wineglass on the floor, Nova leaped for it, at the same moment the butterfly took off again. No longer fluttering aimlessly, the creature shot forward, heading straight for—

Nova's heart stopped.

*The candles.*

It was going to burn itself up. Sacrifice itself rather than be trapped down here. Sacrifice itself so the rest of the swarm could converge.

"No!" Forgetting the wineglass, Nova ran, then dropped to the ground and slid, her leg outstretched, preparing to kick the base of the candelabra.

But just before the butterfly reached one of the orange flames, a white pillowcase fell from the air and scooped the creature from its path.

Nova, however, kept sliding. Her heel struck the base of the stand and the candelabra toppled to the ground. A few of the candles extinguished in the fall, while the others rolled, still burning, across the stone floor.

Panting, Nova watched as the corners of the pillowcase tied themselves together, then the whole thing drifted to the ground. The fabric drooped until she could barely make out the twitching insect inside.

"All this racket," came Ace's exhausted voice, "over a *butterfly?*"

"M-Monarch," said Nova, panting, though as much from the terror of Danna discovering Ace's hideout and going back to tell the others as from her exertion.

"A Renegade," added Honey, her voice dripping disdain.

Ace strode out from where the curtain of bones had parted and let them clatter shut behind him. He stood over the pillowcase. He was still pale, but the bit of excitement had brought a rare gleam to his eye. "Not a particularly menacing shape for a *superhero*."

"It isn't just one," said Nova, standing on her shaky legs. "She transforms into a whole swarm of them." She stood up the candelabra and returned each of the candles to its holder, but as she was about to set in the last candle, it was lifted from her hands. Still burning, it drifted in the air toward Ace.

"Where are the others?" said Leroy.

Nova surveyed the catacombs and the black stairwell, but could see no sign of more. "She must have only sent one to spy on us." *Or me*, she thought.

Nova shivered, spooked by what a close call it was. She wondered how Danna had found them here, but her mind immediately supplied the answer.

Danna had been following her. For how long? What else had she seen?

"Well," said Ace, "it seems easy enough to kill."

He lifted one hand, and the pillowcase floated into the air, nearing the candle flame.

"No, wait!"

Ace peered at her.

Killing one butterfly wouldn't have much of an effect on Danna. The Sentinel had obliterated dozens of them at the parade, and she'd emerged with horrendous burn marks on one side of her body. But to kill just *one* would be no more devastating to her than a paper cut.

But—to *trap* one was a different story. It was her greatest weakness. To return to her human form, Danna needed all of her living lepidopterans to unite. If even one was kept separate, she would be trapped in swarm mode until it could merge with the others.

Nova could only guess how many of her secrets the Renegade had discovered by now. Her true identity would be revealed. Ace would be found. They would be ruined.

She could not allow Danna to reform.

"We need to keep it alive," she said, and did her best to explain Danna's power, her weaknesses, and the risks.

Ace held Nova's gaze for a long moment, then acquiesced. "As you say." The candle returned to its stand and the pillowcase, with the butterfly trapped inside, dropped into Leroy's hands. The butterfly seemed to have gone still inside.

"How many more are in her swarm?" said Leroy.

"Hundreds," said Nova. "Maybe a thousand. And she can be sneaky with them." She peered around again, feeling watched. The creatures were so small. They could fit into such tiny nooks, and so long as they held still, it would be nearly impossible in this darkness to spot them. "But as long as that one doesn't get away, she shouldn't be a threat."

"Oh, good," said Honey, wiggling her fingers. "A pretty new pet."

Nova smiled, but her heart wasn't in it. She couldn't find the strength to believe her own words.

Danna was a Renegade, and a good one.

She was definitely still a threat.

# CHAPTER THIRTY-SIX

THE GALA WAS BEING HELD in an old, stately building that had once been a train depot, all brick and domed glass ceilings and high windows, though for years the station had sat abandoned. Once the Renegades had claimed power over Gatlon City, they had made the building one of their first "community projects." Blacklight, in particular, had insisted that if they were going to get involved in the world of international politics, they would need a place to entertain visiting dignitaries, and Renegade Headquarters wasn't going to suffice.

Besides, he'd argued, it was one piece of the city's history that could be brought back to life with relative ease. The Renegades hoped to restore the city to what it had been before the days of Ace Anarchy—no, they wanted to make it grander than it ever had been before—and this was as good a place to start as any.

Adrian had arrived early, along with his dads, to do what he could to help set up. Mostly he had spent the afternoon drawing lavish flower bouquets for the table centerpieces, and he was just beginning to feel like he would be happy to never draw another calla lily again when Tsunami told him to go get changed. He was grateful for the work, though. It had kept his mind preoccupied, at least in part, when he couldn't stop thinking about the night before.

His skin warmed every time he remembered the feeling of Nova's lips against his and her hand on the back of his neck and the weight of her body in his arms. And then . . . *and then* . . .

Nothing.

Because he'd fallen asleep.

During the kiss? Or after? It was all a blur. He'd been electrified, overcome with sensation. Then he'd been blinking himself awake while movie credits scrolled and Nova smiled at him as if nothing unusual had happened at all.

She'd been so cool about it, like it was no big deal, like it happened all the time, and he appreciated how gracious she was. But still. *Still.*

He must have the timeline wrong. He couldn't have fallen asleep during the kiss. They must have gone back to watching the movie at some point, and then—and only then—did he drift off.

That, at least, was a little less mortifying.

If only a little.

But his memory was unreliable. Nova—kissing—and . . . credits.

He must have been more tired than he'd realized after the fight with Frostbite's team, on top of so many late nights spent working on the mural.

At least she was still going to be his date to the gala. He hadn't ruined it—whatever *it* was. This new terrifying, wonderful thing.

Standing before a mirror in the restroom, his dress shirt left unbuttoned, Adrian peeled the bandaging from his chest to check on the newest tattoo. It was still weeping spots of blood and there was mottled bruising staggered across the left side of his chest. He was becoming used to the healing process and knew that it would get worse before it got better. Soon, the tattoo would enter the scabby peeling stage, complete with a relentless itch that would make him want to attack it with sandpaper. That was always the worst part. At least the tattooing itself—the constant pricks of the needle into his skin—only lasted about an hour. The itching went on for days.

He started to bend over the sink to wash away the spots of blood, but the movement sent a jolt of pain through his side. He flinched and pressed his hand to the place beneath his ribs where he'd been punctured by one of Genissa's ice spears. The wound wasn't deep— his armor had taken the brunt of it—but without the aid of the Renegade healers he knew it would be sore for a while. He had done the best he could to dress the wound, drawing in his own stitches and regularly applying ointment to fend off infection.

He sighed, pressing his fingers lightly against the bandage. The hardest part, as he had discovered since becoming the Sentinel, was simply hiding the fact that he was hurt. Not grimacing when some-one nudged him in the side. Disguising his stiff movements when climbing out of a car or moving up a set of stairs. Smiling through the pain when all he wanted to do was take a couple of painkillers and spend the afternoon reclined on a sofa watching television.

Or kissing Nova again. *That* had certainly taken his mind off his injury.

He finished cleaning the tattoo and patted it dry with a paper towel from the dispenser, then fumbled with the buttons on his white shirt.

He hoped Oscar knew how to knot a bow tie so he wouldn't have to ask one of his dads—or worse, Blacklight.

Adrian wasn't used to feeling this anxious. Sure, he got nervous sometimes. Had, in fact, felt nervous a lot more often since the day Nova McLain had strolled into his life. But he wasn't used to this twitchy, edgy, stomach-twistingly anxious feeling and he was ready for it to go away.

It *was* going to go away. Wasn't it?

He pulled on his tuxedo jacket at the same moment the door swung open. "What's taking so long in here?" said Oscar, his cane clicking against the floor, which was laid with so many black-and-white octagonal tiles it made Adrian dizzy to look at. "Are you drawing your tuxedo on or something?"

Adrian glanced at Oscar's reflection and smiled. "Actually, that's a great idea." He dug through the pile of clothes he had been wearing before and found his marker.

"I was joking," Oscar said hastily. "Please don't strip down and start drawing on new clothes."

Ignoring him, Adrian doodled onto the fabric of his shirt. When he was finished, a crisp, white bow tie rested against the base of his throat.

Oscar huffed. "Cheater."

"We can't all be as naturally dapper as Oscar Silva."

Oscar did, in fact, look extra dapper in a light gray dress shirt cuffed to show off his muscled forearms and a slim red vest. Plus, he was already wearing a perfectly knotted matching red bow tie.

"Is that a clip-on?"

Oscar snorted. "Please. Only villains wear clip-ons."

When they emerged from the bathroom, Adrian was surprised to see that the gala was already filling with guests—lots of Renegades, along with their family members and spouses. He scanned the room but didn't see Nova in the crowd.

A new bout of nervousness struck him.

The space looked great. Massive columns held up the expansive ceiling, and the stained-glass dome at its center had miraculously survived the Age of Anarchy, though the large clock against the wall had to be reconstructed from old pictures.

There were no ticket booths, no boards updating the train schedules, no luggage carts or periodical stands. In their place now stood circular tables draped with crimson tablecloths and glittering glassware. There were lights that bobbed overhead like buoys on an invisible ocean, each cycling through a variety of rich jewel tones and splattering the room in shades of emerald and turquoise. There were levitating trays carrying champagne flutes and tiny hors d'oeuvre, and a stage where a string quartet was playing in front of an empty dance floor.

A high whistle drew his attention toward the coat check, where Ruby was handing over her jacket. "You clean up nice, Sketch," she said, taking her claim ticket and putting it in a small jeweled bag. She was wearing an unembellished red cocktail dress, but its simplicity was offset by the gem she always wore on her wrist, and now a necklace of red rubies too. Her own creation, no doubt. Her hair, a mix of bleach white and dyed black, was pulled into a messy up-do that reminded Adrian of a white tiger. Cuddly, yet fierce.

"He drew on his bow tie," said Oscar. "I'm not sure it counts."

Ruby gave him a sideways look. "You clean up nice too."

Oscar preened. "Ready to show off my moves." He tucked one ankle behind the other and gave a quick turn. "Tell me you can dance in those." He jutted the end of his cane at Ruby's heeled shoes.

"Nice thought," said Ruby, "but we all know there will be no separating you from the free food once they bring it out." Her expression turned serious. "Have either of you talked to Danna tonight?"

Adrian and Oscar shook their heads.

Ruby frowned. "We were supposed to come together, but she messaged me earlier and said something had come up and she'd meet me here. I asked her what *something* was, but she never responded."

"Strange," said Oscar. "But I'm sure she'll be here soon." He started to reach for Ruby's hand, but then froze and settled his palm on top of his cane instead. Clearing his throat, he turned to Adrian. "Nova's coming tonight, isn't she?"

"Yeah, I think so." He glanced at the large clock and saw that the gala had officially started twelve minutes ago. She was late, but not *that* late. And Hugh had mentioned that he'd seen her at headquarters earlier, so she had probably worked up to the last minute. "I'm sure she'll be here soon."

"Come on." Ruby threaded her arm through Oscar's elbow. He stood straighter in surprise, but then Ruby laced her other arm through Adrian's and he deflated again. "My family is excited to see you."

She dragged them into the sea of tables.

It wasn't just Ruby's brothers who were at the gala, but her mom, dad, and grandmother too. Adrian felt like he already knew them, from everything he'd heard from Ruby, and it wasn't long before her brothers were begging to hear about what it was like to take down criminals, and was it true that Hawthorn had a forked tongue, and was it weird living in the same house as the Dread Warden because if *they* could turn invisible they would come up with the *best* pranks.

Adrian was as friendly as he could manage, but he was constantly scanning the entrance, watching the guests filter in. Eventually, Oscar's mom showed up. Their group, including Adrian's dads, who were socializing on the other side of the room, took up two full tables. Adrian saved a seat for Nova, and he noticed Ruby stashing her purse on the seat beside her, too, reserving it for Danna.

Twenty minutes passed. Oscar and Ruby went to stand by the

kitchen doors, where they could be sure to accost the waiters every time they brought out a new tray of appetizers.

Thirty minutes passed. Adrian spotted his dads purveying a long table full of gift baskets and desserts—a silent auction that was part of the fundraiser intended to replace some of the stolen drugs. Simon put a bid down for a latticework pie, though Hugh was the pie lover and Simon definitely would have preferred the chocolate cake beside it.

Forty minutes passed.

Adrian's heart sank, ever so slowly. His smile became more forced. He caught Oscar giving him a sympathetic look, which only irritated him.

One hour into the gala, the guests were encouraged to take their seats and the salad course was served. Adrian stared down at the delicate stems of some unfamiliar lettuce, candied nuts, and glistening purple beets. His fathers joined their table and Oscar's mom looked like she was about to faint from their mere presence. Adrian pushed his salad around with his fork, grateful that between Hugh Everhart and Oscar Silva, no one would notice that he wasn't saying much.

She wasn't coming.

He'd blown it.

It was for the best, he tried to tell himself. There was no way he and Nova could be anything more than friends and teammates. Not if he was going to keep his secret. Already he'd started planning different ways that he could tell her the truth.

But Nova hated the Sentinel. If he thought she would be thrilled to learn his identity, that she would somehow be impressed by him, then he was in more denial than he realized. No. A real relationship would never work, not while he was trying to be the Sentinel too. Not while his loyalties were so divided. Not while—

"Holy smokes," Oscar whispered. "Adrian." He smacked Adrian's shoulder with the back of his hand, dislodging his thoughts. Ruby noticed, too, and they both turned at the same time.

The air left him. Every doubt evaporated at once.

He was just kidding. A real relationship could totally work. He would make it work.

Jumping up from his seat, Adrian made his way through the tables, unable to take his gaze from Nova. She was standing by the doors, searching the crowd, and when they landed on him she started in surprise. He beamed. She smiled back, but warily. Maybe she was nervous too.

Somehow, the idea made him borderline giddy.

"Wow," he said when he reached her. "You look—"

"Don't get used to it," she interrupted. "I'm never wearing a dress again. I don't know why anyone would willingly subject themselves to this torture." She tugged at the hem of the black lining beneath a lacy overdress.

Adrian chuckled. "I'll admire it while I can, then."

Nova blushed and her gaze swept down his tuxedo. She gulped, and didn't make eye contact as she said, "I'm sorry I'm late."

"It's okay. You haven't missed much. I'll show you where we're sitting."

Nova peered into the crowd. Her expression seemed troubled. She didn't follow him.

"Is something wrong?"

"I'm not really that hungry. Do you think maybe we can just walk around a bit instead?"

"Sure," said Adrian. "They actually have a gift shop here, if you want to check it out."

"A gift shop?"

"Yeah. This started to become a popular tourist destination a few years ago, and Blacklight thought a gift shop would drum up extra revenue. It's pretty cheesy stuff, but still fun. Especially if you're in the market for a snow globe, or a new key chain. Or a magnet of the Gatlon skyline with your name printed down the side of the Merchant Tower."

Nova's smile became a little less strained. "I can't tell you how long I've been searching for exactly that."

# CHAPTER THIRTY-SEVEN

NOVA MEANDERED THROUGH the gift shop, her mouth open in disgust. Every piece of Renegade merchandise ever made must have been on display, with an unwholesome amount of shelf space paying homage to the Council—the beloved five.

Thunderbird alarm clocks. Tsunami lunch boxes. Blacklight night-lights. Dread Warden stickers and Captain Chromium . . .

Well.

*Everything* Captain Chromium. From themed dishes to sun visors, guitar picks to action figures, skateboards to refrigerator magnets. There was no product that someone, somewhere, hadn't thought to put Hugh Everhart's sparkling face on.

It was with a sick feeling that Nova realized, if someone was selling this junk, then someone else was *buying* it.

She picked up a snow globe with the Gatlon skyline beneath the glass, prominently featuring the headquarters tower. It made her think of the mason jar where they were keeping Danna's butterfly, at that very moment perched on Honey's vanity back at the house on Wallowridge.

She put down the snow globe.

"Prodigies used to be hated," she said, her attention skipping from shelf to shelf. She inspected a set of Captain Chromium and Dread Warden salt and pepper shakers, flabbergasted. "They used to literally hunt us down and burn us alive. And now . . ." She held up the shakers. "Now we're tchotchkes?"

Adrian grimaced. "Those are disturbing."

"It's weird though, right?" Nova put the shakers back on the shelf. "To be despised for so long . . . and it wasn't all that long ago."

"A lot changed in the last thirty years," said Adrian, turning a rack of key chains. "Ace Anarchy showed humanity that some prodigies should be feared and hated, while the Renegades showed them that some prodigies should be loved and appreciated."

"Appreciated," said Nova. "But surely not . . . idolized."

Adrian grinned at her. "That's human nature, isn't it? People want to put someone on a pedestal. Maybe it gives them something to dream about." He started to flip through a booklet of postcards.

Nova stared at him. There was a tiny speck of lint on the sleeve of his tuxedo jacket, and it was only because her fingers itched so much to pick it off that she clenched her fist and tucked it behind her back instead.

She'd been anticipating another kiss from Adrian, which made her both excited and nervous and even guilty, knowing that this relationship was doomed. But she'd been at the gala for five whole minutes now and he'd made no move, not even to hold her hand.

The conflicting emotions were more than a little alarming.

"What would you have done if you'd been alive before the Age of Anarchy?" she asked. "Do you think you would have hidden your power? Or tried to make a living as a magician or an illusionist, even if you risked getting caught? Or would you have tried to defend yourself and other prodigies, like Ace Anarchy did?"

One side of Adrian's mouth quirked wryly. "I definitely wouldn't have done what Ace Anarchy did."

"Why not?" said Nova, and though she could hear the defensiveness in her voice, she couldn't stop herself. "Back then, you would have been afraid for your life. You would have known that if you were ever found out, they would kill you. For no other reason than . . ." She hesitated. "For no reason at all."

Adrian seemed to consider her point. After a long moment, he said, "I think I would have found some cause that I could have helped. Like making artificial limbs for war veterans, or toys for children whose families couldn't afford any, or . . . I don't know, something charitable like that. And I would start making these things, and donating them anonymously, so no one would know where they came from. But I'd keep at it, and eventually they'd start to think of me as some protective guardian, and they'd be so grateful for all my help and all the things I made, that when I finally revealed myself and they learned all these things were made by a prodigy, they'd see that our powers can be used for good. And maybe it would have started to change people's minds about us." He glanced at a set of Council-themed shot glasses and shrugged. "Just like the Renegades changed people's minds, by helping people, rather than hurting them."

"And what if," said Nova, "after you revealed yourself, they decided that all those things you made must have been the result of evil forces, and they took them away from all those war veterans or children, and they still killed you? That happened, you know. Lots of prodigies tried to use their powers to do good things. Lots of prodigies tried to show the world that we aren't evil, and it wasn't gratitude they got in return."

"Maybe you're right," said Adrian, "but I still would have tried."

Nova bit back her response.

Ace didn't try to change the world. He *did* change it.

But she knew that Adrian meant what he said. He would have done things differently. He would have tried to change the world by helping people. He would have done what he believed was right for humanity.

And though she knew it wouldn't have made a difference, she admired him for it.

When she and Adrian returned to the gala, she was disappointed to see that only fifteen minutes had passed. She needed to spend at least an hour here to fend off suspicion, but the longer she stayed, the more anxious she became. She felt the importance of the night hanging over her head, refusing to allow her to relax. To *have a good time*, as Honey had insisted.

Adrian showed her to their table and introduced her to Oscar's mom, a plump woman with gray-speckled black hair and a smile as amiable as her son's. Nova recognized Ruby's brothers too, who had claimed the seats on either side of Captain Chromium and were bombarding him with questions.

Nova scanned the nearby tables. She recognized most of the Renegades by now, and it was odd to see so many out of uniform. Eating. Chatting. Enjoying one another's company. They did not seem like superheroes.

They did not seem like the enemy.

Her mouth suddenly dry, Nova gulped down a glass of water.

It was too late to back out now. She had a job to do. Ace was relying on her.

Oscar made a joke and everyone at the table laughed, except Ruby, who turned to Nova and rolled her eyes at whatever ludicrous thing he'd said. It might have been an inside joke between them, if Nova and Ruby had any inside jokes.

If they had been friends.

The speakers squealed, drawing the audience's attention toward the stage.

"That's my cue," said Hugh Everhart, flashing one more perfect smile at Jade and Sterling as he got up from the table.

Nova watched him go, remembering how not very long ago, she had tried to put a poisoned dart into his eye.

*Renegades.*

*They. Are. Renegades.*

At the microphone, Blacklight was welcoming them to the gala and explaining what their generous donations would be put toward. He did not mention the hospital heist, though of course, everyone here knew about it. Everyone here knew that they needed funding to replace the stolen drugs, for kids who were sick, patients who were dying. Here was something that the Renegades, with all their extraordinary powers, couldn't fix. Sure, they had prodigy healers who rotated shifts at the hospital, but it wasn't enough. It would never be enough to help save every person who became afflicted with every disease.

But people relied on the healers. They assumed that if they ever had to go to the hospital, a prodigy would be there to take care of them, even though statistics proved that far more people were cured through modern pharmaceuticals or preventative medicine than any amount of prodigy assistance.

There was no profit in pharmaceuticals though. Not with prodigies at the helm. Would there be now, after this theft proved the value and necessity of modern medicine?

Onstage, the rest of the Council joined Blacklight, and the whole lot of them beamed with pride. Nova was transported back to the parade, where they had stood like kings and queens atop their float, basking in the cheers from their doting public.

This was why she was here. To put an end to the idolizing of these so-called heroes and the promises they made but couldn't keep. The heroes who had not saved her family. Who had not saved her. The heroes who had ruined Ace. Who had made society dependent on them.

Her reasons were stuck on repeat in her head, like a mantra, lest she dared forget them again.

Captain Chromium took the microphone from Blacklight, all teeth and dimples.

"I am inspired every day to be working with some of the brightest, bravest, most compassionate prodigies this world has ever seen," he began, "and I hope each and every one of you will leave here inspired as well. Because it is together that we have restored Gatlon City from the despair that once burdened it, and it is together that we will continue to establish a city, a country, and a world that will become better and brighter than ever before. The amount of support we see here tonight is proof of that!"

The audience cheered, and Nova forced her hands together, though every clap echoed with resentment.

They had not protected her family. They had not saved Evie.

She barely heard the rest of his speech. She paid no attention as the others said a few words, and then the winners of the silent auction were announced. The applause was dim in her ears.

She glanced at the clock.

Her heart rate sped. Her blood pounded through her veins, in sync with the seconds ticking by.

A flurry of servers emerged through a side door, carrying trays laden with dinner plates. A fillet of flaky white fish was set before her, drizzled with dark balsamic vinegar and thick orange marmalade, a dollop of mashed potatoes sprinkled with rosemary, a pile of sweet roasted carrots and charred cherry tomatoes. There was even a sprig of parsley, bright green and fresh.

It was the most enticing meal Nova could ever remember having been handed to her, and she had no appetite for it.

Everyone around her was talking about the money that had already been raised for the hospital. Nova forced down a few bites, though her stomach tried to rebel.

The more she thought about it, the more her eagerness grew. Eager to get on with it. Eager for this night to be over. Eager to be on the other side, to be past the dread and the guilt and the uncertainty. Eager to have Ace look at her with shining, proud eyes and tell her it had all been worth it.

# CHAPTER THIRTY-EIGHT

"**S**HOULD WE DANCE?"

The words, whispered almost against her ear, made Nova jump nearly out of her skin. It took her a moment to process the question, blinking at Adrian as her nerves tingled. She had a list building in the back of her thoughts. A dozen lists. Everything she still had to do. Everything that could go wrong tonight.

Adrian gestured toward the dance floor. She spotted Ruby and Oscar already out there. Nova hadn't noticed them leave the table. Rather than letting his cane impede his moves, Oscar was using it as a prop—spinning Ruby away one second, then using the cane as a pretend fishing pole to "catch" her and reel her back in. Ruby shook her head, momentarily mortified, but her laughter soon took over. And then she was following along, puffing out her cheeks and pretending to swim circles around him. Other dancers were giving them odd looks, but the two could have had the dance floor to themselves for all they seemed to care.

"Yeah," Nova breathed, reminding herself to act normal. As normal as possible, anyway. "Okay."

Adrian took her hand as they made their way through the tables. Though his grip was loose, it still sent a series of lightning bolts shooting up her arm.

Only once he'd taken her into his arms and they were surrounded by the upbeat notes of the band did Nova remember that she didn't know how to do this. She had been trained to fight. To kill. What did she know about dancing?

But Adrian seemed no more comfortable than she was, and she was relieved when the extent of his skills seemed to be pressing one hand against her lower back and turning them around in time with the music. Nova observed their fellow dancers. Her attention found Blacklight, who normally struck her as pompous and vain, but she was surprised to see him intentionally making a mockery of himself. One moment he was flourishing his hands in the air, then twisting his hips in imitation of some mid-century dance steps. He looked like he was having fun.

Not far away was Tsunami, who was dancing with a man who was almost portly compared to her petite frame. They were moving way too slow, and gazing into each other's eyes, as if for the moment they were the only people in the room. Was that her husband? Nova had never seen him before, and he didn't at all fit what she would have pictured Tsunami's partner to look like. Too short, too round, too . . . balding. He was about as opposite the mate of a great superhero as she could have imagined, but there was no mistaking the doting glimpses between them.

Her jaw clenched, though she wasn't sure what about them made irritation rear up inside her.

Dragging her focus back to Adrian, Nova tried to school her expression into pleasantness, while inside she wanted to scream. How could Adrian be so nice, so sweet, so authentic, always so damned authentic? How could he be one of *them*?

"Look, Nova," started Adrian, "I wanted to make sure that . . . last night . . ." He trailed off, and Nova's pulse jumped as memories jumbled together all over again. His kisses, his hands, the head-phones, the star . . . "I didn't . . . cross a line, or anything, did I?"

She laughed, though more from discomfort than anything. "I wasn't exactly pushing you away," she said, her cheeks reddening. At the memory of it. At the truth of her words.

A faint smile twitched at his lips. "Yeah, but . . . I just didn't want you thinking . . ." Again, he seemed incapable of finishing his sentence, and Nova wondered what it was she shouldn't be thinking. Then Adrian's thoughts seemed to change direction. "And I'm really sorry about the whole falling asleep thing. I guess I didn't realize how tired I was, and I don't want you to think that I was . . . you know. Bored, or something."

"It's okay," she said, the heat in her cheeks becoming nearly insufferable. "You needed the rest."

He looked away, and she noticed that he didn't hurry to agree with her. He wasn't suspicious, was he? She couldn't tell. Her palms started to sweat and she resisted the urge to wipe them on the shoulders of his tuxedo jacket. She had felt those muscles before, when she'd nestled her head against them moments before falling asleep. She certainly did not need to feel them again. Not tonight.

"For the record," said Adrian, quieter now, so that she had to strain to hear him, "just in case there's any . . . confusion. I really like you, Nova."

Goose bumps erupted across her skin. He was watching her closely.

She swallowed. "I really like you too."

It wasn't even a lie.

Adrian seemed relieved, if not entirely surprised by her confession.

"I'm glad," he said. "Because I know I haven't always been super smooth when it comes to . . . this." He gestured between the two of them.

She lifted an eyebrow. "No, you're clearly a neophyte when it comes to . . . *this.*" She mimicked his gesture.

Rather than laugh, as she expected, Adrian's small smile turned to a confused frown. "Neophyte?"

"Sorry," said Nova, chuckling again, and wondering if it was possible for her to be any more terrible at this. "It means amateur."

"I know what it—" Adrian caught himself, and his frown deepened further. She could see him contemplating something as he stared at her.

"What?" she asked.

Adrian shook himself. "Nothing. Just, for a second you reminded me of . . . someone." He shook his head again and forced a brighter grin. "Never mind."

"Can I cut in?" interrupted Oscar, nudging Adrian out of the way before either of them had a chance to respond.

Adrian gaped at him. "Oh . . . uh, sure?" he stammered.

Nova smiled and allowed Oscar to spin her away. Glancing back, she saw Adrian retreating from the dance floor.

"Before you get carried away," she said, "just know that I will not be *reeled in.*"

Oscar gave her a strange look. "What?"

"That move you were doing earlier? With the . . . fishing pole?"

It took him another second, before comprehension dawned and he let out an uncomfortable, decidedly un-Oscar-like chuckle.

They started dancing, but the ease Oscar had shown with Ruby was replaced with jerky movements and a tense expression.

"Is everything okay?" said Nova, even as her attention strayed to the clock again.

"Yeah. Yeah, yeah. Things are great. Nice shindig, right?"

"Very nice."

He cleared his throat and glanced around the dance floor, then tugged Nova closer to him. "Okay, be honest. How do you think I'm doing?"

She blinked. "Doing?"

"With Ruby. I've been trying to impress her all night but I can't get a read on her. Do you think she's having a good time?"

"Um . . . yes?" said Nova. "You both looked like you were having fun."

"We did, didn't we? I mean, I was. Having fun, I mean. While also feeling like at any moment I could throw up all over her shoes, which—I don't want to do that. They're nice shoes, you know?"

Nova didn't know, but she smiled sympathetically anyway.

"Okay, let me ask you this. Renegade to Renegade. Bosom buddy to bosom buddy."

"Are we—?"

"Don't deny it."

She bit her lip.

"To your knowledge, have the words 'Wow, that Oscar is such a thoughtful and/or studly and/or impossibly irresistible guy' ever passed Ruby's lips?"

Nova smothered a laugh. "Uh . . . not those exact words, no."

He brightened hopefully. "But similar words?"

"I don't know, Oscar. She clearly likes spending time with

you, and you're so good to her brothers. I'm sure she thinks it's really . . . sweet."

His expression turned thoughtful. "Thoughtful sweet or studly sweet?"

"I'm not sure I know what 'studly sweet' is."

"Yeah, me neither." He glanced toward their table, then spun Nova once beneath his arm. She was surprised at how her body reacted to his lead, and it occurred to her that, despite all his antics, despite needing the cane for occasional support, Oscar actually did know how to dance.

"You've liked her for a long time, haven't you?"

He smiled wistfully. "From the first moment I saw her at the Renegade trials. But there's always been a part of me that thought . . . you know, she wouldn't be interested in me like that."

Nova frowned. She'd never, not once, heard Oscar say anything remotely self-conscious before. It was a little bewildering.

He caught her expression and lifted his chin. "Don't worry, I'm over that now. You remember that barista I saved after the hospital heist? I mean, with Ruby's help."

"The 'damsel'?"

"Yeah. I know you weren't there but she was, like, really into me. And it made me think, you know what? I'm a total catch."

Nova laughed as he pulled her close again. "I can find no fault in your logic."

"Right. So. Give me some pointers. How did you and Adrian get out of the friend zone?"

Nova stared at him. Is that how people viewed her and Adrian? That they'd been friends, and now they were something more?

She wanted to believe it was due to her being such an amazing actress, but she knew that wasn't the case at all. As much as she wanted to tell herself differently, there wasn't much acting where Adrian was involved, and there hadn't been for a long time.

She *did* like him. More than she should. More than she wanted to admit.

"You could tell her, you know." She shrugged. "Just tell her that you like her as more than a friend and see what happens."

He shot her a disgruntled look. "Really? That's the best you've got?"

"It's a legitimate course of action."

"I can't just *tell* her. What if she laughs at me? What if it makes everything weird?"

"That's the risk you take. Either you resign yourself to keeping things just the way they are, or you put yourself out there knowing that it could end in rejection."

He shook his head. "Not helping. Seriously. How did Adrian win you over?"

This time, Nova did laugh. Win her over? Adrian hadn't *won* her over.

But then her laugh cut off abruptly.

He hadn't.

Had he?

She tried to think back to when her feelings toward him had started to shift. When he went from being another Renegade, the son of her sworn enemies, to something . . . more. It had happened slowly at first, but then . . . not so slow. The past months blurred together, and she'd witnessed his goodness, his kindness, his talent, his charm. All the little things that made him . . . *him*.

"I don't know," she finally confessed. "He asked me to go to the carnival with him. I mean, it was sort of a work thing, but also . . . sort of a date. I suppose."

"Yeah, yeah, I've tried that. Asking her to go places with me. But she always assumes it's for the Renegades, or we're going with the whole group. She's always like, 'great, I'll see if Danna wants to carpool.'" He huffed.

A nerve twitched in Nova's brow at the mention of Danna, and she thought again of the butterfly trapped inside that mason jar.

"Adrian brought me sandwiches once," she said. "When I was working late at headquarters."

Oscar gave her an appraising look. "I like sandwiches."

"Ruby probably does too."

He spun Nova away from him again, and his expression seemed warmer when she spun back. "Who doesn't like sandwiches?" he said, sounding borderline jovial.

Remembering all the tips that Honey had given her on flirting and the art of seduction, Nova added, "And you should try to find little ways to touch her. Subtle, but not too subtle."

He nodded intently. "Right. Got it."

"And make sure you laugh when she makes a joke. Even if it's not really that funny."

He considered this. "She's not *not* funny. I mean, I'll obviously be the funny one in the relationship. If . . . when . . . well, you know what I mean. But still, she's got a great sense of humor."

"Oh!" said Nova, excited that she remembered so much of Honey's tutelage. "And surprise her with gifts once in a while, so she knows you've been thinking about her. Flowers are good. And jewelry."

At this, Oscar seemed uncertain. "She can make her own jewelry."

"It's the *thought*," said Nova. Taking her hand from his shoulder, she pulled up the lacy sleeve of her dress to reveal her copper filigree bracelet. "The first time I met Adrian, he fixed the clasp on my bracelet. He may not have given this to me, but I still"—her voice faded, almost sadly—"I can't help but think of him, you know . . . Every time I see it . . ."

A hand grabbed Nova's forearm, twisting her wrist around. She tensed and prepared to break the perpetrator's arm—but it was only Magpie, gawking at the bracelet.

"Oh," said Nova, wilting. "You. Funny, we were just talking about that time you tried to steal—"

"What *is* this?" said Magpie.

Nova realized with a start that she'd revealed the glowing orb in the bracelet's setting. She'd forgotten it was there. She yanked her hand away and pulled the sleeve over it.

"Nothing," she said.

"That wasn't there before," said Magpie, pointing at Nova's wrist.

"No. I took it to a jeweler." She started to turn back to Oscar.

"But what is it?" Magpie persisted, grabbing Nova's elbow. "It has a different signature from . . . from *anything.*"

Nova scowled at her. "Signature?"

"Yeah. Not amber. Not a citrine. Definitely not a diamond . . ." Her surly expression was even more annoyed than usual as she tried to puzzle through whatever she was sensing from the bracelet. "But it's . . ." Her breaths became ragged, and Nova didn't resist this time as Magpie lifted her arm and pulled up her sleeve again. "It's worth something. It's worth *a lot.*" Her eyes were wide with . . . with *yearning.*

Nova snatched her arm away again and shot Oscar a baffled look, which he returned in kind.

"Where did it come from?" said Magpie. She seemed desperate to know, but Nova fumbled with what to tell her.

It came from a dream? A painting? A statue?

What *was* it?

Nova didn't know.

The strike of a clock echoed through the room, startling her.

"Nothing," she said hastily. "It's nothing." She linked her elbow with Oscar's. "Let's head back to the others."

He didn't argue, but she could sense him watching Magpie as they left the dance floor. "What was that about?"

She shook her head. "No idea. For some reason, that kid is obsessed with my bracelet. If it ever goes missing, I'll definitely know where to look for it." Spotting Ruby at their table, Nova paused and squeezed Oscar's arm. "Hey, Oscar?"

"Yeah?"

She met his gaze and, after a hesitant beat, she smiled. For the first time she realized that . . . this could be it. She might never see Oscar or Ruby again after this night. At least, not unless it was from opposite sides of a battlefield.

She hoped he would know how much she meant this. "I know this is kind of trite, but seriously, you *are* a catch, and . . . I think Ruby already knows that. Just be yourself. How could she not fall in love with you?"

He stared at her, and for a heartbeat, she could see the depths of his insecurity. Gratitude shimmered in his brown eyes, mingling with hope, overcome with wanting. For the first time, Nova wondered how much of his confidence was an act.

Or maybe that's all confidence ever was. An act.

Then the moment passed and Oscar's crooked smile was back. "*Kind of* trite? Honestly, Nova, did you pull that off the front of a birthday card? 'Just be yourself.' Please. Of all the useless advice . . ." He clicked his tongue as he walked away, using his cane to clear a chair from his path.

Nova shook her head. She was grinning, but it vanished when she spied the clock again.

She had stayed too long already.

Adrian was at their table, too, entertaining Ruby's brothers with stories of all the amazing things they had at headquarters, from the training halls to the virtual reality simulators.

"Adrian," Nova said, settling a hand on his wrist. He jolted. "I'm so sorry, but . . . before I left home tonight, my uncle told me he wasn't feeling well. That's why I was so late. I didn't want it to ruin our night, but . . . I'm a little worried about him. I think I should go home and make sure he's okay."

Adrian jumped from his seat. "Do you want to call him?"

Nova faked a laugh. "I could, but he's so stubborn. He could be halfway to dead and he wouldn't say anything. No . . . I just really think I should go."

"Of course. Can I take you? Or—"

She shook her head. "I'll call a cab. But thanks."

He didn't argue with her, and she wondered if it was because he knew she could take care of herself, or because he had seen her "home" once and didn't want to embarrass her further by seeing it again.

"I hope he's okay," said Adrian. "I'll see you at headquarters tomorrow?"

"Yeah, of course."

There was a moment—the briefest of moments—when Nova thought he might bend down and kiss her. Here, in front of everyone.

And in that breath of a moment, she longed for that kiss. *Just once more.*

But he hesitated too long, and Nova forced a smile as she turned away.

Adrian caught her by the wrist and tugged her back. Nova's heart jumped and then he was leaning toward her, pressing a single kiss against her lips.

He pulled away, a little sheepish. "Good night."

Nova's body tingled and, for an eternity trapped inside a heartbeat, she considered staying.

But the moment passed and she pulled herself away. "Good night."

She moved through the sea of tables in a daze, her mouth burning, her legs like jellyfish. Finally, she shoved through the exit doors and as soon as the chilly night air struck her, her addled thoughts began to clear.

Adrian was problematic. Bad for her conviction. Bad for her loyalties.

Her head would be a lot clearer after tonight.

Because she would no longer be a Renegade. This charade would be over, and with it . . . any ties she had to Adrian Everhart.

"Good-bye, Adrian," she whispered into the night air.

She allowed herself to be the tiniest bit sad as she walked the three blocks to the parking lot where she had agreed to meet Leroy and Honey. The sports car was there, sickly yellow and mottled with dents and scratches. Honey Harper was perched on the hood, buffing her nails. Leroy was in the driver's seat, his elbow draped outside the window.

"How was it?" said Honey, jogging her leg.

"Dandy," said Nova, tearing off her wristband. She handed it to Honey, who peered at the high-tech device with vague distrust. "This will need to be taken back to the house."

"Do you think I wasn't paying attention to all that plotting we did earlier? Don't worry about your precious alibi. I have money for a cab, and I even prepared a disguise." She pulled out a pair of over-size sunglasses and slipped them on.

"In the middle of the night," Nova said, nodding. "Not suspicious at all."

"Not suspicious—*mysterious*."

"Fine. Just make sure you go straight back to the house. No detours."

Honey flicked her fingers through the air, a gesture that only increased Nova's nerves. Maybe she should have given this job to Phobia. Tracking the wristband would provide her with an alibi if anything went wrong. She didn't expect it to happen that way. She had every reason to believe that her lies were at an end.

She would not fail.

It was too late to change the plan now, anyway.

"Did you say your good-byes?" asked Honey, her gaze suddenly piercing as she stood. "I'm sure it wasn't easy."

Nova's jaw clenched. "It wasn't that hard, either," she muttered.

She made to move around Honey toward the passenger's side of the car, but Honey sidestepped, blocking her. Her mouth was still smiling, her eyes remained hidden behind the glasses. "You've seemed distant today, little Nightmare. I'm worried about you."

Nova stared at her. "I've had a lot on my mind, in case you hadn't noticed."

Honey made a disinterested sound in her throat.

"What's wrong?" said Leroy, opening his car door and climbing out.

"You know," Honey continued, ignoring him, "you're proba-bly too young to remember, but we were feared once. Feared and respected. And now . . . we're *this*." She swirled her glossy finger toward the car, with all its rust and dings.

Leroy puffed his chest. "Uncalled for, Honey Harper."

"*Queen Bee*," said Honey, her voice hardening. "And the car is fine, but there was a time when it was the envy of the gangs. When we had jewels and champagne and *power* . . . and now we're scurrying through a parking garage in the dead of night, afraid to show our faces in public. And all because of the Renegades."

Nova spun the bracelet on her wrist. "I'm well aware of that, Honey. They took everything from me, too."

"That's right. They did." Honey lowered the glasses to the tip of her nose, her smoky gaze burning into Nova. "They can offer you notoriety and a fancy pair of boots. They might even give you pretty gems like that bauble on your wrist."

Nova's heart lurched and her hand automatically clapped over the hidden star.

Honey chuckled. "I noticed it when you were trying on dresses earlier. You think I could have missed it?"

"It's nothing," said Nova.

"I don't care what it is. My point, Nova, is that the Renegades can offer you a lot, but they can never offer you revenge."

"Your Majesty," said Leroy, with more than a tinge of irony, "have you forgotten that all of this is Nightmare's doing? Her reconnaissance, her plan. She's risking her life for this mission."

Honey smiled sweetly. "I haven't forgotten, Cyanide. I just want to ensure that *she* doesn't forget, either."

"I won't," said Nova through gritted teeth.

"Good." Honey cupped Nova's cheek in one hand, and it took all her willpower not to recoil from the touch. "Make us proud." Pulling her hand away, she tucked Nova's wristband into her dress and sauntered away into the night.

Nova swallowed, hard. Though the star on her wrist was weight-less, she felt its presence like a ball and chain.

Leroy scrutinized her. "Nova, are you—"

"Fine," she spat. Without looking at him, she yanked open the door to the car. "I'm ready. Let's bring them down."

# CHAPTER THIRTY-NINE

EROY PULLED INTO A SPACE in an empty parking garage one block from headquarters. They had hardly spoken for the duration of the ride.

"Pop the trunk," said Nova, relieved to stumble out of the passenger door.

"When did you become so bossy?" Leroy teased. "This little group doesn't need two Queen Bees, you know."

Nova said nothing. She wasn't in the mood for teasing.

Her shoes echoed on the concrete as she rounded the back of the sports car. In the shadows, she saw a familiar black jacket, her beloved weaponry belt, and on top of the pile—a metal mask, curved to the shape of her face.

Reaching behind her neck, she pulled down the zipper on the dress. She wriggled out of it, then stepped into her dark pants and pulled on the tank top and jacket, the mask, and finally the gloves that she had designed herself. It was always a little disconcerting putting them on and cutting off the most convenient source of her power—if she ran into trouble, she would want her fingers free— but she would need the gloves tonight.

The clothes felt confining compared to the Renegade uniform she'd gotten used to, but once the ensemble was complete, Nova felt . . . strong. Powerful. Almost *invincible*.

No more convoluted loyalties. No more uncertain agendas. No more secrets, no more lies.

She was an Anarchist—a villain, if that's what it made her.

She was Nightmare.

She slammed the trunk shut. "Give me one hour," she called to Leroy. "Drive around until then, just in case we were followed."

"Do you think I'm an amateur?" Cyanide smirked, one elbow hanging out of the window. "I'll be here."

Nova waited until he sped away, tires squealing through the garage. She tugged down her sleeve to make sure the star was covered again, and then she ran.

She stayed in the shadows and the stairwells, checking around every corner, confirming that the streets were clear, the alleys empty. Soon she was standing outside a little-used back entrance to Renegade Headquarters, where deliveries were made and foreign dignitaries were brought inside when they were worried the tourists and journalists would make too much fuss over them. There was a security camera two stories up, but it was angled at the doorway—the building's most vulnerable entrance.

Nova would not be going in through any doors.

She lurked beside a dumpster long enough to be sure no one had seen her approach, then tilted her head up and assessed the climb. The sides of the building were smooth, but there were enough ledges around the windows that she would have footholds when necessary.

It would be difficult to scale, but nothing she couldn't handle.

She pressed the switch on the back of the gloves, sending a jolt of electricity through the material. Suction cups emerged on her palms and fingertips. Nova reached overhead and pressed her hand against the building's side. The gloves took her weight and she started to climb.

As she passed the third story, the fourth, the tenth, the buildings around her began to drop away. She scanned their rooftops and water towers and began to feel exposed, but she knew, logically, that she had little to worry about. The funny thing about living in a city full of skyscrapers was that no one ever looked up.

Besides, the sense of vulnerability was something she'd begun to get used to. Nova had been paranoid from the moment she'd stepped foot into the arena for the Renegade trials. She had been painfully aware of the narrow ledge she was teetering on from the start.

There was a part of her— possibly a big part—that felt more relieved than anxious as she reached the twenty-sixth floor, the first of many that remained unused, and only one floor up from the security offices. No matter what happened here tonight, she would no longer have to lie.

Planting her feet on a windowsill and securing her hand against the exterior wall, Nova reached for the window breaker hooked over her belt. She fit the cylinder into the bottom corner of the window and pressed the lever, releasing the spring-loaded spike.

The window shattered. Tiny bits of glass rained across the sill and toward the street, sounding like wind chimes as it clinked onto the concrete below. Nova used the breaker to brush away the remaining sharp edges and ducked inside.

The floor was as empty now as it had been when she'd scoped it out earlier that day after inspecting the blueprints she'd taken from

Adrian's house. There were no cameras installed here. No sensors. No alarms.

She jogged to the stairwell and slipped down to the twenty-fifth floor. The door opened on a plain beige hallway that was roped off just outside the stairwell, with a sign that read SECURITY PERSON-NEL ONLY BEYOND THIS POINT.

Nova stepped over the rope and crept down the hall. It was lined with closed doors and ID tag scanners. She didn't slow when she heard footsteps coming from the next hallway, though she was surprised when an unfamiliar woman turned the corner. Rather than the gray Renegade uniform, she was wearing a smart navy suit with an ID tag clipped to the breast pocket.

An administrator, Nova guessed. Not a prodigy.

The woman froze when she saw Nova, her eyes widening.

Nova ripped off one of the gloves and leaped for her. The woman sucked in a breath, but her scream never came. The second Nova's fingers touched the woman's neck, her power rushed through her. With a strangled moan, the woman slumped forward into Nova's arms.

Nova deposited her in an alcove beneath a drinking fountain and snagged the ID tag.

She moved faster now, almost running until she came to the room that had been labeled as the security center on the blueprints. She held the woman's tag against the scanner and it blinked green. Nova turned the handle and pushed open the door.

She was greeted by a wall of monitors showing a hundred different views of headquarters, and two empty chairs.

Nova stepped into the room.

Something whipped out from behind the door, stabbing her in the thigh. Nova cried out as the barb ripped out of her, leaving a gash in her pants. She buckled to one knee, feeling like her leg had just had a bite taken out of it. Within seconds the flesh around the wound started to burn, as a trail of blood dribbled to the floor.

"Are you messing with me?"

She looked up. Standing over her, Stingray slammed the door shut, his face twisted in disgust.

"You give Sketch and his loser friends all that trouble, and this is all you've got? I saw you on the cameras the second you stepped into the stairwell." He gestured toward the bank of screens. "What a waste. Thought you were supposed to be some hotshot villain." Sneering, he crouched at her side. "At least we've got a few minutes to kill before that paralysis wears off. Might as well see who we've got here."

He reached for her mask. Nova ground her teeth, resisting the urge to pull away as his clammy fingers dug beneath the sides of the metal.

His fingertips brushed her jawline, and that was all she needed. Skin touching skin.

Realization spread over Stingray's face. The amateur mistake he'd just made. Then he tipped onto his side with a heavy thump.

With him unconscious, Nova returned her attention to her wound. She pressed one palm over it and her hand pulled away damp with blood.

Injured and in pain, yes, but she wasn't paralyzed like Stingray believed.

She rubbed the blood off on the side of her pants and dug a hasty bandage and some healing salve from the kit at her belt, securing it tight around her leg. She could feel the warm press of the Vitality Charm trapped between her jacket and her sternum.

Poison, disease, and evidently venom like Stingray's too. The

Renegades had been fools to stash the medallion away in their vault, without any appreciation. It was just one more example of their arrogance.

With the wound attended to, she turned her attention to the screens.

She spotted Frostbite guarding the main entrance, and Aftershock patrolling the back half of the ground floor. It took longer to find Gargoyle, but finally she spotted him making his rounds near the laboratories on the mezzanine level.

None of them appeared concerned, which was a relief. Stingray must have been confident enough in his ability to take down Nightmare. He hadn't bothered to alert the rest of his team.

Removing his wristband, Nova stuffed it into her belt, then stepped over Stingray's sleeping body. Nova approached the controls. She had studied the installation paperwork at length, the coding, the backup software, the fail safes, the alarms. She had planned for various scenarios until her eyes crossed.

In the end, it took just under eight minutes to disable the cameras throughout the building. She shut them all down, sending the system into dead air.

Eight minutes felt like an eternity, but with the security down, her job would be made a lot easier.

Adrenaline was coursing fast through her veins as she left the security room. She barely gave a passing glance to the sleeping woman beneath the drinking fountain. No one had come for her.

The building was mostly empty, but this woman was a reminder that not *everyone* had chosen to go to the gala that night. There could be more surprises.

She needed to be cautious. Stingray had been cocky and it cost him. Nova wouldn't make the same mistake.

She arrived at the elevators, but hesitated. Changing her mind, she headed back for the stairwell. Her leg groaned, but she fought through the pain. She focused on counting floors. She kept her mind on the job ahead.

She paused when she reached the artifacts department, just long enough to check how her bandages were holding up. A spot of blood had seeped through the wrappings, but the burning sensation around the wound had faded to a dull throb.

She opened the door.

A familiar scene greeted her. The two desks inside the reception area, one sterile and neat, the other cluttered with Snapshot's knickknacks. The lights were out, the floor silent and deserted. Nova marched through the filing room and used Stingray's wristband to unlock the door to the vault. The only sounds were her own footsteps thudding on the floor as she passed among the dimly lit shelves.

She went to prodigy weapons first and claimed the so-called Silver Spear. The Captain's own pike, the one he had used to try to destroy the helmet. Tried, and failed. She hefted it from its shelf— eight feet long and cool in her hand. It felt strong and sturdy, but not too heavy. It was perfect, actually. Elegant. Sharp. Superbly balanced.

She propped it against her shoulder and made her way to the restricted area.

Standing at the end of the aisle, she could see the chromium cube on its shelf, looking exactly as it always did. Shiny, solid, and faintly mocking. Lost in the shadows and the clutter of other random relics. Like the object it contained was hardly worth noting.

Setting her jaw, Nova shuffled the pike from hand to hand. Someday, this weapon would probably live inside a museum, she thought, where people could contemplate the tool they believed had destroyed Ace Anarchy's helmet. They would talk about the good deeds that Captain Chromium had done. How he lifted society from the despair it had fallen into. How he had defeated the most destructive supervillain of all time. People would talk about the first Renegades and how they had been brave enough to fight for a world they believed in, and *that* . . . that was . . .

Nova winced, shaking the thought from her head.

Those first Renegades, including Captain Chromium, might have helped a lot of people, but they hadn't helped *her*.

"Get out of my head," she growled, her fist tightening around the javelin.

On the other end of the aisle, Callum stepped out of the shadows. He was wearing the same wrinkled clothes he always wore. She had wondered, passingly, why he wasn't at the gala. Maybe there would simply be too many ungrateful people loitering around for him to stand it.

He seemed more thoughtful than afraid as he took in Nova, with her dark hood and metal mask and the chromium pole in her grip.

"Nightmare," he said, scanning the shelves. "What are you here for?" He sounded honestly curious. Nova could practically see his mind working, trying to determine which of the hundreds of objects here would be most appealing to an Anarchist who was supposed to be dead. He started to come closer to her, scanning the shelves, until his focus landed on the chromium box and he paused. "It's the helmet, isn't it?"

Nova angled the point of the javelin toward him. "You can't stop me," she said, taking a step closer. He did not move back. "Don't try to be a hero."

His gaze dropped to the pike. Then he came closer to her, putting himself between Nova and the chromium box.

Snarling, Nova marched forward, until the point was only inches from his abdomen. "Move."

A muscle in his cheek twitched, and a memory flashed through Nova's mind. The world laid out before her. The ocean glittering beneath a vibrant sky. A city pulsing with life. A thousand little miracles, and more occurring every day. A million little things to wonder at. And Callum had showed her that. Callum had—

A guttural cry was torn from Nova's throat. She spun the pike around and lunged forward, knocking the butt end into Callum's chest. He grunted and fell to the floor. "Great skies," he gasped. "What was that for?"

"Stay out of my head."

Callum lifted himself onto his elbows. He looked like he wanted to laugh, but he didn't. "I didn't do anything." Then his brow tightened in confusion. "Wait . . . you know who I am? What I can do?"

Nova glowered. "I know my enemies."

He sat up a little taller, rubbing his chest where she had struck him. "Listen."

And she wanted to listen. She *really* wanted to listen. To hear what he would say. What wisdom he could impart from the ridiculous way he saw the world. Because she liked the way he saw the world. She wanted to see it that way too. Somewhere deep inside, she wanted to believe that there might be a way for all the world—Renegades and Anarchists, prodigies and civilians—to coexist inside some sort of harmonious equilibrium. No war, no power struggles. No heroes, no villains.

But Callum's outlook was flawed. It would only work if everyone saw the world the way he did.

And the painful truth was that *no one* saw the world the way he did.

"No," she said, startling him.

"No?"

"No. I won't listen. It's too late for that."

Tucking the pike behind her, she bent over and pressed her fingertips to his brow. Callum didn't flinch, but the flash of disappointment stung just as much.

Once he'd fallen asleep, Nova shook out her hand to rid herself of the sensation of unleashing her power. It felt different this time, using it against someone who she couldn't quite see as her enemy despite what she'd said. Even Adrian, for as much as he filled her with yearning, had always still been the enemy.

Squaring her shoulders, she stepped over Callum's body and propped the pike against the shelf. She reached for the cube. As her hand neared it, the bracelet warmed against her skin. Pursing her lips, Nova rolled back the hem of her sleeve. The star was glowing brighter than it had all day—almost blindingly bright, sending deep shadows dancing over the shelves. She half expected it to explode, or maybe disappear, like it had when she had first tried to grab it out of the statue's outstretched hands. But when it did nothing more than pulse warmly for a few seconds, she turned her attention back to the box.

Inhaling, she lifted the cube and turned it from side to side, inspecting it from every angle. Each side was identical to the others, with no apparent markings or weaknesses.

She set the cube on the floor and picked up the pike again. She took a step back and prepared herself for what she was about to do, though she didn't have any idea what was going to happen. She'd imagined this moment a hundred times since the Captain had made that offhand remark at dinner.

*Or I could make a sledgehammer to take to it, if I was feeling destructive.*

She had hoped that once she was here, holding the pike and

standing over the box, the next step would seem obvious. But all she had was a distant hope that this would work.

"This will work," she murmured, tightening her grip on the pike. "Please, let this work."

She raised the pike overhead, braced herself, and slammed the point into the center of the box.

The contact reverberated through the metal and into her arms, clattering down to her bones. Nova stumbled back.

The chromium box had skidded a few feet away but was otherwise unharmed.

Not even a dent.

Snarling, Nova tried again, harder this time. The metals pinged loudly and again her arms shook from the impact. The box crashed into the nearest shelf, making the whole unit tremble from the blow.

Still, no sign that it was weakened.

Desperation welled inside of her. No, no, no. It could not all be for nothing.

This had to work.

She turned the pike over and tried again, this time swinging it like a battle ax. It thudded hard against the box. Her body jolted from the impact. She swung it again. Again. *Again.*

Reeling back, Nova stared at the pike in disgust. She was panting, though as much from outrage as exertion. This had to work. She needed that helmet and she didn't have any other options.

She couldn't fail. Not *now.*

She hefted the pike over her shoulder and screamed. The star at her wrist flashed, blindingly bright. An electric current shot through her arms and into her fingers as she threw the spear as hard as she could.

As it soared down the aisle, it glowed.

Not silver, but coppery gold.

It struck the box squarely in the side.

The cube shattered.

It might as well have been made of glass.

Nova jumped back as bits of broken chromium were flung at her ankles. The pike clattered to the floor and rolled a few feet away, grayish silver once again.

Her arms tingled from the jolt of energy that had passed through them. Her chest heaved. The wound in her leg was throbbing worse than before.

But all of that was soon forgotten.

A cry of disbelief tumbled from Nova's lips.

The helmet was there, lying on its side amid the splintered box, exactly as she remembered it. The bronze-tinged material still gleamed faintly, reminding Nova of her father, and how the threads of energy would glow like tiny strips of sunlight as he worked. There was a raised band along the center of the skull, ending in a sharp point on the brow, and the opening in the front where Ace's eyes had once peered.

The bits of chromium crunched beneath her boots as Nova stepped closer. She knelt and picked it up, cradling the helmet in both hands.

It did not look dangerous. It did not even look foreboding.

It looked merely as though it had been waiting for her.

# CHAPTER FORTY

R UBY AND OSCAR were dancing again when Adrian left the
gala. Nova had been gone for more than an hour, and he'd
spent some time chatting with Kasumi and her husband and
mingling with a few of the patrols he'd trained with years ago but
rarely saw anymore, except in passing. He'd eaten his dessert—a
sweet and creamy lemon custard—and had given Nova's to Ruby's
brothers to share. He'd danced once with Ruby and once with
Oscar's mom.

But he'd been counting the minutes since Nova had left, biding
his time before he could leave without the truth being completely
obvious.

Without her there, he just wasn't interested in dancing and
small talk. All he wanted was to go home, lie down in the jungle he
had made, and think of the next time he would see her.

The next time he would kiss her.

He couldn't stop grinning as he left the gala and tucked his hands
into the pockets of his tuxedo pants. His marker was there and he
pulled it out and rolled it between his palms.

He should draw something for Nova, to give to her when they saw each other in the morning. Just a little something to remind her of the past couple of nights. The past couple of amazing nights. Something to let her know he was thinking about her. That he was serious about her.

He knew Nova was slow to trust. Slow to let go of her uncertainties. Slow to risk getting hurt. He thought he understood her better now that she'd told him the truth of her parents, and her sister. Great skies, her baby sister. Evie.

His smile faded thinking about it. His heart twisted to imagine Nova, small and frightened Nova, having to endure something so horrific . . .

And though he knew, logically, that there wasn't a person on this planet who needed his protection less than Nova McLain did, he couldn't help the overwhelming desire to protect her anyway. To keep her from ever having to suffer like that again.

He twirled the marker, contemplating what gift he could draw that would encompass all that. His dress shoes were clacking noisily on the pavement, a steady cadence that followed him down the familiar, dark streets toward home.

He had just discarded the most obvious, trivial ideas—jewelry, flowers, a new weaponry belt—when a small movement darted past his vision, nearly smacking into his glasses.

Adrian reeled back. At first he thought it was a bird, or one of those creepy giant moths that sometimes appeared out of nowhere in his basement.

But then he saw it. A black and gold butterfly, dancing around a lamppost a few feet away from him.

"Danna?" said Adrian, scanning the street for more stray insects. The butterfly seemed to be alone, and it crossed his mind

that there was a chance it was nothing more than a common monarch butterfly.

One that just happened to be flittering about in the middle of
the night.

Scratching his cheek with the capped marker, Adrian sauntered
slowly past the lamppost.

The butterfly darted after him. It twirled once around his head,
then alighted on top of a fire hydrant.

"Danna," he said again, with more certainty this time.

The butterfly opened and closed its wings as if in response,
though Danna had once told him that she couldn't hear while in
swarm mode—only see, and . . . *sense* things. It was hard to explain,
she said.

Adrian peered around again, but the street was deserted. Parked
cars and dark shop windows. There were mosquitoes and crane flies
clicking against a neon sign, but no butterflies.

Where was the rest of her swarm?

Where had she been all night?

The butterfly fluttered toward Adrian. He held out his hand and
it perched on his knuckle. Its antenna twitched and it seemed to be
studying him, waiting.

"Okay," he said, pocketing his marker. "You lead the way."

Whether or not it could hear him, the butterfly left his hand,
circled his body one more time, and took off.

Adrian followed.

Two miles later, he wished he had stopped by the house to put
on different shoes.

The buildings changed from glass-and-steel office buildings
to strip malls and warehouses to crammed-together apartments.
Most of the trek was uphill and as the elevation rose, so too did the

affluence of the neighborhood. It wasn't quite the row of mansions that he lived on, but the streets held the memory of quiet suburbia. He could tell people still lived in some of the homes—some even had recently mowed lawns—though like most neighborhoods in the city, it showed signs of abandonment and neglect. Fences needing a fresh coat of paint. Broken windows hastily boarded up. Roofs covered in moss and pine needles from unkempt trees.

The butterfly never flew ahead so far that he couldn't keep up, and it frequently had to pause and wait for him. He racked his brain to think of a reason why Danna wouldn't transform back into her human form, and where the rest of her swarm could be. The only explanation was that the rest of her butterflies were trapped somewhere, preventing her from reforming. Maybe that's what this was about. Was she leading him to her location so he could set her free? If so, maybe this wasn't as ominous as he'd initially thought. Maybe one of her butterflies had gotten sucked into a vacuum bag, or had been captured by a kid and stuck in an empty juice carton for a well-intentioned science project.

But then the hill became steeper, and the neighborhood turned desolate, and he realized where she was taking him.

The hairs on the back of his neck prickled.

He started to notice signs of a long-ago battle and the destruction it had wrought. Scorch marks on the pavement. Holes smashed through brick walls. An entire building with the windows blown out.

And then there were no buildings at all.

Adrian left the crumbling homes and apartments behind and stood at the edge of the wasteland. The Battle for Gatlon had leveled almost an entire square mile of civilization, and the debris had never been cleaned up. A chain-link fence had been erected around the perimeter, warning of possible radiation poisoning, which was enough to keep most tourists away.

In the center of the wasteland stood the ruins of the cathedral that Ace Anarchy had claimed as his home—his headquarters, of sorts. The bell tower was mostly standing, along with parts of the cloister and the northern part of the structure. But the rest had been demolished.

Adrian's fingers twitched, itching to unbutton the top of his dress shirt and open the zipper tattoo that would transform him into the Sentinel.

But even now, he didn't want to risk Danna finding out his secret.

The butterfly flew over the fence, and Adrian saw a place where someone had taken wire clippers to the metal links and pulled it back, just wide enough to slip through.

Curious tourists, he thought. Or some kids acting on a dare.

But he couldn't be sure of that. He had no idea who would come here. This place had been left abandoned since the defeat of Ace Anarchy.

Why had Danna brought him *here*?

Gripping his marker, Adrian ducked through the opening. The metal scratched at his jacket and he felt a piece snag on his shoulder, ripping a hole in the seam. As soon as he was on the other side, he wriggled his arms out of the sleeves and left the jacket draped over the fence so it would be easy to find the opening again.

The butterfly headed toward the cathedral, dipping in and out of the ruins. A second fence had fallen into disrepair, and Adrian passed a DANGER: DO NOT ENTER sign. The butterfly alighted briefly on the sign, then took off again.

"Okay, Danna," Adrian murmured, pausing as he watched the

butterfly's wings swooping around the debris, catching the moonlight. "This would be a good time to indicate whether or not I should call for backup."

But the butterfly didn't answer, of course. She couldn't understand him anyway.

He gnawed on the inside of his cheek. Indecision clawed at him. Should he call for backup? And if so—should he call his team, or his dads?

Or should he transform into the Sentinel and see what he was dealing with first?

The butterfly waited on a fallen pillar, its wings beating impatiently.

Adrian gulped.

If he had been with the others when he'd gone after Hawthorn, then things might have gone much differently.

*There is no I in hero.*

"Fine," he muttered, lifting his wrist to his mouth. "Send team communication. Calling for immediate backup at—"

A sudden wind blew around Adrian's ankles, kicking up a cloud of dust. The butterfly was caught in the draft and sent whirring into the overhang over a collapsed arch.

Adrian's words dried on his tongue. The dust converged. Darkened. Solidified.

A figure stood in a fluttering black cloak, its hood eclipsing the deep shadows where a face should have been, the hooked blade of a scythe cutting across the sky.

Phobia.

Adrian's pulse thundered. For a heartbeat that felt like an eternity, he stared into the nothingness inside Phobia's cloak, dread settling inside his core. Of all the Anarchists, Phobia had long struck him as the most frightening. Not only because his power revolved around the control of a person's greatest fears, but because so little was known about him. No one knew his weaknesses, if he had any. He had never heard of Phobia being wounded, even during the Battle for Gatlon. He had once seen him struck with a giant shard of ice that would have impaled most humans, but Phobia only disappeared for a while, fading into black smoke. The effect had been temporary.

Still, Adrian held his ground. He struggled to think of his options. What could he draw that would aid in a fight against Phobia?

"I have tasted fear like yours before," said Phobia, his voice a rasp and a hiss. "The fear of being powerless."

Adrian tightened his jaw.

Screw it.

He tore open the collar of his shirt, popping a button from the fabric. His fingers pulled the zipper from the ink.

He started to tug it down when he heard someone screaming his name.

He froze.

His entire body caved in on itself. Filling with disbelief. And though he knew deep inside that it was a trick, and it was not to be trusted, there was no possibility of him *not* looking.

Not hoping, for all his miserable optimism.

He inclined his head and saw her.

The thick ropes of her hair framing frantic eyes. The golden cape whipping in the air behind her. That brave, beautiful face that could morph from stern to loving in the blink of an eye. From disapproval to laughter.

His mom was soaring over the cathedral, like she couldn't get to him fast enough. All the horrors of the world were mirrored in her face, and she was coming to protect him, her only son, her life and love.

It was like watching a string cut on a puppet.

She was flying.

And then she was falling.

Plummeting toward the wasteland.

Her cries caught in the wind. Her arms flailed, getting twisted in the cape.

Adrian yelled and tried to run toward her, but his feet were cemented to the ground. It was his worst nightmare, all his worst nightmares come to life. His mother falling to her death and he was stuck, unable to do anything. He was losing her all over again, and he was completely, utterly powerless.

A shadow cut through his mother's body moments before she collided with the earth.

The illusion shattered.

Adrian fell to his knees. Pain spiked through his leg as a piece of sharp stone dug into his shin. He blinked the tears away and watched as the shadow, a blur of movement, pivoted in the air and streaked toward the fence line.

Not a shadow. A swarm. Hundreds of monarch butterflies.

And in the distance, just now shoving their way through the fence, were Ruby and Oscar. Adrian didn't think they had seen him yet.

Phobia turned toward them. His skeletal fingers curled around the handle of his scythe, then he dissolved into a cloud of black crows. They soared after the butterflies, driving them away.

With an exhausted cry, Adrian ducked and rolled behind the fallen arch. He landed on his shoulder. His eyes were watering. His body still shaking from the vision. It had seemed so real. Her voice.

The terrified expression. The way his heart had yearned to get to her, to *save* her.

He took in a shuddering breath, trying to clear the thoughts from his mind.

It didn't work. The memory remained, cloying and cruel.

But he reached for the zipper anyway, and let the Sentinel engulf him.

# CHAPTER FORTY-ONE

ADRIAN FORCED HIMSELF up from the rubble. His legs were still weak, but the suit was supporting him now. The swarm of butterflies was nearly to the fence line and Adrian wondered whether Danna was fleeing for her life or trying to lead Phobia away from her friends. Either way, the flock of crows was gaining on her, their silhouettes almost invisible against the night sky.

Adrian knew the result of that food chain.

The birds passed over Ruby and Oscar. Ruby released a scream of rage and swung her bloodstone at them, knocking two birds from the air. One crashed into the fence, the other crumpled into the ground, one wing twisted at an odd angle.

The others seemed unbothered by their lost companions.

"Danna!" Ruby cried.

Adrian started to run. And then he started to fly, using the tattoos on the bottoms of his feet to launch himself forward.

Flame crackled around his fist. He could feel its heat through the armor, but it encouraged more than frightened him. The fire grew until it nearly claimed his entire arm. White-hot and churning, the flames licking at the air.

Oscar grabbed Ruby by the back of her uniform and hauled her out of Adrian's way.

He blew past his friends and took to the air, thrusting his palm forward.

The fire blazed along his limb and shot toward the gathering of crows. It devoured them, swallowing their squawks and cries, igniting their feathers and talons. Extinguishing them.

Adrian landed hard on the ground just inside the chain-link fence. He collapsed to one knee, struggling for breath.

Beyond the wasteland, he saw a smattering of birds who had escaped the fire turn into wisps of black smoke. They faded away while the butterflies dived beneath the remains of a battered taxicab.

A flutter drew Adrian's attention to the side and he saw one of the crows that had been knocked down by Ruby's stone. Its wing was crippled, and it was staring at Adrian with one beady black eye, intelligent and calculating.

Adrian shuddered.

The bird dissolved into black ash, scattering to the wind.

He released a long, exhausted groan. He was not naive enough to think that Phobia was dead. But he hoped it was the last he would see of the villain today, at least.

A boot crunched in the dirt.

Adrian squeezed his eyes shut, bracing himself, and stood. He turned to face them.

Smokescreen and Red Assassin. His teammates. His friends.

Ruby was gripping her wire in one hand, a ruby dagger in the other. Oscar had a charcoal gray cloud storming around him, obscuring the ground at his feet. They wore matching looks of apprehension.

Adrian could tell they didn't want to fight him, but he didn't think it was out of a sense of camaraderie.

No. They were afraid. They didn't think they could win in a fight against him.

They would be right, he figured, though it was the first time he'd stopped to consider the possibility.

Oscar glanced at Ruby. A brief look, born of worry. He was planning a diversion, Adrian could tell. He would conceal Ruby with his smoke, drawing the brunt of the Sentinel's attack toward himself. It was a risky maneuver, knowing what the Sentinel could do, but it was their best bet to take him down too. It would at least give Ruby a chance to move into a more offensive position. Maybe even launch a counterattack while the Sentinel was distracted.

It was a strategy they'd practiced dozens of times in the training halls. Their tiny gestures, the almost imperceptible way they arranged their limbs, was so familiar that Adrian was tempted to laugh.

Never would he have expected to see those tactics used against himself.

Adrian lifted his hands, fingers spread. The universal sign of supplication.

"I'm not your enemy," he said. "I've never been your enemy."

"Sorry, but we're going to have to let the Council make that decision," said Ruby. She gave the slightest of nods.

Oscar swiveled his hands, aiming to create a wall of smoke between Adrian and Ruby.

But in that same moment, Ruby gasped. "Wait!"

Oscar's eyes widened.

Something fluttered in Adrian's vision, just outside the visor. He blinked.

A monarch butterfly had landed on one of his fingers.

Another quickly followed, perching on his thumb. Then three more on the other hand.

Adrian held completely still as Danna's swarm overtook him, alighting on his shoulders, his arms, his toes, even the top of his helmet, he guessed, though he couldn't feel them. He was afraid to move lest he accidentally crush one beneath a metal limb.

As their expressions morphed from determination to astonishment, Oscar and Ruby gradually let down their guard. Ruby's muscles relaxed, letting the weapons hang at her sides. Oscar's smoke cloud dispersed into the air.

They gaped at him, and Adrian found himself fidgeting beneath their stares.

"Who are you?" Ruby finally asked.

He pressed his lips together. He didn't have to tell them. He could shoo the butterflies away. He could be gone before they would think to stop him.

But was that really what he wanted? To continue with these lies forever? To never be able to trust anyone with this secret, not even his best friends? The team he trusted with his life?

Inhaling shakily, he reached for his helmet.

The butterflies left him. They swirled across the wasteland and took up watch on the toppled statue of a saint, their bright yellow wings the only splotch of color beneath the moonlight.

Adrian unlatched the visor. It hissed as it lifted up, revealing his face.

Their silence was pervasive. He tried to read their expressions, searching for disbelief and betrayal. But mostly they just seemed stunned.

"Please don't tell anyone," Adrian said, and the words came out more pleading than he'd intended. "Especially not my dads. Or . . . or Nova either. I need to be the one to tell her."

"Nova doesn't know?" Ruby said, her own voice carrying a bit of a squeak.

Oscar answered for him. "Of course not. She hates the Sentinel."

Adrian frowned, but couldn't deny the truth of it.

Releasing a string of expletives, Oscar ran his hand through his hair. "How could you not tell us? I thought—all this time!"

"I know. I'm sorry. I wanted to. But after the parade, when Danna got hurt—"

"Because of you!" Oscar yelled. "She got hurt because of you!"

Adrian shrank back. "I know. It was an accident. I would never . . . I didn't mean to."

"And you were there," Oscar continued, shaking his head. "At the library and . . . and chasing after Hawthorn. How did we not see it?"

"Because it's *Sketch*," said Ruby. "You draw things! You don't control fire or laser beams! You can't jump fifty feet in the air! How . . . *How?*"

"Tattoos," said Adrian. "I draw permanent tattoos on myself, and they deliver different powers."

They both gawked at him.

Then—

"*Tattoos?*" Ruby screamed. "You can't be serious."

Oscar, though, had turned thoughtful, his mouth rounding with comprehension. "Tattoos. Holy smokes, dude, that's genius. Can you give me some?"

"No!" Ruby responded. "He can't—you can't—I still can't believe you didn't tell us!"

"I know. I really am sorry. I wanted to—"

"Don't," Ruby snapped. "Don't you even say that. If you wanted to, then you would have." She threw her arms into the air and began pacing, kicking debris out of her path as she went. "What are we going to do now? Next to the Anarchists, you're, like, the most-wanted prodigy in the city. You've been breaking rules left and right. And we're just supposed to become your accomplices in this? We're just supposed to keep our mouths shut?"

Adrian's shoulders sank. "No. I don't know. It's not fair of me to ask it of you—"

"But we will!" Ruby said. She was still screaming, working herself into a tizzy. "Of course we will, because we love you and you're *Adrian*! I know you're not some criminal mastermind who's doing it for the fame or whatever. I know you're a good person, and you must have a good reason for doing all this, I just . . . I just wish you would have told us."

"Wait—Hawthorn," said Oscar. "What the hell, Adrian? They said you—"

"I didn't," he said. "It was all Frostbite and her cronies. I saw them torturing her, and then they killed her so they could frame me for it. It wasn't me."

Oscar rocked back on his heels, considering. His face lightened. "Yeah, okay, I can believe that."

A stream of butterflies whipped past them, then swirled over their heads and returned to the fallen statue.

Pushing her bleached bangs off her forehead, Ruby pointed her dagger toward Adrian's face. "We are *so* not done discussing this," she warned, then swiveled the blade toward Danna, "but we should probably figure out why Danna isn't transforming."

As if in response, the butterflies spiraled upward again, then took off in a straight line, heading not away from the wasteland, but straight for the foundation of the destroyed cathedral. They settled on an assortment of sprawled ruins—a splintered wooden door, the head of a fallen gargoyle.

"I figured she was bringing me here because of Phobia," said Adrian, "but what if there's something else?"

"Or someone else," murmured Ruby.

"No way," said Oscar. "What if Queen Bee and Cyanide are here too? What if this is their evil lair?"

"This was their evil lair years ago," said Ruby. "Who would be foolish enough to come back to it?"

"Phobia was, wasn't he?" said Oscar.

Adrian's brow creased. "Unless Phobia was guarding something."

They regarded the butterflies, their flapping wings glinting beneath the moonlight.

Adrian pulled down the visor. "There's only one way to find out."

# CHAPTER FORTY-TWO

NOVA LAUGHED. She couldn't contain it. The disbelief coupled with the surge of zealous pride brought the laughter tumbling from her lips as she raced up the stairwell and pushed open the door to the abandoned floor.

Leaving the building would be easier than scaling the wall had been. Her ropes were waiting by an open window, right where she'd stowed them, prepped and ready to take her weight.

She would be back on the street in two minutes.

Back in the parking garage in six.

Speeding to Uncle Ace before Stingray or Callum would begin to stir from their slumber.

She was even ahead of schedule.

The chromium pike was strapped to her back and the helmet was tucked beneath her arm as she ran, lightweight and warm to the touch. She could picture the exact smile Ace would give her.

Her body surged with the feeling of accomplishment. She had done it. She had actually done it.

She was nearly to the window when something crashed into her, knocking her off her feet. Nova cried out and rolled a couple times. The helmet fell, tumbling across the tiles. She scrambled to reach for it, but a hand wrapped around her wrist and lifted her clean off the floor.

Nova dangled, panting, all joy knocked out of her.

Gargoyle grinned his pebble-toothed grin.

She tried to use her power on him, but his fist was all stone and she could feel her power striking uselessly against it.

Grunting, she swung her legs, attempting to kick him in the shin, but he held her like one would hold a mouse by its tail—largely unconcerned, but kept at arm's length all the same. He crouched and picked up the helmet, wrapping his burly fingers around its cranium.

"That was a real good try," he said. "But not good enough."

◇◇◆◇◇

He dragged her into a waiting elevator and down to the main lobby. Nova didn't struggle. She knew she couldn't overpower him on force alone, and it was better to reserve her strength. Wait for the right moment.

They passed in front of Max's quarantine and Nova couldn't keep herself from glancing up. She hoped that the lights would be out, that Max would be fast asleep, unaware of anything going on.

But her hopes had run their course for the evening. Max was standing at the window, frowning, curious. His palms were pressed against the glass, the skyline of his city glittering behind him.

Gargoyle yanked on her arm, pulling Nova's attention toward the center of the lobby. Frostbite and Aftershock were there, smug expressions etched into their faces.

Gargoyle tossed the helmet to Frostbite. She rolled it in her hands, peering into the empty eyes.

She passed it off to Aftershock. Carelessly. Like it was nothing. Then she lifted a hand and snapped her fingers. A breeze of frosty air blew through the lobby and the quiet clacks of water freezing over echoed off the high ceiling. Nova looked down. A great block of ice was engulfing her feet. She grunted and tried to kick out of it, but it was already too late. The ice crystallized quickly up her legs and over her knees. Gargoyle released her wrist and she nearly fell, but the ice held her upright. Though her boots offered protection from the cold, her pants did not, and the ice burned.

Snarling, Nova reached for the hunting knife at the back of her belt. She lifted her hand over her shoulder, prepared to throw it end over end at Frostbite, but before the blade left her fingertips, a new block of ice formed around her hand, locking her fingers in their tight grip around the weapon. Frostbite did the same to Nova's other hand, fully enclosing all four of her extremities, rendering her not just immobile, but *freezing*. Nova's teeth began to chatter.

Frostbite paced closer to her. "Don't worry. You'll go numb before the frostbite sets in, and I'm sure the Council will free you when they get here. I can't wait to see the looks on their faces when they arrive and find you so well restrained." She sighed, feigning sympathy. "Of course, you'll probably have to have all of your fingers and both feet amputated after the frostbite destroys them. It won't be a pretty sight. If you're lucky, they'll give you anesthesia before they do it, but . . ." She clicked her tongue. "I wouldn't count on it if I were you."

She stopped a few inches in front of Nova. "Brace yourself, now," whispered Frostbite, "because the loss of limb is about to be the smallest of your worries." She pulled a gun from her waist, one that

Nova recognized from training. Frostbite leaned in close, pressing the barrel of the gun against Nova's chest. "You might feel a slight pinch."

She pulled the trigger, driving the projectile straight into Nova's heart. Nova grunted from the impact and would have fallen if the ice wasn't holding her legs so firmly. She groaned, her chest burning from the puncture. Her hands and legs ached bone-deep from the cold.

She caught her breath and, to her own surprise, started to laugh. An exhausted chuckle that sounded borderline delirious even to her own ears.

Agent N. Frostbite was trying to neutralize her.

But she had shot Nova mere inches away from the Vitality Charm that was hidden beneath her jacket. Nova hadn't been able to test if the medallion would protect against the serum, but now was as good a time as any.

"Thank you," Nova said once the wheezing laughter had dried up. She ground her teeth behind the mask. "I'm not sure I would've had the guts to do this otherwise."

She swung one frozen fist, smashing it against one of the spheres strapped to her belt. The mist-missile crunched beneath the blow and the lever sprang open. A cloud of green vapor spilled into the air, surrounding Nova's body.

Gasping, Frostbite jumped backward, shoving Aftershock aside. "What the hell is that?"

"Your worst nightmare," said Nova. She turned toward Gargoyle, who had stumbled back a step when Frostbite had, but hadn't moved far enough. He was trying to scowl past his confusion. Nova batted her lashes at him. "No darts required, pebble brain."

"Trevor!" yelled Genissa. "Move!"

He did, finally, scooting back three, four steps. Nova counted silently, waiting. They hadn't tested it yet. Leroy's calculations could have been off.

But Gargoyle was a big guy, and it took a long time for most things to reach his brain, so why should this be any different?

Like with the Puppeteer, it started with a surprised widening of his eyes.

Nova grinned. Leroy had figured out how to turn Agent N into a gas, and she had successfully turned it into a bomb. Ace wanted a weapon against the Renegades, and now they had one.

Frostbite cursed and moved back farther to avoid the vapor, though Nova knew it would already be too dispersed to be effective at her distance. The device was spent.

Gargoyle's skin began to morph, losing its crusted, stony exterior, turning splotchy and baby soft. Starting with his head, then moving down his neck, into his shoulders and chest.

He gawked at Nova, stunned.

"Does that upset you?" she taunted.

Gargoyle roared and charged for her, swinging his arm—still stone. Nova lifted her hands. Frostbite screamed.

His fist smashed down onto the solid blocks of ice, shattering them.

His last act before the stone was gone completely.

Gargoyle wailed and collapsed to his knees, but Nova ignored him. With her hands free, she grabbed a second dispersal device from her belt and threw it at Frostbite and Aftershock. It struck the ground and another cloud of green smoke billowed up. Aftershock dropped the helmet and dived away from the explosion while Frostbite fled for the far corner of the lobby. She was screaming orders, but Nova doubted anyone was paying attention to her.

She cursed, doubting either of them had been caught in that cloud of vapor. She had to be more careful—she couldn't waste them.

Reaching over her shoulder, she grasped the pike where she had strapped it to her back, relieved that Gargoyle had been too arrogant to strip her of it. Freeing it from the harness, she gripped it in both hands and drove the point into the ice at her feet. The ice chipped, then cracked. Four more swings and her legs were free.

Nova pulled herself from the ice and stumbled, crashing to her knees. Her feet were numb. Her legs unwilling to follow directions.

Scrambling on her hands and knees, she forced her limbs to cooperate. She was on her feet again, slipping and stumbling. She lunged for Ace's helmet and snatched it off the ground. She tried to pivot, but her feet got tangled together and she fell again, slamming her knee into the tiled floor. Cursing, she used the pike as a support as she forced herself back to her feet.

Her path to the main exit was blocked, so she ran the other way. Toward the sky bridge, the stairs, a back exit. Options scrolled through her mind. A map of the building was etched into her memory. She knew every hallway, every door.

Settling on the shortest route, she swung to the left.

An earthquake rumbled beneath her. The earth split, driving a crack between her legs. Nova fell again.

The crack continued past her, burrowing through the red *R* in the center of the lobby, driving the foundation apart.

Nova gasped as she watched the course of the widening fault line. Straight for the sky bridge.

Straight for the quarantine.

Max hadn't moved. He didn't move, even as the ground beneath him split apart.

Nova screamed, but the sound was consumed by ear-splitting cracks of concrete, groans of metal, shattering glass.

One of the support columns broke—the noise as loud as a tree trunk being split by a battering ram.

The sky bridge collapsed.

The quarantine fell.

# CHAPTER FORTY-THREE

ADRIAN STARED INTO the black hole surrounded by the cathedral's ruins. Ruby and Oscar stood at his side, equally silent. They never would have discovered the staircase if Danna's butterflies hadn't clustered around it, forming a quiet, twitching guard at the entrance. The stairs were invisible until you were right on top of them, expertly disguised amid a collection of fallen wall panels and chipped stonework. It seemed random, but after the fight with Phobia, Adrian knew it wasn't.

How long had the Anarchists been guarding this place? Since they were run out of their tunnels, or even before then? And what could be down there that they wouldn't move to a less auspicious location? A weapon? A storehouse for stolen goods? A boarding-house for wayward prodigies?

"Well," said Oscar, doing a decent job of hiding his apprehension, "I guess I'll go first."

He took one step and Adrian clapped a hand on his shoulder, gently pulling him back. Oscar didn't fight him.

"Oh, right," he said, tapping his cane lightly on Adrian's back. It made a quiet clanging noise. "It probably does make more sense for you to go. But if you change your mind—"

"Oscar," Ruby said, warningly.

He fell quiet.

Adrian started down the stairs. The case was so narrow that he had to angle his body as he went. One flight ended in a short stone landing. He turned and headed down again. His visor adjusted to night vision in the darkness, tinting the underbelly of the cathedral an eerie green. He could hear Oscar and Ruby coming down after him, but their presence kept him tense more than comforted.

He swore to himself that after he told his dads about his secret identity, he would insist that they start incorporating armor into the Renegade uniforms. It could be heavy and clunky at times, but he would have felt better if his friends were half so protected.

A second landing gave way to a slightly wider staircase, and an arched doorway with words carved in ancient Latin.

They passed through a wide chamber. A tomb. White marble sarcophagi lined the opposing walls, watched over by stone figures shrouded in cobwebs and dust. Adrian tried to move with stealth, but his boots clomped against the floor, reverberating through the hollow grave.

A large wooden door fitted with ironwork greeted them at the end of the tomb and around its edges, Adrian detected the faint glimmer of golden light.

Oscar swirled a cloud of vapor around his fingers. At the first sign of trouble, he would fill the space with fog, disorienting potential enemies.

Ruby unhooked the gem from her wrist.

Adrian called forth the slim cylinder on his forearm. The close quarters made him uneasy. It made his springs useless, and a fireball in such a contained space was just as likely to harm his allies. He suspected he would see Queen Bee and Cyanide when he opened that door. His suit would protect him from both, at least for a while, and it would be a quick fight with Oscar and Ruby at his side.

Especially if the Anarchists were caught off guard, though every clapping footstep made that more unlikely.

Adrian placed a hand on the door and braced himself. Behind him, he pictured Smokescreen and Red Assassin taking up position.

Setting his jaw, he yanked open the door.

A skeleton stood on the other side.

Ruby squeaked and swung her gem at it—instinct, Adrian guessed, as much as anything. It struck the skeleton between two rib bones and the whole thing shattered, collapsing to the stone floor with a melody of wooden knocking. Its skull rolled against Adrian's foot.

Heart pounding, he swept his gaze upward. They were in the catacombs. More coffins were surrounded by walls of bones, shelves of skulls. Two standing candelabras held white taper candles that were nearly burned through and a curtain of femurs and clavicles hung across the space, obscuring what was kept behind it.

Phobia? Is this where he returned to when he evaporated like that? Adrian pictured a video-game character being sent back to the start of a level each time they were killed and a laugh stuck in his throat, turning into a choking cough.

The bones at his feet began to shake. They shuffled across the floor and gradually reassembled, until the skeleton stood upright before them again. Its hollow eyes and toothy grin were unchanged, and Adrian wondered if it was only his imagination suggesting irritation coming from the figure.

The skeleton bowed low at the waist and, without lifting his head, gestured dramatically toward the bone curtain.

Adrian stepped inside, giving the skeleton a wide berth. As soon as Ruby and Oscar were inside, the creature climbed up onto a wooden board hung over a sarcophagus, crossed its arms over its chest, and fell asleep. Or, died.

Adrian was still studying the skeleton when the entire curtain of bones fell, crashing into the stone foundation. They scattered to each corner.

He spun around. Air left his lungs. Disbelief mottled his thoughts.

Ace Anarchy.

*Ace Anarchy.*

He didn't fully trust his eyes. He couldn't be entirely sure. There were few photos of the villain without his helmet, and those were largely from his youth—before his rise to power. This man was not young. He did not look powerful either. His pallor was gray and cracked with wrinkles. His hair thin, his body more reminiscent of the skeleton who had welcomed them than the broad-shouldered prodigy who had overthrown an entire government and cast the world into a period of fear and lawlessness.

But his eyes. Dark, nearly black, and every bit as keen as Adrian would have imagined.

He was levitating, his legs crossed like a meditating monk as he hovered over the floor of fallen bones.

And his voice was strong, if also laced with a bone-deep weariness.

"Charmed," said Ace Anarchy, baring his teeth, "I'm sure."

Adrian was thrown against a wall. His back struck the stone so hard it sent rivulets of dust raining from the ceiling. He grunted and strained to move, but while his limbs inside the suit were free, the armor itself was immobilized.

Adrian cursed.

*Telekinesis.*

He'd thought the suit would protect him, but of course it wouldn't, not against a telekinetic like Ace Anarchy.

The catacombs filled with white smoke, so thick Adrian couldn't see past his visor. He struggled harder. If he could just move his arm, he could get to the switch on his chest that would retract the suit—

It was no use. Ace wasn't going to release him.

He heard Ruby's battle cry and he imagined her swinging her dagger-sharp bloodstone at Ace Anarchy's throat, but then her cry turned into a yelp of surprise.

Adrian's entire body tensed, and he fought against the invisible bindings again, but it was useless. He slammed his head against the back of the helmet and forced his muscles to relax. He had to be calm. He had to think.

There were grunts and cries of unleashed fury, and he found himself wishing that the smoke wasn't quite so thick so he could see what was happening.

Adrian urged his heart rate to slow. Think. *Think.*

His fingers flexed and for a moment he thought Ace's control of him was loosening, but then he realized that Ace wasn't concerned about his fingers, not when he had his body secured from neck to wrists to ankles.

He turned his head as much as he could within the helmet. The dust was thick on the wall. It had coated his suit when he had crashed against it.

The smoke was beginning to thin and he spotted Ruby and Oscar a dozen feet away. Ruby was on her knees. Her wire was wrapped around her own neck and she had her fingers curled between it and her throat, desperately trying to keep it from strangling her. Her fingers were bleeding, the blood glinting as it began to crystallize. Oscar knelt beside her, his expression frantic as he tried to help her loosen the wire.

Adrian could see no sign of the villain through the smoky veil.

He curled his armored fingers, pressing a fingertip into the wall. He drew the first thing that came to mind—the simplest thing he could manage. A circle traced into the dust. A single curved line sprouting from its top. A few scratches bursting at its tip.

A bomb.

A wick.

And a spark.

"Oscar," Adrian grunted as he pulled the bomb from the wall. "Take cover!"

Oscar's eyes widened. He grabbed Ruby beneath the arms and hauled her behind one of the coffins.

Adrian let the bomb fall. It rolled a few inches from the wall and exploded.

The flash was blinding. The blast pummeled against Adrian's body and knocked a hole through the wall. Adrian fell forward, landing on his hands and knees. He immediately clapped a hand to his chest and retracted the suit, though he was left coughing from the smoke and dust in the air. The room was darker now. The explosion must have toppled one of the candelabras, extinguishing what little light it had provided.

He crawled across the floor, searching for Ruby and Oscar as he blinked the debris from his eyes.

He found Ruby's garrote first—the wire tangled with a pile of bones. It was coated with tiny red gems from where it had cut into Ruby's skin.

"Smokescreen?" he said. "Red Assassin?"

"H-here," Oscar responded, coughing.

A furious roar drew Adrian's attention upward.

Ace Anarchy was no longer levitating. His simple, loose-fitting robes were splattered with white dust, and the fabric fluttered as he held his arms outstretched to either side. He stood in the center of the catacombs, his face contorted with a rage that had been nonexistent moments ago. His mouth curled, almost grotesque in its anger.

Adrian braced himself for an attack. He expected the sharp bloodstone to fly up and try to stab him, or Oscar's cane to try to club one of them over the head, or even to be pummeled by a thousand bones.

He heard the sound of stone grating on stone.

Adrian scrambled to his feet, unsure where the noise was coming from—until he witnessed the heavy lid of one of the coffins. It slid off the sarcophagus and crashed to the ground, driving a crack through the stone.

Adrian's jaw fell. His heart pummeled against his chest as the entire coffin turned first onto its side, the weight of it shaking the compromised cathedral foundation around them. The bones of a centuries-old corpse were flung from its shell.

Adrian stumbled back a step. He had heard stories of Ace Anarchy ripping buildings off their foundations. Knocking bridges into the water. Sending tanks crashing through store windows.

But that was when he was strong. That was when he had the helmet. Before Max took some of his power.

To actually see him controlling something that must have weighed a ton or more, even now, was petrifying. He could crush them. Easily.

Except, Ace wasn't lifting the tomb.

Adrian peered into his face again. Though hostility burned in the villain's eyes, it was met with strain. His face contorted with concentration. His teeth grinding and his skin damp with sweat.

Perhaps he could move something as heavy as a sarcophagus, but it wasn't easy.

With renewed courage, Adrian charged at him, his fist preparing to swing, even as his brain scrambled to formulate a plan. He and Oscar had sparred plenty in the training rooms, but it was rare that he had to use those skills in actual combat.

In the end, it didn't matter.

Ace Anarchy glanced once in Adrian's direction and the fallen candelabra flew up and caught him in the stomach. Adrian grunted and fell, gripping his abdomen.

He snarled and looked up in time to see the coffin roll over one more time.

Ruby and Oscar screamed and curled into each other. Adrian saw Oscar wrap his arms protectively around Ruby's head moments before the coffin closed over them, sealing them inside. Their muffled yells continued, followed by fists pounding against the inside of the stone prison.

Ace Anarchy slumped and Adrian could see him trying to catch his breath.

"I will deal with them later," he said, wiping his brow with his sleeve. He fixed his gaze on Adrian and cocked his head, studying him. Then his eyes glinted with something like interest, perhaps even amusement, and Adrian knew that he recognized him. He wasn't sure how. They had never met before, and Ace Anarchy had disappeared——*died,* they all thought——when Adrian was just a kid.

But he had been lurking down here all this time. Hiding.

Waiting. Guarded by Phobia, and maybe the rest of the Anarchists too. They could have provided him with information about Captain Chromium and the Dread Warden. They probably would have told him about how they had adopted Lady Indomitable's orphaned son. Maybe they had even brought him tabloids and newspapers, so he could stay informed of his enemies.

"How intriguing," Ace said, eyes narrowed in quiet contemplation. "I do believe you know my niece."

Then he grinned, that same cruel grin, and raised his arms overhead.

Adrian clenched his fist. The cylindrical tattoo on his forearm began to glow—molten hot. His skin warmed.

The shelves behind him rattled and he imagined Ace pulling them down on top of him. Crushing him, or trying to.

Adrian held his fist toward Ace. Peeled open his fingers.

But before he could shoot, Ace Anarchy coughed and fell, crumpling to one knee. The shelves quieted.

Adrian hesitated.

With an enraged roar, Ace slammed his fist into the ground. He swiped one arm over the floor and sent a wave of bones flying toward Adrian. He ducked behind one arm, but the bones clattered against him, harmless.

Ace screamed again, reminding Adrian of a child throwing a tantrum. The villain sat back on his heels, panting and dripping. His eyes, so calculating before, now spoke of frenzied desperation. He waved both arms this time, and Adrian let himself be battered by the remains. There was little force behind them.

Ace Anarchy had exhausted himself.

The villain hissed and crumpled forward again, curling his fingers through the eye sockets of a skull. "Damn you," he groaned.

"Damn you and your Renegades and your Council. *They* did this to me. They turned me into this."

Adrian allowed his arm to sink, though the tattoo continued to burn. "You did this to yourself."

Ace chuckled. "You're a fool."

"What did you mean, when you said I know your niece?"

Ace became calm, his expression almost gloating. "I believe you know her as Nightmare." His mouth stretched wide. "Among other things."

Adrian's jaw twitched. "Then I'm sorry for your loss."

"No, I don't think you are."

Adrian lifted his palm toward the villain and fired.

The concussion beam struck Ace Anarchy in the chest. He fell backward, his legs turning at an odd angle as he collapsed onto the sea of bones, one hand still gripping the skull.

Adrian stared at his fallen body, worried that the blow might have killed him. It had always been intended to stun, more than injure, but Ace Anarchy was frailer than most of the opponents Adrian faced. Silent and still now, it was easy to see just how frail.

But when Adrian stepped closer, he saw that the villain was breathing, if shallowly.

He spun toward the sarcophagus. "Oscar? Ruby?"

"We're okay," came the muffled reply. "Is he dead?"

"No—but unconscious. Hold on."

He transformed into his armor again, though even with the Sentinel's strength it took every ounce of willpower he had to lift the tomb off his friends. They were curled into each other, skin plastered with dust, Ruby's fingers speckled with jewels. Though neither said anything, they seemed hesitant to separate, even when they were free.

Oscar stood up slowly and leaned against the side of the sarcophagus, his breaths coming in short gasps. Reaching down, he laced his fingers through Ruby's and pulled her up beside him. "You all right?"

She gaped at Oscar, dumbfounded, and nodded. "Yeah. Fine."

Oscar nodded back at her.

Their eyes were shining, their bodies leaning toward each other, and if Adrian had ever seen the makings of a kiss before, he was certain he was seeing one now.

He cleared his throat loudly, and the two jumped apart, though their fingers stayed entwined.

"*Ace*," he said, slowly, clearly, "*Anarchy*."

"Right," said Oscar, running a hand through his dusty hair. "Right." Picking up his cane, he stumbled toward Ace and nudged his foot. "What do we do now?"

"We have to the alert the Council," said Ruby.

Adrian considered the destruction wrought from their fight. "You're right. They'll have him taken to Cragmoor. And we still don't know why Danna can't transform. If he had one of her butterflies trapped somehow—"

"Wait," said Ruby. "Do you have your marker?"

Adrian frowned, then removed his gauntlet and handed the marker to her. "Why?"

"I have an idea." Ruby crouched beside Ace Anarchy and started to write something across the skull in his hand. In crisp block letters that weren't at all like her normal loopy handwriting, she spelled out a message.

CONSIDER THIS A PEACE OFFERING.

——THE SENTINEL

"There," she said, capping the marker and handing it back to Adrian with a satisfied smile. "We'll tell them Danna led us here, and this is what we found. The Renegades need to know that you— that the *Sentinel* isn't a villain, and you—he—*you* . . ." She shut her eyes, gathering her thoughts. "*You* should get some credit for Ace Anarchy's capture. Maybe it will help your case. When you do tell them the truth."

Adrian smiled at her, though he knew she couldn't see it. "Thank you," he whispered.

"There's no reception down here," said Oscar. "Let's head back to the surface and let the Council know."

Ruby secured Ace Anarchy's wrists with her wire, ensuring it would take even a telekinetic a while to undo the knot, just in case he woke up before the Council arrived, though Adrian doubted he would.

They were halfway up the stairwell when their wristbands simultaneously blared with alarm, making them all jump.

"What the—" Oscar held his arm away from himself, suspicious. "There's no way they could have heard about this already."

Ruby pulled up the message first. Her face paled. "No. It's not Ace. It's . . ." She hesitated.

"What?" said Adrian, hating the way she looked at him in the darkness.

"It's a message from Max. He says that Nightmare is alive and she's there, at headquarters."

Adrian's heart leaped. "They caught her!"

"No. Adrian. Max says she has Ace's helmet, and he . . . he's going to try to stop her."

Adrian gaped at her.

Max?

*Max* was going to try to stop her?

He shoved past them both, squeezing his way through the narrow passage. "I'm going. Message my dads—about Ace, and Nightmare. They'll send someone."

He didn't wait for a response, just raced to the surface. Away from the wasteland. Back toward headquarters.

Toward Max, and Nightmare.

# CHAPTER FORTY-FOUR

"**M**AX!" NOVA SCREAMED.

Glass everywhere, ricocheting across the lobby's floor. Little glass buildings, glass cars, glass people and street lamps and traffic lights, all fell to the ground and shattered. An eruption of dust and shards so small they sparkled like glitter. Glossy white floor tiles splintered and spider-webbed in every direction.

Where the quarantine had been was now a few bent steel beams and broken plaster.

Where Max had been . . .

Nova stumbled to her feet. Took a few unsteady steps, searching the destruction, but she saw no sign of him. His fluffy hair, his plaid pajamas. Her eyes stung against the cloud of dust, probably tiny bits of glass were lodged in them, but she couldn't stop blinking and staring and searching.

A destroyed city. A few smashed light fixtures. A floor caved in.

As the dust settled, she heard a tiny cry coming from the rubble. It took a moment for her to spot the creature skidding across the ground. Nova watched, nonplussed, thinking at first that it was some sort of baby lizard.

The velociraptor, she realized with a start. The dinosaur Adrian had once drawn into the palm of her hand.

Heart racing, she crouched and held the flat end of the pike toward the creature, giving it something to climb on so she could lift it to safety.

It squealed and dived into the shelter of a collapsed floor joist instead.

The pile of rubble began to shift. A few chunks of plaster skittered and slipped, almost as if being nudged to the side, but still there was no sign of Max.

Her brow furrowed.

A few more pieces of glass clinked together, and the steeple of a church was suddenly crushed beneath some unseen weight.

Nova heard a gasp, and then Max flickered into view. He squeaked in surprise, then he scrunched his face up with concentration and flickered out again.

"Invisibility," Nova whispered. He had invisibility. From the Dread Warden. Of course.

A stream of ice struck Nova's foot, wrapping around her leg. She growled and swung the pike, shattering the ice before it could take hold. No sooner had she pried her foot free than the earth trembled, knocking her off balance. Nova's hip smacked the ground and her wounded thigh screamed at her. Only a few feet away, an avalanche of glass pieces tumbled into the enormous crack running through the tiled floor, clinking whimsically as they fell. Aftershock stood on the other side, glowering at her.

Nova's knuckles whitened, one hand on the helmet, the other on the chromium pike. Her eyes skipped across the destruction. Still no sign of Max and now she couldn't see Frostbite either. Gargoyle had not moved. No, not *Gargoyle*. He was just Trevor

Dunn now, a bully and a coward. His body—large, but no longer larger than life—was kneeling dejectedly where Nova had left him. Nova snarled, disgusted at his self-pity. To just collapse like that. To just give up.

He had never had the makings of a hero.

Nova was grateful for the immunity pendant around her throat, protecting her from Max's power. But even if she did have her power stripped away, as she almost had once, she liked to think she would handle it with a lot more dignity.

Aftershock roared, pulling her attention back to him. He dropped to one knee and prepared to slam both palms to the ground.

With a scream of her own, Nova hefted the pike over her shoulder and threw it as hard as she could.

Aftershock's instincts kicked in and he dodged the pike. It sailed over his head and speared into the INFORMATION sign on the central desk. Aftershock blinked at Nova. He froze, but only briefly, before his face split into an amused grin.

Nova held one of her own inventions in her hand. A blow-dart gun . . . disguised as an innocent fountain pen.

Aftershock chuckled. "You gonna compose a love letter for me?"

"A eulogy, maybe."

Lifting the pen to her mouth, she blew. The dart struck him in the chest, square over the heart, just where Frostbite had driven the dart into *her*. Aftershock looked down, horrified, as the green liquid was driven into his flesh.

"Rest in peace, Aftershock," she said with an exaggerated sigh. "His abilities might have been a seven on the Richter scale . . . but his personality was barely a two."

Not waiting to see his reaction, Nova took off running again, her feet sliding and tripping over the mess of glass and plaster.

She was nearly to the base of the steps that had once led to the quarantine when one of the great steel beams that had been loosened in the destruction swung downward and smashed against her side. The blow sent her flying into a wall and Nova collapsed, her head ringing. She opened her bleary eyes and saw the helmet lying a few feet away. Though her vision was blurred and her bones were still vibrating from the collision with the beam, she forced herself to push off the wall. Her fingers stretched for the helmet.

It was swept away from her and sent volleying through the air. Nova screamed and lurched for it, but too late.

Max cried out in sudden pain and the helmet dropped, landing amid the remains of the shattered quarantine. Max reappeared and collapsed to his knees not far away from it. His body was covered in nicks and cuts, his pajamas shredded. Nova's insides clenched as she watched him pull a glass shard from the sole of his bare foot.

He tossed the bloodied shard away with a hiss, then held out his hand again. The helmet completed its journey, soaring into his waiting arms.

He flashed into nothingness again. This time, the helmet disappeared too.

Nova gawked at the place where he had stood, shocked to realize that Max was the one who had sent the steel beam into her. And now he had taken the helmet.

He wasn't trying to get away. He was trying to *fight* her.

But invisibility wasn't infallible in a room filled with debris, and soon she could detect Max's path as he moved toward the nearest emergency exit. He was trying to be careful, but in his haste Nova spotted the shift of rubble, the disturbed glass in the chaos, smears of blood on the tile.

Pushing herself off the wall, she ran for him. She had no need to be careful, and upon her approach, he started to move faster. She could even hear him panting now, his panic rising as she closed in on him.

She dived, her hands curled into the air.

They found fabric and gripped tight.

Max cried out and flickered back into view as they both tumbled into the destruction. Again, the helmet was sent flying.

Leaving Max sprawled across the ground, Nova pushed herself up and leaped forward. She landed on top of the helmet and curled her body around it, securing it tight against her body before Max could use his telekinesis to snatch it out from under her again.

"No!" Max yelled. A small café table hurtled at Nova's head and she blocked it with her elbow, but the jolt shoved her hard into the ground.

Nova lay there, momentarily stunned, out of breath, covered in sweat. The helmet was pressed into her stomach. Her head was spinning from exhaustion and pain.

But the exit was close.

She was so close.

She would not fail when she was *this close*.

She dug deep into what reserves of strength were left and pushed herself to one knee, then the other. She stood, fighting against the wobble of her legs.

She had taken a single step when an arm wrapped around her throat, drawing her against a solid chest.

"I'm going to kill you," Trevor hissed in her ear. "For what you did to me, I am going to *kill* you."

"Get in line," spat Frostbite. She was standing in the doorway to the nearest exit, blocking Nova's chance of escape. Captain Chromium's pike was in her hand, covered in a thick layer of glistening white frost.

Nova, unwilling to release the helmet clutched in both arms, leaned into Trevor's body, letting him support her as her knees threatened to give out.

"Sorry," she said, her voice slurred more than she would have liked. "But no one's killing me today."

She grasped the forearm around her neck and drove her power through him. His grip loosened and he fell back, scattering the debris with a solid crunch. Nova stumbled and leaned forward, bracing one hand on her knee to keep from falling herself, the other still clutching the helmet.

"Wha—what?" Frostbite stammered. "But you're . . . I . . ."

"Oh, right, this," said Nova, plucking the emptied dart from her chest. "I'd almost forgotten all about that. Looks like it didn't work."

Frostbite's bewilderment changed to rage. Screaming, she gripped the pike in both hands and charged at Nova—a jousting knight ready to impale her opponent.

Nova swiveled to the side. The pike missed her by inches.

A gasp—horrified, shocked—sucked the air from the lobby.

Nova spun around in time to see Max appear again. Genissa had been aiming for Nova's heart, but Nova had dodged, and Max . . . Max was right behind her. Sneaking up on her. His hand even now was stretched out, trying to grab the helmet from her hand.

The chromium spear was driven clean through him.

A scream was ripped from Nova's mouth, splitting into the air. She could do nothing as Max stumbled back. His hand fell to the pike jutting from his abdomen. His eyes were wide, his face contorted in shock.

He fell to his knees.

"No," Frostbite said, her voice etched with panic. "No, no, no!" She released the spear and stumbled back. Her legs shook and she fell, then started scraping against the ground with her heels, scrambling away from the boy. "No! You can't have it!"

And Nova realized that she wasn't worried about Max.

She was worried because she could feel the Bandit stealing her powers.

Ignoring Frostbite, Nova dropped to the ground beside Max. The helmet thumped at her side. The iron pendant felt hot against her sternum. "You're okay. You're going to be . . ."

She trailed off. The wound around the pike was blue and sprouting ice crystals.

*Ice.*

"Take it . . . out . . . ," Max gasped, wrapping a hand around the pike. His eyes were round and his cheeks were wet.

"No, don't," said Nova. "It's stanching the bleeding. If we—"

"Take it out," he said again, more insistently. The ice was frosting over the pike.

Nova gulped. He had gotten some of Frostbite's power. Maybe . . .

"*Please*," he begged.

"Okay," she said, her voice warbling as she gripped the pike. "This is going to hurt. I'm sorry."

He stared at nothing. He said nothing. But when Nova slid the pike from his body, his scream curdled in her veins.

Then the pike was out and he fell to his side, blood soaking his pajamas. Nova's hands shook as she reached for the salve and bandages in her pouch, but when she rolled up the bottom of Max's shirt, she saw that the skin around the wound was covering over fast with small ice crystals. He was stopping the bleeding himself. She wondered if he even knew he was doing it. His eyes had closed, his face white as the broken tiles all around them. His body could have been acting on instinct, using whatever powers he had begun to gather from Frostbite to numb the area and stop the bleeding.

It would not save him, but if it could protect him until he could get to help—

Nova lifted her head. Frostbite had swooned and appeared only half conscious, but Aftershock was there, his arms wrapped around Frostbite's waist as he dragged her away from Max.

Nova didn't think as she grabbed the bloodied pike and charged toward them. Aftershock, startled, dropped Frostbite in a heap and prepared to face Nova's attack.

But the Agent N had taken effect and he no longer had any powers. Without them, he had no idea what to do.

Nova jumped forward, preparing to slam the pike against his temple. He cowered, raising his hands in a pathetic attempt to defend himself.

Nova stopped the side of the pike half an inch from his ear.

Lowering the weapon, she pressed her forefinger to Mack Baxter's forehead. He crumpled.

She spun back to Frostbite. The girl was on her hands and knees, attempting to crawl away from the Bandit. Nova pointed the tip of the spear at her nose. Frostbite paused.

"Go back," Nova growled. "You're giving him your power. All of it."

Frostbite lifted her eyes, but nothing else. "Like hell I am."

Nova snarled. Max was dying. *Dying.* And she didn't care if he was a Renegade, an Everhart, the *very prodigy* who had taken Ace's power and ruined him almost ten years ago. It was Max, and she would not let him die. "It could be the only thing that saves him."

"It's mine," Frostbite growled.

"Fine," said Nova. "I gave you a chance to be noble about it."

Reaching down, she scooped her fingers beneath Frostbite's chin, gripping her throat. A startled groan escaped the girl and for half a breath she struggled to get away.

But then she fell limp. Fast asleep.

Nova dumped her beside Max. She couldn't gauge how fast he was absorbing Genissa's power, but the ice formations over his wound started to thicken.

She thought he was unconscious, but then his eyes fluttered open, meeting hers. She couldn't tell if there was recognition there, but she knew there was a question.

Why was she helping him? She had the helmet. Why was she still there?

"Get away from him!"

Her head snapped up. Her pulse jumped.

The Sentinel stood inside the main entrance, his armored suit haloed by the moonlight reflecting off the glass doors.

Nova stood. Her heart felt brittle, her body on the verge of collapse. But her mind was sharp again, jolted awake when that pike had been driven into Max, and already she was assessing her options.

The pike was only a few feet away.

The helmet was on the ground behind her.

Another dart was loaded in the gun at her holster and she still had two more gas-release devices, though she couldn't be sure the gas would penetrate that suit.

She had one destroyed quarantine, three unconscious former prodigies, and Max—dying at her feet.

"I said," growled the Sentinel, as his right arm began to glow, "get away from him."

Nova took a step back. Her heel brushed against the helmet.

As much as she despised the Sentinel and all his feigned

superiority and self-absorption and the way he had hunted her like some obsessed stalker, she was pretty sure she knew one thing about the vigilante.

He was capable of good things.

Heroic things.

Like rescuing ten-year-old boys when they were dying.

She took another step back.

The Sentinel raised his arm. The concussion beam drove toward her. Nova ducked, barely dodging it, and grabbed the helmet off the floor.

Then she ran.

# CHAPTER FORTY-FIVE

H E WANTED TO CHASE after her.

A big, loud, furious part of him wanted to chase after her. To tear off her mask, to make her face him, to look him in the eye, to tell him why she would do this. To destroy Max's home, his glass city, his everything, and then to attack him— to attack a child! What purpose— What possible point—

But he didn't chase after her.

In part because he already knew the truth.

Max had helped to defeat Ace Anarchy, and now Nightmare had tried to exact her revenge against him.

And he didn't go after her because . . .

Because . . .

"Max," he said, the name overtaken by a sob. He fell to his knees over Max's body and did his best to remember the training they'd had. How to deal with various injuries so they could keep their comrades alive long enough for a healer to get to them.

But he had never seen this before.

Max's shirt had already been pushed up, revealing a deep gouge beneath his ribs. There was blood, but there was also ice. Flakes of brittle white frost creeping across the skin, forming a protective barrier over the wound.

Stolen from Genissa Clark, no doubt.

But even with the ice, the blood beneath Max's body was sticky and thick. The wound was deep, and could have punctured an organ—his kidney, his stomach, his intestines.

How long did he have?

Adrian's arms shook as he scooped them beneath Max's body and lifted him as tenderly as he could.

Nightmare was gone. Despite his fury, he hardly remembered her leaving. There was only Max. Whose skin appeared thin as tissue paper. Whose chest barely rose with each breath.

Holding the kid close, he ran from the building. Out onto the street, where even now he could hear sirens approaching. The Council, the rest of the Renegades, having heard about Nightmare's attack. Rushing to the scene of the crime.

They were too late.

Adrian only hoped that *he* wasn't.

Turning away from the sirens, he ran.

No—he flew.

The healers were all at the gala. *Everyone* was at the damned gala, and the hospital was six miles away and Adrian could think of nothing but the blood on his hands and Max's weak breaths rattling through his skinny chest and the fact that all the stitches he could draw wouldn't be enough to keep the life from slipping out of him.

The ice had bought him time, but still, he was dying. Max was *dying*.

And the hospital was six miles away.

Adrian had never moved so fast in his life. His entire world became a tunnel, pitch-black and narrow. He saw only obstacles—

the buildings in his path and the streets crammed with traffic. He saw only the hospital waiting at the top of the hill, too far away, then closer, and closer, as he bounded from rooftop to fire escape to water tower to overpass. All the while he clutched Max's body so tight he could feel the faint flutter of his heartbeat even through the armored suit. No, he was probably imagining that. Or it was his own heartbeat, erratic and desperate.

There was wind and the hard slap of boots on concrete. Another leap, another rooftop, another building, another city street blurring below, and the hospital—closer, closer, but never close enough. *Don't die, hold on, we're almost there, I'll get you there, don't die.*

And then he *was* there, a lifetime having passed in the minutes—seconds?—since he'd raced out of headquarters. He was moving so fast that the automatic sliding doors didn't have time to register him and so he crashed through, sheltering Max's body as well as he could as glass shattered around them.

Gasps and screams. Bodies leaping away from the infamous prodigy who had just burst into the emergency room waiting area.

A man in scrubs jumped up from behind a desk.

"A doctor, quick!" Adrian yelled.

The receptionist stared.

"*NOW!*"

Swallowing, the man reached for a call button.

Adrian crouched down, holding Max away from his body so he could inspect him. He tried to ignore the boy's frost-covered clothes and the splatter of blood that had dried on the side of his face. It was the pallor of his skin that terrified him most, and the way Adrian could barely see his chest moving, until he couldn't see it moving at all.

"*What's taking so long?*" he screamed, just as a set of double doors burst open and a man and a woman in nursing scrubs appeared, pushing a gurney between them. Another woman followed, pulling latex gloves onto her hands. Her focus landed on Max, devoid of emotion as she took in the blood and ice.

"Let's get him on the table," she said. "Gently."

Adrian ignored the nurses who seemed to want to take Max from him, and carried Max to the gurney himself, settling his body onto it as carefully as he could. It felt like handing over his heart.

The female nurse put a palm on the chest of Adrian's suit, ignoring the smears of blood on the armor. Her gaze dipped to the red S. It had been an R when he had first designed the suit, but he'd changed it after Hawthorn had thrown him into the river. There was no longer any point in pretending that the Sentinel was a Renegade. "I'm sorry, but you can't come back—"

The other nurse gasped. Something crashed. The doctor collapsed against the gurney, her breaths heavy as she pressed a gloved hand against her chest.

Adrian cursed and pushed the nurse away. "Not a prodigy!" he yelled. Grabbing the doctor, he pulled her back from the stretcher, dragging her to the opposite side of the waiting area before anyone could think to stop him. "It can't be a prodigy healer. He needs a doctor—a *regular* doctor!"

The male nurse stood over Max's unconscious body, stunned. They were all speechless—the nurses, the receptionists, the waiting patients and their families—all gawking at Adrian as if he'd lost his mind.

"Not a prodigy?" the nurse finally stammered. "What do you mean, you don't want a prodigy healer?"

"Just do it!" Panic rattled inside his skull until he could barely see, barely think, barely breathe. "Don't you have any civilian doctors?"

"Not in the ER!" the receptionist shouted back, as if such a request was the definition of inconceivable.

"Then get one from somewhere else!" Adrian shouted back. "Hurry!"

The weakened doctor was escorted away. Hot, furious tears blurred Adrian's vision. *Hurry, hurry, what was taking them so long—*

His thoughts stilled. A realization struck him like a bullet.

They *could* use a prodigy doctor . . . if that doctor was immune. If Adrian had the Vitality Charm.

But he'd given it to Simon. It was at home, or Simon still had it, and though Adrian's thoughts spun with desperation, he couldn't fathom how he could find it and bring it back here in time to make any difference.

A new physician in a white coat burst through the doors, harried and breathless at having been called to the ER, which was clearly the domain of prodigy healers only.

The doctor approached the stretcher and began shouting orders. A second later, Max was being whisked away, back into the sterile yellow corridors of the hospital. Adrian could no longer detect his breathing at all.

"Save him," he yelled after them, pleading. "Please. Whatever you have to do. Just save him."

Maybe it was his tone, or maybe it was the sight of Max's blood. Either way, the doctor's frenzied expression gave way to something almost kind. Then he turned his back and the doors swung shut, rattling back and forth a few times before falling still.

Adrian spun toward the receptionist. He noticed for the first time how everyone in the room had moved away from him, crowding against the walls.

"Look," he said, "that kid is a Renegade, and a ward of Captain Chromium and the Dread Warden. They *have* to save him."

The receptionist inhaled deeply. "We are professionals, sir. They will do everything they can."

Shoulders drooping, Adrian stepped away. All his strength left him at once and he slumped onto a nearby bench. It groaned beneath the weight of the suit.

Adrian knew he was being watched. Everyone in the waiting room was staring at him, trying to decide if they should be scared, or if they should alert the Renegades . . . if they hadn't already.

He didn't much care what they decided about him or who came to arrest him. He collapsed over his knees, gripping the sides of his helmet in both hands. The suit felt like a wall around him, separating him from the world. He had built this sanctuary for himself, and now he was alone with his thoughts, and his fears, and the jumbled, chaotic memories of all that had happened.

He was shaking, and his mind returned to anger, because it was the easiest emotion to embrace at the moment. Anger at himself, for not being faster. Anger at Nightmare for daring to attack a kid. *Just a kid.* Anger at the hospital for not being prepared, for taking too long to get a doctor to help. Even more anger at himself for not having the medallion with him so that first healer could have done something.

His thoughts spun to Nova, and how she believed that society was too reliant on prodigies. People expected a Renegade to be around to help them whenever they needed it. To solve all their problems for them.

Maybe she was right. Maybe they depended too much on super-heroes. And what if that dependence cost Max his life?

The memory returned to him, agonizing and sharp. Nightmare crouched over Max's body, her hands covered in his blood.

Adrian's fingers curled into fists.

Why hadn't she been weakened by his power? It didn't make sense.

He would find out. He would uncover her secrets, once and for all. About Max. About the helmet. About her knowledge of his mother's murder.

And then he would find her and annihilate her.

He heard a commotion outside and leaped to his feet. Sirens were wailing, the familiar sound of Renegade patrols on the move.

He glanced at a nearby door that led to a stairwell.

Simon and Hugh would be there for Max, and Simon could give his medallion to any healer who needed it. They could explain its significance and the nature of Max's ability.

Max didn't need Adrian to be there anymore, and he wasn't ready for this confrontation.

He caught sight of flashing lights through the broken glass door, and then Captain Chromium and the Dread Warden were barreling toward him. The rest of the Council was absent, and through a fog, Adrian remembered Ace Anarchy, unconscious in the catacombs.

Clenching his fists, Adrian bolted through the nearest door and launched himself up the stairwell, heading for the roof.

He couldn't hold on to his secret for much longer. There would be consequences for all the choices he had made, the rules he had broken.

But for now, the Sentinel still had a job to do.

Nightmare was alive and she needed to be stopped.

He would not give up the Sentinel until she was destroyed.

# CHAPTER FORTY-SIX

PHOBIA WAS WAITING for them outside the row house on Wallowridge. And all the cheering and euphoria that had overtaken them during their drive vanished with four simple words.

*The Renegades took Ace.*

Nova's heart squeezed. She didn't—couldn't—believe it. Phobia told them everything, and all celebration ceased.

Leroy turned on the car radio and they all stood there, listening, unwilling to believe.

The journalists were beyond themselves, talking a million miles per minute as they repeated every tiny, trivial detail of the capture. The fact that Ace Anarchy was still alive at all was a shock to them, and to know that he had been found and brought into custody . . . not by the Renegades, though a patrol unit had arrived to take the villain to headquarters.

No. Ace had been captured by the Sentinel.

Even thinking his name made Nova's skin crawl with loathing.

Finally, when they could no longer deny the truth of the reports, they trudged through the front door, full of disbelief.

Honey brushed past Nova and headed up the groaning, angry steps. The bedroom door slammed and, seconds later, Nova could hear the start of her wails. For the first time, Nova couldn't write them off as Honey's knack for melodrama.

"You did well tonight, little Nightmare," Leroy said, settling a hand on Nova's shoulder.

She didn't respond, and soon he, too, clopped up the steps to his room. The door closed on squeaking hinges.

Phobia lingered a minute longer, his presence haunting the corners of the room. He didn't say anything. For once, Nova had no fears that he could possibly comment on.

All her worst fears had come true.

The Renegades had Ace. Despite everything, she had failed.

Finally, he too vanished, transforming into a colony of bats and soaring out through the door. It slammed shut in his wake, rattling the weary house.

Nova stood a few paces in from the entryway and stared.

At the garish paisley wallpaper.

At the moth-eaten furniture.

At the nothingness that was supposed to be her home.

The helmet hung from one hand, her fingers punctured through the eye holes like a bowling ball. It no longer felt light and unobtrusive, and as the shadows slowly gave way to the dusty light of early morning, Nova let the helmet fall.

It thumped anticlimactically against the carpet and rolled beneath the coffee table.

Nova let out a shaking breath.

She had failed.

Ace was captured. Ace was gone.

A chime echoed through the silent house, startling Nova from her thoughts. Her communication band. She found it in the kitchen. Her hand was shaking as she picked it up and scrolled through countless messages from Adrian and the rest of the team, and even a global communication sent out from the Council, confirming the truth of the media reports.

> Ace Anarchy is alive and he is in custody.
> The Sentinel was responsible for his capture.
> The Sentinel's identity remains unknown.

The most recent messages were all about Nightmare, also confirmed alive, and the theft of Ace Anarchy's helmet, and the destruction wrought upon headquarters.

The messages said nothing about Frostbite and her team.

They said nothing about Max.

Nova read the alerts about Nightmare more closely, trying to determine if she'd been discovered or not. She hadn't been overly concerned with keeping her identity concealed tonight, believing that by the end of it, Ace would have his helmet back and her charade as a Renegade would be over.

Now she couldn't fathom what would happen next. How long before they figured her out?

She thought of Danna's butterfly, still trapped inside the jar upstairs. If it ever escaped, then Nova's secret would be revealed for sure. And there were a thousand other little lies piling up all around her. A thousand signs pointing to Nova. To Nightmare.

How long did she have before they knew?

Before Adrian knew.

She dropped the wristband onto the table and braced her palms against the back of a chair. Eyes closed, she inhaled deeply. Counted to ten. Exhaled.

Then she went upstairs to change. Honey did not speak, so neither did she as she stripped out of Nightmare's costume, covered in blood and sweat and small shards of glass.

She set her face mask on the vanity, right next to Danna's butterfly.

She could barely look at either of them.

She had to get Ace out. That was all there was to it. The thought made her want to sob, but she bottled it deep inside. Because if that's what had to be done, then that's what she would do. She wouldn't complain about all the work and planning that had gone into tonight. She wouldn't think of how everything was wasted. She wouldn't feel sorry for herself.

She would lift her chin. She would keep fighting.

She went back downstairs, leaving Honey to her solitude. They all wanted solitude. Nova sat down at the kitchen table and stared at the vase of dead flowers, her heart breaking.

It could not all be for nothing. She wouldn't let the Renegades win. She wouldn't let the Council get away with their lies, their broken promises.

And she would not be beaten by the Sentinel.

A knock made her jump. She stood and stared at the front door, choking on her heart. She waited for it to be blown in by the forces of an army of superheroes. She pictured Captain Chromium's fist smashing through the door, leaving it in splinters, or Tsunami's tidal wave bursting through the window and flooding the house.

But the only attack that came was a second pounding on the door, more determined this time.

Then, Adrian's voice. "Nova—it's me. I know you're awake. Please, let me in."

Her saliva became sticky inside her mouth.

Adrian.

Sweet, handsome, brilliant Adrian Everhart.

He knew. He must know. How could she face him? How could she stand to see the look in his eyes when he demanded she tell him the truth? When he dared her to lie to him again?

"Nova? Are you home?"

Her gaze landed on the helmet.

Crossing the living room floor, she stooped and picked it up from the dreary carpet and spent a few seconds turning in aimless circles, trying to determine where to hide it. She settled on the coat closet, jamming the helmet in amid Leroy's trench coat and Honey's furs.

Inhaling a deep breath, she crossed to the door and gripped the knob. Upstairs, Honey's sobs had fallen quiet. The entire house felt deserted.

She pulled open the door.

Adrian was a wreck. His bow tie was gone, and his dress shirt was rumpled and covered in smudges of dirt. His gaze latched on to her, haunted and exhausted.

But not accusatory.

She didn't dare hope.

"Can I come in?" he said, almost meek.

She licked her lips with her sandpaper tongue and stepped inside.

He moved past her and walked straight into the kitchen. Nova held her breath as he passed the closet. The latch, which never closed firmly, clicked. The door drifted open, just a few inches.

Adrian didn't notice. His movements were sluggish as he pulled back a chair and collapsed into it.

"I'm sorry," he said when Nova caught up to him. She stayed in the doorway, terrified. That Honey would make a sound. That some of her bees would fly down from the stairwell and start traipsing across the cabinets. That Adrian's melancholy was an act, meant to lure her into false security. "I know I can't just keep showing up here but . . . I needed to talk to someone, and I knew you would be awake, so . . ." His voice snagged and she noted the bruised circles beneath his eyes, almost hidden by the frames of his glasses.

The night had been long for them both.

"I'm sorry," he said again. "How is your uncle?"

Her heart squeezed.

Captured. Imprisoned. Gone.

But then she remembered the excuse she'd given Adrian when she was leaving the gala—that her uncle hadn't been feeling well and she needed to go check on him.

"Fine," she stammered. "He's fine."

Adrian was silent for a long time. His gaze was fixed on her across the room and Nova couldn't tell what the look meant. Was he inspecting her for the truth? Searching for signs of Nightmare?

"Have you heard?" Adrian said. "About . . . Ace Anarchy? And Nightmare?"

She shivered. "I was just checking my messages. It's true then?"

He nodded. Folding his hands, he bent over his knees, peering at the cracked linoleum floor. "Yeah, it's all true. We got Ace, but she got away, and . . . she took the helmet." A wry laugh fell from him. "I should have listened to you, Nova. We all should have listened to you. You tried to tell us that it wasn't secure, but my dads . . . we were so arrogant about it. And now . . . now it's with them."

Nova dug her fingers into her own thigh to keep from looking back over her shoulder. Toward the closet.

"But we have Ace Anarchy," said Adrian. "That's something." He lifted his head, staring blankly at the wall. "Ruby and Oscar were there when the Council came to collect him. They said they're already planning to have him neutralized, publicly, when they reveal Agent N to the world. He'll be their shining example of how necessary Agent N is, and what it can do."

"When?" Nova whispered. "When will that happen?"

"I don't know. I doubt they'll wait long."

His chin started to quiver, startling Nova. "Did you hear . . . do you know about Max?"

His voice broke and Nova's blood ran cold. She saw Max again, the ice spear puncturing his skin, the blood coating the floor.

He was dead. He was dead. He was dead.

And it was her fault, at least in part. Her fault.

"No," she breathed, not wanting to hear him say it. Not wanting to know the truth.

Adrian extended his arms and Nova couldn't resist the pull of them. She went to him and he wrapped his arms around her waist, burying his face into her stomach. Tears pricked at Nova's eyes and though her body tried to rebel at the intimacy of the touch, she couldn't stop the impulse to cradle his head and shoulders, to hold him closer.

"He's in the hospital," he said, as the tears started in force. "She tried to kill him. Nightmare tried to kill him."

Hospital.

*Tried.*

"Is he . . ."

"I don't know. I don't know. But he has to live. He has to be okay. If anything happens to him . . ." His words dissolved. Nova held him, feeling the damp tears through her shirt, the trembling of his shoulders under her fingers.

"He'll be all right," she said, willing herself to believe it too. "It'll be okay."

"I'm going to destroy her. I'm going to find Nightmare, and I'm going to destroy her." He curled his fingers into the back of Nova's shirt, gathering the material into his fists. "Nova . . . will you help me?"

Grimacing, Nova turned her head toward the front room. Through the doorway, she saw the edge of the coat closet. The dingy wood trim around the doorjamb. The carpet worn nearly to the floorboards beneath.

"Yes, of course I will," she heard herself say as she stared into the empty eyes of Ace Anarchy's helmet, glinting at her from the shadows.

# ACKNOWLEDGMENTS

ONE OF THE THEMES that really started to emerge in this book as I was revising it through multiple drafts is that most things in life are made better when you can enjoy them in the company of people you love. Writing a book is no different. Just like there is no *I* in *hero,* there is no *I* in *book!* I am eternally grateful to have so many people in my life who have helped guide and support me during this journey.

The first person I must thank is my editor, Liz Szabla, who saw the possibilities in Nova and Adrian's story even before I did, and pushed me to delve deeper into this world and its characters. This book and trilogy are so much more now thanks to your encouragement and vision. (Literally . . . it is, like, hundreds of pages more!) And of course, I appreciate all the hard work of everyone on Team Meyer at Macmillan Children's: Jean, Mary, Jo, Mariel, Allison, Rich, Caitlin, as well as my wonderful copyeditor, Anne Heausler, and so many others who work behind the scenes to help bring this and countless other books into the world. I am so lucky to have you all in my court.

To my fabulous agency team—Jill, Cheryl, Katelyn, and Denise—who are not only advocates, counselors, and cheerleaders, but also really great friends. I can't begin to express how happy I am to know and work with you.

Thank you to my intrepid beta reader, Tamara Moss, whose thoughtful critiques are appreciated *almost* as much as nearly twenty years of friendship and camaraderie. You make me a better writer, and for that, I cannot say thank you enough.

Thank you to Joanne Levy, my professional assistant, for a million different things. I don't know how I ever made my deadlines without you!

I owe a very special thank-you to Laurel Harnish, whose character design during a *Renegades* contest served as the inspiration for Callum Treadwell (Wonder). I completely fell in love with Callum and his awe-inspiring power, and I hope you did too!

A humongous thank-you goes to Dr. Tyler DeWitt for being gracious enough to review Chapter 23 and offer insight into the process of electrolysis and metal plating. (Nova would have been mortified if I'd gotten it wrong!) Tyler's science-based videos are as entertaining as they are informative and I highly recommend checking them out on YouTube or at https://www.tdwscience.com/.

And, of course, to my husband, Jesse, our two vivacious daughters, Sloane and Delaney, and to all my family and friends for their tireless support, encouragement, and love.

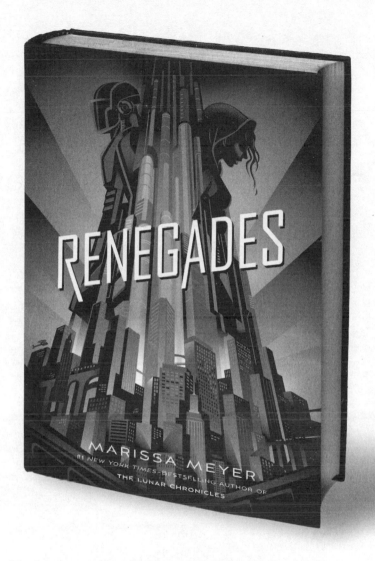

"Exciting . . . perfect for your Fall #TBR list." —PopSugar.com

"Even reluctant fans of hero fantasies will fall for the **smart plot and wonderful world-building**. Prepare to fangirl." —*Justine Magazine*

"**The world is exceptionally well crafted, particularly the complex backstory of the rise of prodigies among humans, and the secondary cast of villains and heroes could give Marvel and DC a run for their money.**"
—*Bulletin of the Center for Children's Books*, Recommended

Praise for

# The Lunar Chronicles

*#1 New York Times*–Bestselling Series

*USA Today* Bestseller

*Publishers Weekly* Bestseller

"A mash-up of fairy tales and science fiction . . . a cross between
Cinderella, Terminator, and Star Wars."
—*Entertainment Weekly*

"Prince Charming among the cyborgs."
—*The Wall Street Journal*

"Terrific."
—*Los Angeles Times*

"Marissa Meyer rocks the fractured fairy tale genre."
—*The Seattle Times*

"Epic awesome."
—*Bustle*

"A binge-reading treat."
—MTV

"Takes the classic to a whole new level."
—NPR

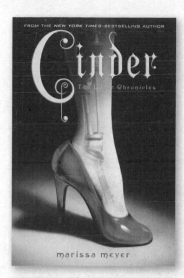

# Cinder
### The Lunar Chronicles

marissa meyer

# Scarlet
### The Lunar Chronicles

marissa meyer

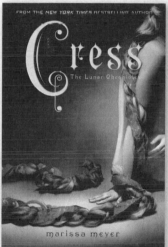

# Cress
### The Lunar Chronicles

marissa meyer

# Winter
### The Lunar Chronicles

marissa meyer

# Fairest
### The Lunar Chronicles
#### LEVANA'S STORY

marissa meyer

# Stars Above
### A Lunar Chronicles Collection

marissa meyer

# WIRES AND NERVE

## VOLUME 2: GONE ROGUE

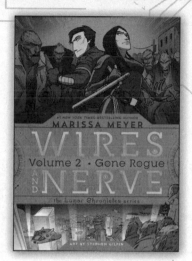

★ "Cinder's friends are in danger at the hands of Alpha Lysander Steele and his pack of Lunar wolf-soldiers, out for revenge against the queen for not reversing their genetic deformations. . . . **Builds to a satisfying ending for all characters involved.**"
—*VOYA*, **starred review**

"Android Iko is still hunting down rogue wolf-soldier Steele, but her quest takes on a new urgency after he convinces Iko's friend Wolf to join his renegade cause. Now Iko and the frustrating (but handsome!) guard Liam Kinney must scramble to prevent a massacre during Cinder's visit to Earth for the annual Peace Festival. . . . **Fans will be delighted to revisit Meyer's futuristic Earth and her young saviors.**"
—*Booklist*

"*In* HEARTLESS,
*the nonsense that is Wonderland
gets a reverential makeover,
full of heart and its own idiosyncratic character.*"

—GREGORY MAGUIRE, AUTHOR OF
*Wicked* AND *After Alice*

Praise for

# HEARTLESS

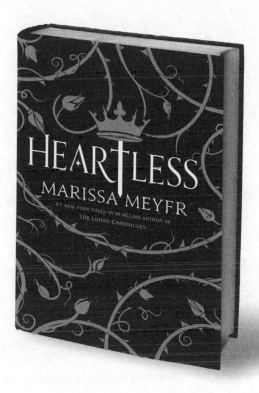

**#1 New York Times** *Bestseller*

*"The Must List,"* Entertainment Weekly

Publishers Weekly *Bestseller*

*"What Gregory Maguire did for the Wicked Witch, Meyer does for
Lewis Carroll's Queen of Hearts, tracing her arc from a teen with
dreams of owning a bakery into a murderous madwoman."*
—People *magazine*